PIROZHKI FOR ONE

Croften Grebe

To Elizabeth Robertson

Acknowledgment

Thanks to Solomon and the rest of the team–Roy Harper, Ron Connor, David Harper, Walter K., Ella Rose, Daisy and Jonathan, my editor for adding in the colours. Last but not least, Tony Duff, Regional President of the Croften Grebe Fanclub; Highlands & Islands Division.

Contents

Chapter 1

The Baroness of Kindeace-Shire had never had the need and, therefore, had never used the emergency communication device before. Her father, never really fully trusting their American cousins to keep their mouths shut, had started installing the secret bases in the early sixties. The state-of-the-art electronics were years ahead of anything that any of the major powers had at their disposal. Lesqueth's ECD had been in place for over twenty years, and in all that time, she had only checked that the latest version was fully active and operational. On the receiving end of her transmission, the operator who had manned this station for nearly ten years had a heart attack. The blinking light, accompanied by the constant beeping, had alerted him. If he had been connected to an ECG, the graph would have looked like a major seismic event was underway. Communication officer P.D. Kerrage immediately raised the issue with his commander. He followed the strict protocol that was laid out in the operation manual and then personally went to inform the head of the station.

General Gunnell Flemings was in the midst of reviewing the latest recordings from the Kunupenny shelter. The orgy of vandalism that Abe Hubstien, along with his gang of riff-raff, had almost joyfully undertaken. This would only create a minor setback for future operations, nothing, nothing at all to worry about. She was interrupted by a knock on the door; General Flemings shouted, giving them permission to enter. Comms officer Kerrage opened the door, awkwardly marched several steps forward, stood at attention, and then saluted. He placed the sealed envelope on her desk, saluted again, about turns, and then just as awkwardly marched straight back out of her office. G-Flem broke open the seal and then read the contents. She punched in the memorised sequence to open the hypersensitive quadruple bio-algorithm armed safe. She retrieved the cypher command module and then transposed the message.

The operation to hunt down then proceed to eliminate Abe Hubstien and company, had now got to be postponed. As the great lamented, General Marshall had once told her a long time ago, "When her ladyship delivers her calling card, you answer. Even if you are in the process of saving the dying planet from certain cataclysmic destruction, you put it on hold and answer the call." G-Flem summoned her adjutants, "Issue an immediate order for the cancellation of the 'Abe must die' operation, then request that all of the commanders must return immediately to general headquarters." She had only once been briefly introduced to the Baroness of Kindeace-Shire, and even then, all these years ago, she had scared the complete shit out of her. As her mama would say, "She was one serious bitch."

Flemings had just gone through the briefing with all the senior commanders under her wing. Each of them had received specific instructions on what was required. The underground system had been reactivated, and they had all been informed that the Kunupenny substation was out of action for now. All of the major stations had all been checked and were fully operational. "Blundell you will head out first to secure the area around station A, check then secure all the roads leading to the point of departure. Smith, you will place your troopers on standby, ready to assist if required. Gentlemen, you all now have your orders." They stood and saluted her as she departed to the comm room.

In the south, Blink and her crew had been travelling for days on end, the days had changed into weeks, and they were now on the second month of the great sea journey. The weather had been, at times, fairly inhospitable, and during these days, they had to take shelter. She had made a big deal of making her crew rest and recuperate. Blink looked at her watch, even after all of these years, it still worked perfectly; much to her surprise, it had even automatically adjusted to the various changes in the geographical time zone. She had just finished her stretching exercises and now sat eating the simple fare in front of her. Blink savoured the fruit and considered that by the quantity of fish her crew consumed on a daily basis, some of them might have been, without any shadow of a doubt, half-fish-half-human.

In this long, arduous journey where they spend most of the day bouncing over the water, not one of the crew had voiced a single complaint. Her mother would have scolded them for not even mentioning it, but that was not her style. Blink was looking forward to finally getting off the boat and then spending some time on dry land. The further north they travelled, she noticed the subtle changes in the landscape. The dense jungles thinned out and then disappeared briefly, replaced by the once booming cities and industrial zones. The jungles then started to reappear, a few sparse clumps of vegetation that gradually transformed into the somewhat threatening walls of impenetrable green-upon-green. The landscape that they were now passing was devoid of all forms of plant life; the barren stretch of sand expanded as far as the eyes could see into the distance. Blink indicated that they were heading inshore for yet another overnight stopover.

She, along with her crew, had experienced a rather unpleasant evening. The area might be devoid of plant life, but the insect population had been more than very active. Most of them had spent the night peeling the creepie crawlies from their skin and crushing them under their boots. Some of her crew were suffering from mild infections where the little blighters had managed to sink their teeth and pierce the unfortunate member of her company's skin. Blink prepared a salve for all those who had been singled out to receive TLC by the little nippers. Sekoyaz was hovering outside; Blink asked her if she had something on her mind. "I was on duty last night, and although I had never seen anything, I had this feeling that something or someone was watching us. I went out at first light, and there were no signs, but I know that I felt the presence of something."

Blink informed her that the next time she thought or felt like something was there, she could come and get her. Sekoyaz thanked her for listening and returned to her duties. Blink was awake during the wee small hours. She had also detected something, for now they were only watching. Tonight, when they rest up, she would inform the crew on perimeter duty that as they were getting nearer to their final destination, they must be ultra-vigilant.

Sekoyaz was correct in informing her what she sensed. Whoever it was that was watching them was almost silent. Today, she thought and hoped that they should clear the desert region and as always, she felt safer when surrounded by the verdant life of the wall-to-wall jungle. Tonight, after they set up the camp when everyone was settled down, she would take Sekoyaz out into the jungle and then test her to what she truly could and could not sense around her. The vegetation was, as always, full of life; some of it slept and some of it only pretended that it was sleeping. There were also the creatures that hid to avoid you and the ones that hid, patiently lying in wait to attack you.

The fuel ship had arrived; after all the boats were resupplied, the crew was changed out, and Blink gave the order to leave. The advance boat had set off just before dawn. She wondered if today would be the day that she received the sign that it was time to go and seek out the one named Enunsha. The old woman with the hooded cloak had empathised that she would save her and come to her aid. Blink thought that the one named Enunsha looked more than capable of looking after herself. She smiled, remembering her mama's words, "Never judge a book by its cover; you might just be surprised at what you will find underneath the dull exterior."

The sea today was relatively calm. The slight breeze was refreshing as it washed over her, removing the last of the sand from her skin. Blink hoped that there would be no more stops in desert regions.

North of London, Commander Essmie had delivered the news to General Miasnikov in person. She had never seen anyone's eyes instantly turn red before. He received the news calmly, then asked her to go through all and everything that she had witnessed at the castle. Vladimir had sincerely thanked her, with all the added displayed emotion, for laying his beloved little sister to rest. He had produced a bottle of the finest vodka from the motherland and then proceeded to pour them both a generous measure. Vladimir asked her to look at the map of the area surrounding the castle. Miasnikov directed Essmie to mark out the route she had taken north, and then they both looked at the road network and the allegedly accurate geographical information displayed on the map. As he studied the terrain in detail, Miasnikov asked her again to retell everything she had seen and more to the point of all the things she had not seen. "If your convoy had come in from that side and witnessed no signs of a firefight, then the attack must have come from the west." He poured more vodka for each of them; together, they looked at all the names of all the possible places where the tribe of mutants could be located.

Vladimir started marking up the areas of interest on the map, then pointed as he spoke. "When we arrive there, we will split up the forces. You will then simultaneously divide your forces to push from the northwest and the southwest. The forces under my command will lie in wait to the east of your position. If it all goes according to plan your troopers will rout out these rebels, then we should be able to capture them just west of the castle. In honour of my sister, I would have very much liked to have been able to feed them, one at a time, to the Siberian tigers. As that option is no longer available, we will just have to think of another suitable punishment."

Miasnikov refilled their glasses, then went over the plan once again, this time detailing what units she would deploy. "I want you to take as many of the mutants alive as possible. I know that you will have to kill a few of them, but you need to leave a bunch for me."

Commander Essmie asked for permission to speak. Miasnikov nodded, granting approval; she suggested that if the rebels were not heavily armed. Then maybe their forces could use the rubber bullets that were often the preferred option in these areas for crowd control. Vladimir thought that this was a splendid idea. He then refilled their glasses, and they drank several toasts to their successful operation. Miasnikov left Commander Essmie slumped unconscious at the table and went off to search for some lucky prisoners to debate with. He picked up a heavy-duty ballpoint hammer on the way out as he marched towards the holding area where all of the unwanted, the unwashed and the ungrateful were kept.

The guards at the gate of the compound quickly snapped to attention as they spotted Miasnikov approaching. Vladimir informed them that he was here to inspect the prisoners and he would very much appreciate it, if they were to take him to one of the holding pens. Vladimir also informed the guards that the prisoners' age, gender classification or ethnic group was, for now, of no importance. As they stopped at the first pen, Miasnikov nodded his approval. The guard asked if he would like them to secure the prisoners and pull them out for inspection. Miasnikov shook his head, respectfully declining their offer. He ordered them to unlock the gate and to kindly close it behind him.

They carried out the request without question, and Miasnikov walked straight in, informing the prisoners that he was there to deliver a present from his sister. Vladimir laid in about them, smashing their heads with the hammer, kicking them, and even headbutting a few of them. He was disappointed that not even one of them attempted to fight back. Some of them had tried putting up their hands to ward off the blows, but it served them no good. Miasnikov relentlessly attacked all of them; once they were all laid out on the floor, he sat on top of them, then systematically bashed their heads in with the hammer. The tool got lodged in the bloody, swollen head of the last one; Miasnikov tried very hard to dislodge it and was frustrated that it did not want to move. He stomped hard on the hickory shaft, determined to drive it as far as possible into the woman's head.

Miasnikov was now covered in blood; fragments of hair, bone, teeth and brain tissue adhered to his face as he ordered the guards to open the gate. Vladimir thanked them for providing this evening's splendid entertainment and bid them all a good night. The guards watched as he calmly walked away. They did not know the name of the tune that he was attempting to recreate with the whistling, but at least he sounded happy.

In the middle of the Irish Sea, Gareth had been down in the engine room, and the mechanics had voiced all of the available options. He was now presenting the latest update to Leena on the bridge. "The parts that need to be replaced, they can try and make and make-do, possibly stripping down some of the other mechanical devices that are strewn over the ship. In the hope of adapting something to repair the engine. They have informed me to let you know that this does not offer any guarantee of success."

Leena asked Gareth for the other option, "We could pull into some harbour along the route, then rape and pillage the parts required from some of the tethered boats." She thought that if they came into contact with bad weather, then they would be well and truly fucked. They would be at the mercy of the unforgiving wind, current and the tide. If that were to happen, it would be an almost certainty that their ship would be cast upon the rocks and almost everyone would be claimed by the unforgiving sea.

After some thought, Leena replied, "I think we should pull in somewhere and try and carry out the repairs. Tell them just to forget about robbing Peter to pay Paul. I know that this is the only available option at this time, but we need to have the pair of functional engines; otherwise, we are just an accident waiting to happen." Leena asked him to relay the news to the team in the engine room, then informed him that a brew would be nice. Gareth was tempted to salute but just nodded instead. Leena had not taken her eyes off the water in front of them. Even though she had the team of watchers scanning at the prow, one collision and they would be scuppered. This was a major worry as, with the current state of the engines, going further offshore was most definitely not a good idea.

Captain Leena caught the attention of one of the watchers on the prow, signalling that they had to come and report to her on the bridge. Leena told them to pass the word that they were going to pull into the first available place. "Have some of the crew scan the coastline, looking for somewhere suitable. The team in the engine room should be able to give you a better idea of what type of boats to look out for." They stood firmly at attention, then saluted. Leena asked where this new routine had come from, "Gareth had told us all that while we were at sea, you expected to be given all due respect that goes with the rank." Leena shook her head, asking them to just salute Gareth from now on, as she, for one, did not need it.

Down, near to where the old international by border used to be, Jackson had everyone in the briefing room; firstly, he welcomed them all to their new accommodation and hoped that they had all settled in. He thanked them all for putting up with all the endured hardships and suffering in relative silence during the long journey that had brought them here. "I know that sitting in the vehicles for days on end was a real ass-busting experience, but believe me, we really had no choice. My main, our main priority is to keep you all safe. In order to do this, you are all going to have to be trained to be capable of doing and carrying out different tasks. Starting tomorrow, you are all going to have to begin exercising, and yes, I will also be taking part. We are not going to be training for the Olympic games, but we need some of you to be able to run from A to B and back again."

Enunsha threw the hat in the ring as the crowd started to mumble among themselves. "There will be several classes taking place, like map reading and the likes."

Someone shouted, asking if they had to participate in all of this. She just told them all straight-up that the people who had messed about with the hydropower station were the real deal, and if they wanted to survive, then it would be a good idea to take part. "We are not going to turn you all into some sort of invincible fighting force, but at the very least, when that time comes, we will be able to hit them back. I cannot say when this time will arrive, but I can wholeheartedly, one hundred percent guarantee that this time will come."

Jackson was now addressing them, "People, we don't have much choice in this course of action, so before you leave the room, check your name on the list and at least give your allocated selection a try. That is all we are asking of you."

Abe asked Jackson what he would be doing. Jackson said, "Just like everyone else, you will be assessed by Perry or one of his team; you never know, Abe, you may have some hidden talent."

Abe replied that he used to like him. Jackson smiled, remembering that he had heard this exact same statement many times before. Enunsha joined at the hip with Spotty had also wondered what they would be tasked with, joining the queue to see where they had been placed on the lists.

Somewhere north in not-so-sunny Scotland, Murray couldn't remember the last time that their house was this quiet. He smiled at the thought of Robbo, who was most likely being harassed in stereo and some about all the items that babies required. Cha asked him what he was smiling about, before he spilled the beans revealing the truth. She told him that he was bad, emphasising that there was definitely a cruel and wicked streak tarnishing his soul. Murray had just made her a cup of her favourite brew and was just about to ask her if he could help. Cha told him that the little monsters were now all sleeping, and she was thinking of partaking in a little afternoon siesta.

Mr. Black thought that was a good idea, adding that he could prepare lunch or take the dogs out for a walk. The look on her face delivered a concise and crystal-clear message. Murray agreed that he was going to take the dogs out, as Frank and Cat were preoccupied with the addition to their family, Remus would be invited to come along. He put his arms around Cha and told her that he loved her. Cha replied that she also loved him but added the confession that she did not love his cooking. As he was heading out with Charlie and Romulus. Murray wound her up by saying that he had been attending secret classes, disclosing up-till-now unsubstantiated revelations that he could now cook in a five-star restaurant. Cha was astounded at his bare-faced lie and thought that if Murray was cooking in prison, he would have to be put into protective custody. They exchanged air kisses, and Murray went on his way to abduct Remus.

He thought about what things were like when they had first arrived here, all these years ago and what the place looked like now. The community had come on leaps and bounds; everything that they had attempted was nearly always successful. Murray was truly thankful that they, as a group, had found a way to live with each other without all the shit that had tarnished the old world. He truly believed that the best part about all of this was that there were no fanatical brain-dead football supporters or religious nutters. Nor were there any politicians trying to hoodwink the population into one of their overly ambitious hair-brained schemes that they steadfastly claimed would benefit everyone, but in reality, it would only serve themselves. Remus was chapping at the bit to get out, and Murray bribed him with the minuscule piece of cheese. In the hope that he would just not fuck off, leaving him standing like an orphaned donkey. Cat and Frank had not asked, but being a good neighbour and friend, it was more than okay to be nice to people in his world.

Cha had given him the heads up that they would have to take it in turns to go up and see the new additions at the medical facility. She had also warned him to be on his best behaviour and to try very hard not to upset anyone. Murray had asked her what she meant by that, knowing fully well that she was underlining the fact that he was not allowed to say if he thought any of the newborns had misshapen ears, making them look like the FA Cup. "Some mothers are sort of emotional, with all the hormonal changes going on inside them. Murray, please try your best to be nice and considerate." He had promised an extra effort to transform into the perfect visitor.

Murray, in tow with his very best friends, had arrived at their favourite spot. He sparks up, watching as the dogs sniffed and ran about. Charlie and Romulus had, as expected, been perfectly behaved around the new arrival. Cha, of course, had wound him up by saying that he would be the perfect husband if he were as well-behaved as the dogs. Murray knew fully well that she did not really mean this as she had not tasted the dog's cooking. He chuckled to himself, looking forward to when he could take the little guys out and about, showing them around the outside world. Murray hoped that he only had to show them the good parts by the time they were old enough. All of the bad things about this world would be well and truly gone forever.

Nothing had come from the old woman in the hooded cloak's cryptic messages. Murray hoped that whatever they were meant to mean, they had just somehow passed them by. He would like to think that they could all just survive here without going anywhere else and that, somehow, their little community could become invisible to the outside world. Charlie barked informing him that they all wanted to go home now. Murray willingly surrendered; on the way home, he asked Remus if he would also like to be fed at his house. Cat's dog did not reply, but he took that as a yes. As they entered the house, Murray asked them all to go into silent mode as everyone was sleeping. The dogs behaved, and Murray fed them. Remus settled in like he had stayed there forever. He put the water on to boil as he looked over at his canine friends; they were all curled up together. Charlie was in the centre with her two sons, lying protectively on either side. Charlie was, as always, awarded the prize for snoring the loudest.

The tea was ready, Murray, now having a few minutes to spare, went outside to smoke. He would not have many of these opportunities in the future, so he intended to make the most of it now. Mr. Black had only sparked up, closed his eyes and took the first sip of the wonderful brew when Karen appeared before him. Murray said hello, asking how things were doing in the construction department. She apologised for not having the work all completed for Christmas. Karen handed him a list, informing him that if he could beg, borrow or steal the following items, it was possible they could move in just after the new year. Murray replied that he would speak to Cha if she was okay with him going out to play, he would try and help. One of the workers from next-door was trying to catch her attention to come and look at some problem. Karen said bye, then headed off towards resolving the pending issue.

Murray thought that he could have worded his reply a little better, thinking that he had sounded like a downtrodden, cardboard cut-out of a husband. He was only trying to say that with everyone else in the medical facility. With the newborn and the dogs to take care of, he could not just fuck off at a moment's notice. Robbo was busy, and as cruel as it sounded, Murray would not be giving him any opportunity to escape the abuse directed at him and his super swimmers. If push came to shove, he could easily drive over to Mark's one morning. Murray would speak to Cha about it later; this could be their first family outing. They could leave early and arrive back in plenty of time for visiting hours at the state correctional facility otherwise known to the rest of the population as the medical centre.

Cora, or more likely one of her staff, had placed a large notice outside the entrance door informing anyone who was passing that they were unable to accept any more flowers. Murray and Cha had laughed about it, and some, when they had heard that there were more flowers in the medical facility than what was in the Orangery. Murray thought that Robbo could very well be the main suspect. He relit his banger, then downed what was left of the now lukewarm tea in one gulp; perhaps the next one he would get to drink uninterrupted. As he smoked, he perused the list that Karen had supplied. Murray thought that Robbo was a cheeky bastard as the state-of-the-art sound system has been placed at the very top of the list. Robbo was just something else; every time Murray gave in, cutting him a little slack, allowing him a little leeway. Robbo always tried to pull a fucking fast one.

It could very well be that he was constantly inundated with ever-increasing, demanding requests from the mothers of his newly delivered brood. But... on the other hand, Robbo could very well just be trying to be a wide-o and pull off another sneaky one. Robbo would never have survived at Wrightson's company in the old world. One thing would have led to another, which would have worked out with Murray having to let him go. He shivered at that thought of the pairing of Robbo and the ever-active man-hungry Primrose. Mr. Black abandoned that thought immediately and went into the house to check on his canine children, hopefully, he would get to make another cuppa. If the Gods were willing, he would not be handed another urgent, life-or-death delivery request.

In what was left of the once famous capital city, Lesqueth had doubled her private guard detail, every gate, every door was monitored round the clock. Anyone not on the list of permitted visitors was to be arrested immediately.

Her security convoy now has an additional two armoured cars, and extra heavy machine guns have been issued to all the other vehicles. The Baroness thought that with the tightened security, not even a mouse could get away with a sneaky, unscheduled visit.

The Baroness of Kindeace-Shire waited patiently until Tesporo and his accompaniment of fetid-smelling brethren had completed all the bowing. Then, the man himself had started to deliver what would no doubt be another overly long, grovelling speech. Lesqueth could only suffer himself and the sycophantic nest of vipers in relatively small doses. Already, she was wishing that there was a secret lever to pull that would make them all vanish quietly via a trapdoor into the shark-infested chamber underneath her feet. The Baroness sighed as, at last, Tesporo had finished delivering the sermon, this time praising her for being the true beacon of eternal light in this otherwise darkened world.

She handed him the report, noticing that he had lost yet another digit. "I need an update on all the numbers, a clear, precise record of what stage the training is at and I need it as soon as possible. There is also a list of equipment that is required to be set up and then fully checked, for that, I have allocated you some of the technicians."

The Baroness reminded him that if he happened to come across something that he did not clearly understand, then he was duty-bound to inform her immediately.

Tesporo and his abhorrent disciples all bowed and almost glided out of her sight. Lesqueth summoned her footman to gather all the cleaners to disinfect the whole room. The Baroness thought that the keeper of the records and his flock had an extreme aversion to soap water and required a training course on the true meaning of being surgically clean.

Chapter 2

Commander Essmie had woken up in Miasnikov's bed. The first thing that she did was to run a check on her memory banks. Essmie was now worried as there was no data recording of her moving away from the table. Essmie lay motionless, scanning the room, desperately trying to track, trace and reconfigure her recent activities. Thinking of the worst scenario possible, Essmie reached down to check if she was still attached to her underwear. The commander was momentarily surprised that she was still fully clothed, still wearing her full uniform, including the boots. Essmie, now fully aware of the severe headache that had just announced its arrival, concluded that she was still in the realm of an overindulgence of alcohol. She blamed the copious amounts of vodka that she had consumed last night; the liquid was very easy, way too easy to knock over. The stuff that Essmie was used to drinking normally burned all the way down to her toes.

Now fearing the worst, she tried to make herself look presentable. Miasnikov was not renowned for his effervescent compassion nor for displaying an understanding nature. By all recent accounts, he is most likely just to reward her with a bullet or a swift slash of a blade. Nevertheless, Essmie, feeling slightly less inflammable, was now going to report for duty and also very possibly a date with mortality. She took a deep breath and stepped into the map room. Miasnikov was lifeless on the floor; blood, fragments of hair, bone, teeth and brain tissue adhered to his face and uniform. Essmie withdrew her service weapon and, with the other hand, checked his neck for a pulse.

The general managed to open one eye and squint at the spectacle in front of him; Essmie was covering his drunken carcass and scanning the room for any would-be assailants. The slight cough emanating from the body beside her made her turn around and look at the general. "My dearest Essmie, most people on finding my blood-soaked corpse on the floor would be outside among the rank and file, announcing a week-long celebration at my demise." Miasnikov had both eyes closed and thanked Essmie for her concerns about his well-being, but now, with both eyes open and sitting up, he asked her why.

"My people are from the Artsakh region; we choose our allegiance carefully and remain loyal forever," Essmie asked if she had offended him in any way, empathising that was not her intention. "I saw you lying there covered in blood, fearing for the worst and was in the process of checking the room before I summoned help." Miasnikov was laughing and explained that he had come to terms with the demise of his sister the only way he knew how. Perhaps in a way that his beloved sister Irena would have fully understood and would have truly appreciated. "None of it was my blood, and thank you for your displayed concerns, but I can assure you that there was no need."

Miasnikov had consumed a fair amount of vodka last night and imagined that Essmie was also like him, a little on the tender side. Vladimir ordered her to go and request two number-one breakfasts with all the trimmings. "If you excuse me, I will go and freshen up and change, can't have anyone thinking that they nearly had cause to celebrate, can we?" Essmie stood rigidly to attention and saluted, instantly regretting it as the contents of her stomach swithered on, selecting the appropriate control measure in reaction to the quick motion. Essmie arrived back in about half an hour as the two full breakfasts were delivered. She looked with abject intrepidation at what was in front of her. The plates were generously heaped with fried food that almost floated on a perpetual sea of grease. The general got tucked into the wonderful culinary delights. "The people of this nation, the English, the Scottish and all the rest of them proclaimed to anyone that would listen that they could drink like no others," Miasnikov ordered her to eat up before the food went cold. "What they did not tell anyone was the hangover cure." Vladimir had demolished the plateful that had been placed in front of him and was now using the bread to soak up the remaining tidal residue.

He insisted that she must follow suit and clear the plate. Essmie struggled with every single mouthful, her system was seriously considering regurgitation techniques for beginners. Miasnikov applauded Essmie, delivering well-earned praise on her being able to eat the vile traditional full English breakfast. He produced a bottle of vodka and poured two large measures. Essmie was now thinking that perhaps it would be an appropriate time to die as she watched him swallow down the contents in a well-practised movement. Miasnikov stuck his fingers down his throat and, as the Scottish say, tickled his tonsils. He had produced the bucket from under the table, which was now in the process of collecting the ejected contents of his stomach.

Essmie heard him announce, "Ah, that was just what I needed!" She did not have to encourage her stomach's expulsion and had willingly puked her guts up into the bucket that he had very considerately placed beside her. Miasnikov informed her that he was going to check that the preparations for the expedition were well underway. He saluted, reminding her that as being now one of his top commanders, her presence would be required.

Somewhere on the west coast of Scotland, Leena was cursing; this barely floating piece of shit that should have been scrapped years ago. Which she was now attempting to sail up the west coast of Scotland. A leak had been reported, giving her more than enough justification in seeking a suitable harbour for carrying out the now urgent repairs. The tub of rust was chugging along, barely making any progress against the current in this part of the Irish Sea. Leena knew that if the determined flow of the current were any stronger, they would be struggling to prevent the ship from going backwards. Gareth was here to deliver the status report from the engine room. Leena thanked him for the brew, then asked him if there was any good news and, if not, just to tell her straight. "The mechanics think if we are lucky that, we will have power for about an hour; after that they cannot say for sure." Leena looked around at the coast. All she could see were rocky outlines with no chance of finding a safe berth. If the weather picked up, they could all be swimming ashore. She asked Gareth to take over the helm, "Just keep her heading dead ahead; if I want you to change course, I will let you know." Gareth somehow knew that now was not a good time to salute, so he just nodded.

Leena was now out on the prow, scanning the shoreline for a suitable place to escape to haul up and attempt to carry out the repairs. If the situation changed, they could always dump the ship and then continue the journey by land. If that were to happen, she would prefer to be able to unload all of their supplies rather than just abandon them with the ship. Leena knew that if the engine packed in and died, they would all be in a perilous situation. She signalled Gareth to change the heading and point to the direction of the coast. She had to find a suitable place to berth, as she was not willing to take the chance of being stuck in the sea without any power. Leena sent a couple of the more experienced sailors to take over from Gareth and to tell him to come to the prow.

She asked Gareth to help her scan the headland, and together, they worked their binoculars back and forth. Looking for a way past the promontory rocks that jut out at irregular intervals, almost daring them to come closer. Any contact with these and the hull would be ripped apart. Leena broke away from searching and signals the helmsman a new course to follow. She was trying to steer them along the coast, close enough inshore to see any hidden place that would allow them safety and to stay far enough offshore to escape the abundant jagged rocks that revealed themselves with the crosscurrent of the waves going backwards and forwards.

She spotted it just in time, directing the helmsman to steer hard to port, Gareth could almost touch the rocky outline as they barely chugged past it. Leena breathed a sigh of relief, knowing that if the tide were going in the opposite direction, they would now all be attempting to swim towards the shore. She directed the ship to back out, back out away from the shore and continued watching all around them. Gareth spotted it first, tapping Leena on the shoulder and pointing her in the direction. Leena gave him the double thumbs-up sign; he thought that she had said, "I will make a sailor out of you yet."

She headed towards the bridge to assume command. Maybe with a little bit of luck and the blessing of Neptune, they would not be swimming ashore after all. The echo sounder, like most of the electronics displayed on the bridge, was dead. All that remained in its place of residence was a tangled mess of multi-coloured wires. Leena had to resort to the old world's almost forgotten technique of measuring the depths. It was hardly the most reliable way, and she would have freely, unconditionally exchanged her soul for the reassuring topographic real-time digital display. The line of crew members from the prow to the bridge as calmly as possible pass the latest information by word of mouth as per the latest indications on the sounding rope. Leena adjusted the speed and the course heading to suit. As the light was now starting to fade; she offered the sea god hers and Gareth's soul in exchange that they would not have to attempt this manoeuvre in the dark.

Down near the Mexican border, Jackson was going through the results of the map reading class with his team. As suspected, most of the phonehead generation had never seen a map before and the only time they had consulted a key plan was when exploring the long-gone shopping malls. No doubt they were all seasoned experts at locating the various wares on display in the department stores—the tools, the games, the sportswear and the ladies' lingerie section. Alas, when it came to calculating how to travel from A to B on the strangely coloured paper with all the never-ending rounded configurated designs that were superimposed to reflect the terrain. There was not one of them that could understand the concept of basic map reading. Jackson guesses that this generation had opted out on mass, in joining up with the Girl Guides, or the Cub Scouts. Forgoing how to read the terrain and geographical boundaries, choosing instead to immerse themselves in the mind-numbing games that inhabited all the various multimedia platforms.

Enunsha approached and caught Jackson shaking his head; she asked him what was up. He puffed out his lips, sighed and then divulged what Perry had just told him. "One of the people on the course could not even figure out how to unfold the map. The guy thought that it was a book and, being unable to open flick through the pages, had asked for a knife."

Perry had duly informed him that it was actually a fold in the paper and the guy was distraught in thinking that Perry was trying to fool him. Jackson had asked what the guy had done in the previous life, and it was revealed that he had been a leading financial analyst in one of them big money houses in the capital. Jackson sat with the guy for a while, and going over the now unfolded map, he explained that it was basically just a grid of numbers. Then he showed him that it was possible to work out just about anything about the terrain within the repeating rounding shapes and the numbers relating to the grid references. Jackson spent a considerable amount of time with him going through the referenceable symbols located on the key plan. At the end of their session, Jackson thought that even though the chap in question had various degrees, he still thought that he would get lost in the back garden.

Enunsha was, of course, without any question the star pupil and Perry had told her straight up that there was nothing he could teach her. Spotty looked at him as if he was invisible, and Perry repeated his statement, this time including the dog in the praise. Spotty turned his head away, almost displaying an act of disgruntled satisfaction. Enunsha reassured Perry that she would speak to him and all would be good.

Jackson was still confronted with the continuous dilemma of finding out what everyone in this group of people was capable of doing and doing well before he put the various groups out into the field. He was dismayed at the abundant lack of basic skills and gave in to the fact that he was not going to be able to get the envisaged number of groups required for what he was planning. At present, he thought that if he were to deploy them into the outside world, they would all get lost and wander about like headless chickens for days prior to them all succumbing to the unpleasant effects of dehydration and sunstroke.

In not-so-sunny Scotland, Murray had asked Cha about the possibility of a family day out and she had instantly rejected the idea. Mrs. Black had reasoned that if he were to go by himself, he would get the task at hand completed quicker, and therefore, they could have some much-valued family time. Cha had reminded him that, at present, they were the only ones in the house and if he played his cards right, then they could have a nice meal for just the two of them. Murray caught on to the idea straight away, told her he loved her, then left to go and fill out the urgent list that had been gifted to him by Karen.

Murray had worked it out that if he left now and then went straight to it, he could be back in time for visiting hour, and then it would just be the two of them. He laughed, thinking about all of the times they had shared in the house. However, he was more than very fond of all the residents that had moved in over the years. Murray had to admit to himself that the best times were when it was just the two of them. The vehicle started up with no problems, Murray put the foot down, heading towards the town which was situated about halfway between here and the farmhouse. He had not ventured into this area for a long, long time and as he drove through the streets, Murray was surprised at the advanced rate of decay, the vegetation had grown leaps and bounds, starting to reclaim the once-paved areas, almost conquering the neat gardens. There were no longer any visible boundaries between the houses; the lawns had spread and overtaken all of the dividing paths. The plants and shrubs that were once pruned on a regular basis had grown wild and then spread in every conceivable direction. Murray thought that within his forceable lifetime, all of the towns would be fully reclaimed by nature, and all that would remain would be a stark reminder that people did actually stay here once upon a time. Murray found the dwelling that he was searching for, hoping that the items Robbo had sneakily added to the urgently needed list would still reside within. He had no intention whatsoever of trying out the various applications or cleaning them. Robbo should be more than pleased that Murray had gone and retrieved them. If he was not happy about that, then as far as Murray was concerned, he could go and fuck himself.

Mr. Black entered the room; it was akin to being an unwelcome explorer walking into some long-forgotten kingdom. The previous owner was still present. Their skeletal form was in the big chair. The once top-of-the-range, self-adjusting headphones were still attached to the skull. Murray did not have the heart to remove them; he disconnected the jack from the amplifier and deposited the neatly coiled cable up beside him.

He carefully checked all the interconnected components and then even more carefully dismantled all the various connections that had been joined to the amplifier, that snaked across the floor for almost forever. The speaker cables, after being very carefully unearthed out of the plastered walls, were rolled up neatly and added to the growing pile. This was once someone's much-loved pride and joy. Murray would like to think that the previous owner would have been overjoyed that it was being rehoused, and the new owner would now fully appreciate the endless joy that the equipment had given them for all those now-forgotten years.

It had taken a little longer than anticipated, but Murray had to show some form of respect. The state-of-the-art sound system had probably been the only aspect that had kept the previous owner's sanity intact. Murray had dismantled it with as much due respect and care as possible. The mess he had created digging out the buried speaker cables was, unfortunately, unavoidable. The sizable vinyl collection had taken up the rest of the space in the vehicle, and hopefully, Mark would transport over the rest of the required items on the list. Murray, for some reason felt terribly guilty about the recent theft and had thought that the crime was almost the equivalent of grave robbing. He sparked up and put the vehicle into gear, wondering what sort of welcome he would be greeted with at the farmhouse today.

The last time he was there it almost very nearly came to an unhappy ending. Murray, since that time, had always double-checked that he had a weapon close at hand everywhere he went; today was no exception. He drew to a halt at the prearranged security check and flashed the lights to declare that he was indeed friendly. This time, his vehicle was cautiously approached by a pair of guards, one covering the other. Murray smoked and casually flicked the ash out of the window, already getting bored with this routine. At last, they recognised him and put away the toys. "Great to see you, Murray; sorry about all this, but after Linda's last fuck up, we had to change everything." Murray pretended to be interested, telling them that it was not a problem and continued on to deliver the list to Mark.

It took much longer than usual as there were more sentries, then even more security points. Murray wondered if, on his return journey, he would have to undergo the same routine; if so, he would need to leave early. Mark met him at the gate; Murray informed him that his biometric passport and his DNA had been checked and then verified to be one hundred percent authentic. Mark asked him if it was really that bad of an experience. Murray shook his head and thought that his people would have recognised him sooner. Mark confessed that they were in short supply of decent binoculars and apologised for the delay. Murray wanted to know where his welcoming offer of tea had gone. Mark smiled and told him to follow.

Now in Marks office, Murray smokes, savouring the exotic brew that was on offer. Mark told his friend that he was, as always, pleased to see him and equally pleased that no one had tried to shoot him this time. Murray chuckled at the remark and handed over Karen's list. "What they never put on the list was furniture and all of the other household shit, like bedclothes, pots and pans, you know, the sort of things that I mean."

Mark looked at the list and confirmed that they had all of the items in stock. Murray asked him if he could send it over tomorrow, and that would give him ample time to dig out the binoculars. "How many sets do you need?" Mark thought that four reasonably good magnified sets would be ample and very much appreciated. Mr. Black nodded, knowing that they had boxes full of them and would hand them over to his driver tomorrow. Murray explained that he was on a strict timetable and had to go soon, but he did remind Mark that he still had an open invitation to come over anytime. Mark was about to say if he could manage to escape for the day, but Murray beat him to it, adding, "When you have some spare time." They updated each other on what had been happening in their communities, and Murray gave him a friendly bear hug before he set off home. Mr. Black arrived home well ahead to keep within Chas' schedule and parked the vehicle outside the ongoing works on the extension. Murray informed Karen that the rest of the required items would be arriving tomorrow, and if she could get some of the guys to help remove the stuff from his chariot, that would be greatly appreciated.

Lesqueth, now deep in thought, walked through the corridors of Buckingham Palace with her hands firmly clasped behind her back. Miasnikov would very shortly address the age-old problem of the Hidden and hopefully eradicate their genetic code from this world. They had, over the centuries, been an elusive quarry, but as her father used to remind her, 'no one can hide forever.' The Baroness of Kindeace-Shire hoped and prayed to the gods on high that Miasnikov would somehow manage to catch some of them alive. Lesqueth would kill them slowly, and even when it got to the stage where they would beg for death, she would deny them instant release and drag their demise out until the very end.

As she rounded the corner, the Baroness nearly bumped into two cleaners who were idly chit-chatting away the day. Lesqueth thought of how many times she had reiterated the rules and must again reinforce the penalty for being captured outright breaking them. One of them had scarpered off, leaving the other one to incur her wrath. The Baroness of Kindeace-Shire did not show any anger, politely held out her hand then introduced herself. The cleaner responded to the kind gesture and accepted the handshake. Lesqueth immediately forced her hand and twisted the cleaner's arm up behind her back. Then quickly forced her to her knees and, in one swift movement, broke her neck without the sightless sign of any emotion. She let the now limp and lifeless carcass fall on the floor. The Baroness now began searching for the one who was trying to evade the inevitable punishment. Lesqueth eventually found her pretending to be ever so busy cleaning pictures in the great hall as she approached the cleaner bowed to acknowledge her presence. The Baroness was extremely upset that she was blatantly trying to pretend that the transgression she had witnessed had not even taken place. Now, with her back turned to her, the cleaner continued with the masquerade, overtly putting lots of effort into removing the invisible marks on the paintings, that only she could see.

Lesqueth reached out with one hand and twisted her around, and her other hand, now clenched into a fist, smashed into her throat as the cleaner lay on the floor, trying to steal her last breath. The Baroness of Kindeace-Shire unsheathed her knife and proceeded to cut her heart out. To be sure that this punishment would not go unnoticed, she jammed the still-beating organ into the cleaner's mouth as Lesqueth cleaned the blade and wiped her blood-covered hands on the cleaner's face and hair. She informed the cleaner that due to unforeseen circumstances, they had to lay some people off. The Baroness continued her solitary walk along the corridors; she found that thinking while walking was a great problem solver. If some cleaners, just by chance, were caught breaking the rules and had to be disposed of along the route, then she simply viewed this as an added bonus. On the other hand, if the Baroness of Kindeace-Shire decided just to kill a few of them on the passing, then she would just see this as a double bonus, a mere perk of the job.

Across the pond, G-Flem was en route to inspect the work in progress by Commander Blundell. Now, sitting in her private carriage, she was, as always, amazed that this technology was not adopted worldwide. General Flemings knew that the main reason the system was not utilised globally was the bare fact, that the leading industrial nations were never offered it in the first place. The magnetic levitation system had always fascinated her, how the innocuous ponds of gel could absorb the hydrogen and the static electricity out of the atmosphere. The Baroness of Kindeace-Shire had merely adapted the foolishly published scientific research papers to suit their own needs. The listed companies involved in the manufacturing of all the equipment and machines spanned all over the globe. All of them were legally registered. No matter how far they were investigated and scrutinised, every single one of them remained utterly unconnected to the families' business empire. The great leapt forward in the advancement of the Magno-L rail system was due to the overabundance of the magnetic properties of newly discovered rare earth elements. That had also, never been disclosed publicly nor to any governmental agency.

G-Flem could almost feel the surge of electricity around her as it powered up the vast array of magnetic rings that allowed this magnificent piece of engineering to function. General Flemings was going to travel nearly a thousand miles on an underground train in less than an hour. She sat back in her seat and smiled, thinking that in the 'not-so-good' old days, this would have been more than a truly horrendous journey. It would not have made any difference which mode of transport she had used; they would have all been truly horrible. There would have been queues of people everywhere, a few patient people, lots of impatient people, clean people, dirty people. The worst of all, screaming children demanding everything, complaining and crying unrelentingly for the whole journey. G-Flem, now fully relaxed, was more than pleased that she did not have to share this journey with a single soul. The general drifted into a sound sleep, dreaming of a world without any irritable humans; why her ancestors had allowed them the ability to think and then question all and everything, never mind allowing them to breed uncontrollably, had always perturbed her.

Flemings had been so looking forward to permanently erasing Abe Hubstien and his followers from the face of this planet. The interaction that had taken place between them and the Kunupenny clan was no big deal if she was going to be truly honest about it. Hubstien had saved her the bother of eliminating the upstart who had aspirations way above and beyond his station on establishing a global empire. General Flemings had thought about capturing the Hubstien crew and forcing them to dig out all the concrete, the shopping trollies and all the other scrap that they had placed down the lift shaft. The only problem that she had with the idea was, did she really envisage them being allowed to continue breathing for that long.

The other problem was the Jackson fellow; she remembered reading the reports, and it was almost as if he had appeared one day and within a short space of time, he was now in charge. Jackson did not have a background in construction work; the files that she had read were clean, way too clean. Jackson, she had made up her mind, would be the first to die. He would be thoroughly interrogated, and she would enjoy every second of every minute, introducing him to a new level of pain he never thought existed.

Chapter 3

Blink had just received the news from the returning forward patrol, she took in all that they had observed and then formulated a plan. The most suitable course of action would be to try and avoid the newly discovered settlement all together. As it is fairly well organised, there was no possibility of her group sailing past undetected. Blink gathered her team and then delivered the planned action; she led from the front and undertook the most dangerous tasks. In deep thought, she knew that her people were untested, nevertheless, she would expect their undivided loyalty in giving them the leader that they truly deserve. The fuel boat arrived as she updated the crew on the new course of action, informing them that there would be no changeover today and at nightfall, they would be sailing out into the ocean. Blink went over the plan, making sure that they all understood what was required, then ordered them all to make the necessary preparations for the night ahead.

The darkness has at last finally arrived; Sekoyaz and Blink had synchronised their timepieces, then having crept into position during the change from day to night, move out. Sekoyaz, accompanied by her small team, had crept for hours through all the discarded shit and debris to get close. Then, at the correct moment, they took out the guards posted at the checkpoints. Blink had told her that they were not to take any lives unless it was totally unavoidable. The guards that they had rendered inactive lay there immobile with the rags stuffed into their mouths to keep them silent.

Blink along her team were now in the harbour, hidden out of sight, amongst the small flotilla of boats moving gently in the polluted water. They heard the shouts of alarm as the fires that Sekoyaz had started had taken hold. In the ensuing panic, the local inhabitants rushed about, attempting to put out the flames. Then started shooting indiscriminately into the dense jungle at shapes and shadows that the gunmen, for some strange reason, thought were the fleeing or approaching saboteurs.

As the chaotic pantomime was in progress, none of the inhabitants had thought about the small flotilla of boats in the harbour. Blink assisted her crew in untethering them, then pushed them all out into the water. As the current started to take hold, pulling them out into the ocean. She gave the signal, and the fuel that had been splashed on all of the decks was ignited. The locals, who were so preoccupied with the fires onshore, had failed to notice the now burning boats drifting out to sea. Blink and her small crew, still unobserved, had disappeared back into the darkness, swimming against the current to rejoin the main group at the rendezvous point.

Sekoyaz, along with her team, had eventually all arrived back safely, now that the complete group was all accounted for and assembled. They sailed further out into the sea than normal, hoping that the noise from their engines would not be heard above the shouting and explosions as the local inhabitants tried to curtail the spread of the flames. Blink was pleased that they did not need to kill anyone in the operation. She suspected that the now burning settlement was deeply involved in piracy and that taking away their boats was enough of a deterrent for now. Her people could have just as easily crept in about them, silently in the darkness and slit all of their throats. She was fully aware that there would be no choice in spilling the blood in the future, and unlike this time, there would be no room for mercy or forgiveness, as they were now well away and clear of the burning settlement, Blink issued the signal for the group to head back into the relatively calmer waters inshore. The old woman in the hooded cloak had been absent from her dreams for quite some time now, and she hoped that they would receive a sign soon. Blink wondered if the Enunsha woman would welcome her group with open arms, hoping that she did not need to remind her of why she and her people had arrived.

Somewhere off the west coast of Scotland. Gareth had been ordered to go below to inform them all of what was happening; he warned them all to put on the life vests and prepare to brace for impact. Alwyn had no idea what that meant; Cinds explained that he was to grab on to something, hold on tight and pray. Several of the crew were now helping Gareth out, locating the seemingly hidden life vests and directing all of the passengers out into the corridors. If the need to abandon the ship arose, then they had all of the people ready in position to usher them quickly out of the ship. Other members of the crew checked that all of the passengers were accounted for and that no one was still sleeping in their cabin.

Leena was on the bridge, steering the helm as per the instructions of the chap with the sounding line. At last, she steered her into the harbour. Leena tried hard to keep the ship in the centre, hoping that this was indeed the deepest point. Now, out of danger of crashing into the hidden rocks, she ordered an all-stop on the engine and to attach lines. She breathed a sigh of relief. They might not be able to carry out all of the repairs, but at least they would not have to abandon their cargo and then swim ashore in the dark. Leena asked for a volunteer to swim ashore to borrow one of the small boats. Cinds was ready in a minute, lowered herself into the freezing water, and, like a contestant in some obscure gameshow, swam across to commandeer the first available small boat.

The rescue zone on the port side was manned, opened up ready to pull Cinds back on board and relieve her of the wet clothes. Alwyn was tasked to go and fetch her a set of dry clothes, and fresh towels. Cinds rowed the small boat across with ease and threw them the line. Once the crew had secured the craft, she was pulled on board. As quickly as possible, they removed the soaking wet clothes and then dried her as fast as they could. Gareth was on hand with a steaming cup of coffee and a hot water bottle to heat her up. Alwyn had brought up lots of clothes from the cabin, and as he was putting the oversized jacket on her, she told him that she was fine and did not need to put on the other two jackets.

No sooner than Cinds had put on the warm clothes, Leena ordered her to cabin up and get under the covers. She informed Alwyn he had to accompany her. He smiled like a Cheshire cat; Leena shook her head, informing the silly boy that it was only his body heat she urgently required. The small rowing boat headed back, looking for something bigger to transfer the crew onto the boats tied up in the harbour and to check that the area was safe. The boat the Cinds had located was manned by two of the crew and they set out to search the harbour area. Leena ordered Gareth to go and inform the passengers that they could all stand down from brace for impact as, for now, they were all safe. When the crew arrived with a larger boat, Gareth would take some of his people onshore to search and then secure all of the buildings in the immediate area. Scruffy, who had been allocated a place on the team that would be going onshore, gathered up all his kit as instructed.

They had returned with a fifteen-foot clinker type of boat; it was not ideal for all the tasks at hand, but for now, it would have to do. Gareth summoned all the people who had been selected to go ashore to check and then secure the immediate area. It took several journeys to get the number of bodies required to man the road that led into the hamlet and enough of his crew to search and then deem all of the buildings safe and secure. Leena's crew members who were doing all the rowing had not complained once as they went backwards and forwards across the harbour, ferrying the various groups to their destinations.

The mechanics had already started searching for all of the parts required for the repairs. Unfortunately, they had not located an engine of the same size. They were of the opinion that if they stripped down and then cannibalised some of the antiques displayed in the harbour, then they just might be able to rattle something up that would be sufficient enough to make the repairs. Now in the calmer waters and with the ship now anchored, the leak was being repaired. Leena went down into the hold to seek out the member of Gareth's crew who had been selected to carry out the welding and was allegedly behaving like a prima donna. She could hear him bitching and complaining long before finding him cursing at the people who were sent to help him. Leena, with everything else going on, had no spare time to listen to his moans and groans. "Hey, shitface, no one has got any time to listen to your never-ending earache, so I suggest that you just zip it and get the fucking job done."

Amazingly, he had shut up and got back to work without issuing another single word.

Gareth was now onshore, and with the entrance to the harbour now secured, he split the crew into two teams; starting from each end of the hamlet, they set out to search the buildings. As the first dwellings were entered, none of them found any signs of recent habitation. The former owners had either moved away, or their skeletal remains had been found in bed or sitting in their favourite chair overlooking the harbour. Gareth was now at the only shop in town, the strangely named sports emporium; it shows recent indications that the front door had been forced open. He checked his weapon and slowly entered the premises. The goods on display had not been ransacked and strewn all across the floor. The fresh handprint on the dusty display case stood out, confirming that someone had been in here not that long ago.

As he exited the shop, Gareth gave everyone with him the heads up that there might still be a person or two in the hamlet, so they had to move carefully during the search for the remaining buildings. All went well and his team had exercised all the due caution required and had not encountered any remainers in the preselected search pattern. Scruffy had led his team on the other side of the hamlet; up till now, they had found no one. He heard the cry of a baby coming from one of the nearby houses and sent word to Gareth that they had some company.

Across the great divide of the Atlantic Ocean, Jackson was thinking about pulling his hair out. The map reading classes were not doing too well. Perry had informed him that most of the candidates were fucking useless, and if they were lucky, maybe about five of them would eventually be able to find their way from A to B. Jackson sat with his head in his hands as Perry delivered his theory, "Most of these fuckers are from the app plus pro no brain generation. The other ones belong to the lost generation, and to be perfectly honest, I think they would all get lost in their sleep." Now, looking at him, Jackson asked if it was really that bad; Perry nodded, confirming that his previous statement was true, "Nothing but the truth, so God help me." Jackson asked Perry if he would like him to pass the sentence now. Perry replied that he would be happy with some suggestions or advice. Jackson poured them both a coffee, asked Perry to relax, and then told him that if that was all they had to work with, then no one could have done any better.

"The five that you think show promise, integrate them into the active patrols and try to bring them up to speed," Perry asked Jackson about the others.

"Transfer them into the other training sessions, and eventually, we will find something they are good at."

Perry asked him why he was smiling; Jackson was now laughing. "Tell all of them that if we don't see any improved results, we may have to remove your guys who are doing the galley duties and transfer back Poison Pete and Doctor Death." Perry did not find this idea amusing in the slightest and told his boss that there was definately a cruel streak deep inside him.

Enunsha had arrived with Abe and Spotty; Jackson told her that she had been a star pupil and that pretty soon, she would be receiving her new posting. Enunsha replied that she liked him so much better when he was bullshiting about the shopping malls that were allegedly open twenty-four-seven. Abe had volunteered to lead the team involved in checking the stock of everything that was located inside the camp. Jackson sensed that he was far from happy and asked him if he would like to do something else now that the stock take was complete. "I have just mentioned to Perry that we are going to start more training sessions, and Abe, you could help us find all the best shots. You have a good idea who is the best among our group, and you could even gather up your original team and then help get their skillset updated. Then, if it is okay with you, your team could start to go out on patrol."

Abe thought that they had lots of patrols out and about in the surrounding areas. Jackson caught his drift, explaining that most of these were static and were merely watching. "What we need is an expanded view of the whole area around us. Soon, we will have teams going out to conduct searches and recon missions; I would like you to help make this happen."

Jackson delivered the bad news, "You will be a controller. I need; we need good people at the base who know what they are doing."

Abe was not happy and complained that he wanted to contribute, but Jackson gave it to him straight. "We know that the underground dwellers were watching us, and they will know that you are an important figure in this community. Just imagine what would happen if they spotted you outside, you know, and we both know that they would come after you, big time. If they have done their work properly, you, Abe, are the star prize; let's not play into their hands."

Enunsha agreed with this and knew that Abe would have a target on his back.

Jackson addressed both of them, "This is your community; you have brought everyone together; if either of you were lost or captured, the community would fall apart. I am only here to help or offer some advice; I can't order you on what you can and cannot do. So please take into careful consideration all of what I have said and, by all means, take active roles, but not on the front lines."

He thought Abe was not convinced, so he took him and the rest of them over to the large map. Jackson pointed and spoke, "This is us right there; we don't know what is in all of these other areas. The bad guys could have observation posts, listening stations and all sorts of nasty things out there. Our job is to find out where they have been and what they are really up to. Abe, I admire your gut instinct to get out there, in and about all of the tasks but it is careful planning that wins battles."

At the watermill, Murray had made himself presentable to go and visit all of his friends at the medical facility. Cha had bribed him to be nice to everyone, and the list included Robbo. She had said that perhaps being a parent would bring out the best in him. Murray smirked, and Cha told him that she did not want to hear what he was thinking about as a suitable reply. He reassured her that he would return with gold stars on his log book and would be back in an hour or so. He had no flowers to hand out, and he was bearing no gifts. Cora's declaration on the plundering of the Orangery was still in effect, and heaven help anyone who failed to obey the stark warning. Murray entered the ward and confessed that Cha had made him promise to behave by disclosing the information that they all now had to sign his report card with glow-in-the-dark, five-star reviews.

After all the pleasantries were out of the way, he asked where Cora was and if everything was okay. Okolo informed him that she had a private room and all was well with both her and the new addition. The twins were looking tired, but all of the women were taking care of them, keeping them from being down in the dumps. As Okolo was the only one who had the experience of motherhood, she had taken over the role of the acting mother superior in the ward.

Cat was beaming, and her daughter, by all accounts, just looked like her. Murray was going to ask about feeding time at the zoo but changed his script at the last second as he did not want to offend anyone. Alicia replied, informing him the really strict matron that Cora had appointed, made them all feed at the same time. Robbo and Frank were noticeably absent; Robbo was with Cora, spending time with his daughter, and Frank was facing a rebellion in the galley and had sent word that he would be up later. Murray asked what all that was about, and it was the usual thing, where some of the population were accusing the stand-in chefs of trying to poison them or put love potions in their food.

Murray asked if they thought that there would be any complaints if he were to volunteer and do some of the cooking. All of them at once held up their crossed fingers as if keeping the devil away. "Oh well, it was only a nice thought." He relayed the info to Okolo that Vincent was doing fine and he was just about perfect. Okolo beamed, knowing that Murray was lying through his teeth, and she knew damn well fine that Vincent when he took the notion, could be just as stubborn as her. She thanked him and made sure and tell Cha that she was thanking her also. "Oh yeah, before I forget, the fancy sound system has been delivered, and the rest of the items on the list should be arriving tomorrow. As for colour schemes and the aspired furnishings, I am taking nothing to do with that, and you can make up your own minds and pass the requests on to Karen via Frank and Robbo."

Murray was sort of sad that Okolo and Alicia would be moving out and confessed that he would miss them. As there had never been any real problems, it was just like one big happy family. Everyone knew that they would just be moving next door, and it was not like they were moving to a continent at the other end of the planet. He had surprised himself with the statement and had almost shed a tear. The twins would find it hard to adjust to the changes, but both Alicia and Okolo had informed them that they were just next door and that they could come and see them anytime. Murray disclosed that Cha thought their children should not be attending the school that was in the process of being set up for the rest of the infants. Due to the special gifts that Mark and Vincent had been displaying, he was advising caution.

"It may not come to anything, and it could all very well just fizzle out, but we have to be careful."

Okolo agreed, and all the other women nodded their approval. Alicia thought that all was going well. They would be allowed to escape in a few days and they were all looking forward to not having to eat the food that Cora had stipulated was for their health and wellbeing. Murray told them to hang on in there, and soon they would be eating fish, fish and more fish. "I am going to go shortly, and should any of you need anything, send me a message, and I will see what I can do."

On the journey back home, Murray looked up at the night sky. At this time of year, the view was nothing short of spectacular. He did not know if it was because they stayed in the far north or if it was just a clear night. He did not classify himself as a stargazer and, sure as shit, could not name any of the constellations, never mind being able to spell or pronounce them properly. Nevertheless, he thought he had spotted something unusual; it was probably nothing, and the chief astrologist Cha or her understudy Cat would surely laugh at him. Then named what he had thought was unusual without even looking at it.

The dogs were pleased to see him, and the exotic meal that Cha had hinted at making was nowhere to be seen. Murray went up the stairs and found them all asleep, Cha and the three infants were all on his bed, dead to the world. The meal was not important enough to wake Cha up for, and he quietly disappeared back down the stairs. Murray stocked up the fire, and the dogs showed no signs of wanting to move; he thought that Charlie was pretending to be dead as she showed no reaction to the going for a walk words.

Murray put the water on to boil and made his favourite brew; for a moment, he wondered what would happen if they ever ran out of tea bags and tea leaves. He had read something a long time ago that in the days of old, they used to grind up flowers, seeds and all sorts of shit to make a herbal drink. Murray thought that it would taste as bad as it sounded, he closed his eyes and took the first sip. Thinking out loud, he announced that it was wonderful and truly nectar from the Gods, and then he took the perfect brew outside and sparked up.

He was smoking very little these days and thought that it was due to a combination of things; he was getting older. The additional responsibilities of fatherhood and the fact that he really could not be bothered. Also, the fact that he had to stand outside in all weather was just making his once favourite hobby transform almost into a chore.

If Cha had noticed she never commented on it, maybe she would have liked the idea. He did not think it would change him any, and he would not really miss it. He looked up into the night sky, and the object he had seen earlier was still there. Murray was pleased that it was not just a figment of his sometimes-overactive imagination. If Cha were awake, he would ask her for an explanation, but whatever he had seen, it could at least wait until tomorrow. Not wanting to disturb any of the sleeping angels, Murray intended to park up on the couch.

He helped himself to a refill and resumed his star gazing; the object he had witnessed was now displaying a tinge of green. At first, he thought that because of his near abstinence from partaking in the weed, with his recent intake, he might be seeing things. Murray rechecked his vision, and as he found nothing else was showing a green tinge, he looked back up into the heavens. Mr. Black was positive that he was witnessing a comet; perhaps the residents of the local star club would be able to inform him of its name. These objects tore through the universe on a huge, repetitive path, sometimes taking thousands of years. Murray wondered that if the last time the comet had passed through their side of the galaxy, perhaps the world would have been a better place to live in. It could have been at the dawn of time when the planet was peaceful and worry-free. Unlike now, where every day, they were all faced with the ever-present uncertainties and possible dangers that could eradicate them. Thus, condemning him and his race of people to exist only as an obscure reference in the pages of history.

At Buckingham Palace, the Baroness of Kindeace-Shire took full advantage of the rain-free day and walked throughout the grounds. Her guards were spread out in front of her and behind her. None of them wanted to incur her wrath should they breach her private space. She was concerned that there was much more to the Hidden problem and ran through everything that had quite recently transpired. Lesqueth made a list of unusual things that had happened in the recent past that the Hidden could have very well, orchestrated. Now more than ever, she wanted them all dead; the last one she wanted to be stuffed and put on permanent display. Her thoughts were interrupted by some of the slaves in the garden breaking the rules and having the audacity to approach her and wish her a happy new year.

The Baroness would have let them off with the offence, but as they had got the dates mixed up, they would have to be punished. Lesqueth thanked them all for their kind wishes and informed them that she had a very special gift for them. The guards, under her instructions, herd up the garden slaves and then escort them to the water garden. This was, at one time, her favourite exhibit to visit when on the grounds and as it was in need of urgent restoration. She summoned the mechanical people in charge of this display and then ordered them to make the necessary preparations for the new intake. The slaves watched, not quite sure of what fate awaited them, as Lesqueth did not want to spoil the surprise in any way; she had them blindfolded.

The Baroness watched as, one by one, the garden slaves were forced down the stairs into the now near-empty enclosure. They trample on the soft bones of the previous visitors and the odd fish that had not managed to escape in time. The prisoners were persuaded to push their arms up through the grate, and as they were handcuffed, all of their blindfolds were removed. Lesqueth nodded in the direction of the mechanics, and the valves were opened. The Baroness of Kindeace-Shire wished them all a belated happy new year and, totally devoid of any compassion, ignored their pleas for forgiveness. The water slowly filled up the enclosure, and now reasonably happy that fresh hands were poking up through the surface, thinking that it was much more appealing to the eyes than skeletal fingers. She looked forward to her next visit when she would witness the fish nibbling away at their rotting flesh.

As always, a group drowning always gave her a healthy appetite, and now, in the banqueting room, Lesqueth read through all the up-to-date information on her future armed forces. All of the children had now received the official stamp that they would proudly display her family's emblem on their skin for as long as they lived. The numbers had increased, and all of the twelve hundred little souls were encapsulated in the sound and vision modules that bombard their brains with their envisaged future. How they would obey orders without question, what they would sacrifice and how they would perform every task to the best of their abilities. Lesqueth would have much preferred a larger number of new recruits, but given the current circumstances, she thought that she would have a sizeable force to be reckoned with.

The troopers who were presently cleansing Merica of all forms of the resident primitive bipeds would add to these numbers. Once all the current problems had been settled, she would instigate a new superior breeding program that would exponentially increase their numbers, enabling her forces to inhabit every continent on this planet. Any remaining members of the indigenous people would be listed as an endangered species. Her forces would search every landform, every tree, every cave, every hiding place and, once and for all, eradicate their seed forevermore.

On the west coast of America, General G-Flem noticed a very small change occurring with the electromagnetic propulsion aboard the Magno-L; she stirred and started to wake up. Flemings found this form of transport so relaxing and almost therapeutic. Maybe one day, she would actually manage to stay awake for the whole of the journey. She pressed the button, and the assistant arrived immediately, G-Flem ordered her much favoured morning nutrition. Commander Blundell should by now have started clearing the transportation network around station A.

She shook her head, remembering the time when he marched into her office like a Roman General and presented the report, even with all the highly advanced munition delivery systems that were at his disposal. Blundell was still of the opinion that he was worthy of being awarded a prestigious accolade for disposing of the Indian nation. G-Flem was of the opinion that he was utterly pretentious and was in the throes of suffering from serious delusions of grandeur. Blundell did not have to muster any of his troops to engage the enemy in a life-or-death standoff, where they would have fought toe-to-toe, holding off a superior force until the last man standing. Commander Blundell did not even have to press a single button. The defensive ring that encircled the CCP, along with all of the other assets was a fully automated system, self-loading and self-arming; it even had a selective detonation sequence where ARI removed the possibility of human operator incurred error. "All I want is a medal," Commander Blundell's involvement had, in fact, been almost negligible. Sadly, only accumulating in providing the supervision who would monitor the replacement of the spent munitions. General Fleming secretly called him Billy Blunderful and was now of the opinion that before their esteemed leader arrived. Mr. Blunderful might just have to be replaced. She was adamant that no matter what fate befell him, he was still not going to be receiving any type of reward even a posthumous one.

Her current mode of transport drew to a dead stop, and she opened the blind for a quick look; as expected, Commander Blundell was there to welcome her. He stood as still as a statue, perfectly straight and displaying the one hundred percent stipulated regulation cap angle required. G-Flem was the thought that he must stand in front of a mirror most of the day, every day practicing his pose and measuring the precise angle of his cap. She guessed that no one had bothered or had the gumption to inform him that they didn't take pictures nowadays.

Chapter 4

Blink looked over at the small flotilla of boats that were all presently tied up, waiting for the fuel to be delivered. The craft that they had utilised to become the tanker was late. Sekoyaz had already informed her that they were now down to the last dregs and could proceed no further. All she could do now was wait; Blink passed out the word that, for now, they could stand down and relax. She added that they should make the most of it as in the next few days, it would be a whole new different ball game. By her reckoning, they had been moving westwards for the last few days and with that came danger. The islands and the abundant peninsulas in this region had always had a reputation for being less than friendly and downright inhospitable. Blink stripped her weapons down, cleaning and then inspecting every part prior to reassembling. She had never liked guns, remembering the advice that had been passed down from mother to daughter. It was only another tool, and like every other tool, it had a designated purpose. The trick with this tool was knowing when was the right time to use it and when was the right time to keep it well hidden out of sight.

Her mother had shown her how to use this weapon, emphasising that it was a beast that had to be tamed. Lucky had taught her everything: how to breathe, how to hold and most of all, how to control. At an early age, she had learned that the weapon had to be aimed, none of this pointing and hoping for the best. The words of her mother rang out in her head. "Every shot has to count; near enough is never good enough. One perfectly aimed shot can win a fight, and one wild shot can lose a war." Blink was now walking around the camp, speaking to all of her team. She knew every single one of them by name and, without question, trusted them all. Blink knew that some of them would never be returning to the village in the mountains, although she would try and save as many of them as possible. She knew deep down in her soul that, unfortunately, no matter how hard had she tried, she would not be able to save them all.

The refuelling boat eventually arrived, all the crew was accounted for, and there were no problems other than the vessel being old and slow. Once all the boats were replenished with the foul-smelling liquid, the makeshift tanker underwent a crew change. Blink gathered them all together and disclosed the possible dangers ahead of them. "After today, we will no longer be using the rusty old tub; we now need to move fast to keep you all out of danger."

She went through the new plan, which now required them to travel day and night to escape the danger zone. "In the next part of the journey, we will be heading across the open sea and from then on in, we will be hopping from island to island. This move does not make our journey any shorter, but it will make it safer." She had thought out this plan over the last few days with the sole intention of hitting them hard to make it crystal clear and to truly understand what was involved. Blink produced the map showing them all the steps that were required.

On the other side of the Atlantic Ocean, Gareth had moved over to the other side of the harbour to join Scruffy and his search team. "What's the problem?" before he had a chance to explain, Gareth heard the baby crying. Taking the lead, then moving everyone away from the front-facing door and windows. He stood to the side and knocked on weather-beaten wood. "Hello, we heard the baby cry. Do you need any help?" There was no reply, and again, the infant was heard crying out. "We are coming in! We mean you no harm!"

Gareth kicked the door in, and the first thing that he and the ones who followed him noticed was the goddam awful smell. The stench of rotten food permeated throughout the small dwelling. "Scruffy, go back to the ship and give Cinds the heads up that we are going to be sending her a few patients."

Cinds had undertaken lots of jobs prior to the arrival of the sickness; one of the ones she did talk about was when she was a nurse. Gareth found not one infant but two, and by the look of them, they were starving. He gently picked them up and passed them over, "They need to be fed and checked over straight away. I don't care if you have to steal the baby formula, but they need to be fed as soon as possible."

He knew that there were a few mothers with young ones on the boat, and he also knew that they might not be too keen on sharing the food. The mothers were out for the count; they had high temperatures, and by the accumulated mess all around them, he guessed that they had succumbed to food poisoning. "We will need a stretcher to get these two transferred onboard." Gareth, seeing that no one had moved, instructed two of the statues to spring back into life and retrieve the required equipment.

He gathered up the weapons that were lying beside the two women, placing them in the bag containing the clothes. Although they were not going to be staying in this hovel any longer than required, he ordered that the rotten fish be removed and dumped in the water. Gareth looked at the creatures as they were being handled delicately, surmising that by the additional lumps on them, they were contaminated and should have never been eaten in the first place. The stretchers arrived, and the two women were taken away for some urgently required medical treatment. On leaving the hovel, one of the women had said something, but he had no idea as to what she was trying to say as it was just a completely garbled unintelligible, delirious mishmash of words. Gareth hoped that they would respond to the antibiotics, and if not, due to the lack of an experienced health professional, they would surely die. Cinds had been alerted and now fully recovered from her immersion in the cold water; she is back on duty. Now, in the process of persuading some of the mothers to relinquish the baby food, "Look, if they don't eat, they will die, and if you don't hand it over, they will die. Do you want to be the one who informs their mothers that you did not want to share?"

Leena had overheard the terse conversation and ordered the women to cough up the required goods, "It's not negotiable, ladies; we all deserve a chance; that's the difference between us and the bad guys that we are escaping from! Hand it over like, right now." Alwyn and Scruffy were looking more than very uncomfortable as they tried to shoo the starving infants.

Leena asked Cinds if she needed anything else.

"Yeah, a change of clothes, some diapers and the other baby things would be fully appreciated."

Leena looked at the mothers again, and this time, she thought that there would have to be no orders issued. Alwyn and Scruffy had been given the feed bottles; now, they looked somewhat relieved as the babies were only making slurping noises rather than bawling their eyes out. They both received knowing looks from some of the women, plus the odd comment that they look like naturals. Gareth passed by, and Scruffy asked him if he would like a shot at feeding the baby. Gareth replied that as he was doing a great job, so why change things? Now red-faced, Scruffy walked up and down, patting the little cherub gently on the back. Cinds had ejected all the items out of her and Alwyn's room; with the sick women now in their beds, she struggled as they resisted the administration of the antibiotics. "If you don't take these, you will not recover, and who will look after your babies then?"

Reluctantly, her patients took the tablets and then fell back into sleep. They are both very weak and both very dirty; Cinds' requests some warm water and a change of clothes. She had made the mistake a while back of informing Gareth of her previous employment status in the old world. Cinds had told him that she once worked as a nurse; what she never told him was that she was a trainee dental nurse, and she had only lasted one full day.

Jackson, accompanied by Abe, was going through the lists of all the items that were available in the vast storage area. "We need to set up a perimeter defense, to ensure that the bad guys just don't march in and take this place over. Perry will be coming to visit you later and will be looking at withdrawing all the items that I have ticked off."

Abe looked at the list, recognising some of the names. "I am guessing that he will not be taking all the stuff in one go?" Jackson replied that Perry would be taking one of the newly formed groups out first to reconnoitrer the surrounding areas. Then, once they have established the probable routes that the bad guys will use, they will come back for the goodies. "I am sure that he will give you a heads up on what he and his group need first."

Hubstien looked at him, knowing that the last statement could probably, most likely translate into I need some of these, some of them, and could I get them all now. Jackson noticed Abe's unease. "Why don't you go and see him? And he will put you in the picture, then you will have a rough idea of what he is thinking about doing."

Abe nodded, thinking that he could persuade Perry to allow him to accompany the group outside. The thought of escaping the camp for at least a couple of hours would be, as far as he was concerned, a wonderful idea. He mentioned this to Jackson, and Jackson gave in, "I guess that everyone should really be aware of where they can walk and where not to walk."

With a new spring in his step, Abe, now delighted, went in search of Perry to deliver the good news.

Enunsha had been coerced into teaching some of their people how to shoot; like everything else, she was a natural. Some of the people were reasonable. Others were nothing short of hopeless; one shot would miss the next would be perfect. All of her newly enrolled students had one or multiple faults that she had to try and attempt to rectify. Poison Pete, along with his forever shadow Doctor Death, the former camp culinary specialists, were the worst students, struggling to hit a single target. "If you don't get this right, I may have to recommend that you are both transferred to the camp maintenance department. As they already have most of the skilled people that they require, that would equate to both of you fixing and cleaning the toilets. C'mon guys, I need you to at least try."

"Peter, we've all seen you coaxing, endlessly handling the pumps with all the due care and attention. These guns are just other machines that need to be treated the correct way.

Give your gun one of your ex-girlfriends' names, then treat her nice."

Poison Pete tried again; Enunsha watched over him, noticing him inadvertently twist then jerk the trigger rather than gently squeeze it. She got down on the ground beside him and made him cringe as she exaggerated his motions. "That's what you are doing, Peter it's not good enough." She had brought on the rest of her students from being truly awful to reasonable, but she was confident that by the end of the week, they would all be able to pass the test. Poison Pete and Doctor Death, she doubted if they would improve any. Enunsha hoped that they would be good at cleaning toilets. The one place that they would not be transferred to was the galley; both Abe and Jackson had agreed that they would have a riot on their hands if that happened.

Perry had agreed to take Abe out on a short-guided tour, where he showed him all the areas where the munitions were going to be placed. Abe was banging on about how he missed being out and about in the wide-open spaces. Perry informed him that although he fully appreciated and truly understood what he was saying, he made a point of telling Abe that he would not like to be in his group. Abe wanted to argue the point, reminding Perry about all of his outdoor skills and how he thought he could be a team player. "I have four teams in this area who go out on forty-eight-hour duties. Do you think that you could do that? These guys lie in one position, eating, sleeping and shitting for two days on the trot. Abe, I think you would hate that duty; like Jackson said, you are way too important, and the people here need you." Abe looked as if he was trying to formulate the information and fully understand what Perry was saying to him. "Put it another way, you have been two feet away from one of the teams, and you never even noticed."

The two team members lying in the scrub coughed and gave away their positions. Abe, in his defense, said that he did not know that it was a test. Perry shook his head. "Every step, every breath out here is a test; we know they are out there, and we just have to be ready when they come." Abe took his point, finally admitting defeat. Perry pointed out all the obvious paths in this area, then pointed out all the unobvious paths the trained bad guys would take. "That is what we need to be able to counter; it is not some untrained horde that is going to be attacking. These guys are highly trained and super-efficient at covering their tracks, and we are going to beat them. It might take months; it might take years, but either way, we will beat them."

Jackson was inspecting the perimeter of the camp, checking out for all the blind spots and pinpointing the areas where an attack would not be anticipated in being launched. He would pass this information on to Perry when he returned from his guided tour with Abe. Jackson knew that Abe was desperate to get out and about, and although he kept telling him, Abe did not seem to be getting the message. Hopefully, Perry would have convinced him that they were looking after his best interests and keeping him in the compound. When they both returned, he would take the two of them around the outskirts, and Abe could help formulate the plan. That, at least, should keep him and his brain occupied for a few days.

With this issue being resolved, Jackson then made his way over to Enunsha; her group was hard at it, shooting away at all the targets. He asked her how it was going, and she told him all the details. He listened, agreeing with her on the recommendations that Poison Pete and Doctor Death should be transferred. Jackson knew that she had been trying hard to bring them on, and he also knew that there was no toilet cleaning detail in the compound. Well, at least, not just yet, but with everything else that could change in the very near future. Jackson was aware that some of the accommodation blocks could be cleaned, plus a coat of fresh paint or two, and the dynamic duo's name was stamped all over them. He just hoped that they were more adept at painting and decorating than they were at cooking.

At the watermill, Murray was entertaining the children, trying to make Mark eat. Charlie and Romulus lay with their paws over their eyes, not wanting to witness another performance of 'here comes the train.' Cha shouted incoming, throwing the feeding bottle over for Murray to catch. He was now in the process of feeding Alfie and tormenting Mark to at least swallow one mouthful. As always, Vincent was an angel, eating away without any fuss or any of the applied amateur dramatics. Mr. Black had previously observed that Cha did not have to go through this rigmarole at feeding time, and he thought that it must be a man thing. Cha was rustling up some grub, and this could be the last time they had the chance for a quiet meal for two, as it was strongly suspected that some of the prisoners from the medical centre could be released the next day. Murray mentioned the comet, and Cha made a promise of sorts to have a look if she got the chance.

It was Cha's turn to go and visit, and he had been roped into babysitting. He was thinking of bribing them into going for a walk with the dogs, but already he was having second thoughts. As soon as Cha left the room, Alfie screamed as if there was a serious crime in progress. Murray thought if he played some music, then maybe that would calm him down, and perhaps then he would think that his dad was not the bad guy. Mark thought Daddy was not looking and stole a handful of his food. Murray was impressed and handed Mark the spoon. The baby smiled, realising that he had been left to his own devices to feed himself without the ongoing audition for the pantomime.

All the banging and hammering, including all the other associated major construction underway noises, had almost ceased. Cha and Murray both thought that Karen's work crew could now be decorating the new abodes. It would take at least another couple of weeks to finish everything, making it fit for habitation. Robbo had spent most of his time in there, helping out where he could. Murray suspected that he could possibly be the oldest tea boy on the planet, but fair doo, at least he was there. The delivery from the farmhouse had just arrived, and Karen was delighted that all the items on her wish list had been supplied.

Murray opened the door and invited the driver to come in; as he had Alfie in his arms, he could not pick up the package to be delivered to the farmhouse. "Mark asked about these the last time that I had seen him and please tell him that we only had a dozen pairs to spare."

Cha informed Murray that the food was ready and that if it got cold, she would be angry. Murray thought that it was his birthday, Christmas, and every other celebration all rolled neatly into one. Cha was bemused as he had not even tasted it yet. "You look awfully pleased with your meal."

Murray smiled, confessing that it reminded him of the early days when it was just the two of them. Cha laughed and shook her head. "You never did ever take me away for a weekend, promising no end that I could have any food I wished for via room service."

He replied that it was not really his fault and that the sickness had put an end to all the hotels, adding that as soon as things got back to normal, he would take her away immediately.

Cha countered with, "You are just so full of shit sometimes."

Murray declared that was why she loved him so much and complimented her on yet another sumptuous dish. He was just about to ask her if he would ever be allowed to cook for her when she interrupted him before he even asked. Telling him that if hell froze over and he had somehow managed to win the international Chef of the Year award for the tenth time running, she would still not allow him to cook for her.

"I hate it when you invade my thoughts," Cha retorted, saying that it was just as well that he was as honest as the day was long.

Karen knocked and came in. "Sorry to disturb you both, but I wanted to ask if we can work through the night decorating next door. If we complete all the work tonight, the houses could be ready to move into sooner."

Cha and Murray had no objection but told her that there was no need to get her crew to work all through the night. It was a very nice thought, but really, there was no need. Cha poured her a cuppa, and Murray made his escape for a much-needed smoke. He was thinking about his famous two-pan shuffle, but he did not think that it was that bad. All the same, he laughed when he thought about Chas's initial reaction. At one time, he thought about asking her for the official translation of what she had said, but on second thoughts, perhaps it was really not a good idea.

As he went back into the house, Karen had Alfie in her arms. Mark and Vincent were splayed out on the floor, cuddled into the dogs. Karen had just asked if they were ever worried about the dogs biting or scratching the babies. Murray burst out laughing, declaring that he worried non-stop about the babies scratching and biting the dogs. He explained to Karen that the dogs were great with the children, even when Mark and Vincent stole their food.

Murray asked if all of her projects were going well and apologised for not keeping up to date as they had been busy the last while. Karen seems to be in another world as she gently soothes Alfie, who has now fallen asleep in her arms. Cha told her that she was good with him. Karen smiled but looked sad at the same time. Murray, the diplomat, instantly changed the subject by asking if there was anything that she needed help with.

Karen, now back in the present, nodded. "Funny you should mention that there was something I was going to mention. A while back, Robbo had the idea about the solar power."

Murray thought that this subject was null and void, on the general understanding that Robbo had no earthly idea what it was about. "Well, as he has been working away with the team next door, we sometimes talk about this and that." Murray was waiting for the next idea, Robbos' latest brain fart, to surface. Karen explained that the plan that Robbo had explained to her might just actually work, and she admitted that it was not as far-fetched as it sounded, as it seemed perfectly feasible.

"Robbo had warned me that you would not want to listen, as he had gone off on multiple tangents when he initially found all the kit." Cha had taken Alfie, put him upstairs to sleep and was now making a fresh pot.

Karen continued, "Robbo had presented all the facts and figures, then, much to my surprise, showed me all the diagrams. He must have driven Okolo and Alicia mad with this as it was evidently clear that he had practised the presentation."

Cha provided them with a fresh brew; Murray, feeling that his head was about to explode, rattled one up.

The conversation continued outside, and Murray smoked as he listened to what she had to say, or more to the point, what Robbo was proposing. Karen had now produced the diagrams and talked through the plan. "The hydro plant produces electricity, even when we are all sleeping. This plan will enable us to store that energy; the best part about it is that we do not have to go and rummage into dangerous territories for all the parts that are required."

Cha asked her why; Karen explained that all the parts were here already, and all they had to do was connect them.

Murray asked a few questions while pointing to the diagram, and Karen answered all of them with ease. It was the case that all the parts were there, and with minor adjustments, they could, in fact, store the energy. "Robbo had no intentions of just going ahead with the idea without it being run past you and until it had received your approval. Up till now, everyone has held back from switching on appliances, especially in the morning, as they are afraid of causing a power cut. This plan would enable people, within reason, to switch things on any time they wanted. I would like you to approve this and then agree that you will help out when required. Our population is growing, and with that, so will our electricity consumption."

Cha asked if the initial plan that Robbo had for the solar panels was now dead in the water. Karen took a deep breath, confessing that Robbo was still working on that one. "The good news is that the panels have never been used, and they are all still wrapped up in the protective coating that was administered prior to their departure from the manufacturers."

Murray sparked up another one as he tried to wrap his head around this new piece of information. Looking at Karen, he asked if the solar panels would actually produce any juice. "These panels were the latest technologically updated models to leave the factory. They work on light, not heat, and yes, they will produce."

Cha thought that, for now, they should go ahead with the battery installation. Then, until they received all the facts and figures about the panels that part of Robbo's electrical dreams could wait. Murray drifted off for a few seconds, and as he returned, he was aware that they were waiting on his decision. "Okay then, we go ahead with the battery installation for now." Karen thanked them for listening and let it slip that she had reassured Robbo that he would agree. Murray thanked her for the vote of confidence, informing her that she could deliver the good news to Robbo.

Now, on their own again, Cha checked on Alfie, who was still sound asleep, and Murray checked that the dogs had not been abused by the other two monsters, who were still snuggled into them. Cha asked what he really thought; Murray thought that one day, sometime in the future, someone was going to come in requesting outside lights to neatly line every single street. Cha informed him that in another world, he would have been a Luddite.

Murray disagreed and thought that he would have been the chap the establishment burnt naked at the stake for proclaiming that this planet was not the centre of the universe. Cha was going to go for forty winks, and Murray prepared his brain to fully submerge into Robbos' electrical diagrams. He took his time, allowing for the permissible mistakes, and went through them all, agreeing that they were possible. If they had to venture into what must now be nothing but a hostile world for parts, he would have instantly vetoed the project. In the past, they had gone into the remnants of the old world, and these journeys were always pretty awful and somewhat dangerous. Now, he thought that they all had a most definite no-go area stamped all over them. Not one of these other groups that they had encountered in the past had made any provisions for the future, and with that, he thought their parasitical world would be an absolute nightmare to even attempt to travel into.

Mrs. Black had come back to the land of the living, and just in time. Mark and Vincent had just announced that they were awake, declaring to all of the known universe that they were very hungry. Murray wondered if their mothers had warned them about his cooking, so Cha came to his rescue and offered to make them something. The bottle was ready for Alfie, and Murray took a turn at feeding him. The baby intently stared at him during the feed, never once taking his eyes from him.

Murray reminded Cha about the comet he had seen, "Perhaps on the return journey from visiting the inmates at the penal colony, you could have a look at the heavens?"

Cha replied, "Oh, you mean that moving object up in the sky with the green tail?"

Murray was sure that she was taking the piss and also thought that he was just making it all up. "All I am asking is that you take a look, nothing else. It could just be a simple case of the onset of vision problems, which is why I am asking you to look, nothing else. Just a plain, simple request to confirm what I have seen."

Cha gave in and promised to have a look; before she left, he was reminded to wash himself and the children before their bedtime story.

She arrived at the medical facility just in time for the allocated visiting hour. All of the prisoners were pleased to see her, and Cha was informed that if she was quiet, they could show her the new additions. Cat led the way; Cha was almost on tiptoes as she followed her, accompanied by the rest of the mothers, through the double doors. Alicia and Okolo both had healthy baby boys, and all of the rest of her friends produced healthy girls. All of the new additions looked like little angels, and all of them were sleeping except for one whose eyes followed Cha around the room.

Cha just knew without asking that this was Cat's child; she looked at her Cat's beaming smile, confirming what she already knew. Okolo, assigned to the position of the lookout, gave them the word that the strict matron was on her way, and they all sneaked back into the ward. All of the inmates managed to get back into their beds, and Cha sat and chatted with Cat as the matron, aka the chief of the secret police, popped her head in to check on them. The women had to curtail the giggles at nearly being caught breaking the somewhat strict rules. Cha asked Cat if she had a name picked out. "I was thinking about naming her Sammarra, but Sam for short; I have not mentioned it to Frank yet, but I think he will agree."

Knowing full well where Cat got the name from, she put her arms around her and told her that she will be a fantastic mother.

Chapter 5

Lesqueth, surrounded by her retinue of guards, was out for her morning stroll. She was overjoyed by the sight of the fish feeding on the flesh of the slaves, now fully immersed in the water gardens' main feature. The Baroness of Kindeace-Shire made a mental note to remind herself not to leave it for so long the next time before she replenished the food source. Now, back in Buckingham Palace, she mulled over the projected outcome of the Enhancement project. She followed the sequence of the predicted, somewhat variable results, although this experimental theory had never been tried or tested. Lesqueth was going to initiate the start-up. It could be a catastrophic failure, possibly eliminating all life on this planet and reading the results at the end of the predicted outcome. This could very well empower her children to be the most powerful species to have ever existed on this planet.

If this experiment were indeed successful, there would no longer be any limitations on what her people could achieve in the future. Her long-forgotten ancestors had travelled through dead space for years upon years to reach this place. The Enhancement project was only the beginning, unlike the indigenous species of this planet, which were content to make small steps. The Baroness of Kindeace-Shire was fully intent on taking numerous gigantic steps forward.

Tesporo, along with his nest of fetid brethren, had been extremely busy in finalising all the preparations required to celebrate the passing of the comet. The keeper of the records was overwhelmed by the more than generous gift of the fifty-four prisoners. Tonight, they would honour their great leader, the Baroness of Kindeace-Shire and sacrifice all of the prisoners in her name. All the work that had been carried out to celebrate this momentous occasion required lots of planning and coordination. The preparation involved gathering the six heavy lift cranes and getting them all on-site was itself a task and a half. By hook and by crook, they had managed, albeit Tesporo may have cut a few throats belonging to the petulant, ungrateful mechanics. As far as he was concerned, their unfortunate demise accounted for nothing at all in the aid of progress. Compared to the progressive expansion of their species accumulated over the last fifty thousand years, it was only a small price to pay.

The original plan had to be remodelled, not from the point of view that it would not work. Building the massive structures would have required huge amounts of materials and many skilled workers, which was an impossible undertaking. Tesporo doubted that even in days before the great sickness had descended, they would not have been able to procure the number of tradesmen required. He was surprised their great leader had not labelled the ones that were still fully *compos mentis* as a protected species. After undergoing many trials and even more modifications, the enormous darts were at last deemed fit for purpose. The one stumbling block that remained was the timing, Tesporo wanted a simultaneous release of the projectiles and an all-inclusive scream from the unsuspecting participants.

After a few summary executions, eventually, the operators were persuaded to pay more attention to the flag movements. That was issued by the septic, foul-smelling brethren in the centre spot of the once-hallowed football ground. The secure patients in the chemically induced sleep had first been experimented on with a selection of drugs. These results were very poor, way off the expected recovery rate, and as they all had awakened at different times, this method was abandoned. A new method to produce the much sought-after communal awakening had to be devised.

All of the fifty-four sleeping patients were carefully carried out into the football ground. One of the keepers of the records brethren now lay bleeding. He had been chastised, then received multiple non-lethal stab wounds for thinking out loud that the participants looked so peaceful and in an almost angelic state. Tesporo had constantly lectured his flock that these people would still be primitive bipeds if it were not for their species' intervention. "These truly repugnant vertebrates would still be living in caves and trees if it were not for our ancestors meddling with their DNA. Their uncontrolled breeding should have been curtailed centuries ago; they are ungrateful unapologetic, and now they are nothing but undesirable species stealing our oxygen with every fresh intake of breath."

The first group of six prisoners were laid out in the assigned areas; each one of them was placed in the north-south axis point. The second group of sleeping volunteers were hoisted up and, with barely an inch between them, placed on top of the first group in the east-to-west axis point. With each additional group, the legs of the beds were extended to repeat the stacking process, and with the ninth group finally in place, Tesporo raised his arms, requesting his followers to kneel before him.

"50,000 years ago, our species set out on the great walk from the unforgiving desert sands to breathe life into these hallowed lands. Our ancestors toiled for untold generations, transforming the fetid swamps into the splendorous paradise

Tesporo gave the sign, and the trio of brethren placed in the centre of the football ground, resplendent in their white-upon-white hooded robes standby, ready with the flags. On the first signal, a single black and white chequered flag was raised, and all the engines of the cranes and the generators were instantly fired up. On the second command, the other black and white chequered flag was raised. All of the fifty-four sleeping participants received a more than sufficient electrical shock. They all jerked uncontrollably, held in place by the restraints attached to the beds. The power was switched off, as the fifty-four captive subjects were now all in a slightly disorientated but fully awakened state.

Seconds later, the third command was issued, both of the chequered flags were raised, and the six cranes simultaneously released the suspended loads. A front-weighted six-inch diameter pipe, fitted throughout its five-meter length with perpendicular lines of protruding razor-sharp blades resembling a mythical monster's fangs, descended like arrows delivered from the gods themselves. The prisoners who had looked to their left or right could see the other sets of participants and the fate that was being unleashed upon all of them.

They had time to issue a final scream before the projectiles passed through them, obliterating their spines and major organs. Then, one after another, the weighted razor-sharp dart joined them all in death. The member of the brotherhood who had dared to issue a sympathetic comment on the humans was dragged to the centre spot of the football ground. Tesporo and all his faithful followers urinated on the near-to-death brother, doused him with a flammable liquid and set him on fire. Not one of them looked back upon their fallen brother as he writhed about in his final death throes and left the grounds. As the sky darkened, the keeper of the records thought that the fifty-four prisoners now entangled together in the mess of distorted animals, with severed spines and decapitated body parts did put on a rather splendid display.

Miasnikov was on the road, which would eventually take him to not-so-sunny Scotland. He thought that the hardest part of the journey ahead would be clearing the stationary lines of dead traffic that almost jammed up every single road in this country. In his wisdom, he sent a detachment ahead a few days ago to try to create as much free space as possible. Not only had his ancestors made the mistake of allowing humans to breed and vote, but some fool in the past had also allowed them to own vehicles and given them access to almost unrestricted travel. A disgruntled Miasnikov thought out loud, "Cars, cars and more cars, did these fuckers never walk anywhere on foot?" His convoy stretched for almost a mile; taking no chances, he was bringing everything that was required to subdue and conquer the country that was responsible for the death of his sister.

Irena, he realised, could have very well brought her demise upon herself. In her homeland, she was hardly noted as a charismatic figure in society. On being let loose in Scotland, her uninhibited displays of barbarism and cruelty would certainly not have won over any friends in the locality. Miasnikov thought that if he had supplied her with more guards, perhaps it might have produced a different outcome. On the other hand, knowing that his beloved little sister may have subjected them to the same treatment awarded to the locals, it would not have ended differently at all. Either way, he was duty-bound by the family rules to seek revenge and retribution on those who had murdered her. Bartram, the deluded lover in her life, was of no concern to him.

Miasnikov thought that his last words would have been something along the lines of "Please take care of the works of art."

In his humble opinion, these were nothing but pieces of painted scrap metal that sold for ridiculous sums of money. Miasnikov also thought that the fan club, consisting of the delusional rich and famous, almost came in their pants when viewing these alleged works of art. Without any doubt whatsoever, they should have been nailed to the walls with a sign hanging from their necks displaying the words guilty of appreciating delusional, overpriced scrap metal. Now, that would have been an exhibition worth queueing in the rain for.

Miasnikov would devise a plan for dealing with Irena's unruly neighbours once he had apprehended them, and then he would review all of the damming evidence. Essmie's report hinted that it was very likely that his sister, along with two others, were burnt alive. He had ruled out any repeat performance as this would be way too easy and far too quick a death for the perpetrators of this crime. He ordered the convoy to halt and then summoned his scribe and despatcher; Miasnikov was obliged to send regular updates to the great leader, the Baroness of Kindeace-Shire. He noticed a commotion up ahead and sent one of his subordinates to investigate.

On returning, he saluted and delivered the report. "Sir, the locals up ahead were demonstrating, welcoming the return of everything going back to normal. They also sought permission to line the road and wave as the convoy passed. "Miasnikov agreed to the proposal as the subordinate rushes off to deliver the good news to the well-wishers. He gave the instantly revised order to be passed down throughout the ranks. The convoy started up, slowly moving forward. All of the locals, much to the astonishment of the passing army, cheered and waved; some of them even passed over bunches of flowers as a gift of appreciation. Miasnikov, on reaching the last of the locals and celebrating the return to normality, brought the convoy to a halt. Without mercy, the crowds of well-wishers were all gunned down, troopers searched among the fallen, and anyone who was not killed outright was rewarded with a shot to the head. The locals were left where they lay, and totally unperturbed by the violence, Miasnikov ordered the convoy to advance.

G-Flem would quite happily stay on the Magno-L and wait until she returned to the CCP, but alas, duty was duty. She disembarked to be greeted by the now saluting commander Blundell. General Flemings, as expected, inspected the retinue of troopers standing all spik and span-like statues. Billy Blunderful was now accompanying her as she walked up and down the ranks. G-Flem asked Commander Blundell if he had any news on the whereabouts of the elusive Abe Hubstien and the mysterious Jackson chappie. A flustered Blundell replied that he had cancelled the 'Abe must die campaign' on her orders, and with that, he had also withdrawn the reconnaissance patrols. General Flemings, armed with the damming admission, now had enough of Billy Blunderful. If their great leader had been privy to hearing this admission of guilt, the Baroness would have eliminated her on the spot.

G-Flem asked his second on command for his name; he stood and shouted out his full name, "Christopher Alistair Walker Emmerson." General Flemings had instant misgivings about this one and asked the next in the chain of command his name. "Jack Green, mam," and he stood to attention, gave a prompt salute, and then stood at ease. G-Flem informed him that he had been promoted. Commander Green was then ordered to remove Billy Blunderful, along with the ex-second in the chain of command, who owned the overly long name, sidearms. General Flemings was impressed, someone who knew what to do and someone who knew when to do it.

Commander Green enquired what the general would like done with the prisoners. G-Flem asked how they disposed of the local inhabitants once they passed their sell-by date. The newly appointed commander ordered the arrest of his former superiors and had them frog-marched down to the canal. Commander Green slashed them with his regulation blade, then had them pushed into the water. They did not have to wait long until the tell-tale movements of the water-borne creatures revealed their presence. The blood of the former commanders had quickly dispersed, and the alligators homed in on the newly available food source. Billy Blunderful was in the midst of appealing for clemency when he suddenly was pulled under the surface. His second in command with the overly long name was attempting to swim out of the way. A monster of a creature surfaced immediately in front of him. The former second in command had no time to scream as its huge jaws clamped down on his head and pulled him down into the murky depths.

Green, fairly confident that his former commanding officers were gone for good, orders several of his squads to prepare the reconnaissance patrols to locate the whereabouts of Abe Hubstien and that chap called Jackson. Commander Green now escorted G-Flem and gave her a guided tour of all the work underway at station A. He asked to be excused for a minute and apprehended the lazy bastard worker who had taken an unofficial break. Commander Green shot her in both legs, and she was dragged over and unceremoniously admitted into the alligator feeding program. G-Flem thought that the newly appointed commander would do well and continued with the guided tour. She did not have to ask any questions as Green blasted out all of the facts and the supplemental figures without being asked.

Down south, Blink and her crew awaited the arrival of the rusty old tub, and they had taken the opportunity to rest. She had informed them that they could be resting for a couple of days as there was a storm on its way towards them. Sekoyaz looked up to the clear blue sky that was present in every direction, although she did not doubt what her leader had told them. She wondered how she just seemed to know these things when there were no signs of the storm on the horizon. Blink, aware that her group would like to eat something other than fish, allowed a small contingent to go out hunting.

She warned them to maintain constant vigilance on the new area as it could very well be inhabited or patrolled by hostile inhabitants. Blink requested that Sekoyaz accompany the hunting party, adding that they should only kill what they need to sustain them for a few days. Blink scanned the horizon as always; she was overly concerned that the rusty old tub would not make it to the scheduled stopover. Her people would be pleased that they no longer had to take turns travelling in the slow vessel. All of them told her the story about the engine that, almost without fail, regularly threatened to die on the hour, every hour. Blink noticed the plume of smoke in the distance and was overjoyed that her people had safely made it to the rendezvous.

The crew have already found places to shelter during the expected storm. This time, they were going to have to pull all of the boats onshore and secure them from the high winds. Blink had guessed that it would take at least two days to pass, and then after that, the stretch of water would be safe to cross. The first island-hop would take them at least one full day and one full night. She had no doubt that they could make the crossing, but to do so, they needed calm waters.

The area they were now in was notorious for being subjected to the onslaught of tropical storms. If they were caught off guard in the open ocean during one of these events, then none of them would survive. As her mama had reminded her often, 'it is always better to be safe than sorry.'

The sky was starting to darken as the old rusty tub limped into port; Blink thought that it was a good idea and some to abandon her now as it was a foregone conclusion that any future journeys in this craft were decidedly inadvisable due to the increasing onset of mechanical problems. She welcomed her people all by name and then joined in assisting them in unloading all the remaining fuel. Blink is trying to figure out why they have stopped the work when she notices them pointing up to the sky. The comet with the green tail was slowly moving across the heavens, and one of her crew asked if it was a good omen. Blink replied that it was only a celestial object passing through the universe, which had been an ongoing process for thousands of years. Then assured them that it was nothing, nothing at all to worry about. She told them to get back to work, and if they hurry up, they could be under cover before the storm arrives. Sekoyaz, along with the hunting party, had arrived back in the camp; they had several animals tied on poles. Blink thought that by the techniques on show, her crew would have no problems integrating into a long-forgotten tribe of their Neanderthal ancestors.

Blink answered the question before Sekoyaz had asked it, repeating the words that she had offered up to the crew of the rusty old tub. Sekoyaz asked Blink if there would have been people like them who had witnessed the passing of the comet the last time it was in this part of the universe. She thought for a moment, then replied that there would have been people, but they would not have been anything like them. Blink shouted, instructing them all to hurry up, "The rains along the strong winds are on their way, so move it and let's all get under cover."

Somewhere in the small harbour in the west of Scotland, Gareth informed Leena of what they had found. He also told her that they should put out the word, warning their crews from eating any of the creatures in the harbour as they are contaminated. "The two sick women we have recovering in Cinds' care had been feasting on lumpy, misshapen fish and crabs."

Leena asked if they were going to recover and if Cinds' the head nurse, thought that they would pull through. "She has dosed them up on antibiotics, not sure if the types that we have in stock are suitable. Cinds' has, as a precaution, given them both types."

Leena knowing Cinds' sketchy background, somehow thought that these were aptly named the green and yellow ones, then the big fucking ones that were a pure bastard to swallow.

Gareth added that, for now, that was all that they could do. Hopefully, they will pull through. Leena agreed and then asked him to accompany her to check the progress of the various repairs underway. On the way down to the engine room, they opened the door and checked in on Cinds'. Alwyn and she were in the process of bottle-feeding the new additions to the crew. Leena just complimented Alwyn on yet another hidden talent and, not wishing to disturb them, left them to it. The patients, were still running high temperatures, taking turns to intermittently utter some incoherent words in between their unconscious states. Cinds' had no idea what they were trying to say or if, in fact, they were trying to say something or just moaning about the way they were feeling. Alwyn had offered a translation, making out that the two guests were telling them that they did not want to eat any fish ever again.

Leena was first to enter the engine room with Gareth close on her tail. The blue light bounced about the walls, and a set of aggressive invasive sparks, fumes, and light belonging to the welder repairing the leak. The other set of unpleasant attributes belonged to a thin woman cursing the repair on the driveshaft. "Bastard, so the next run will be going in hotter than hell, and just to let you know that when you were made, you must have been named the bitch from hell."

Leena asked if all was good. The welder replied that this type of metal required a high temperature and that she would manage with what she had. Pointing to the driveshaft, she explained that they were only discussing what was coming next as the parent metal was stubborn. Leena informed her that she was doing a great job before she and Gareth hastily retreated. She asked him what he thought, and Gareth replied that her parents originated from the Glasgow area. "In that neck of the woods, the conversation that we had overheard would be viewed as being perfectly normal and one hundred per cent acceptable."

The mechanics overhauled the engines did not speak to the metallic parts as they rotated, checked and torqued up the assemblies they were working on. They did not have the correct tools, but they were fully accustomed to the UK's endemic engineering malpractice of not supplying the workers with the correct toys they made do with what they had available. Gareth apologised for interrupting them, asking if they needed anything or if he could help. The guy lying under the engine informed him that several barrels of oil onshore needed to be transported to the ship. Leena butted in and told them that she would take care of it and if there was anything else needed, just holler.

Once they had escaped the repair crews, Gareth mentioned that as they had time, he intended to go out in the morning to shoot some fresh game. Leena mentioned that steak would make a nice change. Gareth promised to try, but they could have recreated their first meeting if he failed. Leena told him she would cook if he only managed to bag some rabbits.

After being fed, the youngest additions to the crew were now fast asleep. Cinds was pleased to report that they seemed healthy enough, considering what they had been through. She persuaded Alwyn to help her change the sheets on the adult patients' beds and explained that it was easier with two people. Alwyn did as he was told, then moved the woman that way as Cinds' performed the hard part. She informed him that when she was washing the women, their backs had been subjected to what seemed like torture. Alwyn asked her what exactly she meant. Cinds described that there were patches where the skin had been removed, and perhaps, they had been subjected to someone repeatedly burning them.

One of the women stirred and woke up, Cinds' quickly inserted the antibiotics into her mouth, informing her that if she wanted to recover, she had to swallow them. Cinds' placed the straw in her mouth and watched the woman gulp down some water. She mumbled something. Neither knew what it was meant to be, but perhaps she said thank you. The head nurse informed the woman that the children were both doing well and had nothing to worry about. Alwyn and Cinds' noticed that the woman, sort of, nodded before falling back asleep.

Leena found Gareth on the deck, and for a change, she brought him a brew. "Was that you trying to get into my good books?"

Leena replied, telling him that it was a bribe for him not to cook the rabbits, which, if he cared to remember, he had burned them to a frazzle the first time they met. Gareth chuckled and retorted that he was just trying to put her off-guard and impress her with his cooking skills. Leena pointed upwards and asked if he had added the new addition to the sky to impress her. Gareth pleaded not guilty and saw that no one was about. They disappeared into their cabin for some much-needed us time.

In the morning, after checking that all was okay and that there were no more problems, Gareth and Scruffy went ashore and set off to hunt down some fresh game. The repairs were still ongoing, so he did not set a deadline, stipulating what time he had to return. Leena waved them away and then organised the crew to bring onboard the barrels of oil that the mechanics had requested as the able bodies manhandled them off the pier into the transport boat. She called out the orders, and the crew assembled in the rescue zone of the ship to pull the cargo across the harbour. She also added the dingy to this list of items to bring on board as they did not possess a craft to enable them to go ashore. This would be dragged onboard once the loading and storage of the oil drums was completed. Leena hoped that Gareth returned with steak as she was not too keen on a rabbit, but failed that, she would settle for lamb.

Cinds continued to attend to her patients. She thought the women's high temperatures had decreased, but as she had no access to a thermometer, Cinds only guessed. Every time the women woke up, she fed them the antibiotics, hoping they might recover soon enough and take care of their kids. The way she saw it, she had other duties to attend to and being allocated to the head nurse and pediatric technician position was not on her list of desired jobs and attainable skillsets.

Once she had all the tasks well-organised and underway, Leena returned to the engine room. The welder, who had been conversing with the drive shaft, was absent.

Leena took that as a sign that the work was completed and the woman if off to do something less stressful. The mechanics were still hard at connecting the various assemblies. She couldn't help but notice they were still not shouting nor having any serious conversations with the machinery, assuming that everything was going well, Leena left them to it.

On the dry land Scruffy had been allowed to drive the vehicle. He informed Gareth that it was an unresponsive piece of shit. Gareth asked him what he expected as the car had been idle for like forever. They drove a couple of miles away from the quaint little village in the harbour before any animals were spotted. The first one they encountered was a cow accompanied by a single calf. Scruffy nor Gareth had the heart to shoot them; their thinking was that there were more than enough motherless children and childless mothers in this world at present. They continued driving for another couple of miles. Gareth spotted them first, and Scruffy halted the vehicle without complaining. A couple of hours later, they had enough sheep to last the rest of the sea voyage, skinned, then loaded into the car. The journey back to the harbour was uneventful, and Leena had the boat ready to transport them and their much-anticipated haul onboard. As they climbed back on the ship, Leena informed them they could leave on the next high tide if all went well.

Leena left them to it, making good use of the time by going about the passengers and crew. She tells everyone she met they were doing whatever was required to get the ship moving again. Leena also promised them that wherever they ended up, it would eventually, after lots of hard work, develop into a great community. One where they could settle down and then raise children in peace and tranquility removed, as far away as possible from all the dangers that had forced them to flee from their previous settlements.

Chapter 6

On the other side of the Atlantic Ocean, Jackson was relieved that Abe had finally capitulated on realising that going out on the designated regular patrols was not for him. Enunsha had immediately understood the stark reality of what could be waiting for them out there; never once had she badgered him to rescind the decision. Jackson had them with him now and placed the names on the sectors he had marked up on the huge map of the surrounding area. With the aid of pins and thread that Abe had just happened to come across. Now accompanied by his platoon leaders, Perry had just come into the operation room to join them. Jackson nodded to welcome them all. Spotty got up off the floor, issued a single bark, and then deposited himself back, assuming guard detail beside Enunsha's seat. Jackson took to the floor; with the aid of the half pool que, he pointed directly at the numbered areas while he talked.

"This area marked up as number ten was where we used to reside not that long ago." Then, moving the pointer to where they are now, "This area was marked with number one. The areas on the map between our new location and the old one were marked with single digits. Perry, we need to know where your teams were and what areas had been cleared. Look, people, we know that the bad guys are out there; therefore, it was just a matter of time before we find them or they find us." Jackson continued, "Perry, we must find other suitable areas where our people can shelter. This place was ideal for now, but we all know it is only a temporary refuge. When the fighting starts, we need to be able to keep two steps away from them otherwise, we would just be wiped out. For sure the bad guys have a base, most likely several bases from where they launch their operations from. This country was so vast that it could take years to locate these places, but if we are careful, we could find them." Jackson asked if there were any questions, as there were none. He wished them all a safe journey, telling them he hoped to see them all soon.

Abe asked if he thought it could come down to them moving every few days to avoid the underground dwellers. Jackson replied that it was just a simple matter of the number of people affected and the availability of resources. He reminded Abe of when the subterranean people had fucked them over at the hydro plant. "That required men, machines and lots of planning. Our foe is cunning, elusive and there could be many of them." Jackson continued, "If it comes down to it, we will hit then continually move for as long as it takes." Abe now understood what was in store for them, went to the map, and then double-checked the locations set out by the coloured pins. The dungeon dwellers could be anywhere in this vast country, and he, along with this group, was now stuck in the bottom corner.

Poison Pete with his sidekick Doctor Death had been allocated to their new jobs. They had been assigned to clean and apply paint to the unoccupied accommodation blocks.

At first, they were a little miffed at being denied reinstatement into their previously esteemed positions in the galley. Peter asked the Doctor if their cooking was that bad. The Doctor replied that Spotty had threatened to report them to the animal welfare officer or run away if he got wind of them returning to recreate their culinary delights. For the record, Pete proclaimed that when he was in prison, none of his customers had ever complained. Doctor Death asked him that when he was there, was it his recipes they were conjuring up daily. Pete replied that it was a set menu with every single item provided. Doctor Death scratched his head, "Man if you were allowed to make things from scratch, half of the prison population would have opted for the chair or the chamber. The other half would have tried to escape, and then the National Guard would have been called to quell the rebellion. You would have been put in solitary confinement for the rest of your life."

Poison Pete thought his companion had made several unfair but nevertheless true points. He had to admit that the food they now eat was way much better than the barely edible concoctions they used to rattle up together. Just to get even with the Doctor, Pete asked him if he remembered the time he had lost his false teeth in the pot of chicken Gumbo. The Doctor took the hint, offering to go for the coffee. As he passed him, he promised not to spit in his cup. Pete got on with the cleaning, thinking that maybe one day he would tell the Doctor what gives his coffee that special taste. It was not that bad here, and he does not attribute any blame to Jackson for banning them from the kitchen. The food was more than nice, and they did not have to partake in any washing up. His old friend returned, and Pete thanked him for the coffee. They sat and shot the shit about the old days. Poison Pete pulls a crumpled-up packet from his pocket, then offers Doctor Death to make the first selection. As they light up the blunts, Pete said it was like prison. The Doctor agreed but added that the food here is so much nicer.

Perry was worried; this was the first time he had placed the new team members on an active patrol. He had paired the newbies up with one of his old teams to make it a success.

They made part of the journey in the vehicle then, after applying camouflage, the allocated pairs headed out to their assigned positions. The forty-eight hours of being out in the scrubs would be the true test; not everyone can do it, and this way, he could select the best of what was available. Now, all they were doing was scouting out the immediate areas, and hopefully, when the time arrived for the long-range missions, all of his crew would be ready.

He had overheard his crew talking about the school teacher; he guessed they had applied the name to Jackson. If only they knew what this guy had been involved in; he was a service legend. He thought Jackson would like his new name; he was the ghost in the old world. The mere mention of that name would scare the living daylights out of the would-be bad guys and their homegrown regional commanders. Jackson had never once spoken of the old days or hinted at the name of his old employers or even his job title. He thought Jackson was that skilled; he could have easily slipped into being a genuine school teacher without missing a heartbeat.

At the watermill, Cha had returned from the medical centre; Murray, much to her surprise, was still awake. She laughed as he presented her with the report cards he had knocked together for all the children. He told her that Robbo was in for a while before returning to go and continue working on the new houses. Murray had thought he was working on his new abode but admitted that he was quite surprised to find out that he was concentrating on finishing the home for Cat and Frank. Cha thinks his actions were highly commendable, doing all these extra hours for the new arrival. Murray replied that Robbo had mentioned in the passing that Remus would need a new home just as much as Frank, Cat and the new addition to their family.

Murray asked if any new names were being issued. He knows; she also knew it would take him forever to remember them all. "Cat has called her daughter Sammarra, but you are allowed to call her Sam." Murray thought he should know where this name came from as it sounded more than familiar. Cha, energised his failing memory banks, reminded him of the woman who grew up without her mother. Then, was briefly introduced to her just before dying. Murry now remembered, "Okay, I will call her Sam. Does she look anything like her mother?"

Cha replies that she possessed those eyes that capture everything and follow you about the room. "I think she was going to be very smart, almost like she had been here before."

Murray asked her if that translated to her being as scary as her mother. Cha shook her head, "No, much scarier; Cat is a cat, Sam will be a lioness and, without any shadow of a doubt, the unquestionable leader of the pride." Murray had made her tea, and now standing still, she asked him if there was something on his mind, perhaps something that he wished to talk about. He pointed to the fake report cards and asked her if his tea-making skills would be reviewed and marked up accordingly. Cha tells him that he was sometimes unbelievably childish, puts her arms around him and confesses that was why she loves him so much. Murray can't help himself, puts on a serious face, and then replies that all the women in his life have said the same thing. Cha kneed him in the balls and informed him that she did not love him that much. Murray lies recovering on the floor, waiting for the pain associated with the unexpected assault on his wedding tackled to subside. When his speaking capabilities had returned to functioning level, he changed the subject, asking if she had managed to take a quick look at the green thing in the sky.

Cha helped him back onto his feet and confirmed she had seen the new addition to the night sky. Murray was pleased that the vision was not just a figment of his somewhat fertile imagination. "We could go up to the Orangery later and treat the children to the once-in-a-lifetime chance of seeing it in all its displayed splendor and glory." Cha thought they were a little on the young side to fully appreciate it but gave in to him, agreeing that they could try it. She would mention that they would be wasting their time if it were overcast and cloudy. In doubting that he would have even listened to her in the first place Cha bit her lip, remaining silent. She rustles up a fresh pot, then joins Murray outside.

As he looked up into the night sky, not even a measly single star could be seen. "Maybe tomorrow night it will be clearer; we can't see anything up there just now." Cha nodded and agreed that it was a good idea. "The inmates are getting out tomorrow, so that we would be busy most of the day. As the houses are not quite ready, everyone will be moved in with us for a while." Cha mentioned that all the patients had asked if that would be okay with Murray. "I told them it was your idea, so you must be on your best behaviour for the next few days," he exhaled, and Cha empathised that it was only for a few days, not forever. Murray replied that he would be an angel for as long as it took to obtain the perfect score, represented by all of the ticked boxes on his report card.

Cha left him to it; all the children were sound asleep upstairs. She checked that they were all okay, and even though all of their eyes were firmly closed, she felt that they were all aware that she was in the room with them. The dogs had been sleeping outside their door, almost as if they were on guard duty. Cha persuaded them to move, opened the front door then shouted incoming. Murray accepts the hint and takes his best friends out for a walk. Remus seems sad, Murray tells him that Cat will be back for him tomorrow and all will be good. He doubted if the dog had listened to a single word, never mind understood what he had said, but Murray felt it was important to pass on the relevant information. A house full of dogs was one thing; a house full overflowing with repugnant smelling diapers and all incessant, twenty-four-seven baby talk was another thing.

Murray breathed a sigh of relief when they all reached Charlie's favourite spot; together, they looked up into the heavens, and for a brief moment, the comet was visible. Charlie just looked at him with that 'so what' face. Murray sits on the rock and sparks up; in the coming days, he thinks that to escape, he will go on more walks, possibly even longer ones. Robbo had been noticeably absent from their house, supposedly being very busy getting everything spic and span for the move. Murray hoped that it would all work out for them, but if push came to shove, he, without any doubt, would always be on the side of Alicia and Okolo. He would miss them but simultaneously realised that they had their own lives to lead. The good thing was that Cat would be next door. They would all be next door, so he came to his senses and thought he was turning into an old tosser for worrying about nothing. He whistled at his canine friends, apologised for not being his usual self, promised that he would do better the next time, leads them all back home.

On arrival, Cha was nowhere to be seen; without checking, he knew she would be sound asleep with the young ones upstairs. Making the most of it, Murray rattled up a banger with the perfect accompaniment of a fresh brew. After he consumed them outside, Murray stuck on the headphones, turned the volume up to seven and disappeared out of this realm of existence. He would freely admit to all the gods of old his weakness; some guys liked fishing, and some liked football. Murray liked getting ripped, putting on his cans and merging into his secret world of ancient rock music full of sad songs and wailing, gut-wrenching, face-melting guitar solos. He smiled, thinking that the previous world would have perhaps been a far happier place if all the politicians had played guitars. One of his favourite songs came on, and he instantly rescinded his previous thought. Thinking out loud, he said 'fuck it' and turned the volume up to eleven. The headphones almost bounced off his ears with the sheer volume, but he could not care less. Murray had not done this for a long time; everyone needs private space. This was his moment; the guitars and drums came the reach the well-orchestrated ending. He received a gentle tap on the now silent cans.

Cha had not been sleeping after all. She stood before him, dressed in clothes that should only be seen in the bedroom. Murray removed the headphones, giving in to the fact that there were private and there were intimate shared pleasures. He carried her up the stairs, and they went into one of the other bedrooms, making the most of the opportunity. When all the patients are discharged from the secure mental health facility, it will not be as easy to steal a moment like this. Both of them remembered the time when they could do this freely. It was now quite a long time ago, but the imported thing was that they do indeed remember. Murray knew for sure that without her, he was nothing, nothing at all.

Cha was up before him in the morning; the smell of breakfast had almost magically reached his subconscious, enticing him to return to the land of the living. He was greeted with "Good morning, handsome." He wrapped his arms around her, telling her that he loved her. The children did not applaud the performance but studied it very closely.

Murray spoke to them as they understood. 'Well, kids, today we are going to be joined by other people, and if I have to behave, then so do you." None of the children react; the dogs have ignored him and are pretending to have died. Charlie had gone one step further and had placed her paws over her eyes.

Mr. Black informed her that he was truly heartbroken by her blatantly displayed uncaring attitude, but Charlie surprisingly did not respond. Many inquisitive eyes watched Murray as he entertained his audience with his solo version of "here comes the train." Cha asked him that when the children were older, they were asked to recollect their earliest memories. "Do you think they would shiver and squirm in abject terror at the mere mention of here comes the train." Murray looked hurt; Cha put her arms around him and told him she was only joking as she was sure that at least one of them would like it. Murray told her she was the cruelest woman he had ever known. As he had finished stuffing his face, she got him involved in assembling all the feed bottles. He asked if she was considering starting a business, "How many of these will be consumed in one sitting?"

Cha responds, "Alfie, aka greedy guts, would scoff two per session; the others will eventually want the same. That worked out to a possible twelve per sitting, leaving a spare eight as a contingency."

Murray knew he shouldn't but had to ask anyway. "A contingency for what? Well, they might want more; if one wants, they will all want." Murray was on a roll and enquired if that would be the same for diapers. Cha told him that he was unbelievable in the things that he asked. She gave him the good news that all the used ones can go straight on fire, and he did not need to wear a fully enclosed enviro-suit.

Murray made excuses to all present as he stood outside partaking in his dual hobby. Karen appeared accompanied by an army of cleaners. All of them said good morning; some even congratulated him and Cha on the new addition to the family. Murray was glad they did not want to shake hands, as his fingers would have throbbed. Karen continued to speak to him, "Robbo had bribed them all to come and clean everything in sight from top to bottom." Murray couldn't think of anything that would have been a suitable offer to make them volunteer. Karen let it slip that Robbo had told them that it was traditional in the old world for all the neighbours to come and clean the house of a mother with a new baby. Adding that would lead to happiness and good fortune for all undertaking the task. Murray thought there was more to the story than what Karen had admitted; he asked her if he had told them anything else.

Karen looked embarrassed as she added in the final details, "He also mentioned that those women who had wanted children but had not managed to conceive were sometimes blessed with the gift of motherhood." Murray, for a minute, thought that Robbo had promised to unleash his super swimmers upon them all. Even Robbo would not be that stupid as he knew that Alicia and Okolo would happily remove his wedding tackle. Then place the offending items in a jar if he ever thought about sowing his overactive seedlings into the population.

Karen told him that she would see him later. Murray, now left alone, thought that Robbo was just a fucking chancer. Although he would be moving out sooner than expected, Murray thought that it was a good idea as he could only take so much of his bullshit. If it was the other way, Murray would have stayed awake for days and cleaned the new house alone. He went back into their house, disclosing the latest exploits of Herr Robbo. Cha thought that it was funny but noticed that Murray was far from amused she changed the subject quickly. Cora had said that any time after lunch would be a suitable time to collect the term-served prisoners. "I told her we would take turns collecting the twins and Cat," Murray asked if she needed him to help with the sleeping arrangements; Cha told him that she was thinking of sorting out some bedding and then perhaps letting all the children sleep in one room. "We could take it in turns to watch over them, as all of the new mothers will be tired and need some much-deserved rest," Murray told her that he would agree to whatever they decide, he would do anything to help without question, nor complaint and also take his fair share of the babysitting duties.

Frank had appeared, and even Murray noticed that he had tried to tidy himself up. "Are you sure Cat will recognise the new you?" Frank almost laughed, knowing that if Cat was blindfolded and in a dark room, she could still pick him out in an identification parade.

Cha informed Frank that he looked smart. "When Murray had come to pick up me and Alfie, I thought he had stolen his clothes from the scarecrow. I could never be able to pick Murray out by his attire; I would have to rely on smell." Murray told them there was not one fragment of truth in that statement as he had changed one of his socks sometime last week. Cha puts her fingers to her nose. "I could never really figure out why animals liked you so much, I guess with the recent admission that we all know why."

All of this was to put Frank at ease; he was overjoyed, but he was also scared. They both took turns reassuring him that everything would be okay and he would easily merge into the delights of being a parent. Murry empathised that it was best not to worry about it and to let things happen. "Honestly, it was the best thing that can happen to a man. You would wake up in the middle of the night thinking that your child is not well and be greeted with a smile that would melt your heart, but it would last forever." Cha told them that it was time.

For the first time, Murray shook Frank's hand and welcomed him to the father's club. Frank freely admitted that he did not know what to say. Murray replied that he did not have to say anything as they knew he would be an outstanding father. "Frank, get your bride and daughter before we start crying." Cha had left Murray in charge of the young ones and drove Frank up to do the collection, "He is quite a guy." Cha joked that she much preferred the dogs. Frank was astounded until he realised, she was only joking; she drew the vehicle outside the medical facility. Frank took a deep breath and set out on the first steps that led into his new world.

Sammarra, on setting her eyes on her daddy for the first time, immediately held her arms up; Frank held her like he had done this all his life. Cat wiped away a tear confessing that she had told Sam all about him, what he looked like. He put his other arm around her and thanked her with all his heart for this wonderful bundle of joy. Cha did not fuss over them as they entered the vehicle; when they were settled in, she drove them slowly to the house. Remus immediately noticed their arrival and patiently awaited them to enter the house. As soon as they came in, he whined gently, welcoming his new best friend to this world. It was too much for Murray; he escaped outside and tried to hide the tears that streamed uncontrollably down his face.

Cha settled them in, letting them know this was also their house. Make yourselves at home; we will sort everything out later. She whistled at the dogs, and reluctantly, they got up and followed her. Cha found Murray outside; his eyes showed signs of bubbling, but he was assured he was fine. Cha told him it was okay to cry and there was nothing to be embarrassed about. "Frank thought the world of you, but I had to tell him the truth and confessed that I much preferred the dogs." Murray smiled, then told her that he believed her.

"Take the dogs for a walk and you can go and pick up the twins when you return." Murray nodded, shouted at his friends and walked them, telling them all about Sammarra. Cat asked if Murray was okay, Cha told the truth, letting them know that he was just so overjoyed with emotion for the both of them. She joked that they would need to put buckets out for him before the twins arrived home. Cat thought that it was a terrible joke but laughed all the same. Sammarra looked at the other children; they all looked back as if they were waiting for her to say something meaningful.

Murray wiped his face before returning home; he welcomed Cat, gave her a huge cuddle, and, like Cha told her, just treated like place like home. He drove to the medical facility to collect Beth, Debs and their little bundles of joy. As luck would have it, he passed Robbo and his entourage on the way there; Murray waved hello but did not stop. On entering the facility, he was informed that the twins were not quite ready yet. Murray told the head nurse they all suspected she was a former member of some foreign secret police force. She stared at him as he uttered, "I hope that all of their attempted escape plans were not too much of a problem?"

He made good use of the time to go and visit Cora; Murray knocked on her door and entered. "Just thought I would pop in and say hello." They chat about this and that; Murray senses that she is uneasy about something; he can't say what it is, but he knows something is bugging her. "Cora, if you ever need anything, all you have to do is ask. Here in our little community, we all look out for each other; we all try and help each other. When you are up for it, feel free to come down and visit us. All the children were the same age, and they needed to mix. Otherwise, your daughter would end up like me, possessing the social skills of a single-cell organism."

Cora thanked him, promising to take him on the offer one day.

Murray asked her what she was worried about; Cora asked him if it was that obvious that something was troubling her.

He nodded, letting her know it was okay to let it go. "Everyone has to talk to someone; keeping it all inside won't do you, nor your daughter any good." Cora lets it out, revealing that she was worried as they all have special blood groups and all the tests, she had carried out on them revealed that they were all sort of special. "I know I am being silly in thinking I have contributed to making some super child who will turn out truly despicable and then take over the world."

Murray laughs, "Cha would not allow that; none of the mothers would. The children are special; all of the children are special, and the daughter you have brought into this world will truly be special in her own unique way." Cora stared as if Murray would reveal she would have some special power. "Your daughter and you will have the special bond that only mothers and daughters have. No matter what this world has in store for us, no one will ever be able to take that away. Treat each day as special; everyone single one counts. I can assure you that all of your worries are completely unfounded." Cora thanked him for listening to her moans and groans. Murray confided in her that she could come and see him anytime she needed to talk. The head nurse appeared, informing them that the twins were ready. Murray was tempted to reply and stand to attention, then salute with an extended right arm pointing upwards towards the horizon. He changed his mind and cuddled Cora at the last possible moment, telling her he would expect to see her very soon.

Beth and Debs were dressed identically, and to confuse matters even more their babies were dressed out in similar attire also. Murray had always thought that they would have been stars in the old world. "Okay movie stars, time I took you all home. In case I forget to mention it, you all look great." Debs and Beth informed him that they wish for a private group cuddle before they leave for home, as this was a special moment in their lives. Murray did not refuse them and stretched his arms around them as much as possible. The twins thanked him for being nice to them since day one and said that they would never forget the kindness he had shown them, but most importantly, for never being angry at them.

Murray told them that it would be very difficult to get angry with angels as perfect as them. They climb into the vehicle, and in their usual way of speaking, they tell him, 'Home, James.' By the time they arrived home, all the sleeping arrangements had been sorted out. The women had arranged an area in the front room for the infants. Eight little beds were spread out on the floor. Murray asked which one was his. Cha replied that due to the shortage of available space, they had held a vote in his absence and he was to sleep outside. Okolo, Alicia and all the other new mothers look very happy at being released from the medical facility. Most of them were exhausted and needed a good, undisturbed sleep to recharge their batteries. Cha volunteered herself and her other half for the first night shift duty. Murray took the hint and lied, accepting the full credit for the plan being his idea. It was time for the first mass feeding, as suspected, when the newbie witnessed Alfie's greedy chops having a double helping, and as Cha had suspected, they all wanted the same. Sammarra watches everything around her. Remus as still as a statue, sat beside her the whole time. All the new mothers waited until their children were settled, then, one at a time, sneak upstairs for a much-needed rest. Now alone,

Murray asked Cha if it was a suitable time for her to fill out his report card. Cha smirked and informed him that once he managed to perform the task of changing the diapers without pretending, he was a pearl diver trying to break the world record for holding his breath, then maybe.

Chapter 7

Lesqueth decided that it was high time to review in person the status of her new armed forces. Tesporo had deliberately not been informed of the intended visit. On good faith, she had received the signed, sealed and delivered documentation. Tesporo had staked his soul along with the future of the brotherhood, in guaranteeing that all the information that had been supplied was accurate. Should it be found that the keeper of the records and his inherent nest of vipers were less than honest in this, their version of the truth. There would be no arrests, trial or charges issued, it would qualify all of them for instant dismissal. The Baroness of Kindeace-Shire sheathed the sharpened blade, just in case she had just cause to issue a complaint. At the given signal, the elite guard detail appears out of nowhere, forming an impenetrable shield around her. The unit proceeded with all undue haste to the infant indoctrination unit situated within the grounds of Buckingham Palace. Any of the workers in the vicinity of the oncoming storm hastily removed themselves from her intended path, in the prewarning thought that out of sight, out of mind would keep them alive for at least another day.

Two of Tesporos acolytes had rushed forward clutching umbrellas, which they intended to activate and shield the great leader from the onset of the downpour. They did not make it; unfortunately, her guard detail had not been informed of the intended curtsey. Seeing the individuals approaching with what could have been viewed as weapons, the guards reacted instantly and eliminated the threat. Tesporo and his now not-so-white-on-white sycophantic disciples follow what must have been a well-rehearsed, choreographed charade. As she walked past them, they kneeled on the ground, bowed their heads and clasped their hand in a silent prayer. Lesqueth, as always, enjoyed the overt display of blind obedience but wondered why on earth they were performing this stunt in the rain. Their clothes were thin, not suited to this type of weather. Perhaps the collection of unscheduled surgery along with the bucket loads of painkillers had numbed up all of their senses, and they never even noticed the weather change.

The Baroness patiently waited for the arrival of Tesporo inside the building, She watched as he almost glided effortlessly across the floor. The keeper of the records and his accompanying lackeys had changed their robes, the white-upon-white delegation was spotlessly clean, but the ever-present stench of decaying flesh followed them about the room with every step they undertook. Lesqueth puts on her mask, and the troopers pre-empt the next move, spraying some perfume to defuse the rancid odour emanating from the hooded figures now in front of them.

Tesporo informed the great leader that, as per her instructions, they had edited the proclamation that the infants' thoughts were saturated on an hourly basis. Lesqueth requested to hear the new version, Tesporo uttered some undecipherable, almost hissed gibberish accompanied by strange hand gestures to his fetid companions. They instantly obeyed the issued command, and as they retreated, the smell normally associated with dead, decaying animals almost permeated out of every single one of their pores. Lesqueths nodded to the guards armed with the perfume to refresh the space around them from the stench of decay that Tesporos' helpers had involuntarily dispersed into the surrounding atmosphere in their wake.

The curtained area was opened up, revealing multiple viewing screens, all positioned together like one giant television. The sombre military music resonated throughout the room as the troopers active on display stopped and stood to attention. The screen changed intermittently from being multiple messages, being displayed at the same time or just a single message that stood still and did not flicker. As the music merged into the background, the complimentary accompaniment of the militaristic action scenes was overlayed with the orator's authoritarian, booming voice. With the skills of a seasoned thespian, he varied the tone along with volume to empathise with the truths and the expectations. That the intended audience is wholeheartedly, without any exceptions, was expected to fully endorse.

'Children of the present, you have been selected to represent our great leaders armed forces of the future. On this great leap forward in which, our esteemed leader has engineered our race to establish complete domination of this planet. You would play an important role in establishing our people as the apex species. The projected allocation of the indigenous bipeds would only be utilised as slave labour. As they grow old beyond their useful years, they would be eliminated when the first signs of them being unproductive appear. Show them no compassion, no kindness, award them with the utter contempt that they deserve. Never allow them basic education, keep them dumb and keep them down in the gutter where they truly belong.'

'Your fellow compatriots were never to be viewed above nor beyond suspicion. If your immediate supervisor or commanding officer was lacking in displaying true commitment to our perceived future, complain, report and

above all, question. Your leaders expect the best results from you at every order issued. Do not hesitate. Your undivided loyalty would be gratefully rewarded and fully appreciated by our great leader. Go forth from here and grasp with open arms your destiny, our undeniable future, and destroy without remorse or question all that would deny us our unquestionable place in history.'

Lesqueth compliments Tesporo on the presentation, but has nevertheless added a few additional changes that she would like included in the pictorial display. The keeper of the records now directed the Baroness to the infants that were in formation marching to a repetitive single drum beat. The Baroness acknowledged her approval, and Tesporo led the great leader along with her entourage to the dining hall. "This age group had completed the morning training sessions. As per the stipulations regarding rank and status, they were the first to dine," Lesqueth asked about the spaces at the tables where only an empty plate along with an upturned drinks container resided. "These represented the children who did not make the required grade, thus serving as a constant reminder that failure equates to being expendable."

Tesporo politely enquired if the Baroness would like all the details of Marshall's progress. Lesqueth was aghast with the audacity of the request.,"Tesporo if I was to exhibit even a miniscule of aspiration towards maternal instincts. I would expect that General Miasnikov would unquestionably carry out his duty and shoot me on the spot. On the other hand, if my son, the one named Marshall, had displayed or displayed in the future any signs of paternal yearning. I would expect that his place at the dining table would exhibit another empty plate!" Lesqueth, now more than angry, asked the repugnant leader of the brotherhood if what she had said was crystal clear. Tesporo repeatedly nodded like his head was attached to a spring.

The Baroness thought that what the keeper of the records had previously stated about expendability was a fine example to lead with, she unholstered her sidearm and shot his two accompanying associates in the head. "Perhaps that demonstration would set an example for our future meetings to be attended only by non-foul-smelling brethren who do not disperse a designer bouquet reminiscent of the dead. Lesqueth commented on the fact that none of the infants had batted an eyelid on hearing the weapon discharged. "Remember, if there was any hint of a stench emanating from you or yours the next time, I would shoot all of you without any hesitation." As she vacates the premises, Lesqueth wishes the keeper of the records a good day.

Miasnikov had just issued a complaint that the progress was just not good enough. Commander Essmie informed him that when she had previously travelled north, her convoy had consisted of only half a dozen vehicles. "General Miasnikov, with all due respect, your convoy is a mile long, and a fair percentage of the vehicles were wider. We cannot just push them through the small gaps presently available, and that meant that we had to create an opening in this endless sea of now redundant forms of transportation." Miasnikov had listened to her explanation and now wanted to know what she was going to do to enable them to advance more speedily. "If you agree, we could have the allocated tracked moving equipment with a detachment of guards working throughout the night."

General Vladimir Miasnikov wanted to know if he implemented the order, would they get to their destination any quicker. Essmie thought that they, at a push, could have arrived about thirty-six hours earlier than the current forecasted time period. Vladimir wanted to eat his lunch in peace for a change and ordered her to make the arrangements. As she was leaving his command vehicle, he advised her only to wake him up if she really had to. Essmie knew him well enough now to translate the message, which in the real world equated to: I am now going to get seriously drunk, and if you disturbed me without a reasonable excuse, I will kill you.

Commander Essmie delivered the updated plan to her squad leaders, having only just started to brief them on the additional nighttime activities. Her inspirational delivery was interrupted by a bottle being thrown out of the command vehicle and smashed on the ground at her feet. She ignored it, then continued to give them the details. "As you were all aware, this entire route was ideal territory for an ambush. Check as many stationary vehicles as possible, then place the guards out in front." Essmie collected another bottle of the once extravagantly overpriced vodka favoured by the insanely rich and the equally insane politicians, then carefully placed it inside the command vehicle. She thought that this would keep him quiet for a while, and if they were all lucky, General Vladimir Miasnikov would hopefully drink himself to sleep.

On the other side of the Atlantic Ocean, G-Flem, now completely satisfied with the progress underway at station A. She stands to, then salutes the newly appointed Commander Green, reminding him that updates had to be brief, regular, and above all else, represented the truth. Commander Green personally escorted General Fleming to the Magno-L and stood to attention along with everyone present as the train departed on route back to the CCP. G-Flem thought that her new commander could perhaps just turn out to be okay. However, should he acquire the same dysfunctional attributes as his predecessors, she would quite happily personally introduce him to the alligators.

The squads that Commander Green had sent out to search for Abe and his gang of rebels had just reached the hydropower station. They find no one about and also noting that Abe's crew had not attempted to fix the damaged machinery, they assume that the project had been abandoned. Under cover of darkness, they had encircled the camp, and the scouts had crept stealthily forward. In the hours that it had taken them to breach the perimeter undetected, the forward patrol had advanced only to be disappointed to find that the camp was, in fact, also abandoned. All of the houses were searched, and every squad reported the same findings that the houses were left intact. Some were still displaying plates left out on the table.

Commander Green search and destroy units next paid a visit to the former Kunupenny underground shelter. They were astounded by the amount of damage; both the stairwell and the lift shaft were now permanently out of service, having been completely filled in by cement. All of the troopers spread out, looking for clues that would determine which direction the community had travelled in. The whole of the area around the former underground shelter was a mess. Concrete trucks had emptied their loads where the vehicles were abandoned. Any visible signs that would have revealed the direction the group had travelled in had been completely obliterated. The squad leaders called in their troopers, informing them that they would have to widen the search grid. It was agreed that they would call a halt to today's activities and recommence the search first thing as dawn breaks.

On the uppermost tip of the continent of South America, Blink and her group had sheltered from the hurricane for two whole days. On surfacing from their shelter, the place where they sought refuge was almost unrecognisable. The sheer, unrestrained force of the storm had decimated building after building, then uprooted many trees as it carved its trail of destruction through the small town. As soon as the storm had abated enough to allow safe movement, she had ordered her crew to place the boats into the water. Blink kept her eyes on the expanse as she waited for the dawn to arrive. The ocean was still recovering from the tropical storm, but the good news was that it was starting to calm down just about enough for her and her crew to safely resume their journey.

This next crossing would be the last time that they would have to travel across a large body of water. After that, they would be exposed to the pleasure of hopping from island to island, then hugging the coast of America as she looked for a sign that would lead her and her crew to Enunsha's location. Blink had unquestionable faith that the old woman with the hooded cloak would not let her down.

She prayed to the old ones, lifting her hands to the universal mother of life, in thanks for delivering them and watching over all of them. Blink whistled on Sekoyaz, the big smile on her face giving away the fact that she did not need to inform her to get all the crew ready for departure. The dawn sky had not blessed them with its presence yet, but Blink knew that it was going to be yet another beautiful day. All of her crew were now on board their crafts, and she gave the order, and all the engines fired up simultaneously, then headed out into the waters that would take them to the islands in the Caribbean.

Blink had warned them that they might not see any land for at least two days. She had ordered them to split up the activities on the inflatable, some were to try and rest while the others steered the craft in the correct heading. Blink had constantly reminded them not to be tempted to place their limbs in the water, as the sharks in the area had a well-documented history of pulling people from boats and eating them. She had made the last part up, but not to make a fool of them, just to make them all fully aware of the dangerous creatures that had freely existed in these waters around them for thousands of years.

Somewhere on the coast of western Scotland. Gareth had clambered back on board, along with Scruffy, and with the aid of a few helpers, they had carried the meat to the galley. The gathered crew had given them a standing ovation on the very much appreciated contribution to humanity. After handing over the valuable treasure to the cooks. Gareth played to the crowd and delivered a thank you, fuck you all speech. He then persuaded Scruffy, along with the other members of the crew who had helped them, to join the curtain call to their adoring public.

Leena was the one who was clapping by far the loudest. She, for once, loved it when Gareth was subjected to some friendly abuse. She waved, grabbed his attention, "Cinds' along with her assistant nurse, need a break." Gareth looked at her and pretended he did not have any remote idea of what she was going to say next. She closed her eyes, then shaked her head. "Okay, smarty-pants, I had volunteered for us to go in and take over their duties. It's only for a couple of hours, so really no big deal." Gareth asked if he had to. Leena just ignored the childish remark, informing him to get a move on; otherwise, he would be going ashore for good.

As they entered the cabin, Cinds' thanked them for giving them a break. Alwyn, delighted to escape, said nothing, then, as quick as a flash, left the room immediately. Leena asked if he had a problem, and Cinds' mentioned, "The tortoise was popping it's head out."

Gareth held his hands up, declaring that the last statement was definitely, "Too much information."

As she made her way out, she informed them that the charges had been changed and washed. Now, on their own, Leena told Gareth to relax as all the hard work had already been done. The infants were awake, required food. Gareth asked heads or tails? Leena told him that she could quite happily strangle him sometimes. He mumbled something about as the infants had no names yet. He thought that heads or tails was slightly more suitable than, "This one or that one." Leena, after checking the temperature of the bottle, handed him a baby along with the liquid nutrition. Gareth, having played this game before, displayed the expert touch. The infant snuggled in and sucked away. Leena watched his performance, commenting that if he fell asleep before the baby, he would be getting keelhauled.

"I guess you have done this before?" He nods, empathising that he was not blessed with having any of his own.

"Nieces, Nephews, all that sort of thing," Gareth asked Leena if she had any children.

"Nope, just never got around to it, I guess. It was either the job I was in or the fact that the guys I went out with at the time never really stayed around for that long. I thought it was really a blessing in disguise. The sickness was bad enough, but just think of all the destroyed families."

Gareth, not wanting to dwell on the misfortune of others, asked if the two women had any form of identification on them. Leena replied that they had no papers, no nothing that could reveal anything about who they were or where they had come from. He thought that was fair enough as no one carries anything like that anymore. "After the sickness, I carried my mobile phone about for quite a while, somehow thinking that one day it was going to suddenly come back on line and I was going to start to receive messages. Even if there was some of the government still left alive and in charge, they would not have told you anything."

Gareth laughed, thinking about the time the party in charge at the time of the viral infection had introduced a search and text system. "It was hopeless, never performing as promised. At that time, you could order a parcel from Timbuctoo, and through the various apps offered, you would even be informed when the courier was having an unscheduled tea break. Every step of the journey was constantly updated. Right up to the point of informing you, that as you were not at home when they delivered, and they had left it with the thieving bastard who stayed next door."

Leena let it out that she was not a member of the online shopping fraternity. More than that, she confessed that she considered shopping just another mind-numbing chore. "On the phone, things, I remembered that there was a big thing in the media about a nationwide alert going to be initiated. It was just another bullshit campaign, pretending that they cared and that should a dangerous situation ever arise, the general public would be kept up to date. I can't recall ever receiving the message about the great sickness that had descended and then wiped out the biggest percentage of the population overnight. Imagine that you lived next to the neighbour from hell, who had been an absolute nightmare like forever and some. Then, all of a sudden, you receive an emergency alert on your phone, informing you that a dangerous situation was about to occur nationwide. Any normal person staying next door to a nutjob would immediately do what was required and eliminate the potential threat straight away. The nutters would also be having a field day. How many people do you know who would have loved to kill their boss, the bank manager, or even their mother-in-law? The resulting death rates would have all of a sudden increased exponentially nationwide." Leena noticed that Gareth's charge had finished the feed, reminded him that he had to get the infant up, then gently rubbed their back until it burped or puked. He told her that he was just testing her powers of observation and was pleased to announce that she had passed the test with flying colours. She was intent on informing him that he was so full of shit but stopped mid-thought as one of the sick women suddenly stirred and tried to say something.

Neither Leena nor Gareth understood what she had attempted to say. Gareth, nevertheless, replied that the babies were doing fine and there was nothing at all to worry about. The woman had fallen back asleep, none of them sure if she had actually heard them or if she had even understood what they had said. Leena thought that she sounded foreign, perhaps from one of the eastern European countries. Gareth was unsure as he was unable to detect a relatable accent or a single decipherable word. A knock on the door interrupted their conversation. Cinds' along with the assistant nurse, have returned. "If you want some of the lamb, I would hurry before Scruffy and his cousins scoff the lot."

They made their way to the galley and just managed to get in line before Scruffy, along with his forever-hungry cousins, joined them for a second helping. Gareth found a table for them in the corner, "five minutes later, and there would have been none left. Scruffy had told everyone that he had caught all the sheep by hand, and he was entitled to a double share." Leena wondered if being full of shit was a communicable disease, rampantly spreading among his group.

Leena thanked him for his comments, "Does Scruffy have a special power that allowed him to run at speeds beyond the normal human range to catch wild animals."

Gareth replied that the only special power Scruffy was blessed with only applied to his tongue. "He never stops talking; Alwyn had thought when he first met him that Scruffy breathed through his ears."

Leena could feel the slight vibration on her feet. "The mechanics must have fired up the second engine. They would be jumping about down there, checking that all was well. Rather than going to annoy them, we should have let them run all the tests, then assuming that everything works, we could be leaving on the next high tide."

Gareth asked if they would have to depart in the early hours. Leena nodded, informing him that she thought it would be about three o'clock in the morning. "When we travelled with only one functional engine, it was a nightmare. Now that we hopefully have two working units, the ship would be easier to handle on the open water. As we have some spare time, I was wondering if you would like to come to my cabin and look at the maps."

He agreed without any hesitation. As he took the plates over to the cleaning hatch, Alwyn having arrived just now, was informed them that the women they had rescued were now awake. Leena shrugged, and informed Gareth that she, too, was also disappointed, but they could go over the maps later. He nodded, knowing full well that later translated to when they could manage to steal some private time together. It could be hours or even days later, sometimes especially at times like these, he wished he could press the magic button. That would make everyone suddenly disappear and leave them in their own private little world. Alas, when duty called, they both had to be responsible and immediately available to address any arising issues. Maybe one day in the future, maybe in another life. Gareth hoped that Leena and himself would be living on a remote, uninhabited island with a temperate climate completely hidden from the rest of humanity. He knew that this thought was only a dream, and it was most likely never going to work out that way.

Anna had woken up first; she was at first startled by her new surroundings; the grey walls and the metallic furniture had initially thought that she had been imprisoned. As she slowly became more aware, Anna noticed Olga lying in the bed beside her, then the babies who were being cared for by the two complete strangers. If she were in one of Miasnikov's prisons, they would have already transferred the infants into Lesqueth's indoctrination programme. She holds her hands out, wanting to embrace her child. Alwyn tried to pass over the one he had been nursing; Anna shook her head, indicating that it was the other child, the one named tails.

Cinds' obliged by passing over the correct child. Anna cuddled into her baby and thanked them for taking care of the children. Olga had come to, and without being asked, Alwyn had passed over her little bundle. Olga asked if they were in a hospital and was astounded by the reply that they were now on a boat. Cinds explained the circumstances in relation to the state they had found them both in and educated them on the fact that they had consumed contaminated seafood. "If it was lumpy, you don't even think about eating it." Alwyn had left them to discuss the rudimentary do's and do not list associated with inshore fishing. He had returned ten minutes later with Leena and her shadow. Gareth was about to start asking them questions when Olga issued a very big thank you for saving all of them.

Leena told them that they were welcome, "If we had arrived twenty-four hours later, you would have never made it. Did you not notice that the fish, along with the seafood, was contaminated?" Anna admitted that they were village girls, never having been to the coast before, and had no idea that the lumps and bumps on the food indicated that they were contaminated. Olga added her part, "They tasted okay-ish; by all means, they could have been tastier, but I thought that perhaps the taste could have been a testimony to Annas' unrefined cooking skills."

Gareth wanted to get down to the nitty-gritty, asking straight out about the damage on their backs. Olga started to remove her clothes, and asked him if he would like to see the other parts of her body where she had received the additional rewarded for not freely cooperating with their captors. Gareth, not wishing to see the results, held up his hands, indicating that she could keep her clothes on.

Anna did the talk, "We were both working in London at the time the sickness came about. I was a service desk operator working for a company that required someone with Russian and English language skills. The company was owned by one of the oligarchs associated with the president and all the other companies he owned. I suspected that it was just another front company laundering huge sums of money for all the big boys who were then supposedly taking care of our country."

"I had never met Olga before I met her in the prison, the guards took an interest in us. At first, we thought that this was because we could speak the same language. Unfortunately, this developed into an unhealthy interest as soon as they realised that we were not going to give up what they wanted for a measly bar of chocolate. The guards decided that we were going to be entertaining them wherever, whenever they wanted. Sometimes, they would take us out of the prison, we watched them drink, and then they would beat and torture us. There were times when we would wake up at the prison, having no idea what had happened. They had drugged us, the aches, the pains and the resulting bruises issued us with a clear indication of the abuse that we had suffered. This continued for weeks on end, then one night, they had drunk too much and forgotten to drug us.

"We waited until they had all fallen asleep, then we slit all of their throats. The journey to the little village was our plan to escape the armed forces that were actively destroying every village, town and city that they had come across. The main roads were a mess full of abandoned vehicles, so we travelled cross country and eventually ended up there. In order to survive the onset of winter, we collected all the provisions that we thought would see us through the cold snap. On realising that we would, due to our advancing pregnancy, be unable to drive and forage efficiently, we holed up there.

"It wasn't easy getting to this place. Some of the local people we had come across were animals, almost just as bad as our guards at the prison. Yes, we defended ourselves, and yes, we killed people. Would you not have done the same to protect your children?"

The head nurse interrupted the conversation and informed the two women in the beds that they needed to take their antibiotics. Cinds' handed them the tablets, "Even though you were wide awake, you still had to complete the course." The women acknowledged the request, making disgusting facial gestures as they swallowed the medications. Alwyn had prepared the bottles, and now handed them over in allowing the mothers to feed their offspring.

Leena thought that it would be a goodwill gesture if they left the room and allowed the women some privacy. "If you need anything, just shout, and Alwyn or Cinds' would assist you," Olga asked if they were now their prisoners. Leena took a deep breath and asked her if she was restrained or if there were any bars on the windows. Olga replied, "Okay, but I still had to ask, these days, it was hard to tell the difference between who was friendly and who was only pretending to be friendly."

Leena motioned for her tribe to leave them to it, out of earshot, she asked Gareth what he thought. "Their story would explain the wounds and why the weapons that were in possession were spotlessly clean. Otherwise, they would have burned and mutilated themselves in order for the cover story to ring true." Leena asked him if that is possible. Gareth sighed, "In all of the things we've witnessed since the sickness, nothing would surprise me these days. However, pregnant women taking turns in repeatedly mutilating themselves somehow seems a little unlikely. If you want my opinion, we should be giving them a chance."

Leena asked the same question to the head nurse and her trainee, and they agreed with Gareth's opinion, "The wounds were fairly serious; it was hard to imagine two pregnant women taking turns mutilating each other over a period of time to achieve the desired effect. The areas that were damaged looked as if they were achieved with something very hot, which was, by the looks of it was, repeatedly applied to the same areas."

Lenna thanked them but wanted a close watch maintained at all times. She knew that they had all inherited a fairly unpredictable world, but the thought of giving someone permission to disfigure you freely beggars' belief. Leena, for one, thought that no matter how desperate one's situation could be, this action for her would be a most definite no-no.

Chapter 8

Jackson found Abe, along with Enunsha, looking intently at the large map pinned on the wall. He asked them if they thought about a much dreamed-about holiday destination located in some far-away exotic land completely unaffected by mankind's unrelentless barbarity. Abe retorted that he wished that was, in fact, true, but let it slip that if they played the role of the bad guys, where would we hole up. Jackson looked at them, "Considering that they had many years to prepare for this and vast amounts of money at their disposal, they could be absolutely anywhere."

"They are connected all the way to the top and avoided all the planning applications and inspections. I think that they must have hoodwinked the military officials and the president's office that they were involved in building some form of defensive structures that would have guaranteed the survival of the country. Just think, if the Kunupenny complex was a minor structure, that alone would have taken years to build. I suspected that the other hidden kingdoms are larger, better equipped, and far more complex, and they would have started construction at least in the early sixties. They could be absolutely anywhere, just bidding their time to surface and take complete control. The one question that I cannot figure out was why they have not already done so. The only reason I can think of is that there is a far larger plan in play. Possibly, they are waiting on instructions being issued down from the chain of command. So, taking into consideration all of what I have mentioned, they could be anywhere."

Abe couldn't believe that they had remained out of sight for that length of time, totally undetected, building massive underground complexes. Enunsha would love to tell them that these people had been unseen among them since the dawn of time. That would have led to many questions that she did not want to under any circumstances have to address. One day, she would have to tell them, Abe would not understand, and that would be a problem. He had never mentioned his family background in detail. If she revealed their undeniable involvement in the past along with her secrets it could be the end of them. The old woman had told her of the woman from South America who was coming to save them. Enunsha knew that when this time arrived, she would have to tell them something. Jackson would want to know everything, absolutely everything, with as many of the relevant details as possible. Enunsha loved Abe and liked Jackson, but she was indebted to the old woman with the hooded cloak. Her family had been persecuted for centuries because of their involvement with the Hidden. To just disclose this all of a sudden to the men in her world, would make life very difficult for all of them.

Enunsha, to escape from her thoughts, asked for news on the various active patrols that were now stationed out in the wilderness. Jackson had nothing new to tell them; sector by sector would be searched, and if the bad guys showed up, we would hopefully be able to deal with it accordingly. Abe thought out loud that people who fucked them over at the hydro-plant won't hide forever. "We must have at least pissed them off when we dumped the cement, denying them access to venture above ground. You would think that they would be already out looking for us, seeking revenge for our actions." Jackson was pretty calm about it. "Time will tell; they will be out searching, slowly checking from where we used to reside. Moving from area to area and looking for signs of recent habitation. As we left no visible traces of our evacuation, they will be searching for quite some time before they come across this place. All we can do is prepare ourselves and make sure that we give them the welcome that they truly deserve."

Poison Pete, accompanied by his constant shadow, Doctor Death, was now sitting back and admired their handy work. Not one of them had much to offer in the way of required skills, but all the same they were of the shared opinion that they had done a rather splendid job. They were now reduced to smoking normal cigarettes as the stash had been just about depleted. Pete had hoped that by now, they would have found some of the special herbs growing out in the wild. Even though this was an army camp, there must have been at least some part-time smokers. As of yet, they had not found anything, but Pete told his friend that they would find some soon. They just haven't looked hard enough. Doctor Death informed his friend that, at least in prison, there was always someone to ask as there was always something available. Poison Pete agreed, but at least here, they did not have to pay the price of joining the Brotherhood or relinquishing the ownership of their souls in exchange for an unconditional affiliation to one of the other gangs.

In not so sunny Scotland, Murray had woken up to the sound of the motherhood conversations, checking that Bobby was not on display for all and sundry. He announced his arrival on the new day. "Good morning, ladies," locating Cha in the middle of the throng he moved towards her to receive the ungently required customary cuddle. He did not think that he was needed today as there were many hands available and all of them have vastly superior baby skills than himself. Cha supplied him with a cuppa, informing him that he had missed breakfast. Murray was not bothered. He was more than happy with the supplied liquid; he grabbed his jacket on his way outside. It was a beautiful day, nowhere near summer, but at least the weather was not cold enough to freeze your balls off. Cha joined him and informed him that the infants thought that there was a wild animal asleep on the premises. He asked how loud his snoring was on a scale of one to ten. Cha pretended to think about it for a minute or two, then came up with the number fifteen. He told her that, as always, it was a subconscious thing, and he had no real control over it. Cha disagreed, revealing her theory that a plastic bag placed over his head, then secured very tightly around his neck, could very well provide a permanent cure.

Murrays lowered his head, loudly informing all of the known world that his life was full of unrelenting misery as he had fallen in love with a cruel woman. He confided in her that they were team-handed with lots of people to look after the new additions to the household. As his services were not required, Murray was going to make some space to install the batteries beside the workings of the watermill. "I would need to find an alternative storage space for all of the weapons that you and Okolo placed in there," Cha asked if he had any ideas. Murray thought that where they had recently discovered the escape route might be the perfect place, but he would have to go and check. Cha put her arms around him, reminding him that he didn't have to carry out all the work himself. Murray promised that if he needed help, he would ask. "Robbo would be busy with all the other more important tasks, so I won't be asking him. He would be getting the houses ready for the new occupants. If I took him away from that, Okolo and Alicia would not be happy. But I do promise not to do all the lifting myself. Karen would supply what was required if and when I ask her for reinforcements."

Mr. Black would have invited the dogs to come along, but as he was aware that, for some reason, they did not like it up anywhere near that place. He made his way up to where they found the hidden access that had led to the escape route. In his absence, someone had installed a ladder. He took that as a good sign and switched on the torch as he descended into the chambers. Murray made his way all the way down to where they had pressed the symbols on the wall that had opened the secret access to the tunnel. The door that had taken a long time for them to figure out how to open had now been closed back into its original position, as well as the huge slab of stone that had blocked their retreat. He remembered not pressing any additional sequence on the way through the long tunnel and the only thing they had touched was the door at the very end. Murray thought that it was possible that with exiting at the other side, perhaps this could have closed the entrance. If not, then the opening mechanism could have been on a timed sequence and could have closed automatically. Mr. Black made his way back up the stairs. There was more than enough space available to store all the weapons without having to disturb the bodies of the Hidden. He intended to run the latest information past Alicia when he returned to the house. She had always provided a reasonable explanation when they had come across problems that defied logical thinking. Murray now made his way to where they had stored enough weapons and munitions to equip a small army.

He saw Cora in the distance and waved enthusiastically to attract her attention. Murray made a slight detour to go and say hello. She was slightly more upbeat since the last time they met. They exchanged pleasantries, but the doctor was still looking worried. Murray suspected that she slowly came to terms with the fact that her daughter may be talented in unusual ways. Cora was not her normal self, Mr. Black cancelled the job at hand and took over the buggy controls. Murray had purposely steered them towards his house, thinking that if the new mother interacted with the others, it would do her the world of good. Cora was hesitant at first, making every excuse possible, finally adding that she was just really not too keen on just turning up unannounced. Murray reassured her that they had nothing to hide and she was welcome anytime. "C'mon on in and at least have a cuppa. I don't know about you, but I would love one."

The doctor gave in and surrendered to his effervescent charm. Murray selected the correct lever that puts the buggy into automatic parking mode and, like a perfect gentleman, held the door open for her. The first thing that she noticed was the dogs just lying there among all the infants, almost as if they were guarding them. Murray knew what she thought and told her that they were just practicing for when the babies move onto solids. Cha welcomed Cora with open arms and invited her to sit and join them in the meal. The doctor protested. Cha told her that they always made more than they needed, and she would be offended if she refused. "Cora, please don't worry. Murray has been banned from cooking for like forever." Everyone made her feel at home, and even the twins took great delight in her being there. They had placed her daughter down with all the other infants on her arrival. Now that all the new additions were together Cha had noticed that there was a very faint hum emanating from their vicinity. Not wanting to freak Cora out, she did not mention it. Murray acted like her personal butler and brought her over a plate of food.

"It had taken me a lifetime to teach Cha how to cook properly, and I hope you enjoy the meal," Okolo asked him; if Cora ever had the unfortunate experience of tasing his famous two-pan shuffle, would she believe him? Alicia piped up, informing Cora that the dogs even refused to even look at his cooking. At one time, they had threatened to contact the organisation that prosecuted people who mistreated their animals. Murray stood up, confessing to all present that he was probably the worst cook on the planet.

Cora complimented Cha on her culinary skills and confessed that her daughter, when she was older, would think that she had attended rudimentary classes at Murray International School of Toxicological Cuisine. The twins told her that would not be the case as they were available to give her lessons anytime, she felt up to it. Okolo vouched for them and stated that they could cook the pants off anyone in there. Cora looked at them, agreeing that they could show her once the little ones were up and about on their feet. "But could we start off on the easy meals, I am not quite ready for gourmet cuisine."

Robbo was noticeably absent, still getting the houses spick and span for the new tenants. Murray, after he helped with the dishes, had disappeared outside to smoke. Alicia had followed hot on his heels, "Did you notice the hum when all the children were together?" He was just about to reply when Robbo appeared. Murray said hello and asked if everything was okay and if he wanted some help. All he had to do was ask. Robbo replied that all was good, but if he would show him how to unravel the enigma of connecting up the components of the sound system, that would be greatly appreciated. The good news was that Cat and Frank could move in tomorrow. It was all ready, all clean, and everything in their house was almost brand new.

Alicia told him that it would be a great idea to bring Frank over and then deliver the goods news to him and Cat at the same time. Robbo stole a smoke from Murray, promising to go over and get him once he finished. Murray thought that Robbo had done well putting other's needs before his own. Robbo asked if the kind act of unselfishness would grant him the offer of sainthood. Murray informed him that he still had a long way to go before he received his wings, but at least he was on the correct path. Murray promised not to move from the spot and guaranteed his silence. "You should be the one to tell them as you had done all the hard work." Robbo asked Murray if he could fix the sound system soon, "I could do it anytime you wish. We could even wire it up when your neighbours were viewing their new house." Robbo shook his hand, confirming the done deal. When Robbo went to lure Frank across, Alicia asked Murray if he had forgiven Robbo of all his crimes. Murray closed his eyes and then nodded, "Okay, anything to keep the peace, although there was one condition." Alicia asked him just to give it to her with both barrels. "I would like you and Okolo to remember that we were your friends and promised to visit often and not forget about us." His comments quite touched Alicia, and she promised to visit often and frequently. She cuddled him. That was from Okolo and me, "If we lived for a million years, we would never forget you. Murray, sometimes you were so fucking stubborn, almost like a wild animal. In times like these, I realised that Cha was very lucky to have you." He was quite touched by her comment, wondering if Cha had been privy to the same disclosure.

Robbo had returned accompanied by a perplexed-looking Frank. Murray was surprised that Robbo had not just placed a hood over his head and then frogmarched him over at gunpoint. Now in the house Robbo announced that he would like to propose a toast and he would really appreciate it if everyone joined in. Cha took the hint and called her stray husband to heel. Murray had the distinct impression if he resisted in any way at all, she would have dragged him in by the ears. They were handed a glass as they entered the house. Robbo, who has promoted himself as the master of ceremonies, thanks everyone for their presence. "The future is always uncertain, but with friends, mothers and babies, the future always shines brighter." Robbo handed Frank a set of keys, "If you are going to stand there all day, I would take the keys from you and move in myself." Robbo raised his glass to Frank, Cat, Sammarra and their new house. Everyone clapped, and Murray was by far the most enthusiastic among them. The couple had no idea that they were top on the list and had expected that Alicia, along with Okolo, would have received the first option. The lucky couple have to be almost pushed to go and view their new abode.

Sammarra was reluctant to go. Cat just reached down and placed her in her arms; Remus followed the three of them without any question. Alicia looked over at Murray, and he nodded acknowledging that the hum produced by the children had ceased immediately when Sammarra had left the room. Robbo asked Murray if now was an appropriate time to resolve the brain-numbing enigma of the cables that would miraculously resuscitate the sound system. Murray told him that it was not a problem, then leading the way discretely they left to go and sort it out. Mr. Black was surprised that Robbo's new abode was spotless and looked like it was almost ready to move into. Murray was presented with the box of cables; it took him less than five minutes to connect up all the components. "All you have to do now was give it a test drive." Robbo thanked him, confessing that he had tried then failed miserably, all the different types of connectors just gave him a migraine.

Murray gave him his place and the privacy required when one was test-driving their newly acquired sound system, reliving distant memories that came alive when playing old favourite songs. He arrived home, informing Okolo and Alicia that their very own private DJ in residence was selecting the forgotten sounds of yesteryear for their entertainment. Alicia thought that their ears would now be constantly bombarded with German heavy metal death bands, or whatever the fuck they all called. Okolo corrected her and delivered the proper genre that Robbo's much-favoured sounds belong to. Alicia suggested that they should go through and select what they would like to hear. Okolo nodded, thinking that she would like something soothing, not something that felt and sounded like your head had been placed in a vice with an angle grinder being used to reconfigure your eardrums. Cha wished the women good luck on their quest. She thought that she was quite lucky as Murray played his awful-sounding music with the cans on, which she supposed was really a blessing in disguise.

Cora asked her if their house was always this busy. Cha replied that there were people here most days and that she thought that it would be pretty awful if it was quiet. The twins speak in their accustomed way. Cora, not at all used to them, moved her head left and right as they spoke. "Have you picked out a name for your daughter?"

Cora replied that it was a nightmare, taking into consideration that children could be so cruel and often play with the associated names. Beth nor Debs didn't understand and Cora explained, "Because I am a doctor, all the names that I liked were out of the question. If I had wanted to call her Maxine, the other children would call her Maxine the vaccine, and the other names don't sound any better. I have gone through all my favourites and added on all the cruel jibes that would have inadvertently followed, Eloease the disease, Lorraine the pain and lastly, Edwina the oedema. My daughter, in her later years, would be more than very angry if I had picked any of these. After all of that, I thought of calling her Echo."

All of the women present thought that it was a great name. When Murray received an under-the-table kick from Cha, he also wholeheartedly agreed. The twins loved the name, informing Cora that it sounded so nice and gentle even though they thought privately that the girls' friends would no doubt call her Echo the Gecko.

Cora grilled the twins on any forthcoming names for their daughters. At first, to were a little reticent on disclosing any information on what they had been thinking. The twins knew that they were now under the spotlight now had to spill the beans. They go through the motions involving the routine of "you tell them first; no, you could go first." Murray asked the dynamic duo if he was allowed to have three guesses. Cha shaked her head, politely informing him to put a sock on the grand inquisition.

Beth gave in, informing all present that she was thinking of naming her daughter after Cat. "Before you all jump down my throat, I know that it was impossible just to name my daughter Cat. I also know that she never used her real name, so I have shortened it down to Terina. In future years, my daughters' friends could antagonise all they wanted about her name at their pearl. Because if she was anything like her namesake, they would be calling her Terina the misdemeanour."

Beth could hear Murray's cogs churning away, and she shot him down in flames before he said a word. "Murray, I really don't want to hear the words that you think rhyme." Mr. Black held up his hands, surrendering to her wishes. Beth turned to her twin, "Okay, sis, now it's your turn for the revelation."

Debs took a deep breath, confessing that it had taken her a very long time to come up with a name that she liked. "After much thought, I am going to call my offspring Lyla. Not because I thought that Murray would never be able to find a word that rhymed with it. But because I really liked the name, it sounded nice and peaceful."

Cha thought out loud and informed the twins that both names sounded fantastic. "Murray would never get them right, and please don't be offended if it took him years to stop mixing them up. Just the other day, he was getting his son's names mixed up with the dogs' names, so please be patient." Cora asked Murray if that was true because if it was, it could be a sign of the onset of a severe, life-changing medical condition.

Murray smiled and replied, "Cora, Cha always took the piss out of me, especially when there were other people around. I think she does it because I am a nice guy and could laugh along with everybody else. Either that or she hated my guts and was trying to prove that I am really a neurotic psychopathic bastard."

Cora thought now that Cha's story was true and that perhaps Murray was covering up his symptoms of the onset of dementia. He may be a little on the crazy side, but certainly not a real bonafede, one hundred percent psychopath. Cha Forever the umpire, broke the ice and asked if anyone would like to eat. "As far as I am aware, Murray was still under a lifetime ban and sorry to inform you all that he would not be doing the cooking tonight."

Cora thanked Cha for the offer, professing that it was time to take Echo home. "You know the deal, feeding time, bath time, storytime, then the best bit, some mummy me time."

The women hooted at the last comment. Murray complained that there was no mention of Daddy time. Cha looked at him straight, "I have been told that there was fresh fish on the menu tonight. We were going to go over to enjoy. Do we really need to have a discussion, followed by a vote to decide who was nominated for babysitting duties?"

Murray stood to attention, volunteering for the said duty. Without being prompted, he offered to take Cora home after the meal. Cha asked him if he had forgotten something, and Murray scratched his head. "Of course, I would go and ask Cat to bring in Sam while you all get ready."

As he headed out the door, Cora asked her how long it had taken to house-train him. "Oh, that was still an ongoing work in progress. He was still under secret quadruple probation, but I have not told him yet."

He had returned with Cat along with her daughter. Murray placed Sam beside the other bundles of joy. Cat wanted to know if everyone was ready as she, for one, was starving. Murray stood at full attention, saluting them all as they left. As the women arrive at Frank's place, they received an invite to join Okolo and Alicia. Cha informed the company that the male folk have to be good at something. It was just so hard to find what that good something was. All of them took the rise out of Murray, impersonating his 'Oh no! it's fish tonight' face. They discussed the names that had been chosen, asking Okolo and Alicia if they had come up with any suitable ones yet. Okolo takes the lead, "I like the name, Albert, Robbo thought that he would shorten it to Alby, but that was okay also."

Alicia confessed, for some strange reason, that she can't quite put her finger on that she liked the name Norton. "I honestly don't know why. It just sort of came to me, and no doubt his dad would try to shorten it to Norrie, Orton or something equally silly. But I have warned him that he would use the full name or else."

Cha informed the company that she expected to find Murray sound asleep on the floor when she returned home. "He will be lying there surrounded by books, when waking up later, he will resolutely assure me on all things sacred that he read every single page at least three times. When in reality, he had fallen asleep halfway through the first one." Alicia had the chair confiding to them that Robbo had the intention of educating the children on the obscure history relating to the German industrial metal bands. Okolo nodded, indicating that it was indeed a true story. "He would have tried, but between us, we gave him a list of approved books that he was permitted to read," Alicia added that he was also banned from reading them anything to do with re-mortgage evaluations and delayed repayment schedules. Cora thought that they were just as cruel as Cha, perhaps even more so.

Murray had not fallen asleep and was in the process of impersonating animal noises. He had tried reading them several stories, but as they had just stared at him, Murray had decided that they needed entertainment. His animal noises probably sounded nothing like the real thing, but at least the children smiled at them. The women return from the under-the-water eating extravaganza at, which Murray was delighted at not having to attend. He was in the midst of his performance, caught outright impersonating the sounds of ducks. Cat asked him if his ducks were suffering from sore throats, as they sounded a little on the croaky side. Murray replied that they were smoking ducks, "The reproduction of their sound is authentic, and one hundred percent accurate."

Cha informed him that Cora, along with her little fluffy duckling, was requiring an escort home. "Perhaps, after you take the curtain call for your more than appreciative audience, you could walk them home." Murray performed his bow like a seasoned thespian. He was unperturbed by the fact that all of his adoring fan clubs were fast asleep. He took over the duty of driving the buggy. Now fully accustomed to the vehicle, he knew not to bother seeking out the overdrive controls. As they meander back towards the medical facility, Cora thanked him for making her day. She admitted freely that she had not laughed that much in ages.

Murray smiled, confessing that they laugh at him most of the time. "I am the blunt of the jokes almost twenty-four-seven, but as I laugh the loudest, it does not really matter. The way I see it, a happy house is a healthy house, and I would not have it any other way." Murray was happy that Cora had brightened up somewhat, "Don't be a stranger, Cora; you were more than welcome to pop in anytime you were passing. We all needed someone to talk to every once in a while, as well as Echo could mix with the other children. I think she was the most appreciative of my animal impersonations." Cora looked at him, wondering if perhaps he urgently required some tests to confirm that he was mentally stable. The doctor thanked him for an enjoyable day. Now arriving at the medical facility, she bids him a goodnight.

Alicia and Okolo, on returning home, witness first-hand what Robbo had been up to. His ad-hoc painting class had left a trail of destruction throughout the newly decorated house. They found the abundant display of little and large handprints adorning the walls, on every wall resplendently decorating every single room. They find the main offender sitting out the back, quietly puffing away, looking quite at peace with himself and the world.

Okolo asked if he had enjoyed himself. A beaming Robbo declared that Vinny, Orty, along with cousin Alby had a great time leaving their imprint for all posterity. "Just think that when the handprints are viewed in the future, they will see a recorded moment in time. We could even add to the collection on display by making other prints when the children get older. Not forgetting to introduce yours and Alicia's into the collage."

Alicia had listened to his theorised hypothesis, suggesting to Okolo that now could be the perfect time to reintroduce Robbo to electric shock therapy. Okolo told him straight to his face that he was a wanker. She noticed his hands and asked to see them. Robbo held them up, with the palms facing her. The bright red paint, was very much evident and has completely dried. He told them that there was no need to panic as he had covered up all of the children's hands in the white wood glue prior to immersing them in the pot of paint. As the women were far from being amused, he offered to make them a drink, then added he would get up early and perform the breakfast duties without complaint. Robbo gave in, asking them what he could do to appease them. They issued a joint statement requesting a vow of silence, empathizing that it came into effect immediately.

Chapter 9

Tesporo, with the assistance of his rancid brethren, had completed the task of preparing JJ's corpse for interment into the mausoleum. The Baroness of Kindeace-Shire praises the keeper of the records, declaring that the monument will stand forever to the test of time. "It will remain a splendid reminder to all of the future generations, that heroes do indeed exist and they were not just confined to the ancient history books. These unbelievable volumes upon volumes of fantasy-driven self-praise, were nothing but pure, unadulterated waffle, balderdash and piffle. Portraying that these vastly inferior primitive bipeds arose from the fetid swamps then conquered and tamed this planet all on their own."

Lesqueth commanded him to halt and pay close attention to what she was saying. "Tesporo, I want all of these ancient tales corrected to display the truth. Make it your top priority to establish the true factual events, highlighting how our race steered their collective ineptitude. Make sure that you included a passage depicting that if it were not for our intervention, they would still be living in caves, forever thinking that the ability to start a fire was the ultimate human achievement." Lesqueth walked away, and Tesporo took this as an indication that the one-way conversation was over.

The Baroness had entered the mausoleum, intent on saying a few words to the fallen general. Two of the keepers of the records disciples hovered around her and delivered an indecipherable incantation along with the truly unwelcome smell of decay. Lesqueth looked around the room for their leader, but unable to locate his whereabouts, she went outside to hunt him down. The Baroness, still not being able to find him, instructed her personal guards to retrieve the elusive quarry and bring him to heel. She was infuriated that these loathsome creatures had the audacity to approach her and violate her private space with their irrepressible stench.

Lesqueth had previously made it crystal clear to Tesporo, letting it be known that she had found their permeated odour intolerable. This time she would be issuing no warnings, no permissible, nor probationary period for atonement. The keeper of the records was in the process of being frogmarched over to attend the summons. The guards arrived and threw their captive onto the ground before her. Tesporo started uttering pleas for clemency for whatever crimes he had unknowingly committed to displease her as he started to deliver the much-practised grovelled speech. The Baroness commanded him to refrain from speaking.

"How many times do I have to repeat myself? How many times have I complained about that awful smell that followed you and yours everywhere like a stray dog? You and your nest of vipers, with all the in-house body modifications that all of you enthusiastically perform on yourselves. Dissipates the smell of death and decaying flesh into my private space from now on, before you venture outside of your little fucking cave. Your church, chapel, monastery or whatever the fuck you wanted to call it was dedicated to the fallen, the vanquished and forgotten. You would wash away all the smells of your perverted, distorted aspirations of attaining sainthood."

"Then and only then would you or yours be allowed anywhere near my presence. Failing to do so would result in you or your follower's untimely death. I was going to issue orders decreeing that if my guards detect one unpleasant whiff of your unusual cologne, then they'll have carte blanche permission to remove you or your breed from this plane of existence." The Baroness instructs Tesporo to nod, just once, if he understood all of the full implications. The keeper of the records unquestionably obeyed his instruction and remained still on the ground.

"As I was preparing myself to deliver my farewell speech to the acclaimed fallen hero, the unquestionably brave general John Josiah Atkin. Two of your reptilian acolytes breached my private space, and this was unforgivable and, therefore, punishable. Let this be a permanent reminder of the consequences that will automatically follow when the rules are not strictly adhered to." Lesqueth ordered Tesporos' assistants to be removed immediately from JJ's mausoleum.

The Baroness waits patiently while the human slaves were drafted into sanitised and cleansed JJ's final resting place from top to bottom. On completion of the task, they kneeled as per their instructions. Lesqueth recited the prayer in the ancient tongue to the fallen, the vanquished and the forgotten. She lit up one of her small cigars, then produced her hip flask and took a stiff pull at the brandy. Lesqueth poured the rest of the flask's contents onto the casket and wished John Josiah Aitken an unhindered journey into the afterlife. She balanced the small still burning cigar on the casket lid, then very sincerely thanked all of the slaves individually for cleaning the final resting place of her dear departed friend. Lesqueth produced her blade and then proceeded down the line of the kneeled figures. This time she grabbed them by the hair, then, one by one, she slit their throats. The Baroness of Kindeace-Shire bowed to the casket containing JJ and then exited the mausoleum.

Tesporo was still lying prone, face down in the dirt. She ordered the head viper to stand up and gather up all of his snakes. Lesqueth pointed out, "The two who had the audacity to invade my private space will stand over there." She barked for Tesporo now, accompanied by all of his disciples, to watch closely and pay attention. Lesqueth put on her gloves and calmly walked across to the waiting recipients. She head-butted the first one, then kicked his companion in the stomach. As they were lying on the ground, the Baroness awarded them with a series of full-force kicks to their heads and bodies. Now, slightly satisfied with the initial beating, Lesqueth grabbed the first one by the ankles. Leaned back and then slowly started to rotate him around her, synchronising and then increasing her footsteps until they had gained enough momentum. Lesqueth gauged the distance of the perceived trajectory, then suddenly let him go. The white-upon-white robed serpent's head impacts the corner of the building. The area around the recently inflicted head wound changed colour as the crimson fluid was absorbed and spread into the white material.

The Baroness was bitterly disappointed in the lack of sustainable damage. She had to repeat the process multiple times until the first recipient's head was a swollen, distorted, bleeding mess. Lesqueth spat on the corpse, leaving the victim where they lay. The second recipient, after being awarded the severe beating, was slowly starting to come around. He had just managed to open his eyes when Lesqueth announced in an almost sexy voice, full of intent and promise. "Well, hello, you." Then dropped a rock with added force on his head. Lesqueth found the process quite exhilarating, almost therapeutic, as she continually smashed their head to pulp. When the Baroness was finished, the head was totally unrecognisable. The rock had fractured and had broken, then pulverised the skull completely. Lesqueth gave the corpse one final kick, then reminded Tesporo and company, "No matter what anyone else tells you. I can resolutely assure you all that cleanliness is indeed, next to Godliness."

Several thousand miles away across the vast expanse of liquid, otherwise known as the Atlantic Ocean. Commander Green was confident that all of General Fleming's orders would be carried out to the letter. He showed no remorse for the untimely demise of his predecessor and his sycophantic sidekick with the overtly pretentious long name. If he was going to be really honest about the whole thing, Green was planning to vanish them anyway. All the yes sir, no sir replied to the ludicrous and banal orders had reached the outer range of his bullshit meter. Green had just about depleted all of his peace and goodwill to all the superior officers allocated ration. Then finally, his resolve was broken by the fucker who wanted his name said in full with every fucking conversation, every fucking sentence, including every fucking reply to every fucking issued order.

Commander Green had overlooked the thought of disposing of them via the alligator canal. Jack had envisaged a good old-fashioned poisoning, perhaps even an unfortunate transport accident. In which any and all the evidence that could have possibly been connected to him would simply be incinerated along with his former superior officers. Green had just received the latest squelch transmission from the search squads, out trying to locate the whereabouts of the somewhat elusive Abe Hubstien and his fellow conspirators. They reported that the area surrounding their last known location had come up null and void. However, as they had expanded the area under investigation, they had found some evidence. The recently disposed the quantity of trash could very well be an indication that the hydro-plant people had travelled southwards. Adding that if this were the case, then a sizable convoy would have been utilized. In order to increase the search parameters, the squadron leader requested permission to split the group into several teams. They were also making enquiries about the possibility of employing tracker drones and sensory optics.

Jack Green started to prepare a reply squelch. The decision to approve the deployment of tracker drones was way above his pay grade, and without going into all the details, he denied the request. He did, however, agreed to supply the sensory optics, and added in the rendezvous coordinates. Commander Green would be more than pleased if he could present G-Flem with all the captured hydro-station gang. Jack would have filled his dreams of the fugitives, all chained together. Looking thourarly miserable and broken as they awaited in the torrential rain to be loaded into the animal wagons now being used as prison carriages. Commander Green would wave enthusiastically as the Magno-L rail system energised, transporting Abe, whatever his name was, along with all of his buddies to their final destination at the CCP. The only downside would be that he would not be present to witness nor be actively involved in the subsequent interrogations, involuntary dissections and executions. Jack thought that this was truly unfortunate, but who would know and, more to the point, who would actually care if he accidentally, on purpose, sort of inadvertently misplaced a few of the prisoners. After all, there was entertainment for all and sundry, and then again, there was uncurtailed private, very private entertainment.

Blink and the rest of her crew had been on the water for far too long, she thought that they would all be relieved when they reached dry land. She drifted off, reminiscing about the stories her mother Lucky had told her. Her adoptive grandmother had passed down tales about the islands in the Caribbean. It was almost impossible to believe that Gabriella Serrano was actually a police officer,. Blinks' mother had often told her that they joked about her grandmother's almost gangsterish-sounding name. Lucky had confessed to presenting her with a fake rap sheet, which depicted the alleged list of felonies that she had committed, as a birthday present. Blink would have given anything to have spent some time with her. The love that she passed on to her mother was always omnipresent, and even in her dreams, Blink would witness the bright aura that surrounded them.

The island chain that they were traveling towards was famous for many things, most notably the ever-present musical culture. Her mother and grandmother loved to dance to the four upon four rhythms, with the with heavy accent placed on second and fourth beats. Blink found the genre as appealing as captured cats screaming to escape from confinement within a closed canvas bag, which had been placed in the centre an intense oil drum fire with a sealed lid. Her mother had also passed on the important message that these islands were perhaps, possibly one of the most dangerous places on earth. The stark warning was underlined, declaring that not all of the indigenous people's habitual customs and practices were listed in the index, contained on the back pages of the various tourist guidebooks.

They had been blessed with calm seas and pleasant weather, but it had still been a rather long, arduous journey. Sekoyaz gave her the heads up that the land was in sight and surveyed the stretch of coastline in front of them through the military grade binoculars. Blink replied via hand signals to ready their weapons, even though the scene in front of them was just as serene and pleasant like the perfect picture postcard. The hair standing on the back of her neck informed her otherwise. What lay before them was as far removed and as far away as possible from depicting an ultra-tourist-friendly beachfront property. Almost enticingly charming unwary travellers with beckoning arms into the ex-shanty town boy's version of a fully inclusive, unforgettable onshore entertainment package.

Blink issued more hand signals and then delivers the briefest of nods, for the operators to redline the engines. In the remaining space between their crafts and the beach, the other crafts fan out and match her speed. She hoped that the majority of the local inhabitants would be reluctant to partake in early morning alarm calls. At the last moment, all of the propellers were lifted out of the ocean, as the boat's momentum glided them over the final stretch of water and propelled them onto the beach. Sekoyaz had alighted from her boat before it stopped and now rushed forward to take up a defensive position. The rest of the crew, with weapons out, readily followed suit. A welcoming petrol bomb was launched, and it started to arc through the morning sky towards them. Blink destroyed the flaming projectile with one shot from her 9mm automatic before it reached anywhere near them. She was slightly disappointed at not noticing it sooner, plus the fact that the locals were still not fast asleep.

More petrol bombs were launched towards them on mass, and the expected reign of fire that the dread-headed locals had planned to unleash upon them was a complete failure. All of Blinks' people were accomplished marksmen, and all of the missiles had been eliminated prior to entering the danger zone. Several of the islands' residents ran around in flames, having received one of the returning gifts that had engulfed them in liquid as they were preparing other cocktails. Blink leads from the front, killing anything that moved in front of her.

The inhabitants of the beach apartments, resplendent in red, yellow and green attire, had been encouraged by their defacto leader to attack. The group that Sekoyaz leads was confronted by a mob wielding rusty machetes. She was slightly perplexed by the attempted onslaught, but nevertheless ordered her companions to open fire on them. Blink had not been so fortunate and was now being attacked by a mob brandishing machine guns. She had nowhere to go to take cover and evade the oncoming fire. Blink stood her ground. As the assailants had never participated in any formal training to use their weapons. They still retained the bad habit of closing their eyes when the firearms were activated. The shots that had been fired at them from the attacking mob travelled in every conceivable direction but the intended one.

The fighting did not last long; it had taken her highly efficient crew just a few minutes to completely eradicate the problem. As the strange eerie silence, almost seeped out of the ground then completely blanketed the area, Blink ordered that the dead should be gathered up, as there was no available mechanised equipment in the vicinity they would be cremated. If the now departed had not been lying in wait, to attack them she would have happily negotiated a peaceful outcome. All that her crew required was fuel, food and some much-needed rest. They had not crossed the watery expanse to create any form of a regime that required her crew to conquer then systematically subdue the local population into servitude. After everything and all that the people of the planet had gone through, she thought that the waste of life was appalling. Sekoyaz approached and informed her that all the bodies had been stacked up, prepared for burning. Blink thanked her for informing her, and then, together, they walked towards the funeral pyre. Even though it was not their people, she felt duty-bound to pay respect to their souls. All of her crew stood with their heads down and their hands clasped in front of them as they collectively recited an ancient prayer for the recently departed.

Sekoyaz was just about to ignite the kindling material to incinerate the dead when Blink issued the alarm. They all snapped out of the prayer and then followed her as she started running forward. Blink reached down into the pile of discarded weapons, picking up a pineapple-shaped object, pulled in the lever with one hand and pulled the pin with the other. As the modified pick-up truck with the mounted heavy-duty machine gun arrived. Blink threw the projectile, which exploded, almost instantly obliterating the gunner and the driver. The other vehicles tried frantically to manoeuvre out of the way of their companion's badly damaged truck. They all had been driving way, way too close together and ended up in a car jam. As they fought with each other trying to scramble and claw their way out of the crashed vehicles. Blink's crew stepped forward into the ensuing melee and proceeded to kill most of them. A handful of them had successfully managed to pry themselves out from the wreckage, only to be mown down seconds later by Sekoyaz and her ever so vigilant teammates.

This lot of fallen attackers were not allocated the dignity of a funeral pyre nor a prayer, and their bodies were dragged and then discarded like rotten meat into the backs of the wrecked, bullet-ridden vehicles. Blink was utterly disgusted that they had attacked when they were in the middle of paying homage to the forever lost souls of the fallen. She now requested that they load up with fuel and provisions to enable them to vacate this area as soon as possible. There was not an issue with the fuel, an abundant supply was located nearby. A human chain was created to pass the near-empty containers to be replenished by the liquid and then returned to the boats.

The only suitable source of food that was found was located in several run-down, almost semi-derelict coops. The black throated pheasants were not an indigenous species to this region. It was most likely that they had imported to the island and bred for sporting events in the more affluent times. Sekoyaz wrings the necks of a dozen birds, then walks away deliberately, leaving all the doors fully open. Once the funeral pyre and the vehicles were ignited, Blink issued the signal to leave. She hoped to find a safer area to hole up and rest several miles up the coast. That was not inhabited by people who wished to snuff out her and all of her crew. As they coast around the island, Blink wondered if she had made the wrong call. Rather than continue up the coast of central America, in her wisdom she had decided that island hopping would be a safer alternative. The countries on the upper half of the southern continent were deemed risky and extremely dangerous. She hoped that the next island, maybe even all the islands that they were next venture to, would be inhabited by friendlier people or perhaps only full of once, semi-domesticated animals.

Blink knew for sure that they had been very lucky during the previous attacks. This was mostly due to the remarkable ineptitude displayed by the attacking forces. The next time, sooner or later, they were going to come into contact with a cohesive force that would be more than capable of mounting a sustainable, well-planned attack. She thought that her group would be unable to survive unless they had heavier weapons. If and when it was possible, they would conduct a search for these items.

On the west coast of Scotland, Gareth, still with his eyes closed reached out with his hand and turned over in attempting to steal a share of Leena's body heat. Her side of the bed was empty, and the cold space indicated that the captain had vacated this life raft at least several hours ago. He guessed that the conversation in which he was going to ask if it was a Caribbean or a Pacific Island where she dreamed of escaping to could wait until another time.

As he gets dressed, Gareth chuckled at the obscure thought, musing that in the far distant future, an archaeologist would find their dusty bones. The maps that they had studied to find that envisaged dream location would have perished, almost having turned to dust. After an extensive subatomic search on the remaining fragments of paper, which would take like forever and ever. The historical enthusiast would be perplexed as to why the couple, found in a cave in a remote location in Northern Scotland, were looking at maps of the Caribbean and Pacific Island chains.

As he left the cabin, he gave his hand a single kiss and then taped the top left of the door frame for good luck.

Gareth carried out his first scheduled task and grabbed a couple of mugs of steaming hot brew to deliver to the bridge. Leena was, as expected, very busy, arse deep in some conversation about the current status report regarding the engines. "All that I want to know was do we have two working engines? Can I request full power without the delegation from the engineering debating society arriving and failing to answer, here is your starter for ten?" The mechanics confer in hushed tones, and one was waving his arms passionately empathising what his children can and cannot do. His companion was looking like he desperately required a larger-than-life silver crucifix, to hold up and ward off the devil himself.

Gareth handed Leena her tea. He was going to salute and wish the captain a very good morning but changed his mind. Thinking that when the ongoing pantomime announces an interlude, and if he was quick, he might then have a brief chance to speak a word or two. The mechanics abruptly ceased all of the applied theatrics. Gareth looked at Leena's hands checking to see if she was in possession of the magical remote control that had the pause button enabled. Leena asked the mechanics if they thought that she was gifted with the powers of telepathy. The two guys with the oil-stained clothes, hands and faces look at her as if she had all of a sudden beamed in via the red planet. "Okay, guys, here are the simple questions! Do we have working engines? Will they be able to supply full power if and when requested?" She added the next one with pure unadulterated sarcasm, "The last one on this round was a team question, therefore please feel free to confer with each other on this one, and please give me a fucking answer!" The mechanics nodded in unison, doubly confirming that they were indeed good to go. Leena wanted to line up all of the crew along with all the passengers, fuck she would even bring the sick women and their babies to join in with the bastarding standing ovation.

As they left, Gareth hoped that the supplied tea would extinguish the fire in her breath and maybe even depressurise and curtail the plumes of smoke emanating from her ears. Captain Leena eyes glared at him, almost daring him to say something. As the air raid siren sounds off at maximum volume in his head, it warned him that the not-so-subtle hints of the fluctuating behavioural characteristics that were being blatantly advertised by the captain. It is an unequivocal confirmation that Leena had psychopathic tendencies, as all of his ex-wives had displayed the exact same symptoms. Gareth thought that he could be lucky; this could just be a temporary change, given the fact that Leena had assumed all the burdens of responsibility and was under intense pressure.

The alternative thought was that Leena was just plain nuts, leaving him with the choice of abandoning the vessel like now or wait until the ship reached the northern shores. Then just getting up early one morning and walking off into the horizon without saying a word.

In the old world, he had several failed marriages and multiple doomed relationships. Gareth put this all down to his former somewhat socially unacceptable occupation. His former wives and forgotten girlfriends would tend to get a little upset when the regional crime squad blessed him with an unexpected visit. This usually occurred about three in the morning, why they picked this time was a complete mystery. They would use the battering ram that had the stored kinetic power of a raging bull elephant to separate the front door from its hinges. Then, team handed they charged into the house, ran up the stairs, then stormed into the bedroom. "Armed police! do not move!" was the usual standard greeting, maybe every once in a while, just to add some niceties, they could have at least said good morning.

Then, inetably the charges would be issued, followed by the trial. Some but not many of his former partners would turn up to support him. The other ones just fucked off as soon as the police vehicle, which he was secured in, turned the corner and left the street. Gareth would receive the odd piece of correspondence when he was banged up, it was usually in the form of a begging letter or a divorce certificate. The visits were few and far between. Many times, he had waited for the promised visit only to be informed by the duty officer that the appointed person was a no-show. Gareth did not retain any bitterness or resentment towards any of his exes, and he had never offered nor promised a planned secure future to any one of them.

Although he was by trade an armed robber, albeit not a successful one, he had never taken his work home with him. The aggression was always kept for work only, never to be displayed in the home or with relations. He had sincerely hoped that this relationship would be different, perhaps even be the one. To avoid any confrontation with Leena, Gareth took the now empty mugs, escaping the confined of the bridge before she vented her anger and frustration towards him. He never asked her, nor had she informed him about their imminent departure. The vibration of the engines being put through their paces reverberates throughout all of the ship announcing to all that they will be attempting to leave very shortly.

Gareth found an empty table in the galley, pleased as punch at not having to sit and go through all the sometimes infernally mundane 'Hi, how were you?' conversations.

Now, deep in thought, ignoring the fresh brew in front of him and all of the other people now around him. Cinds' plonked herself down on a seat beside him. He did not move nor indicate that he had even noticed her arrival. She ignored his mood and chatted away, "Looked as if we will be on our way soon. Alwyn has told me that northern Scotland was beautiful." She got no reaction whatsoever from him, "I was going to inform him that all the guys up there were rumoured to be extremely well endowed and if that was the truth, I am going to unceremoniously dump him." Gareth turned around in his seat, looking straight at her. He replied that she does not half talk shit sometimes. Cinds' welcomed him back to the land of the living and asked if she had to line up everyone in the advent of an emergency evacuation.

Gareth replied that there was no need as they would be going out at high tide and with the displayed full moon there should not be any issues. Cinds' asked him if he had just made that up. Gareth pleaded guilty to all charges, letting her know that Leena had issued no orders requesting the stand-by procedure. "You could always go and check with the captain, perhaps she can give you an estimated time of departure. Otherwise, the people could be standing holding onto the rails for hours." Gareth asked her how the patients were in the sick room, Cinds informed him that they were much better and they would like to thank him for rescuing them. He finished the brew in one gulp, half-mumbled that he would visit them once he had supplied the mechanical elves in the forbidden kingdom with fresh tea. Cinds nudged him and asked him if he was okay. Gareth closed his eyes giving a hardly noticeable nod of his head, "Yeah, just fine, no problems." He got up, then collected the tea for the dungeon dwellers, mouthing see you later as he passed.

The engines were now in blast mode. Even if you shouted at a full screech, you would not be able to hear shit. Gareth put the mugs down and used hand signals to inform all of the elfin figures that he had just delivered the hot drinks. The control bell sounds and the engines were engaged into the all-ahead slow setting. He informed them that he would deliver food and refills as soon as possible, about turns and leaves them to it.

He knocks on the door, and Alwyn knowing that Cinds' had spoken to him about the nameless refugees', shouts out, "Who is it?" Gareth retorts that he can fuck right off, stop being a dick and open the fucking door. He did as he was told and issued a good morning to you also to Gareth. Alwyn went out as he entered, going to check if Cinds' required any assistance.

Anna does most of the talking. Olga just added bits in the conversation with her Eastern European accented bad English. "We would both, all of us would like to thank you for saving us. In this day and age, in these uncertain times, most people would have just raped us, mutilated us, then just left us there like discarded pieces of flesh." Gareth replied that they could blame his dearly departed mother for his manners. They did not register the slight humour in his reply. Gareth enquired about the babies. The women light up, "The boys were getting stronger every hour, and we want to ask if we could repay the kindness and name them after you."

Gareth thought that they had implied that they were going to condemn the children forever with the names of Gareth One and Gareth Two. He explained at length, sometimes having to reword his explanation several times and add in some grunting noises just for effect, that although it was indeed a great honour there was no need. Gareth asked them if they could possibly name their children after the grandparents. Both of the women let it be known that their fathers had abandoned them while they were still very young and they would rather name them after the devil. Gareth really did not know what to reply with, changed the subject and asked them if they were hungry. They both nodded, saying that they would eat anything at all as long as it was not fish. He explained that if it was fish, it would be so much nicer than the version that they had feasted on previously. Anne and Olga shook their heads reinforcing the joint commitment that they did not want to eat fish ever again. Gareth surrendered, understanding and agreeing to their sentiments. "Okay I will see what's on offer and try and arrange the feed bottles."

It was almost as if Alwyn was waiting outside the door. He knocked, then entered, producing the bottled feed like an amateur magician presenting his next trick on a talent show. Gareth made his excuses, then departed to see if he could acquire them and the elves down in the engine room some food. If need be, Alwyn could help them to select the names, and if that fails, they could always rope in Cinds' to toss her hat into the ring. Either way, whatever names they finally chose will be a whole lot better than burdening them with G-one along with his best buddy G-two.

Chapter 10

Spotty was unsettled. He looked at the monitor attached to the receiver, tilted his head one way, then the other then went back to lie at Enunsha's feet. Abe witnessing the canine's inquisitive mannerisms asked what that was all about. Jackson mentioned the well-known fact that a dog's hearing range is vastly superior to theirs. "Does that work the same as the receivers' bandwidth?" Jackson asked Abe to explain what he meant. "Well, if we couldn't hear what the dog is hearing, can the bandwidth not be tweaked to reconfigure a search and then reconstruct the sounds on a different waveform," Jackson said out loud that perhaps in the old world that machines equipped with advanced modular frequency analysers capable of switching between all of the known variable parameters probably existed. The machine we had here in front of us could not switch unrelentingly backward and forwards between Khz, MHz, microwaves and zoo-zoo sounded structures. Then, reconfigure all the bits per second into multiple sequenced sound bites and then reassemble them into something understandable. Abe, in other words, and please excuse my French, we can only piss with the cock we have."

"The technology in use in the day would have involved a huge dedicated team, breaking up the signals and sharing them between different departments. All of them specialised in detecting the various wavelengths and the appertaining bandwidth signatures allocated to their particular departmental specialists. I would have imagined that the new shit would employ more than one of them quantum spectrometer analysers. That would have been more than capable of picking up a gaseous discharge from a fly, then being able to identify the said fly with its relatable signature. Spotty could very be hearing something that is outside our hearing range and our equipment's reconfigured display. Sorry Abe, I wished that it was that simple, but rest assured, the bad guys would have very possibly been using technology that we had never heard of, even seen or used."

Spotty had fallen asleep and had just dropped one. Enunsha declared straight away that she was not responsible for the smell. An almost smiling Spotty wagged his tail a couple of times, pleading guilty as charged. Perry had just returned from the first active patrol; he sniffed the unusual fragrance and looked at Enunsha. The trio joined him on the map as he marked up the areas they intended to search. Jackson asked how the new guys performed; Perry was reluctant to speak, eventually informing him that the new guys were a walking major accident and emergency ward just waiting to happen. "We were going to have to scale back the planned patrol schedule. These guys we had put out had just completed the course, but yet they seemed to forget even the basics, once they got out into the field. I had to be really honest here and tell you the truth: the bottom line is that none of the new recruits can cut it in the real world. They fuck up continuously at the easy tasks. God help us if they were ever involved in a firefight. Seriously, Jackson, we can't put them out in the field. It is just not gonna work."

Jackson had listened to everything Perry had said. He did not like the results but had enough respect for Perry to understand that he was making a fair and valid recommendation.

"How about we keep all the season guys for the advance patrols and the guys and gals who completed the training will be kept on the perimeter duties. The newbies could be reassessed weekly, monthly and once you think that they are up to speed, we could try again."

Perry agreed to give it a shot but empathised that it was him and his guys that were out in front. Jackson asked if he had anything else to say on the subject. Perry knew that Jackson was reading his reactions,

"Taking all that into consideration, I would like to have the final say in the operational patrols. Of course, we would retrain, then re-evaluate, but if they couldn't cut it, then they couldn't cut it no matter how many times we trained then retrained them." Jackson told him that he had a deal, and they shook hands on it.

As they looked at the maps, figuring out the new proposed searches Abe informed Perry about the comms the bad guys are using. Perry listened to all that Jackson had said on the subject and agreed that all of his points were more than valid. "Even if we managed to somehow pick up one of their comms devices, there would be no guarantee that it would work."

Enunsha asked if it was because they would be assigned to an individual operator. Perry informed her that it could be more stringent than that, "perhaps the devices are biometrically linked to a certain individual and may self-destruct if tampered with or used by non-registered user."

Perry continued, "Just before the sickness, we were involved in a trial where all the weapons were biometrically indexed. I know that it sounds far-fetched, but I can assure you it was designed to stop civilians going postal with semi-automatic weapons. The system worked with no problem for all the army personnel, as they were all registered to the weapons that could be used by one and all. The gangsters, the drug dealers, and the homegrown and international terrorists were faced with weapons malfunctioning, resulting in instant self-elimination. So, we don't really know what the bad guys have got to play with. That's why we have to be ultra-careful."

Abe piped up and mentioned that with Perry had said, any thoughts about them using the handheld radios for communication between the patrols and the base were now totally out of the question. "I am guessing, but would I be correct in thinking that they would no longer require more than thirty seconds of dialog to pinpoint our transmission location."

Jackson lit up a cigarette, as he exhaled; "if they had access to all the singing and all the dancing kit that we could only dream about. Then, without any doubt whatsoever, I could guarantee that they would be able to locate and confirm our position within several seconds." Perry asked Jackson if he was thinking what he was thinking.

Abe cottoned on straight away, "If push comes to shove, you are deliberately going to lure these guys into a trap. Purposely drawing them into a chosen location where it will not be an action on their behalf. But in fact, a well laid out plan to trap and apprehend them."

Jackson put out the foul-smelling cigarette and confirmed that Abe had indeed won a cigar. Now, the four of them pour over the map, trying to figure out where and when the proposed action will take place. Spotty had now woken up, stretched then barked, informing Enunsha that he was hungry and would like to be fed. Spotty thought that the future plan, the future action, could wait, and also much more importantly that his stomach could not wait much longer.

Doctor Death had taken his turn, and without issuing any complaints, he went to collect the lunch for himself and his brother-in-arms. He and his compadre, without a doubt, thought the culinary delights on offer far superseded anything that they could have rustled up. If they ever unfortunate enough to appear in front of an investigative hearing. He thought that they would have no choice but to agree that some of their concoctions were as appealing as regurgitated dog shit. Even though the pair of them, at several points during their illustrious career in the kitchen, actually thought that they were superstars. Destined for far greater things, well, that was until the new guys showed up, and boy, oh boy, could they cook. Someone had remarked in the passing that it was rumoured that Spotty, blindfolded with his legs hogtied, could cook better than the pair of them and some.

Poison Pete had been busy. He had planted some seeds and finally dried off the crop that he had quickly uprooted when they had left their last home. Pete had tried in vain to save his crop. Most of the plants had withered and then died. The couple he had managed to save were flourishing in the warmer climate, and he had even given them names. He did not think that he had lied to Doctor Death; he had merely rerouted the said facts. He was of the mind, that if he had declared that he still had some product. DD would have wanted to smoke all of it, but just like the time when they were incarcerated in one of the gladiator schools, 'Some, is better than none.'

Doctor Death had returned from collecting the food, and Poison Pete asked what was on the menu.

"I just got one of each, never bothered to look at the names; either way, you just know that it is going to be more than good."

Poison Pete was a bit grouchy, not knowing the names of the food that Doctor Death had returned with. DD informed his former cellmate to stop being tetchy, open up the containers and just pick whatever one he fancied eating. Now that the hard part was out of the way, they savoured the culinary delights. Both of them exclaimed, "Man, that was goddam awesome."

Poison Pete reached into his pocket and offered his friend the peace offering of a ready rolled blunt. DD was about to ask questions. Poison just held up his hands, "Sorry brother, I was keeping it for a rainy day. But seen as it is Friday, I thought we could celebrate."

Doctor Death sparked up, asking if it was indeed Friday. Poison Pete lit his smoke up, then replied that he would be fucked if he knew what day it was, but they could just pretend that it was Friday. They wish each other a very happy whatever the fuck day it was and puff away.

Death informed his partner in crime that one day, they would have to invest their hard-earned cash and splash out on a sound system. "Nothing fancy, just something we can work away to and something we can chill out with."

Pete confessed that he once was nearly engaged to a set of cans. "They were so good; they made you feel like you were actually in the band."

Death asked, "Why nearly?"

"Well, the shop owner got a little on the upset side when I tried to walk out of the shop without paying for them and called the cops. But they were that good. I had wet dreams about them for years and years."

In not so sunny Scotland, Murray woke up to Cha's face staring right at him. Before he had a chance to say anything he was greeted with, "Good morning, my little duckling," and a huge grin. He put his arms around her, "Okay honey, let's hear the rest of it."

"Well, baby, I had a really terrible sleep last night. I just could not get settled. Every time that I felt as though I was going to drift off, you would start again."

Murray asked her if his snoring was really that bad. Cha can't hold it in any longer and informed him that it was the constant quacking. She jumped out of bed and ran around the room, flapping her arms, quacking and laughing. Murray pressed the eject button, jumped out of bed and proceeded to chase her down the stairs.

Cha pretended that she was petrified, shouting out to all of the planet that the mad duck with the resequenced DNA had taken over her husband. "Someone please help me; someone please save me and save my children."

As she entered the kitchen, she was met with Debs and Beth sitting at the table. Cha instantaneously reverted back to her normal self, "Good morning, girls, how are you both this fine morning." Murray had jumped the last couple of steps and landed with his arms stretched out, ready to deliver more impromptu scary duck noises. Just in time, he noticed the twins and adapted instantly from the resequenced DNA monster to being a reasonably normal being. The twins looked at him as if he had finally lost his threadbare grasp on reality. Cha shrugged her shoulders, matter-of-factly issuing the statement that he woke up like that. "Would anyone like some tea?" Murray replied yes, please, wished the twins a good morning and moved towards Cha for the much-needed morning kiss and cuddle.

Cha participated for a second or two, then told him that was all he was getting as he had snored all night. Murray ignored her, put his arms around her, and squeezed her tightly towards him. He leaned over to her ear and delivered a whispered quack-quack. She told him that sometimes he behaved like a five-year-old. Murray replied that he was more like a four-and-a-half-year-old. Cha shook her head, "Six months difference, no big deal, you are still a wanker." Murray smiled and told her that he would love her forever, till the of time no matter what she thought about him.

Beth and Debs had concluded that both of them were certifiable and without any shred of doubt perfectly suited for one another. They delivered the appraisal in their accustomed way, one starting the sentence and then the other finishing it. Cha pleads with them to stop, otherwise, Murray would think that he was the perfect specimen. Mr. Black stood up and thanked the twins for their accurate summation of the said facts. He then informed Judge Cha that he intended to plead not guilty to all of the alleged offences committed against humanity. She ignored his latest outburst, pointing to Charlie and Romulus, who were sitting patiently at the door. "It would appear that your lawyers wish to confer with you on some of the finer details in private."

Murray got ready to take his other children out and delivered a rather flamboyant royal bow to Cha before he took the dogs out. The twins asked Cha if they were always this happy, "He gets a little grumpy and sullen from time to time, but unfortunately that is a pure Scottish genetic trait that would take generations to breed out. Apart from that, yes, he was just about perfect, but I would never dream of telling him." Beth and Debs laughed and confessed that all they ever heard was that everyone thought that they were the perfect couple. Cha smiled and replied that drunken conversations don't really count. The twins both disagreed and invoked the firmly held belief that Murray would do anything for her. They knew it, she knew it, and probably what was left of the population knew it, too. Cha told them to stop it again and help her prepare breakfast for the soon-to-be-awake children.

Charlie and Romulus ran about peeing and sniffing at anything in their path. Murray loved his dogs just as much as his children. He hoped that when Mark and Alfie were older, they would enjoy these walks as much as him. Remus whizzed past and tried to catch up with his brother and Mother. Murray waited for Cat as she strolled along the well-worn path that only the dog people seemed to use. He stopped and sparked up while he waited. She greeted him with a good morning and asked him if there was any truth to the rumour that he was starting an evening class. Murray asked what he was going to allegedly teach. Cat delivered a quack-quack and blamed him for Sammarra refusing to sleep unless Frank and her supplied constant duck impersonations. Murray did not believe her, strongly suspecting that she could do a better sounding of the birds calls than what he ever could.

She admitted that she was only pulling his leg but was all the same well impressed with his baby-sitting. All the children never took their eyes off you when you were delivering your animal kingdom renditions. I told Frank all about it, and we both agreed that you were number one on the sitting list. Murray was quite chuffed and informed her that they both knew that they had an open invitation to pop in anytime. The dogs were all sitting and waiting patiently for them when they arrived at their favourite spot. All three of them were looking over the spectacular view as if they were almost waiting for something or someone to arrive. Cat asked him if this was normal behaviour.

Murray thought that the dogs were just impatient like him, waiting for the warmer weather to finally arrive. Charlie barked and informed Murray as well as her offspring that it was time to return to the house. Murray asked Cat to pop in with Sammarra so she could spend some time with Cha and the twins, "Better than sitting by yourself all day, bring Remus. Children should mix with dogs and it will do them and you the world of good."

Cat quizzed him and enquired if he was being secretly sponsored for a humanitarian award. Murray said no, he was just being nice to everyone, and maybe one day people would be nice to him. "Seriously Cat, don't be sitting in there all day by yourself. We are only next door, not a continent away. I will even make you lunch!" Cat shook her head, "No way, even my dog would leave home if he knew what you were offering." "Well, you could always persuade Frank to deliver some goodie bags for all the refugees. I think that Alicia and Okolo are also intending to come over." Murray let the dogs in, and he heard the noises of the children as their favourite friends entered the house, Mark was shouting out for Cha-Cha. Talking to himself, "And there was me thinking that I was the favourite!"

The infants of terror have been fed. Murray had arrived just in time for them to be changed, at first, he had thought that Cha had said chained. Thinking to himself, that perhaps some of the children would possibly end up being incarcerated, but not his angels. He had some stuff to try and sort out. Murray made some gracious duck noises and left them all to it. Mr. Black would require some assistance from Karen and her group to shift the weapons stored in the utility corridor that gave access to the generator housing. He was going to attend to it quite a while back, but with one thing and another, it was just one of them jobs that he had never gotten round to doing.

First, he had to locate Karen. Murray thought that maybe Frank could have an idea, and if not, he could scrounge a bite to eat before searching for her. He could have also left word as in where he could be located, should Karen happened to pop in sometime later. Frank had something already for him as he entered, "Cat told me you would be popping in for a sneaky." Murray thanked him and sat to eat. Frank couldn't join him as he was busy organising to get ready to receive the expected consignment of fresh fish. Murray hoped that he had enough time to finish his grub before it arrived. He would be duty-bound to inform Cha of the statistical update on the repulsive food group, but Murray knew that Cat would have already told her. Mr. Black thought that as he would be entertaining the children tonight, perhaps he could entertain them with the sounds of the Amazon jungle. Murray was positive that there were some CDs that contained these and similar sounds hiding in the house somewhere. Hopefully, he would be able to obtain the treasure map in time to locate them. Either that or he would have to tell them stories or sing some songs.

If he was really struggling, he could dig out the guitar and play for them. Murray had not seen the instrument for quite some time and strongly suspected that Cha had sacrificed it to the Gods of music in a secret pact with the devil to stop him from ever singing again. He thought that the children would not be particularly fond of his taste in music. Murray had to be honest about this and admit that no one on the planet was particularly fond of his somewhat peculiar taste. He thought that it was especially fine and a somewhat eclectically refined, selective pick and mix from various genres. That weaved through various music groups with several notable exceptions, the dreaded country and western songs along with reggae and the mind-numbing, brain destroying dance music. Murray would find it easier to dance to the finite tones of a pneumatic drill being inserted into his brain than that other shit that people used to jump up and down to for hours on end too.

Mr. Black placed his plate at the to-be-cleaned hatch and thanked the staff for yet another lovely meal and catering for him outside of normal working hours. Murray plonked himself outside, accompanied by a rather nice cuppa. He rattled up a banger, enjoyed the smoke, and savoured every single sip of the just-about-perfect brew. Frank appeared. Murray took his arrival as an imminent warning that the smelly underwater creatures were inching closer by the second. He finished the brew, informing Frank that his cuisine, as always was fucking spectacular. "If you happen to bump into Karen, could you mention that I was looking for her. I will be over at the storage area where we generate the power." Frank took the mug from him, "I was thinking that you would stay and help out with the fish?" Murray just looked at him, then walked away without uttering a single word.

Murray can't remember the last time he was in this place. It felt like it was in another lifetime when Okolo along with Cora and all of their trucks had arrived. Then, they had spent weeks moving and making the weapons safe for storage. He thought that there was a detailed list that contained everything that was hidden in the boxes. It was an Aladdin's cave full of nearly every imaginable weapon. Murray doubted very much that they would ever need to use them, but at the same time, he and the others understood why they could not just leave them. The more he thought about it and looked at all the boxes it seemed like it was yesterday when a fat Cha and an even fatter Okolo would waddle over here, preparing an accurate inventory of all and everything on display. Machine guns, landmines, parachute flares and all the rest of the kit and caboodle that is more than enough to equip a small army.

He thought that there were also some of them undated, emergency ration packed that the dogs growled at. Murray smiled and thought that the lack of a use by date meant that they were good forever. He had the unfortunate experience of tasting the contents and was prepared to swear on all things sacred. When he offered to share with Charlie, she growled at him for the first time ever. Perhaps the emergency ration bags could be used by the building department, or maybe they could be used to be scattered on the ground to scare off wild animals. If this community was ever held to ransom and a food shipment was required. They could pay with the emergency ration packs, in doing so maybe even scaring away the would-be invaders forever. Murray had located the extensive list, and he looked at all the boxes. He estimated the space that it would take up. Thought that Karen would have to supply a few trucks and have a sizeable crew on hand to help shift all of this.

A familiar voice sounds out, "Hello, where are you?" Karen had arrived, like him, she was looking at all of the kit. Murray told her that he knew that it only seemed like yesterday when she, along with all of her crew, had arrived here. She sort of agreed, but mention the fact that they had also achieved many things in that seemingly short space of time. Karen was still looking at all the boxes containing all the weaponry, thinking of all the mayhem and carnage that would have ensued if they had left it behind.

Murray interrupted her thoughts, "We recently discussed Robbo's battery project, and as you have guessed, this is where we would need to place them. I don't know how much work you have ongoing at the moment, but if you have some spare time, we could walk through what I have in mind."

Karen, still looking at all the kit, told Murray to show her what he was thinking.

"We could have moved all these items up to where we found the hidden chamber that led to the emergency escape tunnel. There was plenty of space underground to store all of this equipment. As you quite rightly surmise, I would not be able to accomplish this all by myself and would need a considerable amount of assistance." Murray asked if she had a flashlight handy, and he suggested that they went up and look at the chamber. "I take it that it was you and your crew who installed the ladder." Karen pleaded guilty, informing him that Robbo had requested the work. They drove up to the recently discovered chamber. Karen activated the flashlight and descended into the void. Murray talked as she bounced the light around the room. "I think that there is more than enough space available here to store everything, and we do not need to venture any further down the stairs." Karen agreed with his findings but added that it would be a nightmare to load all the weapons and ammunition into here via the ladder. Murray asked her what she was thinking. "Well, for starters, if this is an emergency escape route, how are all the people going to be able to access it. I mean, we could not really expect them to form an orderly queue. It could be in our lifetime, or it may well be in a future lifetime, but either way, we really should allow for that possible contingency."

Murray agreed with all that she was saying and asked her to please continue. "We will need to erect a building above the enclosure, complete with a stairway that will allow people to access the escape tunnel, on mass Also included in the design should be some form of lighting system. Let's face it: everyone cannot walk about with a flashlight forever. On the subject of lights, it could be an emergency system that could be activated by the Robbo's batteries. I thought that it was possible to have some of them rigged up here. Therefore, if the main power supply was for some reason inoperable, there would still be enough power in the batteries to light up the stairs that lead down to the entrance."

Murray asked her if all of that just came out of her head. Karen nodded and confirmed that it was indeed all true. "I know that where we live everything is nice and makes for a relatively easy lifestyle. Not everyone will have this option, and I mean, just think of all the various types of animals that are still out there. In the wilderness, foraging, plundering any groups they come across for food and supplies. They will not give a hoot about the future; their expectations will only be set for a day-to-day survival routine. They will eventually arrive here maybe not tomorrow, maybe not even in our lifetime. But rest assured, Murray, they will eventually come knocking at our door." Murray asked her if there was anything he could do to help with the newly envisioned projected works.

Karen replied that she would need approval and the paperwork stamped.

Murray told her to start as soon as possible, he had agreed and that is all anyone needed to know.

Chapter 11

General Vladimir Miasnikov was at last very near to the castle where his little sister, Irena and her strange husband with the even stranger than life interests had perished. His memory banks had been thoroughly scanned but lack most of sufficient information related to the journey. As he was blind drunk for most of the time, the recent events were just about totally blank. He had retained some fairly sketchy, unconnectable data that floated about in his grey matter and pertained to destroying several vehicles. Miasnikov could only guess that they contained either rebels, innocent bystanders or perhaps even his own troopers. All he could remember as the fairly large and very noisy explosions as the escaping vehicles had been blasted out of this realm of existence by his tanks at almost point-blank range. If the incident were somewhat relatable to an important issue, he was sure that one of his commanders would have enlightened him, filling in all of the missing details. As no one came forward, he presumed that it was all in a day's work, or perhaps it was just part of one of the many drunken dreams. Miasnikov ordered his transport to halt, he stretched his arms as he pissed standing in full open view to anyone in the street. The guard detail suddenly appeared, taking up position, protectively surrounded him against any unseen danger.

Miasnikov directed curses at all of them, asked once if it was possible to expel liquid in peace and quiet for a change. Commander Essmie informed him that he should have been aware that they were now officially in bandit country. "While I am here, you will be protected at all times. Our great leader would, shall we say, be more than rather displeased with your untimely demise. I had informed these troopers to be with you twenty-four seven until ordered otherwise. It would be me who would have to undergo Lesqueths' not-so-subtle interrogation techniques, so the guards stay." Miasnikov wanted to know if he was allowed breakfast. Essmie informed him that the sumptuous delicacies were currently being prepared and would be served shortly. Miasnikov thought that the building with the green roof across the way was extremely ugly and urgently required a salvo or two to reduce it to rubble as he walked on the way to being fed. He had a closer look at all of the buildings, and on reflection, Miasnikov thought that he immediately required the skilled services of an accomplished demolition team.

The breakfast was as unappealing as the rest of the menu and was just nondescript and as tasteless as his new bland surroundings. Nevertheless, he forced it down his throat and hoped that it would remain down there long enough to soak up the remaining alcohol hibernating in his lower intestines. Miasnikov thought that he would absolutely hate it here, he would hate the food, hate the people, hate the weather, and most of all hate the country. Why his sister had elected to stay in this inhospitable, barren wasteland, he would have never been quite able to truly understand. The location was just as bland and genetically sterile now as it was before the great sickness. All of the leading armed forces inhabiting this globe, at one point, had strongly objected to the use of atomic weapons. Right here, surrounded him in all directions, could very well be the one true possible exception. A mega-ton or two of unleashed atomic energy, in his humble opinion, would have brightened up the whole area. Although the land would be uninhabitable for several centuries prior to the reduction in radiation levels, at least it would have looked a whole lot more appealing to the eyes.

Vladimir exited the command vehicle and expelled the foul breakfast food that he imagined was very difficult for the chef to replicate. The authentic culinary equivalent to that of a regurgitated premature canine embryo must have had taken many hours to prepare. Now requiring the services of a scribe, he shouted out and demanded that their presence was required immediately. The unfortunate woman selected for this position jumped to it, appeared with the writing implement firmly clenched in her hand. Vladimir ordered her to write down the usual formal greetings to their esteemed commander in chief. "'Inform her that we had just arrived in the vicinity of the castle, the attack will be commencing very soon. Due to the crimes that were committed by the rebels, there would be no prisoners taken. Also, please consider that, if possible, we should have had perhaps left a long-term reminder to the region, informing them that we do not forget nor do we forgive. If we were to detonate several atomic weapons in the area, it would deliver in no uncertain terms our statement of intent. The tribes in this area should carry the pain for killing our people."

Miasnikov informed the scribe to butter up his message with all the long-sounding, encoded managerial speak that Lesqueth employs. "When you finish, bring it back for my signature." Commander Essmie approached, stood to attention and delivered the regimental salute perfectly, then requested to go over the attack plans. Miasnikov greeted her with open arms, informed her that he was all ears. Essmie pointed to the map, indicating the location of the areas that they were attacking from. "As we discussed previously, your forces will be positioned on the eastern side of the castle. Our other forces will enact a pincer movement from the north west and the south west. This, we anticipate, will drive the rebels towards your position, where they will be subsequently subdued and apprehended. I have split up my original unit, reallocating half of the personnel under your direct command. These people are familiar with the area. Lastly, the patrols have located the rebel headquarters, confirming that they appear only armed with machetes and axe-type weapons." Miasnikov asked her when the proposed attack was going to commence. Essmie stood to attention and saluted, informed him that it was the General's prerogative, and she awaited his orders.

"Okay, Essmie, you can relax, please sit down. I think we should attack at dawn; the bastards should still be asleep when you start your approach. Drive in fast, if you happen to run over a few of them that does not really matter. What was important is that you scare the living daylights out of them, making them think that they were escaping. We will lie in wait until the last possible moment, then unleash a barrage of rubber baton rounds and the immobilising nets. As for the captured prisoners, I'm not sure how they were going to be rewarded, but I should have a better idea after we capture them. You could go now and prepare your units for the early morning advance." Essmie stood and saluted.

Miasnikov would have disposed of her, there and then, if she had even suggested a time for the attack. In him asking her, almost baited her was only another one of his little tested to see if she was still truly loyal. It was sad but a true fact that some of his previous commanders had gotten too big for their boots, thinking that their opinions and stratagems were far more important than his. Then, finding out the hard way, usually from a great height, that he was the boss, that he was still the one in charge.

Vladimir thought that Essmie would last longer than most, although he knew that eventually she would succumb to indecision or transform into the grossly inflated alter ego version. When that day arrived, he would have disposed of her there and then without a second's hesitation. Vladimir would like a drink, but refrained due to the proposed early start. He went out, walking around his troopers and wished them all the best of luck for the fight tomorrow. Privately, he thought and hoped that for just once, perhaps even this time, the locals would have stood up and faced him rather than play hide and seek. Ducking and diving at every opportunity, hell, if that were to happen, there was a strong possibility that he would let some of them go. Miasnikov would have removed one of their legs or one of their feet, but he would still let them go. He knew that these fuckers would not be any different from the rest of the recidivous locals of these hallowed isles who had all adopted the cowardly hit and run tactics. General Vladimir Miasnikov found it hard to fall asleep, dug out his sketch pad, jotting down a few ideas on what he could capture the prisoner's imagination with.

At precisely five minutes before dawn, Essmie aimed up to the heavens and discharged the oddly shaped pistol. The green parachute flare ignited, almost momentarily held time in freeze frame as it slowly drifted way above the tree line. Announcing to one and all that the attack was now underway. The troopers that were positioned in the overlying hills ignited the petrol-soaked ground in the areas behind them, then steadily advanced towards the settlements.

Commander Essmie's mechanised units charged forward, unleashed a barrage of munitions designed to cause as much chaos as possible. The ordinance designed to confuse, stun and damage eardrums exploded in the once-upon-a-time pretty gardens, driveways and anywhere else where Essmie's troopers wish to place them. Over the years, decline and neglect, had transformed the residential area into a weed-infested sprawl of urban decay. It was almost impossible to differentiate between occupied dwellings and derelict houses. Commander Essmie's ground troops, on reaching the dilapidated buildings, forced opened the doors, charged in, cleared them from room to room, house to house. Rigorously enforcing that all of the former occupants flee, seeking sanctuary in the surrounding fields.

One of the first houses that was cleared had a shrine dedicated to the woman from the north who ran naked through the forest. The walls were adorned with many shrunken patches of inked skin that were once attached to someone's back. An overweight rebel was in the process of attempting to outrun one of the tanks. The driver, without any readable expression of emotion, incrementally adjusted the vehicle's direction. Increased the pressure on the gas pedal, then, exercised no due care or caution, ran straight over the top of her. In coordinated movements, Essmie's troopers moved in from the north west and the south west destroying everything that was in their path. The rebels had no room left to manoeuvre, leaving them with only one viable option available to travel east.

When her troopers were confronted by a group of rebels, they were subjected to a few salvos of rubber baton rounds. The immobilised nets fired at close range took care of anyone left standing. Miasnikov's troopers lain in wait and patiently watched the ground in front of them for the imminent scheduled arrival of the rebels. Essmie's forces pressed forward, the forced action persuading the rebels to retreat further towards Miasnikov's position. Essmie's troops lined up and unleashed salvo after salvo of rubber batons rounds into their crowded mass. As her group gained ground, any stragglers were bound, beaten unconscious, then chucked into the back of the trucks. The rebels were now aware that they were doomed, as a far superior force was chasing them, pushing them forward into the waiting line of armed troopers. Led by Tally, who, seeing no possible way out of the ensuing fray, issued the war cry as they had all charged at full speed towards General Vladimir Miasnikov's troops.

He was delighted, almost applauded as Tally and his unwashed and mostly unarmed mob surged towards them. Miasnikov ordered his troops to steady up and hold fire until he issued the order. He allowed Tally's rebels to get within twenty-five yards of them, then gave the order to fire. General Vladimir Miasnikov repeatedly ordered his troops to reload, fire then advance. The weighted round encased in hardened industrial rubber travelled at seventy feet per second. In coming into contact with a human being at such a close range, the baton rounds broke bones, shattered facial structures, knocked out and subdued all of the attacking force. Commander Essmie forces closed in from behind and unleashed a few salvos of baton rounds along with a few of the immobilising nets, finally curtailing any hopes of the rebels' retreat.

Miasnikov had never been this elated whilst being sober for longer than he could remember. He wished to meet the rebel commander to bestow his sincere congratulations for launching the charge against him. Miasnikov searched for them among the now-bound prisoners, and he asked out loud for their leader to reveal himself. The general was only greeted with silence; not one of the newly conquered issued a single word. They all glared at him as if he was shit residing on the sole of their shoes but still nobody uttered a word. Miasnikov changed his tactics and informed the bound prisoners that he wished that all the other invertebrates inhabiting this shithole of an island nation had displayed as much balls as them. "What a pleasure it was to actually come against a group who did not run away and were prepared to stand and fight."

"Unfortunately, due to the fact that you burned my sister alive, I have to punish you all. I am not going to waste any of your time, or any my time in questioning you as you won't tell me fuck all, anyway. As you have been such a gallant foe, I am guided by my ancestral heritage, duty-bound to award you something special to truly honour this momentous day. A steadfast, honest reflection on who you were and what you have done." Vladimir now wished to speak in private with Essmie and signalled her to follow him. He congratulated her for perfectly execution of the planned attack. Miasnikov asked her to show him where she had located and then buried his sister's bones. Commander Essmie led him to the place of his sisters' unfortunate demise, then backed away to allow him some private space to pray.

She retreated far enough away from him so that she could not hear any of the privately spoken words. Essmie stood with her head bowed, closed her eyes, and offered her own prayer to the fallen, the vanquished and the forgotten. As she opened her eyes, she found Miasnikov directly in front of her. Vladimir stated for the record that, without any doubt, his sister was perhaps a total sociopath with underlying psychopathic tendencies. "She was family, and I, by tradition, had to say a prayer; most people who knew her would be celebrating in full at her demise. It was very considerate of you, but I assure you that there was really no need, as even I know that Irena should have been drowned immediately at birth."

Essmie, kind of lost for words, asked him to come and look at the rest of the evidence and revealed what other atrocities the locals had inflicted on some of their people. She took him to the castle; he viewed the skeletons that were nailed to the walls on both sides of the stairwell. "You know that they were alive when they were crucified?" Miasnikov nodded and understood what the victims had endured in their last moments on this plane of existence. Essmie took him into the main room. Miasnikov noticed the stone tigers straight away and knew that, without any question, the Hidden, after being absent for centuries, were now back among them.

The three tattooed skins hung together, and he knew that these were his sisters, Bartrams and their chief of security, a French chap by the name of Ernesto. Essmie informed him that all of the gold and priceless antique jewellery had been left untouched and had remained in place. Miasnikov stared at all the hideous objects that Bartram had allegedly spent hours, even days, looking at. His sister's husband had thought that these misshapen, gaudy colourised pieces of scrap metal were indeed refined works of art. Miasnikov thought that perhaps Bartram required glasses and regularly induced high-voltage electric shock therapy to realign him firmly back within the realms of reality. Vladimir asked her if there was anything else that she wished to show him. Essmie commandeered a vehicle and, accompanied by several escorts, she took him up to where they had located the shrine.

He looked at the crucified figures that had been preserved in the tarlike substance. Miasnikov just knew that they were once loyal troopers. Essie led him into the building, and he looked at the wall-to-wall coverings of all the tattooed skins that were once attached to the troopers' backs. Essie pointed to the bold lettering inhabiting pride and place on the wall. Vladimir read it out loud: "Dedicated to the woman from the north who ran naked through the forest." Miasnikov agreed with her assumption that it almost looked like a shrine. Adorned with all the offerings, the seemingly obscure gifts of dirty cups, glasses, one pair of panties, threadbare socks and half-loaded ashtrays. All neatly laid out in front of several candles, overlooked by several crude, childlike pictures of the alleged heroic figure swooping down from on high to smite the enemy.

Vladimir reached down, picked up the panties, closed his eyes, and as he sniffed them, Commander Essmie asked if he wanted the place demolished. Miasnikov shook his head and placed the panties carefully in his pocket, then asked her to take him back to the castle. As they exited the building, he had a closer look at the garden, and someone had spent a considerable amount of time putting all of this floral display together. The only odd thing was the wild mushrooms that grew among the plants. He picked these and joined Essmie in the vehicle. Miasnikov was deep in thought on the return journey and showed no facial expressions, nor issued a single word. When they arrived back at the castle, he asked Essmie to summon all of the subcommanders. Miasnikov waited till they were all present and asked how many prisoners they had. As always, Essie was on the ball and informed him that they had eighty-four still kicking and breathing ones.

Miasnikov informed the assembled leaders that he intended to kill all of the prisoners, but he wanted to kill them real slow. He showed them the mushrooms; these ones would give them a blinding headache, all sorts of aches, pains, and if we were lucky, some festering sores. Miasnikov produced the other type, which will induce severe stomach cramps along with all the other associated symptoms. Then, after three to four days, their kidneys and livers would stop functioning. They would go into a coma and then die. I would like to make their last days extremely unpleasant, a truly unforgettable experience. With all that said, we required eighty-four reasonably sturdy wooden seats, eighty-four metal buckets. Several bails of industrial-type wire, some hammers and nails. Miasnikov opened a bottle of vodka and poured the liquid over the hand that had touched the second exhibited mushroom.

"Do not eat any of these, half of one was enough to kill a horse. If you touch it with your bare hands, you must wash them immediately. Please inform the cooks that we will be cooking for all of our guests, and hopefully, they will not get the ingredients mixed up, so perhaps we should add separate cooking and eating utensils to the list. We were going to be here for at least another five days, get all the troopers to assemble enough firewood for the duration, informing them that the fires will be burning twenty-four-seven." Miasnikov dismissed the officers but asked Essmie to stay behind. He told her to relax as she had done nothing to displease him.

"I have a special job for you, take your original squad out on a tour of the nearest towns, every town and city in this wretched land has music shops, even if all the locals can't play anything worth a shit, they have them everywhere. I would like you to acquire as many pairs of drumsticks as possible and see if you could find lots of things that you put in your mouth that produce those goddam infernal sounds. We were not talking saxophones and trumpets here, just the cheap fucking things that you would give to the children of relations that you don't particularly like. Do you know the instruments that I am talking about? The ones that the kids play with all day long, making incessant noises that never have a tune or display any recognisable rhyme or rhythm." Essmie nodded and indicated that she knew exactly what he was talking about. Miasnikov dismissed her reminding her not to forget the copious amounts of vodka and all the other shit that the troopers liked to consume in vast volumes. As she was still within hearing distance, he raised his voice and advised that she take two trucks for all the supplies of alcohol.

Miasnikov made his way back to the castle and looked at the more than dreary, almost suffocating landscape that surrounded the area. He was resolutely assured within himself that even if he were to set off a nuke, it would have been hard, almost impossible to detect the discernible changes. The prisoners just lay on the ground and perhaps silently reflected on their inevitable fate. He noticed that a few of them were sleeping, others laid in strange bodily configurations, trying to get as comfortable as possible without aggravating the broken bones, then receiving jolts of pain. The firewood had started to arrive, as the accumulating bundles grew in size and untidiness. Miasnikov ordered one of the commanders to heel, and he showed her where to place the cut timber. "I want it all placed in a straight line, starting from this point and running all the way down to here." She stood to attention, saluted and then continuously delivered a resounding "Yes, sir" in reply to almost every single word. Miasnikov walked away and thought that perhaps she had only received the promotion because she was present in someone's wedding album. The General was surprised when a truck arrived, and he had to give credit to Essmie when required to do a task, and she certainly pulled out all the stops.

Vladimir watched as the troopers unloaded the cargo, and the various unmatched sets of dining room chairs were hauled out and dumped on the ground. Vladimir ordered them to be arranged around the line of firewood, "I want them close enough to feel the heat, but not so close that they will burn." Miasnikov sat down, and as his troopers placed the rest of the chairs as per their instructions. He tried to imagine what the planned event would look like when in full swing. Miasnikov's thoughts were disturbed when one of the troopers approached him and offered a plate of food. The general asked if the meal on offer contained any mushrooms, and the trooper confirmed that there were none.

General Vladimir Miasnikov tucked in, having not eaten properly for several days, and he was rather peckish. When finished, he chucked the plate along with all the utensils onto the pile of firewood. Commander Essmie had arrived accompanied by several trucks, and she approached to deliver the report. Miasnikov invited her to have a seat so that he would not strain his neck looking up at her. "We have found everything that you requested. The two trucks with the alcohol will arrive later today." As they conversed, some of her troopers' carrying boxes were making their way over towards them, she informed the general that they were delivering the wire. Vladimir whistled at his commanders and asked them to watch closely. Under his direction, one of the prisoners was roughly manhandled and then placed on a dining chair. Miasnikov thanked her for accepting the dinner invitation, then proceeded to wire her up to the chair. He applied an arrangement in which the wire was wrapped around her neck and connected to the backrest. The head was held firmly in a straight position, restricting any upward, downward or sideways movement. Vladimir continued to demonstrate how to secure the arms and legs. On completing the task, he asked his commanders to repeat the process with all the remaining prisoners.

Essmie asked if he would like to select a set of drumsticks and had first choice in picking out one of the various infernal noise makers. Miasnikov quietly replied that, as all of them would be equally annoying, it does not really matter; therefore, anyone would suffice. The boxes contained the hammers, nails the various coloured metallic buckets not requiring an immediate allocation were placed near at hand. Miasnikov, accompanied by Essmie, walked up and down the line as the dinner guests were secured into position. He offered some instructions every once in a while, and requested that the selected guest require the tension around their neck to be increased. Vladimir, at the end of his inspection, was fairly satisfied that his troopers had sufficiently carried out the said instructions. Then stood at the head of the imaginary table and welcomed all of his notable guests for travelling vast distances and accepting the dinner request on rather short notice.

He clapped his hands; swarms of his troopers started to arrive with the specially prepared meals. "Ladies and gentlemen, I hope you all enjoy this splendid fare. In view of your overly sensitive pallets, I could assure and resolutely guarantee that all of the ingredients have been sourced locally." Every prisoner was spoon-fed by one of the troopers; any refusal to partake in the more than sumptuous delights on offer was rewarded by an instantaneous slap or three in the face. If that failed to encourage them to consume the delightful food on offer, the trooper engaged in the ritual feeding, raised their hand. Seconds later, the reward team arrived and hammered nails into various regions of the guest's body until they relinquished the rather hastily made decision on refusing to eat. The chopped-up timber that runs along the full length of the esteemed diners was set alight. With the meal finished, all of the now empty plates along with the eating implements were unceremoniously discarded into the flames.

The metal buckets were now placed on all of the prisoners' heads, and for a few minutes, all was silent. In that time, the pairs of drumsticks were shared out along with the noise-making instruments. Miasnikov, stone cold sober, wanted to retain this glorious event in his long-term memory, opened the proceedings where he had chanted, then hit out a rhythm on the surface and the sides of the bucket with the drumsticks. Now that he had demonstrated his version of the said rendition, he would like his troopers and all of his commanding officers to join in. On the count of three, the assembled company beat the metal buckets, some played the infernal noise devices, and the remainder sang in unison. "Oh, we're all going to Blackpool, Oh, we're all going to Blackpool Da-na-na-na, Da-na-na-na." Miasnikov hoped and prayed that the sound would infuriate and drive the prisoners crazy. Soon, the poisonous mushrooms would come into effect, and the onset of the headaches would arrive first. Followed by the aches, pains and if they were really lucky, the festered sores. The drums and the infuriating noise devices would be operated continuously on a twenty-four-seven basis. When the fever started, the severe stomach cramps along with the associated symptoms arrived, the prisoners were inundated with the continuous bedlam sounding out in their head, along with the uncomfortable heat, they would think that they had arrived at the gates of hell.

They will recover for a few days, then as their liver and kidney functions will start to falter then finally pack in. The prisoners would completely lose touch with reality as they suffer delusions and start to hallucinate. He ordered his troopers to make continuous, unbearable noise throughout the whole mind-numbing process. Firmly ensured that the fire burns intensely fierce and convinced the prisoners to think and, more importantly, feel as if they had indeed arrived in the devil's hallway. Miasnikov informed his troopers that over the next few days, they could drink as much as they want, work whatever shifts they want. "As long as the fire was kept going and the prisoners were entertained continuously without any breaks, then all would be okay."

"Make as much noise as you want, beat the shit out of the buckets with the drumsticks. If you wanted to use your hands, use anything as long as you were driving them insane. The noise makers you could all play different tunes, play the same tune, play the same fucking endless note for all I care, but play something and play it non-stop. Sort yourself into groups, day shift, back shift, twilight shift whatever shift that you fucking want as long as you and the commanders supply twenty-four-seven coverage I will be delighted. I would like our honoured guests to think upon these events as a truly unforgettable experience. So go ahead, get drunk and make some noise."

Commander Essmie had listened to all of his instructions. At first, she was concerned that he was not drinking. Perhaps it was because he was seeing this event as his sisters' funeral wake. She had seen the look of resignation on his face when he had at first noticed the stone tigers, and she now thought that he was not drinking for another reason altogether. Miasnikov signalled her to come over, and he asked her why she was not drinking. Essmie replied that she was not what you could classify as a serious drinker. Vladimir informed her that her view was permissible, but whether she likes it or not, she will have to join in with the celebrations. "In a few days, the prisoners will start to die off. When that occurs, I would like to be informed. I would really like to be there, to witness their final moments, after all, it was really important to say goodbye." Essmie nodded and pretended to agree and understand his request, not really knowing what Miasnikov had hidden up his sleeve for these final moments.

As with all of the other members of the armed forces, she had heard lots of the tales relating to her leader's treatment of prisoners. He had been quoted in many of these stories as saying, "A special prisoner requires a special reward." Essmie thought that this was something that he had said to cheer himself or the prisoner up. Everyone was well aware of the fact that Miasnikov had no aversion to barbarity and cruelty. The general had at times invented punishments on the spot, using whatever materials were available. Essie knew that for the grand finale, Miasnikov would be rehearsing their final moments, to ensure that the closing scene would be truly remarkable and beyond all of the prisoners' comprehension of what was in store for them.

Chapter 12

On the other side of the Atlantic Ocean, Blink, along with the small flotilla, had coasted around the island looking for a safe place to haul up for a few days. The first few places that they had scouted out were either way too dirty for them to stay in or seemed almost impossible to defend. They had all hoped that after the fairly long voyage across the ocean that they would be able to rest immediately. None of them had expected that they would have to go into action straight away. Blink scanned the landscape and hoped to find somewhere suitable before the arrival of nightfall. The place where they had first come ashore was less than friendly, resigning herself to the thought of the distinct possibility that the whole island chain could just be as unwelcoming.

The next inlet looked promising. Blink posted Sekoyazs' crew on lookout as she, along with the rest of the group, checked to see if the location was secure and a confirmed viable location to rest overnight. The area was thoroughly searched for any evidence of recent human habitation, satisfied the now deserted industrial estate was adequate. Blink ordered their boats to be hauled ashore, keeping them hidden well out of sight of any passers-by. Sekoyaz had sent a messenger and requested that she come to the shoreline immediately. Blink arrived there just in time to witness the frigate, accompanied by several large, well-armed motor launches, pass. She knew that they would have had no chance of survival if her people had been caught in the open waters by this group.

This new disturbing development drastically changed everything. They would not have been able to outrun them or outgun them, and if caught in the open, they would be like sitting ducks at a fairground shooting gallery. Their small boats would have been easy prey, waiting to be either rammed or capsized. Any of her people attempting to swim away, desperately trying to escape the carnage would be instantly churned into fish food either by the propellers or by the large-calibre machine guns. Blink was left with a difficult choice: make them relinquish ownership or destroy them. In order to do anything, she would have to find their base of operations. This alone was a huge task in itself, as the boats could be anywhere, stationed on this island or maybe on one of the neighbouring ones.

Blink knew that they could do nothing about it for now, as the crew needed some rest. Once they fully recuperate, she would put a plan into operation that would hopefully solve the immediate problem of the larger boats. Blink had that feeling when the hairs on the back of her neck stood up and made her think. The heavily armed boats may have actually been searching for her and the crew in revenge for killing their friends. She gathered her team together and explained that for now, they needed to rest and recuperate. Blink wanted the opening to the inlet manned constantly, if the patrol and search boats were working to a routine scheduled search. Then she needed to know the times of the patrols and any changes in the number of boats actively involved in the search.

She delegated who was sleeping, who was watching and when the changeovers should happen. Blink found a quiet spot, sat down and thought about how she was meant to overcome this problem. It would need to be something simple, as they had limited, almost sparse resources around them. Blink thought that if they had been fortunate enough to find a naval base, then the solution would have been on hand and readily available. Now, here in the middle of nowhere, in a disused factory that looked as if it had been abandoned a long time ago. There was nothing on hand that could possibly help them. All around them was an impenetrable wall to wall of jungle, full of poisonous insects, toxic plants, trees and vines that almost stretched forever.

Blink fell asleep, easy, really considering that she had been awake for God knows how long. In her dreams, she pictured huge sways of the interconnecting vines that reached up into the sky. In the process of being chopped down, separated out to locate the stronger sections, then reassembled into strong ropes. These, she thought, could be used to slow down the patrol boats and hopefully force them to stop and carry out urgent repairs. All she had to do was formulate a plan that would have enabled her crew to take command of the stricken vessel or vessels. This was the hard part: would the patrol boats all stop, or would they all depart from the scene, leaving the boat requiring repairs on its own. Blink had to come up with something that would be all-encompassing, covering all the possible unseen eventualities.

She must have been sleeping for quite some time, as her joints were aching. Blink got up, stretched and then went through all her exercises that kept her nimble and flexible. One of her crew approached and delivered some fresh fruit and water. Blink thanked her for the gift and asked if Sekoyaz was up and about, as she would like to speak to her. Added that if Sekoyaz was fast asleep, she had not to be disturbed, as it was not that important, and the conversation could wait until later on. Now fully revived, Blink walked into the surrounding jungle. After about a hundred yards, the vines were abundantly displayed. She had only reached up to untangle what she thought was a particularly fine example. When she sensed the presence of the poisonous creature, Blink held her breath and reached down for her blade. The animal was still not visible, but she was certain that it was very near, getting ready to deliver the fatal blow. A brief glimpse of movement, detected from the corner of her eye, was all the warning that she received. In less than a split second, the brightly coloured snake launched towards her. Blink grabbed it behind the head, held it against the trunk of the nearest tree and removed the head in one stroke of the blade.

Now removed from the danger, Blink pulled and hacked away at the overhanging vines until there were sizable portions to work with. She separated the good fibre away from the rotting and entangled mess, then searched for a suitable spot to conduct her experiment in making the test piece. She selected one of the branches on a fallen tree and chopped away, removing all the excess foliage until there was a suitable space. Blink separated out the good fibre into three near-even widths and secured them onto the cleared branch one at a time. Then started to plait the clean stranded into a rope and used the blunt edge of her blade to pack her handiwork as close and tight as possible. It was a time-consuming job, but at the end of a couple of hours' work, she was left with a reasonable length of what she hoped was a fairly strong rope.

Blink made her way back towards the camp, stopping off at the disused factory, she looked for something to strengthen test the adhoc device. Sekoyaz and a few of the others had spotted her entering the building and wanted to know what was being planned, followed their leader in. Blink knew that they were standing behind her and informed them that she was searching for something heavy to test the strength of the rope. "Your help would be greatly appreciated, just stop standing there like statues, come and join in." Blink directed them to do her bidding, as the crew tested the strength of the rope. She was not entirely satisfied with their efforts as they played tug of war and told them to hold up. "Find somewhere to tie the rope off on, then something that we could apply some weight with." The remaining section of an overhead platform acted as the anchor point, and the various bits of scrap metal that were tied together acted as the suspended weight. When the experiment was all prepared and ready, Blink gave the order. Sekoyaz, assisted by a couple of crew members, shoved the makeshift weight, and it was pushed off the platform. They all watched as if almost in slow motion as the rope tightened, then stretched, but managed to hold the weight without breaking.

Sekoyaz asked her boss if she was going to let them in on the plan. Blink replied that as soon as she received the details of the patrols, Sekoyaz asked her what she wanted to know. Blink informed her that she wanted to know every single little detail, as the more they knew, the better their chances would be of stopping, maybe even stealing the boats that were hindering their escape from this island. "The frigate and the motor launches mostly travel together, usually about every three or four hours. This was normally around mid-morning or mid-afternoon.' Sometimes the frigate was on its own, but mostly she was accompanied by the three motor launches." Blink asked her some more questions, and Sekoyaz supplied the additional details. "Oh yeah, the frigate stays at least about three to four hundred yards away from the shore. The other boats sail in real close, fifteen to twenty yards off the beach, travelling in a loose formation, one in front, two behind. At all times, they have the machine guns manned, keeping within sight of each other."

Sekoyaz was going to ask, but Blink beat her to it and started to unravel the plan. "The channel leading to our temporary base was not large enough, so we have to find somewhere to accommodate a motor launch. While that was ongoing, we will need to make a start assembling the traps that will force the motor launches to stop. That was when we would hit them and take over the boats. We will also need to locate where they harbour the frigate, as it would be a suicide mission, doomed to failure if we attempted to take her over in open water. The search will begin tonight. Once the berth is located, it will be manned round the clock to find any weakness in the guard's routine." Blink selected the team that was going to search for the frigate and ordered them to go and prepare.

Blink marked out on the sand, illustrating her idea on how they could halt the motor launched as she explained all the ins and outs of the plan. Blink confessed to the assembled members of her crew that she didn't know if it was going to work, but it was certainty worth a try. "I need you to go into the surrounding jungle, chop down all the good vines that you find. Please be careful and watch out for the snakes; one bite could kill. Also, while you were in the jungle, try and locate any tube-like plants; these may be of some use." Blink wished them all good luck, walking towards the group stationed on watch at the entrance of the inlet.

She wondered if perhaps this entire mission was doomed to failure. Even in her dreams, the old woman in the hooded cloak had been noticeably absent. Deep down inside, Blink was worried that they would be marooned on this island forever, with no hope and no future. As she approached the crew assigned to the watch detail, Blink made her worries vanish, displaying utmost confidence. She could not be seen to be dismayed and had to be viewed as being extremely confident, projecting that all would end well. Blink squeezed into their makeshift hide and asked them how they were, then getting to the point and asked for an update on their recent observations. She asked them to set up a marker that would indicate reasonably accurately, how far the motor launched travels from the shore. "We will need to be certain that when the trap is laid down, it will be lying waiting in their path. There should be an outer and an inner indication roughly depicting the motor launch's distance from the shore. It does not need to be anything fancy, a stick protruding out from the sand would suffice, as long as you could easily pinpoint a reasonably accurate distance."

The crew that was tasked with collecting the vines had started to return with the goods. Blink, not wanting to sit and watch, needing something to keep her occupied, made her way over towards them. She helped out by separating all the good fibre from the tangled mess. Over the next few days, she supervised the building of the traps to ensnare the motor launches. In the middle of the following week, the crew received some good news; at long last, they had found the location where the frigate was berthed. All the preparations currently underway for plan A were put on hold. Blink explained to them all that with the newly received information, she had devised a new plan. She thanked them for carrying out the work that involved going into the fairly unpleasant jungle. Blink had roughly drawn the movements of the planned attack on the factory wall by digging into the plaster with a flame-hardened stick. The crew followed her through every single action until she was satisfied that they all knew where they would be positioned. Then, more to the point, to ensure that they would all know the sequence of events and the part they would all be expected to play.

It took several long and careful days to reach where the ex-navy boats were harboured. Blink waited until the sky started to darken, then gave the order for the mission to commence. They entered the water and then swam out to sea, keeping well away from the shore patrol, with their dogs and lights. Blink had her crew treading water several hundred yards offshore until the sound of the party onboard the frigate subsided. She gave the signal, then they slowly moved in towards the target. It surprised her that although they ran almost daily patrols searching for her and her crew, they only had one person on active duty.

The solitary figure walked slowly along the length of the frigate, almost as relaxed as if he were out for a leisurely morning stroll with the dog. He stopped every once in a while to shine the flashlight onto the motor launches. James Gardener was well pissed off; he had been selected yet again for the dead hours' security detail. All of the other members of this posse had been partying, most of the day and most of the night. Jimbe-man thought that because he had the foreign-sounding white man's name, they had excluded him from the celebrations. Mr. Gardener was born and bred on this island, and cursed his mama for having a one-night stand with the holiday maker. He stopped the utterly uninteresting routine, then, after fishing in his pocket, lit up a homemade cigarette. After Jimbe-man finished his initial burst of coughing, he cursed everything and everyone he knew.

They had waited, as they had watched in the darkness, after confirming that there was only one man on patrol. She had gathered her crew together and informed them in hushed whispers of the moves ahead. Blink had been previously informed that vessels were normally patrolled by a squad of eight well-armed guards. On seeing that tonight's patrol consisted of only one man, they had changed everything that they had rehearsed for. The opportunity, now laid before them, was almost a gift-wrapped present waiting to be taken. They had practised storming the boats, using as much force as required to eliminate the guards. Now, as it was only one man who stood between them and the prize, Blink and her crew could have afforded to be more subtle in acquiring the motor launches.

Jimbe-man, still pissed off with his compatriots relieved the stashed bottle of white forked-lightning from its secret hiding place. He took a decent swig and instantly resisted the urge to vomit, praying that the vile liquid would stay in his system long enough for the alcohol to take effect. Now slightly happier, he reflected on how his friends had ended up. The ones who had pretended to fall in love with the old bags of flesh and bone. He had the chance to make the play with a very old lady from the UK. All he had to do was pretend he was head over heels in love with her, then go through the sham wedding ceremony and all of the other ghastly performances that were required. Once in possession of the fabled passport, he had it made. Jimbe-man had been informed that he did not even need to work. The people in the women's country were so gullible; all he had to play was the racism card. If he were really lucky, one of them bleeding-hearted liberals would sanction his cause, and he would have nothing to worry about.

James Gardner forced down more of the rocket fuel, dreaming that if he had pursued this course of action. He could have possibly achieved the ultimate dream of getting to see his beloved team, the great Glasgow Celtic. That alone would have adequately compensated him for having to put up with all the never-ending stares as he walked hand-in-hand with a woman who was older than his grandmother. Not to mention fighting off the woman's family members, who quite rightly would have suspected him of being on the make. The only one play that would have given him any problems would have been making love to the two breaths away from being a corpse woman. His friends had bragged that it was so easy, 'Just keep the lights off, close your eyes and dream of someone younger and someone prettier.' The more he thought about doing the dirty deed, the cold feeling ran up his spine and made him shiver as if someone had just walked across his grave. His friends had tried to console him and informed him that as soon as the one with the wrinkly skin and the false leg perished. He would, if he had played the game correctly, inherit all of the money. The house, the car, and then he could do what he wanted. Over many beers, his friends had taught him all the tried and tested lines. They were far from amused when he enquired if he was allowed to ask, 'Honey, why can't you iron your skin?'

Jimbe-man laughed and thought that he had not played the game well at all; in reality, he had lasted about five seconds. All the women he had dated before were pretty good looking, pretty dam smart and the best part about them was that they took no shit from anyone. He fished in his pocket to rescue another homemade cigarette, then sparked it up. Jimbe-man stood frozen like a statue with a look of astonishment and didn't believe the vision of the perfect goddess in front of him. The reefer slid free from his fingers without him even noticing. Jimbe-man was too far gone, way beyond any hope of beaming back into the realms of reality. His feet may as well have been welded firmly to the deck. Jimbe-man was now in a transcendental state of existence, mesmerised by the legs that stretched all the way to heaven, the long blonde hair and the perfectly formed breasts.

He did not know that there was anyone behind him until his head was forced back and the blade sliced clean through his throat. Jimbe-man had just about enough time remaining to witness the goddess starting to put her clothes back on before he bled out and died. Once Blink was fully clothed, she went in search of the connections used when the vessel was bunkering. Her crew had already securely fastened all the door locking wheels. That made them all completely inoperable. No matter how hard the now-imprisoned crew tried, all exits remained impossible to access. Upon reaching the bunkering inlet, the package that had been carefully transported through the water was now opened, waiting for her arrival.

Blink dished out the goodies, which would be simultaneously placed in the bridge, the forward-facing cannon and the inlet for loading the fuel. She carefully placed the package as far down the pipe as possible, then dropped down some of the twenty-millimetre ammunition. Blinks stuffed the petrol-soaked rags mixed with the shredded material to take up any of the additional leftover space, then laid out the makeshift fuse. The motor launches had been taken over without any force, checked, fully laden with fuel and ready to roll 'n' roll. Blink delivered the signal, flashing the handheld torch and indicated that they were all set for the final stage. The three motor launches fire up their engines simultaneously, and two of them headed out and maintained position three hundred yards offshore. The third boat arrived on the port side of the frigate and waited for Blink and her crew to descend the embarkation ladder. As the motor launch arrived, they ignited the fuses and then abandoned ship onto the waiting boat.

Blink made sure that all of her crew were accounted for and was the last to disembark. The motor launch, hightailed it out to sea, followed closely behind by the other two sister ships. They watched behind them as the explosions lit up the sky; the damage sustained will place the frigate permanently out of action, marooned in the harbour, unable to pursue them.

It had taken them a couple of days travelling stealthily under the cover of darkness to reach the harbour where their small boats were berthed. Even though they had stopped to pick up their small inflatables, they still made it back to base just before midday. A small boat arrived first and informed the crew stationed at the base that the motor launches were now under new ownership, and they had to refrain from opening fire. Everyone whooped and hollered and delivered Blink a hero's welcome as her boat arrived. She thanked them but also made them aware that it was very much a team effort, many parts making up the whole deal. She ordered everyone to get ready to abandon the temporary base. Blink informed them, "We still have enough daylight left to make it to the next island. So come on, people, get a move on and let's get out of here!"

Sekoyaz was pleased to see her, "I prayed to the Gods for a safe mission and for them to deliver you along with all the others back here safely." Blink thanked her and confessed that they were very lucky and that the previous owners of the boats had been lazy. Both of them joined in assisting with the loading of the vessels. Blink ordered them to abandon all the small boats that they had used to travel here. She cajoled her crew to hurry up and make fast the preparations to enable them to leave this horrible place, promising that the next port of call would be nothing short of sheer unadulterated luxury.

On the west coast of Scotland, Leena was busy on the bridge continuously manoeuvring the ship backwards and forwards. The dungeon dwellers were worn out, almost asleep on their feet. On receiving the repeated orders of all ahead slow, stop, all reverse slow, stop, until the captain steered the ship into the correct position. If the harbour had been larger, Leena could have slowly sailed the ship around in a circle. As it was on the small side, the repositioning was carried out in miniscule movements. The last thing that anyone wanted to happen was the boat being damaged or permanently beached beyond any possible hope of repair in the harbour. Leena knew by the thuds of the water on the hull that, as the tide was still coming in, they had been lucky to turn the ship around. Otherwise, they would all have had to stay at least another night here or possibly even longer and depended on the tides. Leena, for one and wanted out of here 'El-Pronto' as far as she was concerned, the bad guys were on the move, and her group had made little in the way of progress on escaping from them. If they were unfortunate enough to be apprehended, there would be no such thing as a fair judicial process, only torture, then execution.

Leena shouted down for the people who inhabit the darkness to move all ahead slow. The ship struggled to clear the harbour against the high tide, and she called out for an increase to half speed. As the engine controls were adjusted immediately, Leena nudged the helm and altered the course heading a small increment at a time to clear the rather tight harbour entrance. She thought that Gareth was being a selfish, moody bastard for not even delivering a much-needed cuppa or even coming to say hello. Maybe she had pissed him off earlier, if she had not been so busy Leena would have hunted him down and got whatever the problem that bugged him, right out into the open. She switched off from her current relationship problems and concentrated on navigating this rusting heap of junk out of what was possibly the smallest harbour on the planet.

Alwyn, accompanied by Cinds, was playing the name game with the two sick but improving every day passengers. Anna and Olga wanted to give their sons names, and they have insisted that the names sound like the children were from the British Isles. Both Cinds and Alwyn had asked them about perhaps using the names of their fathers or brothers. Both of the eastern European women had disliked this idea immensely. Informed the originators of the suggestion that they would rather name their offspring after stray rabid dogs than use the names of any of their male relatives. Alwyn and Cinds had been at this for hours, going through every name that they could think of. Everyone that they had suggested had some sort of problem or another. This had frequently resulted in that Anna or Olga had thought the suggested names were shit or they both had lots of trouble with they thought were almost impossible pronunciations. Alwyn had sort of politely mentioned that "There was no point in using a name that they could not say correctly, as the child would think that they were either an orphan or that they had been kidnapped."

Cinds' offered to go and retrieve some sustenance for all of them. Alwyn thanked her, Cinds' wished him good luck on the almost unachievable quest presently debilitating their mental health. Anna and Olga both agree that they wished for a simple-sounding name, but at the same time, it had to be strong and a real man's name. Alwyn tried them out with shortened versions of all the names he could think of. The only problem was that he had to clearly explain each and every single one of them. He could vividly imagine these two in the old world, being labelled as nightmare customers to every shop that they went into. He could also imagine if they were this fussy when they went to get their hair done, that the hairdresser would be tempted to either cut their throats or commit suicide. Alwyn was allowed to think it, but he would never dream of revealing these inner thoughts to their face. He tried again, "Okay, girls, what about Edward, we could shorten that to Ted, Tedds, Teddy, Ed or Eddie." Anna shouted out, "Bingo." Alwyn went quiet for a second before realising that she was actually agreeing to a name. He had to explain that she was only allowed to pick one, as they could not use them all. Anna repeated the name Ed. Alwyn wished that the ship had a PA system which he would happily activate, then announced the news to the whole of the crew.

He continued, "Okay, Olga, now we have to get your little cherub sorted." An hour later, almost at the point where his tongue, along with his brain, was just about to refuse any additional co-operation. He, out of the blue, came up with the name Robert, and Alwyn spelt out the variations for her. 'Rob, Robbo, Rab, Rabbie, Bert, Berty, Bob, Bobby?" Olga replied, "Yes!" He went through the whole process again and explained to her that she was also, as in the same as Anna, only allowed to pick one. Olga nodded her head and agreed, and opted for the name Bob. "I wish to call my son Bob." Alwyn now wished that the ship had a workable radio that would have enabled him to connect him to a worldwide network. So that he could have broadcast to everyone one the planet that at fucking long last Olga had picked a name for her son.

There was a knock on the door, Cinds had returned with the provisions, she asked Alwyn if all was good. Alwyn smiled and informed her that the enigma that was seemingly destined to remain unsolvable had been, by the grace of God, or possibly by divine intervention, miraculously sorted out. Alwyn was tempted to ask Cinds' if she wished to join him on a tour of the ship. Where they would have been greeted with untold waves of scented flower petals as they were cheered on by the crew. He refrained as he announced that Anna and Olga had chosen good, strong names for their kids. Cinds' congratulated the women on picking good masculine names for their sons and explained that it was quite a daunting task. The women shook their heads in unison and agreed with every word that she had said. Anna and Olga thanked Cinds' for all of her help and apologised profusely for taking such a long time. Alwyn pinched himself and confirmed that he actually did not exist and was not just a hologram with an enabled dictionary function.

Gareth had spent his time feeding and keeping the spanner monkeys that lived in the bowels of the ship supplied with ample supplies of hot liquid. He thought that they had just taken his kind nature for granted, never once thanking him for the services provided. Gareth had decided that he had been avoiding Leena long enough, and perhaps, just perhaps, she had deactivated the imminent DEFCON one warning. He prepared her a fresh brew, took a couple of deep breaths then made his way to the bridge. On purpose, he did not knock on the door to warn her of his presence. Gareth just walked in and delivered her hot drink, "Thought you could do with one of these."

Leena sharply retorted without any feeling that she could have done with a cuppa ages ago. Gareth closed his eyes for a brief second, "If you want, I could take it away and come back later or if you so wish I could fuck off right now and not come back at all." He continued, "I kept out of your way as you were a psycho woman earlier on and thought that I was going to receive the same treatment as the diesel monkeys." Leena realised that their relationship was teetering on a course of no return. She looked at him, "I was all wired up earlier on, and I would never speak to you like that."

Gareth informed her that he thought that they had something, something that he never thought he would ever find. "I just can't do the aggressive thing with someone that I am in love with." He continues, "You can either cut me some slack or cut me loose; it is up to you. I was a criminal in the old world, doing hold-ups, but I never took that attitude back home with me." Leena wanted to know if he would have given her a place on his crew, Gareth told her nicely to shut the fuck up, put her arms around him and tell him that she loved him. Leena replied that she would gladly do what he asked, but he would have to come closer to the helm.

As the ship was going through the motions to escape the harbour, hidden from view an old man accompanied by a little girl watched the whole of the proceedings. When the vessel had finally sailed into the open water of the Irish Sea, the little girl tugged on the Macdhiarmada's sleeve. She did not say the words, only pointed towards the ship and indicated that they should follow. The old man asked her if she was absolutely certain that this was what they should do. The girl nodded and repeated the single word, "Sure."

Macdhiarmada had found her by complete chance, as he had come across the wrecked vehicle. The little girl had uttered no cries, nothing at all to attract his attention. Something out of his normal sense of reasoning had drawn him over to survey the distorted and tangled metal. At first, all he had noticed was the dead troopers and the smashed bottles, then just as he was about to walk away, he had spotted her in among the mess of the interior.

Chapter 13

Across the Atlantic Ocean, at the camp near the Mexican border, Jackson was checking up on Poison Pete and Doctor Death. Knowing full well that the dynamic duo would be involved in some form of skulduggery, rather than make an appointment, he thought a surprise visit would be more appropriate. They were in mid-conversation discussing the appeasing characteristics of the applied colour scheme. Doctor Death was in the process of delivering an in-depth version of all the possible painting and texturising techniques to fully enhance the rather drab architecture. Poison Pete listened intently, and when his ex-cellmate finished, he replied, "I don't think that we have any just cause to apply any of the postmodernism or the pseudo, almost retrophilia styles."

Jackson threw his ten cents' worth into the ring. "Does that translate to, you just have to sometimes make do with what was available?"

Poison Pete asked Jackson if he was happy with the work that they had already completed in the unused accommodation. Jackson knew that the pair of them had been swinging the lead, but was also more than well aware that he couldn't place them anywhere else. "I think the whole place needs another coat or two." Doctor Death asked Jackson if he was being serious or if he was pulling their leg.

Jackson replied that he wanted them to apply a recoat to everything that they had finished. "I will be back to check on the progress at the end of the week." Jackson finished off and informed them that, apart from that, they had done a great job.

Now that he had gone, Poison Pete gave Doctor Death a blunt to spark up. He congratulated his friend, "That was good timing, spotting the school teacher sneaking in like that."

Doctor Death lights up, "Just plain bad manners if you ask me, at least in the old days, the raid was usually accompanied by the sirens and flashing blue lights."

Jackson, on his way back towards the command post, bumped into Enunsha, Abe and Spotty. He wished them all a good morning. Spotty, as per normal, just ignored him. He thought it could be a dark, foreboding day, full of thunderstorms accompanied by torrential rain, and this couple would still brighten up the day. Jackson related the tale of his recent encounter with the dynamic duo, and they all laughed as he recounted the pretentious word play that they had obviously constructed solely for his ears.

Abe reckoned if the duo had been that inventive in the kitchen, maybe they would still be working there. Jackson, Enunsha and even Spotty instantly stopped in their tracks and then reacted with strange looks in reply to Abe's somewhat overenthusiastic comment. Abe held his hands in the air, "Okay, I wish to retract that statement and change it. Maybe if they had not been that inventive in the galley, they would still be employed there."

Spotty accepted the revised comments for all of them and wagged his tail and barked. Jackson praised the dog's intelligence, but Spotty totally ignored him and turned his head away as if he had been mortally insulted.

At the command post, Perry had prepared his reports, chalked up the coordinates and had the coffee machine gurgling away and awaited their arrival. Spotty was first to arrive and delivered a welcome back bark and a complementary wag of the tail. Perry ignored the displayed affection that the dog had bestowed on his former owner. He waited till they were all seated, poured the barely drinkable coffee, and Jackson nodded to let Perry know he couldn't start when he was ready.

Perry took a sip of the coffee and winced at the texture of this particular blend. He excused himself and poured the offending drink down the plughole. "I think that someone has mixed up some pebbles with the coffee beans." He returned to the table and pointed to the newly highlighted parts of the map and informed his audience that the bad guys had been spotted. "It was the dust clouds from their transport that gave them away. I thought that with all that they had done in the past, they would have moved during the night. Remaining as hidden as possible from being observed. As you can see, the bad guys just drove around as clear as day, planting objects in the ground. We were able to spot them from miles away, so now we know for sure that they have tech, transport, and they want us to know that they were looking for us."

Perry added, "Going by what was on the reports, they were expanding their search parameters every few days."

Jackson asked if the patrols had spotted anything unusual in the sky.

Perry replied that no airborne devices had been heard or spotted, "But that does not mean that they don't have them, I would hazard a guess that it equates to them just not deploying them."

Abe wanted to know what devices the underground dwellers were positioning along the grid coordinates. Jackson assumed that they were most likely some form or another of sensory detectors with a limited range; otherwise, the bad guys would have already arrived here.

Perry added, "If we were to go and investigate the devices, it would only lead to the patrols giving away our position. We have discussed this in the past about luring them in, but for now, I think we should wait until we have more information about what we were really up against. Then, when we hit back, we hit them hard and fast from all sides."

Enunsha pointed at the map, "Are these coordinates that indicate the search patterns of the bad guys going to be updated soon? If not, I think we could be waking up to a surprise one morning, finding out too late that they were already on our porch."

Jackson knew what was coming and pointed to the map and asked Enunsha to let it rip. "We should not wait, they were going to come for us no matter what, I think we should go back to the plan of luring them in."

Enunsha expanded her idea, "A little bit at a time, look at the map, we can try and figure out where they were going to appear next. Hit them, there and then. I have listened to all of the thoughts pertaining to those see all, read all devices, we don't have to bring them home here. We can place them along with their dead troopers somewhere we can maintain complete control over the given situation."

Perry and the rest of the team thought that the proposed action was a viable plan. Spotty barked nonstop to inform every one of his seal of approval. They all gathered in and huddled over the map then devised a plan from a series of all the what if we do this, what if we do that questions. At the end of the session, Jackson thought that they had a workable scenario; he ordered Perry to gather in the advance patrols and informed him that they were going to be busy for the foreseeable future.

In northern Scotland, Murray had woken up early, rather than making any noise or non-environmentally friendly mess in the kitchen, he had decided, much to the delight of Charlie and Romulus, to go for an early morning walk. They ran about non-stop sniffing, then pissing on everything that Remus had left his unmistakable scent on. Charlie was informing her siblings that even though they all ran about here freely; she was without any question the boss. Murray thought that having dogs was almost as good and perhaps even a greater blessing than having children. Cha would have probably wanted to remove his family planning unit, then nail the block and tackle on the wall for the thought, of it but luckily for him and Bobby, he had no intention of telling her.

As always, the excited dogs' antics lit up the morning. Murray would rather be dead than, heaven forbid, become too old and infirm to take part in this ritual. They had been out playing for quite some time. He had taken up by the river, then reversed the direction, now ending up at their favourite spot. Charlie had always loved it up here. She sat with her tongue hanging out, panting away, looking out over the view in front of them.

Murray was in deep conversation with her, reminding his dog of the time that she had disappeared, leaving him totally distraught, almost without a soul. "Charlie, to this day I have no idea where you went, but I need to tell you that you were my best friend and I would freely give up my life if you required it." Charlie was now lying on her back, indicating that a much-needed belly rub was way overdue. Murray, agreed and obliged, just as he began, Romulus had decided that he would like a chin rub. The dogs received one hand each, Murray talked non-stop and informed them that they were the best dogs on the planet. "Don't you two be listening to that bad woman named Cat, who thought her dog was perfection in fur. You guys were the best and don't ever forget it." Charlie had had enough of Murray talking and rolled back to the normal position and stretched, then barked to inform him that breakfast would be greatly appreciated. Murray gave Charlie a final pat on the head and informed her yet again that he loved her before they set off home.

The dogs ran off in front of him. Murray thought, however, if they were given the choice between him and breakfast, that he would come in a close second. Charlie and Romulus had already been fed and were now lying on the floor pretending that it was okay for all of the children to use them as pillows. Murray arrived home, and it was already a full house today. All of the children were there, and all the mothers, with the exception of Cora. Murray had to carefully navigate his way through the obstacles to ensure that he did not step on any of the little monsters. He finally reached Cha to deliver the much-needed morning kiss and cuddle. Murray was just about to speak when Cha piped him at the post and informed him that his breakfast had mysteriously vanished. Cat stood up, pleading guilty to all charges and freely admitting to several previously unrecorded criminal offenses.

Murray just smiled, "Okay, not a problem. I think the guy on the door will take pity on this poor undernourished soul, and allow him to eat at his fine establishment."

Okolo jumped into the conversation and declared that she was going to join him. Murray delivered a gracious bow, then, like a true gentleman, held open the door for her. On the way over to Frank's, Okolo described all the gory details of Robbo's red hand gang. "I mean, Murray, me, and Alicia thought Robbo would just read the children a bedtime story. You can imagine our surprise when we opened the door to be greeted by the caveman style, look at what we did on our holiday's pictures. The red handprints were fucking everywhere; he had managed to get a duplicate full set on the ceiling. Have to give him some credit though, as he had glued up their hands with water-removable adhesive before the start of the painting class."

Just as they sat down with the food, Murray informed Okolo that his answer was no and was not open to renegotiation or any form of appeal. Okolo stared at him, wondering if he was afflicted with some decaying mental function and asked. "What the fuck are you on about?"

Murray smirked, "I am not going to teach him how to make duck noises, not now, not ever."

Okolo delivers the normal greeting, "wanker." "You had me worried for a bit there, I was thinking that you were starting to suffer from the onset of senile dementia."

Murray replied, "Well, not as yet, though I am getting restless sitting about not doing much. You know as well as I that this place almost runs itself."

Okolo agreed, "We all have seen so many changes, since we arrived here."

She asks if he remembers the first time that they met.

Murray raised his eyes, pretending to think, "In real life or in the dreams?"

He responded before she reacted, "Yes, I remember the day you arrived with your gang. As always, you were accompanied by your forever shadows, and you stared at me, wondering if I really was the wild animal that Cha allegedly kept on a leash."

Okolo denied his unfair recollection. "I never thought anything of the kind; however, I did think that you were a blast from the past. Perhaps even that you had always been that way, almost like forever. Never changing with anything or adapting, as you never quite see the point."

Murray bowed his head, acknowledging her fair and just observation.

Okolo continued, "We all worry about you, especially me."

Murray asked, "Why? Why worry about me? There were so many other things that you could worry about. Like the children and what the future has in store for them." Murray assured her that there was no need to fret about him.

Okolo pushed her point across, "What about the shakes, have you told anyone about it? I would bet that Cha, nor Cora, had not been informed about your condition."

He confirmed that she was correct, but as the shakes had ceased, there was no need to discuss it with anyone. Murray continued, "I guess that what I am really saying was that the case was closed, no further action required."

Okolo replied immediately, "I came here with absolutely nothing, just a faint glimmer of hope in a whispered dream. I took the chance, reached out, and you were there for me. It did not matter to you where I came from, what I was in my previous life. Above all, you made sure that I was well taken care of and looked after. Hell, Murray, you practically gave me the keys to your house, after what, about five minutes after knowing me."

Murray smiled, "If I can get a word in, you were kind, you were honest, and most of all, Charlie liked you. I think anyone would have done the same in that given situation. I have never asked where you were from, or what your chosen profession was in the now-gone world. What was important was that you were here, here with all of us, to start something new. Okolo, what was also important is that you were always part of us and that won't ever change."

Okolo asked if he would like to know what she had done to make her stamp on her past life.

Murray replied, "No, but now that the food was gone, a mug of tea and a smoke would be nice, what do you think?"

Okolo surrendered, halting her questions, offering to go and fetch the fresh brew. Murray saw it as a joint effort, gathered up the plates, and then returned them to the hatch. He thanked the staff for yet another really nice breakfast, joking that he thought his wife was trying to poison him.

Okolo had overheard him, "What do you think Cha would say if she heard that?"

Murray said, "I think she would laugh, as everyone knows, including her, that I married her for her cooking skills."

Okolo put the cups down on the table and informed him that he really was a wanker. He took the first sip with his eyes closed, and when he opened his eyes, Okolo handed over a joint. After they sparked up, Murray opened up. "You know what I think will be really hard?" He exhaled, took another sip, then, in between smokes and drinks, he let it all out. "What if we ran out of cigarette papers? Then God forbid, we ran out of tea? What kind of world would that leave us? Just imagine drinking some brew that was made from dandelion flower heads and some other shit. It would be truly fucking awful, I for one would be terrified at the thought of getting up in the morning. The cigarette paper shortage would be truly apocalyptic, a most definite sign that civilisation had truly declined."

Okolo was not biting, "These problems are, I think, solvable, well, at least in the short term. I am sure that you have not plundered all the local shops for teabags, tealeaves and Palm-Finns. Therefore, it was possible that we could be drinking tea for a while yet."

"There was also the other option, considering that fact, most people in this country kept the sacred leaves of eternal life in sealed tins. There was, without doubt, an undisputed fact that every household will contain an uncontaminated supply of tea. As to whether you think that this, yet to be accounted for supply, was suitable for your delicate taste buds. Or you will think that certain brands will taste like cats' piss remains to be seen."

He asked Okolo for a compromise, "If I go and acquire refills, you could skin up. Then, when I am back sitting at the table, you could tell me what you were really thinking."

Okolo nodded and confirmed that they do indeed have a deal. She handed over his reward for the fresh brew. Murray thanked her and commented that her rolling skills have somewhat improved. Okolo burst out laughing, "Alicia has been teaching Robbo, and you will be pleased to know that his joints no longer look like a burst couch."

He shook his head, imagining the ordeal that Alicia had to endure on this task. "Okay, Okolo, what's on your mind?'

She replied that Alicia and she had thought about approaching him for a while, and as now seems the correct time. "We were thinking that the whole area could be searched for all the items that we need, every shop, every supermarket, every house and home. We don't need to cross the river, and we should be able to find most things on this side of the bridge. I am talking shoes, diapers, kiddies' clothes all the shit that we were going to need in the future.

But, while we were out and about in all the houses, we could take the tinned food and any other useful items that we find."

Murray looked puzzled, and Okolo put him out of his misery. "Sewing kits, tools, knitting needles, everything that you could possibly think of. Up till now, we have only sorted out the food and power issues. Now we had to think about when we were going to have to make things, and in saying that, certain items were going to have to be completely relearned from scratch."

He freely admitted that he was not looking forward to wearing woolly jumpers, sheepskin jackets and perish the thought, homemade shoes. "Okolo, I don't think that we shall will ever see these times. We still have plenty of clothes and footwear from the old world, albeit there may come a time when we will have to search far and wide to locate them. When this changes to the items not being freely available, we will be long gone. Our children, our children's children, will, unless they learn to make things pretty quickly, will be the ones dressed in homemade clothes. These items will be limited to what material was available locally, and as far as I can tell, we don't grow any plants capable of producing the correct fibres to make cloth. This was not just a long-forgotten skill, and it was a long-forgotten industry residing in the pages of some obscure history book."

Okolo offered him a hand-rolled cigarette to stop him talking, as he lit up, she offered her opinion. "That was exactly what I am saying, we need to put these things solidly in place. There will be no one left for our children to ask for any advice on how to produce all of these items that we take for granted on a daily basis. Our future generations will need some help, and at the very least, we should provide them with a contingency." Murray asked her if that equated to plundering all the houses for apparel to be stored for possible modification in the future.

She confirmed that his statement was correct, adding that the tinned goods, assorted tools and implements would also be added one way or another into the just-in-case plan. Murray was going to mention that he was not that keen on robbing the dead, but thought that Okolo would mention the recently rehoused sound system. Now knowing that he does not have a possible counterargument to her sound proposal, Murray spoke up. "Okay, Okolo, I think all of what you have said was pretty reasonable and also pretty sound. It was only fair that we should let the others know what you were thinking. You never know, perhaps someone will know what type of plants to grow to produce a clothlike material. Someone might even know how to prepare and make the cloth." Murray hesitated for a second, biting his lip, "But I don't know if anyone will be able to tell us what crop to plant to produce shoes." He laughed at this remark, Okolo does not even smile and informed him that he was without any doubt a true wanker.

Once she had calmed down, Murray calmly informed her that if and when they went out and about plundering. It would only be fair if they informed their neighbours what they were doing. He continued, "Hey, M was the resident farm expert, she might even know what the name of the plant is, what it looks like and if it requires any specific growing conditions. As this was by all accounts yours and Alicia's baby, you could both go over there, then deliver the news and along with that, the intentions of why we were doing it." Murray could tell by the look on her face that she did not like that idea, one little bit. Okolo let it slip that the last time she had been in contact with Mark, it was just after the shooting incident. "I was not too friendly towards Mark or Ellie; I don't think I even looked at him when we were speaking."

Murray acknowledged her statement, "At the end of the day, he was our neighbour and rightly or wrongly, we have to give him his place. I can understand that you were upset, thinking that I was going to die. But here I am, alive and kicking, bygones were bygones, all sins were forgiven. One day we will need to go to them for help, or one day they will have to come for assistance from us. It would be easier for all involved if we could all speak to each other. Therefore, after you have the talk with Cha and the others, it would only be fair if you, along with Alicia, went to deliver the talk at the farmhouse."

"I can't make you do this, but it would be more than nice if you were to knuckle down and approach Mark. Time was marching on, perhaps we should go over to the house now, otherwise they would think that we have run away from the prevailing smell of the wet and sticky diapers." Okolo waited for Murray to hand in the now-empty mugs and to deliver his almost fan club appreciation of yet another splendid brew. On the way over to the house, Murray asked Okolo if she was good. She replied that she was fine and they didn't have any problems. He thanked her, "I have always thought that you have always been honest with me, always saying what you think rather than saying what I would like you to think. Okolo, please don't ever change that." She smiled and reminded him that he would always be a wanker just before she slipped through the door ahead of him.

The first thing that they noticed on entering the house was the ever-present faint humming sound. Sammarra was in the middle of all the other children, Vincent and Mark, even though they were slightly older, appear to be just as enthralled along with the other infants. Cat informed the newly arrived couple that the hum subsides a little once they have been fed. Murray asked Cha if she had missed him, receiving the curt reply that she never knew that he had left. Murray knew that she was just playing for the crowd and held his chest, pretending as if he had just received a mortal wound to his heart.

Cha informed him that he had to do better, as if he had a heart in the first place, it would be on the other side of his chest. Murray just shrugged and said that Cha was always this cruel and that was the real reason that he loved her. "I am just continually attempting to curtail her evil ways and create a happy household for the sake of our children's peace of mind," Cha asked him if she told him that she loved him, would he promise to keep quiet. Murray went on his knees and held the other side of his chest where his heart was actually meant to be, and replied that he would promise to be silent forever if she were to say the meaningful words.

Cha handed him Alfie along with the feed bottle, "How about I make you some tea?" Murray told her that she was a wonderful woman and that he never once believed the horror stories that were adorning the walls in every cubicle of the gents' toilet."

Murray was interrupted by Alfie, who was hitting him and indicated that the bottle had to be placed in his mouth. Murray apologised to his son, paying more attention to the feeding routine. He talked to him almost as if the infant were twenty years older than his actual age was at present. Okolo has informed Alicia that she had put across the idea that they had been thinking about, and they have been given the task of presenting it to the others. Alicia asked for everyone's attention, "Okolo and I have been worried about what the future holds for our children and, more to the point, what we can do to ease the burden of the transition from a modern society that has changed into a society that has almost nothing." Murray raised a hand and informed the speaker that although it was great to hear her voice, Cora and Karen should be present to witness and take part in the presentation.

Alicia thanked Murray for his input, adding that it was great to also hear his voice. "I have already run through the idea with the doctor and Karen. They have both agreed on principle that all the points that I am about to raise were both valid and important."

In reply, Murray stuck out his tongue and crossed his eyes, then returned to paying attention to feeding his son. Alicia, with the assistance of Okolo, laid out what they have envisaged for the children's future. "The years ahead for them will not be easy, and we should provide them with as many skills and resources as possible. I know that we will not be able to furnish them with every item, nor with every piece of information that will be required. But at the very least, we had to try and provide a sustainable future where they will not be toiling to survive every single day of their existence."

Okolo took over, going through the items that would not be freely available in the shops and empathised that the missing quantity could be supplemented by searching houses. "If they don't knit, they sew, and if they sew, they will have buttons, threads and needles. The list was endless, anything you can think of, they have in one form or another. Nails, screws, tacks, pins not to mention a supplemental list of suitable tools required to do the various jobs. Everything was out there, and we just had to gather it in, making it safe. So that when the time arrives when the collected items need to be used, they will not be all rotten and corroded beyond any hope of their ever being salvageable. We can build sheds to store all the items, keep them from getting damp. It will take a while to gather everything, but our children, and our children's children will appreciate the fact that we did not just abandon them with no foreseeable hope for the future."

Chapter 14

Miasnikov had just been informed by Essmie that the prisoners were now starting to show the symptoms of acute liver and kidney failure. Vladimir insisted that his senior commander join him to partake in this rather splendid lunch. Essmie hesitated and offered a rather futile excuse. Miasnikov promised her that the excellent fare on offer did not contain any mushrooms. "The prisoners will all be dead soon enough, and I insist that you join me for lunch." Miasnikov put on a little song and dance routine when he delivered his next impromptu mini-speech. "Then you can watch as I demonstrate how to burn off excess calories and dispense with unwanted baggage at the same time." Essmie thought that his singing and dancing were a sure, undisputed sign that her superior was, in fact, insane. Nevertheless, feeling that she had no choice in the matter, graciously accepted the invitation to dine with him.

She couldn't fault him for his impeccable manners during the ordeal of the midday meal. Miasnikov had even perfectly performed the skills of a sommelier. A little on the dramatic side for her taste, as he self-congratulated himself on removing the cork without the popping noise. The general regretfully had to inform her that due to the local greasy spoon cafe was temporary out of action. They would not be serving the indigenous populations a flavoured deep-fried chocolate bar. Essmie took the news as a blessing in disguise, just the thought of seeing the mentioned sweet alternative, never mind actually tasting it, made her want to puke her guts up. Miasnikov gulped down the wine, then announced that perhaps on the return journey, they could find someone who could make the aforementioned delicacy.

Essmie replied that it would be very nice, but for some inexplicable reason, she had a vivid image of a battered, deep-fried dog-shite floating around her brain. The lunch was almost finished when they were interrupted by a knock on the door.

One of the sub commanders stood to attention and presented them with the report that they had captured several prisoners. Essmie had placed some guards to watch the alleged shrine for any activity. Miasnikov complimented her foresight and asked for the prisoners to be presented before him. The sub commander informed the general that they were pretty smelly and suggested that perhaps the prisoners should be cleansed first. Miasnikov threw caution to the wind, ordering them to be admitted. The man was a big fucker; the two even bigger women could have perhaps been ex jail birds with the number of homemade tattoos on display. They were all more than very dirty and as smelly as reported by the sub commander.

Miasnikov offered them some food, and was momentarily transfixed as his new guests behaved like cavemen and crammed the food into their mouths with their dirty fingers. One of the women grabs a knife from the table, then lunges towards Miasnikov. Essmie shot her twice in the head before she had gotten anywhere near him. Vladimir sighed and informed the remaining guests that they had spoiled what he had hoped would turn out to be a rather jolly get-together. Miasnikov now ordered the prisoners to be cuffed, then led them out to where their fellow compatriots were seated. The remaining female prisoner hissed and spat like a wild animal. Vladimir having put enough of her group's errant behaviour for one day. Removed his sidearm and informed her that he could not really comprehend why she was complaining. He resolutely assured her that he would deliver something that was justified to actually complain about.

Miasnikov had her dragged outside and shot her in both ankles, then in both of her knees. He turned towards Essmie and the remaining prisoner, "Shall we go? I believe the rest of your friends were patiently waiting for the party to start."

The woman he had shot was left to bleed on the ground. Miasnikov thought that if she withered and then died, that was fine, or if by some miracle she dragged herself away and managed to beat the odds. Then that was fine also, either way, he could not care less. The remaining prisoner was manhandled towards where his former colleagues were situated. He could now clearly hear the metallic drum beats, accompanied by the irritating noises emitted by the cheap musical instruments. The prisoner thought that maybe the locals were in the process of being entertained by the invading forces. This idea was kicked into touch when he saw what lay before him.

All of the eighty-four prisoners were equally separated into two lines. A huge fire blazed in-between them. As they drew nearer, the prisoner noticed that all his former friends had metal buckets placed on their heads and they were semi-permently attached to the chairs with wires. They all appear to be dressed in damp looking clothes, but as he got closer, he could differentiate between the smell of body odour, the smell of stale pish and the rancid smell of shit. Miasnikov completely ignored the unusual aroma, and he looked with unequivocal admiration as his troopers beat the drums. At present, they were going through the call-and-response routine. One group would play a certain rhythm, only to be answered by a slightly different rhythm seconds later. His troopers mixed it up a little and applied subtle variations in which two troopers played drums, the next two waited and repeated the process, which multiplied all the way throughout the two lines.

Essmie was of the opinion that any normal person would see this as wholeheartedly ill-conceived madness. As she wanted to remain breathing, she said nothing and held her mouth firmly closed. Miasnikov made sure that the prisoner had a grandstand view and held his hands into the air and signalled for the activities to cease. He addressed the dinner guests the somewhat now poorly, dinner guests, "Ladies and gentlemen, I would like to thank you all from the bottom of my soul for attending this dinner party. But with a sad heart, I have to inform you that the celebration is unfortunately coming to an end. I could lie through my teeth, promising that we could do this again sometime in the near future. But I really don't think that you would believe any word that I said. So, without any further ado, I would like to deliver the presents that you all well and truly deserve."

The General asked for the hammer and the nails to be delivered. He asked him troopers to sniff out who had the most miserable, unhealthy guest. Several pairs of hands go into the air all at once, reminiscent of primary five school kids being asked a question that they actually knew the answer to. Vladimir removed the buckets from their heads to have a quick look, inspected the hopeful recipients of the prizes to fully ascertain if they were near passing into the next world. After several false calls, he announced to one and all that yes, indeed, they do have a winner. Miasnikov held his hands out to be furnished with the tool, accompanied by the implements of death.

Miasnikov lifted the metal bucket up and bent over, then whispered. "This is my gift to your entire tribe in repayment for what happened to my sister." He replaced the bucket and then drove a six-inch nail through the base. Vladmir doubted whether this was enough and then continued adoring the bucket with several more nails in various locations. As the blood became visible, Miasnikov held his hands out to his assembled troopers. As they were all pretty dam well drunk, he had to give them the appropriate hints that he was expecting a round of applause. Miasnikov bowed like a seasoned thespian and then announced, "Okay, an encore you shall have."

This time, he sharpened up a pair of drumsticks while waiting for his troopers to select the next in line to vacate the party. Miasnikov played to the crowd and asked them if they were one hundred percent sure that the guest should be allowed to leave. He wound them up until they were all shouting, "Let them leave! Let them leave!" Vladimir held his hands up again for silence, then plunged the sharpened drumsticks one at a time into the recipient's gut. He was not completely satisfied that he had inflicted enough pain upon them. Miasnikov proceeded to decorate the metal bucket and ultimately their head with more nails. Some went past through the sides of the bucket, some went straight in through the base.

He issued orders for his troopers to continue and pleaded with them to be creative, "Make it interesting, be inventive, delve into your dormant artistic aspirations and try and make their demise as unpleasant as possible. I want to see my sister smiling and happy at your efforts. Go ahead, guys, make my sister and me proud."

Miasnikov watched from the side and realised that they would get a much better view if they toured the site. He has the prisoner dragged to witness the demise of all of his friends. Vladimir nodded his approval as one of his troopers opened a hole large enough in the bucket to force a drumstick into their head. He was overwhelmed with joy as a pair of his troopers got really inventive and delivered a pair of sharpened drumsticks into the prisoners' ears in stereo.

Miasnikov was overheard above the noise shouting, "Out fucking standing."

Vladimir was very impressed with the accumulated killing skills that were being blatantly displayed in all shapes and forms. He announced to his men to get drunk, as they would all be resting for several days before continuing north. Essmie's presence was required; Vladimir instructed her to provide the prisoner with a suitable vehicle. Miasnikov dragged the prisoner aside and righteously hissed in his ear, "I don't care what your name is. I don't care if we have just ended every single person that existed in your pathetic little world. You go north and let your friends know that I am coming for them, be sure to tell them of everything that you have seen here today."

As the prisoner departed, Miasnikov informed Essmie to spread the word that they would be heading north in the morning. "Hopefully, the advance guards will pick up his trail, and if we are lucky, he will lead us straight to them."

The General looked at all the dead prisoners and wondered whether, in years to come if life around this area was to eventually return back to normality. Perhaps some botanist in the future would be extremely perplexed in thinking that he had actually discovered a new species of plant. They would be looking at the inverted metal bucket with the protruding nails, along with the weather-beaten white structured covered in intertwining greenery. Almost represented a plant that grew in two perfectly formed lines, and most strange, it appeared as if it actually grew in the upside-down position.

Uno, the last surviving member of the swamp people, had been on his way to pay his respect to the shrine dedicated to the woman who ran through the forest naked. When he was apprehended by the invaders, they had made him witness the farewell party that involved the last surviving members of his tribe. Uno thought he had a greater chance of being struck by lightning on a clear sunny day, than seeing this one out. Then the fable that the leader of the invaders had disclosed about being true to his word, he knows for sure that they would have their people out looking for him already. Uno asked for forgiveness as he placed one of the dead swamp people in the vehicle, then set the simple fuse. After the people from the north had departed, it was agreed by the council that, should the need arise, his people should have vehicles available to escape. Uno was traveling towards one of the secret exit points. He occasionally stopped and looked behind him, watching for the emerging flames coming from his supplied vehicle.

This, he hoped, would put off his would-be pursuers, perhaps convincing them that he had no longer any association with this realm of existence. Uno had no idea where Okolo and her crew resided; all he knew was that it was somewhere up north. Uno was also aware that the invaders would be watching all routes leading in that direction. He intended to travel southwest, hopefully they would not see him, but if they did happen to spot him. Uno hoped that they would think he was running away. He would give the rouse a few days, then turn about and change his heading. Uno has at last reached the emergency escape vehicle, he opened the door, jumped in, and secured the seat belt. As the vehicle was parked at the top of a steep hill, he bumped-started the monster. The motor chugged at first, trying to come back to life, after what felt like a lifetime, it fired up to normality. Uno drove the wreck around until he reached the turn-off. He very nearly switched on the indicator to signal, but stopped at the last moment. He hit the road that would take him westward and hopefully leave behind all the madness that had wiped out all of his people.

Uno periodically checked the back mirror and looked to make sure that he was not being followed. He intended to stop in a while, perhaps after the vehicle had fully charged its battery. Then he would attempt to pull over to a secluded spot, just rest up for an hour or two. To watch, then wait for any would-be pursuers attempting to play the cat and mouse game. The drive towards the coast was relatively easy; every once in a while, Uno had to slow down and then perform the various manoeuvres required to squeeze around the rusting hulks. These vehicles would have at one time been someone's dream car. The owners would have lovingly cared for them, every rub of the cloth applied to shine the already gleaming bodywork would have been administered with TLC. Their children and friends would have been prohibited from eating, drinking then most likely sternly advised to refrain from speaking and breathing in their pride and joy.

All that remained of them now would reduce the previous owners to tears. The flat-on-flat tires, smashed windscreens, along with the indigenous plant life and fauna that were now adapting to flourish in their relatively new habitat. Uno just saw them as obstacles; he chuckled as he remembered the days of his youth when someone asked what type of car his parents or friends drove. He would reply most sincerely and honestly that they drove a red one or a blue one. Uno for sure did not know any of the specifications, had no clue about the manufacturer's guidelines and the shed load of recommended modifications that the vehicle aficionados could recite in their sleep. As far as he was concerned, it was all just unnecessary information that he saw no valid reason in even attempting to absorb.

He kept his eyes firmly glued to the road ahead; these days, one could never be too careful. In the old days, he found driving nothing but a complete brain-numbing chore. Never quite being able to figured out why people found it relaxing and pleasurable. Even when he had travelled through the night on just about empty roads, Uno still found the task totally unrelaxing and anything but a pleasant experience.

Uno had nearly arrived at the coast; several times having pulled in to a partially hidden layby, then patiently waited and watched for any pursuers. In the weeks before the sickness had arrived the residential area ahead of him had received the accolade of being voted the most depressing, rundown shithole of a town in Scotland. As he drove through the decaying urban sprawl, the area had surprisingly not changed that much. If anything, the somewhat noticeable absence of people, dead junkies floating in the water and rabid stray dogs fucking on the main drag actually brightened the whole place up some.

He slowed down, clunked through the gears then after an intense period of trial and error sped back up as he exited the rather sharp corner. The last thing that he expected to come across was an old man accompanied by a young girl riding bicycles, travelling on both sides of the road. Uno stomps hard on the brake pedal, quickly turning the steering wheel to avoid a collision. He completely forgot the situation that they now lived in, gets out the vehicle and delivered the what the fuck do you think you were doing speech. The harsh words in the old forgotten world would have been socially unacceptable, but to irate drivers like himself, they would have been totally normal and harshly delivered in the uncompromising macho man style. Uno realised his mistake of being in the old world and instantly apologised and muttered some words about sometimes we forget where we are.

The little girl walked towards him, "If you were going north, you would have to turn about, as the road ahead is blocked and impassable. As we were going north also, we accept your most sincere apology and forgive you for very nearly running us over. We shall take you up on the very kind offer of inviting us to accompany you on the journey."

Uno was speechless, and for some strange reason, agreed that giving them a lift was a splendid idea. When he was back in the vehicle, Uno thought about what had just happened, and he scratched his scalp in bewilderment. Did the little girl just charm him or order him to take her and her companion with him? He did not know them; he had never met them before or even heard of them. Uno did not even know their names, but there they were, fast asleep in the back of his vehicle.

On the other side of the Atlantic, Commander Green had arranged for the delivery of another batch of sensory optics for his units. Who were out in the wilderness attempting to track and apprehend Abe Hubstien along with his merry band of saboteurs. G-Flem wanted as many of them as possible captured alive for questioning. Green would, of course, try and follow her orders to the letter, but these were somewhat difficult to maintain in the heat of battle. Once he had gathered all of the information relating to the strength and the exact location of the enemy it may just be possible to round them all up. As per his company's last incursion into their territory, if he remembered correctly, they were somewhat prone to operate in the daylight, possibly even against night time patrols. This time, his troopers may just swoop in on their camp during the hours of darkness and capture them all in their nightclothes.

Commander Jack Green thought that he would rather just face Abe and his compadres in a straightforward battle. Troopers with machines against troopers with machines, a fair battle to see who had the best tactics. The commander knew that for some reason, most likely because the opposition were sneaky little fuckers, the ensuing battle will be anything but fair and equally mismatched. He was fully aware that his superior wanted results sooner rather than later. Taking this valid point into careful consideration, he sent a message to the advance units advising that he expected some results in the very near future.

Green summons his driver and informed them that he wished to view the preparations that were underway to ensure that their great leader arrived on schedule without any problems or delays. He noticed that several workers were crossing the road ahead of them. Green advised his driver not to slow down and encouraged her to floor the gas pedal. If they get a move on and escape being knocked down, then ten out of ten for them. On the other hand, if the driver was lucky enough to run any of them over, then that would be ten out of ten for her. Green thought that the workers should be overjoyed that he was in a good mood. Otherwise, he would have stopped the vehicle, broken their legs, then had them inducted into the alligator feeding program down by the canal.

At last, they have reached their destination, and Green stared at the sentries on duty. They carried the explicit inspection to the letter, knowing full well that if they did not ask for a valid form of identification. The sadistic bastard in front of them would have no hesitation in executing them instantly. Commander Green waited patiently while his document was verified. The trooper returned and handed over the paperwork, then saluted as the barriers were reoriented to allow the vehicle access to the base.

He scanned the immediate horizon, watching as the lines of regimented autonomous land drones slowly moved in unison and cleaned the surface, removing any unwanted material from the stretch of reinforced asphalt that almost stretched as far as his eyes could see. Green, on one of his first days of his newly awarded promotion, had changed his predecessors' orders. Billy Blunderful had requested that the sweep was only to be conducted before the transport departed, and then carried out again prior to their esteemed leader arriving in the event of any part of the plan to permanently relocate the Baroness of Kindeace-Shire and her entourage. As for faltering or failing along the way in anything remotely related to a successful operation.

Commander Green was more than fully aware of the unavoidable punitive actions that would be immediately sanctioned by his less-than-forgiving commanding officer.

He would be the first in line to be punished, and Jack Green thought that being fed to the alligators would be fairly pleasant compared to the unimaginable fate that G-Flem would instigate upon his bag of water and bones. To ensure that his part in the mission was a resounding success, he has ordered that the autonomous land drones work twenty-four-seven until the Baroness of Kindeace-Shire, their great leader, Lesqueth Bretton, has arrived safely on these fabled shores.

Commander Green had updated this information and subsequently forwarded the report to General Fleming, and added that this and all additional changes to his now dead and gone predecessors' orders were open to a thorough inspection on her command. Jack knew that G-Flem will read it knowing that this was only a cover your arse document blaming his former superior for being transparently negligent in performing the duties expected from a senior commander. Now satisfied that the over precautionary cleaning process was functioning as per his request, Green ordered his driver to proceed to the next port of call.

They arrived at the huge hangers; the sub-commander stood to and saluted, informing his superior that all of the required modifications had been carried out. Adding the inspection team from the CCP had performed a function check, and she was pleased to inform him that all of the work carried out had passed with flying colours. She elaborated, "A complete bill of health with no added comments or recommendations." Commander Green offered his congratulations to her and the crew involved in the task. He informed her that he would like to see the test reports for the inflatable bladders. Then, once he had read them, perhaps she could show him all of the modifications that were performed on the vehicles to transport the twelve hundred inoculated infants. Commander Bryan led the way so that he could see for himself all of the work that had been carried out. It was only rumoured that this action was going to take place, and only recently had it been passed down the chain of command, confirming that this operation was actually going to commence.

Bryan had been through everything with an ultra-fine-tooth comb since she was transferred to this project. Sub Commander Bryan was confident that she had missed out on nothing and knew that every installed item had been checked and rechecked more times than she cares to remember. Even the inflatable bladders had been subjected to an intensive series of pre-tests prior to the scrutinisingly exhaustive inspection performed by the CCP delegation. When they arrived, the company delegation had point-blank refused to speak to her and requested absolute privacy while they carried out their duties. As per the stipulated regulations, the governing authority insisted that her troopers and mechanical technicians were to be placed under guard on the base until the completion of their work. The consignment of CCP roboticized personnel had subsequently checked everything, every nut, every washer and every type of fastening to ensure that every single component matched perfectly with the required specifications.

They had even gone to the extent of comparing all of the components that Bryan's technicians had used against samples from their own stock. To ensure that there were no deviations in the pre-coded stock index. In a space of three intensive months, the team from CCP had dismantled various sections of the work carried out and performed destructive testing on the various category red installations. Commander Bryan had thought that the bastards had cross-referenced every applicable manufacturer's specification guide to find a possible infringement. When the ghosts from the CCP had completed their inspection, they just upped sticks and left without uttering a single word. All that Commander Bryan had received in the form of notification that the works were stamped and approved was a mail from General Fleming informing her that the inspection team from CCP had accepted and endorsed the said modifications.

Commander Green walked in and about the modified transport units, asking about this and asking about that. Bryan replied to all of his questions immediately, and as the test reports relating to the inflatable bladders arrived, she handed them straight over to him to scrutinise. Green quickly scanned through them, asking about the working pressure in relation to the storage pressure. Commander Bryan replied to his set of questions, using bar pressures and then changing it to pounds per square inch to ensure he fully understood what information she was putting across to him.

Green nodded his head a few times as he digested the incoming data, which flowed off her lips without a set of referenceable notes. Green asked about the relationship between the PSI compared to barometric pressure. Commander Bryan correlates the answer in her head, explaining that all the tests that were carried out had taken every possible scenario into consideration. Pointing out that all the test pressures were set at either one and a half times the working pressure or one point one times the system pressure. Bryan added that the stipulated liquids were used as per the appropriate system under test. The liquids that would be stored were subjected to a weekly purification test, and that they have a sizable reserve set aside for any unforeseeable contingency. Commander Jack Green stood to attention and saluted, and shook the sub commander's hand. He informed Bryan that she has done a tremendous job and he would be referring to this project, outlining his glowing praise in the report that he intended to submit to General Fleming.

Jack Green was completely satisfied that all was as it should be at the base. Instructed his driver to follow the route that their great leaders' convoy would take when they journeyed towards the Magno-L embarkation point. Green curtly reminded his driver that it was not a race and she had to drive steadily to make sure that he found any and all of the imperfections along the route. As they drove along the highway, the first offending items that caught the commander's eye were a group of indigenous workers seemingly far too happy at their work. Jack issued a request for his driver to pull over, and CG got out of the vehicle and walked towards them.

The workers were involved in erecting a fence, which at eye level would block out the offending landscape as

Lesqueths' convoy drove through the area. All they had to do was install a certain meterage, easily achievable within the timeframe of the working day. As Commander Green approached, one of the workers arrived from the other side fence. She sniffed and wiped her nose several times. Jack asked her a question, and the slurred speech as well as her eyes rolling upwards gave away what she had been up to.

He ordered her and all the other workers to line up along the completed part of the fence. Commander questions all of them; the ones that he thought were fit to continue working were dismissed. The remaining slightly dazed workers slouched on the fence while Jack searched for the appropriate piece of equipment. He raised his voice and ordered the others back to work. The ones that were segregated were permanently attached to the fence with the cartridge-powered nail gun. Commander Green informed the remaining working group that they would be drug tested in the morning. Adding that if any of them think that they would fail, they could always save some time and commit suicide.

Now at her family home, Lesqueth had instructed all of her personal guards, apart from two of them, to take position outside of her family home. The other two she took inside and made full use of them as they assisted her with packing all the items that she wished to take away with her. All the framed photographs, the mementoes from a bygone era passed down to her from her ancestors, were placed neatly and efficiently into the crates. Lesqueth had already selected the attire and jewellery that she intended to take with her on the journey overseas. The Baroness watched them like a hawk as they diligently obeyed her latest set of instructions. Finally with all the packing complete, she ordered them to follow her down into the basement. Lesqueth had packed away some items that had been privately held by her family for generations. The boxes ancient artifacts, that no one outside her close circle was even aware of their existence, were hauled up to the temporary staging point with the rest of the baggage. As she intended retain the secret of the inheritance they returned one last time to the basement, the Baroness issued a short sigh and shot the two guards through the head. "Sorry guys, there was trust, and there again, there was complete trust."

The Baroness made her way to the ECD, presented her palmprint for verification, then types in two letters, two numbers, then pressed the send button. She thought that this was possibly the last time that she would ever use this device, and most likely the last time that she would ever be in the family home. Lesqueth summoned the remaining guard detail and instructed them to load up the packing crates. They did not ask about the two missing guards, and the Baroness offers no explanation in relation to their up-to-date medical status nor their current whereabouts.

Chapter 15

On the other side of the world, Blink had just ordered her crew to approach with caution the newly spotted landmass. As she viewed it through the high-powered binoculars, at this distance, it all appeared rather peaceful. Blink requested half speed, and all the motor launches immediately slowed down. She instructed Sekoyaz to make sure her people are scanning the beach for anything that appears slightly unusual. As the recent island adventures had been less than friendly, the crew were preparing themselves for another battle. Blink had not issued an order to that effect, and in reality, she couldn't really blame them for thinking that way. On the other hand, she was hopeful that maybe this island would be different. If they were lucky, it would only be inhabited by docile herds of semi-domesticated animals that just wandered about and hoped that someone would stop by to feed them, or perhaps even be inclined to adopt them. Sekoyaz delivered the heads up and reported the activity on the pier. Blink activated the zoom option on the device to get a better view of the unfolding events.

The middle-aged woman stood alone, looking towards them. She had no visible weapons on display nor any warriors standing by ready to obey her commands.

Blink thought that the woman looked rather relaxed, almost as if she was expecting visitors. Sekoyaz asked if she wished a crew to get ready for a seek and search mission. Blink replied that she wished one of the inflatables were made ready and someone to take her ashore.

Sekoyaz urged caution and pleaded with her leader to send someone else to land on the beach first. Blink thanked her for the cautionary remark, but reminded her that she was responsible for all of them.

Blink asked Sekoyaz what the woman is doing now. "She is now sitting at a shaded table with a pitcher of juice, two glasses and by all noticeable accounts appears to be waiting for your arrival."

The motor launched came to a halt about a hundred meters from the shore. Blink climbed down into the dingy and she told Sekoyaz not to worry needlessly, then ordered the pilot to take her ashore. Sekoyaz watched the woman sitting somewhat relaxed on the pier, then ordered the other members of the crew who had the other sets of binoculars to scan the area. The inflatable reached the pier without any incidents, and Blink ascended the ladder to go and meet the welcoming committee that was still sitting at the table for two. On reaching the top, she turned around and gave Sekoyaz a wave before she walked towards the woman.

As she got closer, the woman stood then delivered a warm welcome to her island. "My name is Uuvla, and rather than stand exposed to the elements please have a seat." Blink watched her every move, ready to spring into action should the present situation show any signs of anything untoward about to happen. Uuvla, informed Blink that they don't receive many visitors, especially ones as relaxed as herself. Blink accepted the compliment and replied that there was a distinct possibility of being introduced to cannibalism on the last island that had visited. Uuvla, smiled and informed her that, as there is an abundant supply of fresh provisions, she should not be expecting her to change her diet now. Uuvla, informed Blink that she liked the boats and freely admitted that she never really cared much for the previous people who crewed them. Blink asked her if she had met them. Uuvla, replied that she had heard the various stories about them, and that was more than enough reason to avoid them. The older woman poured the drinks and offered one to Blink. "Take anyone you wish; I can drink out of both of them to prove that they are not poisoned." Blink took one and had a few sips.

Uuvla, spoke freely, "You look as if you have travelled many miles and for many, many days to get here. I don't think that your journey is quite over yet, and you still have many miles to travel. I would be thinking that you, along with your crew, would like to rest for a few days and resupply before recommencing your quest."

Blink, not taking her eyes off her, calmly replied by asking Uuvla, if that would in any way be inconvenient. She smiled slightly, closed her eyes for a brief moment, then replied with a voice as cold as ice. "We have had many visitors here, some were nice, some were not as nice as others. Some wanted to just come and take over, others wanted just to do as they pleased. You have that old world feel about you, perhaps you and yours will be different, perhaps not, but either way we shall see."

Blink had listened to every word that had been said, and more importantly, she had underlined all of the words and phrases that had not been said. Uuvla, still attempting to portray that she was in complete control of the situation, slowly pulled one of her fingers down the condensation on the glass as she waited for a response.

Blink replied the only way she knew how. "I suppose that we could sit here for days playing chess with words, and you would give nothing or give very little away. Rather than skirt around, evading the issue, why don't you just get straight to the point and in that, just tell me what it is that you want."

Uuvla, thought that this one had never attended any of the posh schools that were frequented by the brats of the various bankers or criminals who used to stay or evade extradition on this island chain. "What we want is a chance to survive. Presently, we have no menfolk, everything that we do here is accomplished by the women. Eventually, we will fade away and perish in the dust. It would be nice if we could perhaps plant the seeds for the next generation."

Blink asked Uuvla, to get straight to the point by avoiding all the frilly phrases. "We need men, not just any men, but healthy, disease-free men to help us repopulate this island. The ones who all came before you were unhealthy, unwashed and more than particularly unsuitable. You look clean, very healthy and if you are an example to go by, then I am thinking that the men on your crew will be more than adequate for what I have in mind. Your people must be hungry by now, why not bring them ashore and at least permit your crew can sample the delights on offer."

Blink asked Uuvla if that equated to her wanting to view the men on her crew to tick the suitable for breeding box. Uuvla nodded and confirmed that it was about the truth of it. She added that for now her crew are only coming to eat, and anything that happens after that will be open to discussion. Blink raised her right hand, and the motor launched moved towards the pier. Uuvla turned around and waved both her arms. Moments later, the women on the island start to ferry out all the tables, chairs and all the other items for the banquet.

Both of the women knew that if they had used other signals, things could have been so different. Blink cuts to the chase, "I am of the opinion that you are in favour of artificial insemination rather than actual copulation? If not, we would be here forever, or you would have to take my menfolk prisoner."

Uuvla, confirmed Blink's theory. "If your chaps are deemed suitable, then all we require is a deposit in a sealed container. No mess, no fuss and the best of all, no drama. The rest we can do in the small laboratory, and before you know it, we will have an increased population. At present, we have some males on the island, but they are still too young to take part. Once your crews' contribution is added to theirs, then we think we should have enough active variables to sustain a healthy population."

Blink watched as all the equipment was brought out and put in place. She noticed the small tents currently being erected at the end of the pier.

Uuvla, noticed her interest, "Oh, don't you worry about them after the meal, the guys can pop in and deposit the required sample." She continued, "All going well, your boats will be fully resupplied and fuelled first thing in the morning, all ready to go."

Blink noticed her crew now climbing onto the pier, excused herself to go and meet them. She delivered the information to Sekoyaz, who does not fully understand. Blink explained the test-tube baby routine, accompanied with the rudimentary hand movements Sekoyaz could hardly believe it and asked Blink if that was really how they did it. Blink confirmed that this is the way they do it here. Sekoyaz was given the daunting task of explaining to the guys the type of tip they have to leave behind in appreciation of the meal. Sekoyaz was also given the nod to keep an eye on things. They were both aware that some things that appear nice and comforting are nothing but deceptive illusions in a carefully planned manoeuvre to distract one as far away as possible from the true picture.

Uuvla, welcomed Blink back to the table and asked her if all was good. She replied that everything was just fine and added that she, along with all of her crew, were absolutely famished and hoped that the food would arrive soon. Uuvla, assured her the sumptuous banquet being held in their honour would be served shortly. Blink did not know for sure what this woman was up to, but the longer this charade continued, the more the hairs on the back of her neck stood up. Blink was still watching the older woman sitting opposite her like a hawk. Uuvla, was cool, calm, all present and correct. Sitting there, all smiles and welcoming. Blink thought that if she asked her the question, the woman in front of her would without a moment's hesitation swear on all things holy that her shit did not even smell.

Like a well-oiled mechanised assembly line, Uuvla's people marched towards them with the generously piled salvers of food. The brightly coloured ornate plant table decorations add to the splendidly displayed fare on offer. Blink could hear her people thanking them, issuing very complimentary remarks about the food on offer to the staff who had delivered the banquet to their tables. Blink stood and offered a toast to Uuvla and her people for the more than generous display that was on offer. Blink informed her host that she and her crew could not possibly eat all of what was placed in front of them. "In this day and age, it would be viewed as an unforgivable mortal sin to leave food uneaten, to leave good food that would feed many to go to waste. I would like Uuvla, and her people to come and join us in this feast." Uuvla, was momentarily lost for words, but her facial expression was as clear as day and there was no intention of either her or her people joining in. Blink stared her out while Uuvla, searched for the words. While she was patiently waiting for a suitable reply, Blink raised her left hand and the all-motor launches simultaneously fired up their engines, and moved into a defensive position.

Blink gave Sekoyaz the signal, and she withdrew all of their crew to the end of the pier. Now having the distinct feeling that this is not going to end well, Blink continued her little speech. "Unlike the last owners of the boats, we were not stupid, and they may have seen things in black and white, where we see things in vivid colour. If any of your group made one step towards us, the guns on the boats will eliminate all of you." Blink stepped forward, put the knife to Uuvla's throat, and turned her around to face her own people.

Blink informed her to order her people to deliver the fuel for the boats. Uuvla, did not even try and stood defiantly, refusing to issue the order. Blink quickly turned her head to check if her people had all boarded the boats. In the brief seconds that she had taken her eyes off of Uuvla, her people had started to move on mass towards her. Blink slit the woman's throat then pushed her bleeding corpse towards her people. She ran towards the end of the pier and dived into the water. Sekoyaz noticed her leader's predicament at once and ordered one of the motor launches to move to the centre of the pier and the other two into positions covering the left and right. As Uuvla's people produced weapons and started to fire at Blink in the water, Sekoyaz ordered the paired machine guns on all boats to open fire. The .50 calibre bullets ripped the pier and the people to shreds. Blink was pulled onboard the centre boat, and the three motor launches continued to fire until all visible movement had ceased.

She waved to Sekoyaz and indicated that she was unharmed, then informed her that they were going back to claim the previously promised fuel and provisions. She had no idea what Uuvla's end game in all of this was meant to achieve, but whatever the plan, it had failed miserably. The motor launches got as close to the beach as possible, and Blink's crew waded the remaining distance to the shore. This time, they were all fully armed, ready to deal with any arising issues. Sekoyaz detailed a squad to go and deal with the mass of dead bodies on the pier. They were ordered to search them, then to dispose of the dead and the dying into the water. The last time they had tried to be civilised in holding prayers for the deceased, it had never quite turned out the way they had expected. The general opinion among them now was, why take the chance in the first place? The bodies being exposed to the heat would start to rot immediately; the quicker they get rid of them, the better.

Blink led her crew towards the various buildings, one or two armed residents were cut down in the brief of machine gun fire, prior to issuing a challenge. Her crew spread out and started to search the buildings. Some sporadic gunfire can be heard as various buildings were still occupied or being defended by armed female residents. It did not take long before the all clear was issued. Blink wanted to know if all of her people were safe and sound. Sekoyaz reported back that all of the crew are accounted for, adding that they have suffered no casualties. One of the crew shouts over to attract their attention. A prison block had been located, and the crew member thought that they should come to see for themselves what was inside.

Sekoyaz arrived first, and she was shocked and dismayed at what lay before her. Blink arrived shortly afterwards and noticed the worried look on her second in command's face.

She knew that something was not quite right. Uuvla, and her supporters did, after all, have a contingency of the male population; unfortunately, they were all prisoners. Blink requested that all of the prisoners be released from captivity, as some of them were in need of medical attention, and she ordered them to be taken care of. The men had been beaten, and all of them were suffering from malnutrition. At first, all of them were reticent to speak, but as they witnessed all of the cell doors being opened up, then as their fellow males received medical care and attention, they started to open up.

The story about what had transpired on this island started to unfold. After the disease arrived, Uuvla, had taken control of the survivors. Then, after many gender-related speeches. She had subsequently blamed the previous all-male government for being solely responsible for all of the wrongs in her their life. She ordained that no male should ever again be allowed to attain a position of authority. She stipulated that if the men wished to live in this new world, they should be kept in cages and treated like animals that all of their gender truly deserved.

Many of the prisoners had openly declared that they had done nothing at all to deserve this type of treatment. The only thing that they were all guilty of was being born a man. That was more than enough to get them incarcerated for life without parole. If they worked, they were fed; if they got too old or became unfit to work, they perished. Uuvla's regime was totally unforgiving, and no man was allowed to speak to a woman without first being given permission and failure to obey this rule resulted in severe punishment. One man with a badly healed leg was punished for allegedly looking at Uuvla, 's toes. He recalled that during his show trial, his crime was classified as an uncontrollable desire for wanton male sexual gratification. He was allowed no defence in the hearing, and the jury consisted of Uuvla's most ardent followers. John was rewarded with a broken leg for his alleged crime, which was never set properly and resulted in a limp that he would now have for the rest of his life.

Blink had got some of her crew to prepare a meal for the badly underweight ex-prisoners. She had told her crew that if any of the recipients of the meal were hesitant to eat that they should grab a plateful themselves to prove that it was okay to eat. One of Sekoyazs' team had found all the packets of heavy-duty painkillers that had been added to their welcoming meal. Uuvla's grand plan must have been that once Blink and her crew were sound asleep, she would have divided up the ranks, the males were going to prison, and perhaps even imprisoning or disposing of the females who refused to co-operate in the madness. Blink took time to reassure all of the newly released prisoners that Uuvla, along with her diehard supporters, were gone forever. She also pointed out that she was not here to take over where Uuvla had left off, and as soon as they refuelled, they would be leaving.

John, who seemed to have been appointed the leader, asked what were they meant to do. Blink replied that they will have to do whatever it takes to survive. John stated for the record that there were no women here, and eventually, the population on the island will die off. Blink informed him that he and his group can either stay here or take a vote to leave. John asked if that meant that if they wanted to leave, she would take them away on her boats to somewhere nicer. Blink told John to hold up right there, "We have rescued you, then freed you all from your imprisonment. We don't have room on the boats for any extra passengers. I am sure that there must be some other boats stashed somewhere on this island. All you have to do is find them; there is an abundance of food growing, and by the look of the spread, your recently demised leader put on display an ample supply of domesticated livestock. You and yours do not need me nor mine to help in any way. We are leaving and wish you all good luck. There may be women and other people inhabiting the nearby islands who were scrapping out a day-to-day existence. They may even want to come and join you in this paradise, but that avenue you will have to investigate for yourselves."

Sekoyaz approached and informed Blink that they had bunkered the fuel, replenished the drinking water, food and ammunition. Blink gathered her people up and informed them that it was time to leave. She shook John's hand and wished him and all of the people good luck, and left. Once aboard her motor launch, Blink set the course for the next island. She did not wish that it were completely uninhabited; whatever awaited them, no matter how dangerous or inhospitable, her crew would cope.

Across the other side of the Atlantic, Gareth was at the helm. He had agreed or thought that he had most likely been conned by Leena to take control for a shift. The captain had told him that she was plum worn out and needed a rest. Gareth thought that Leena had promised something wonderful in return as a just reward, but he was not one hundred percent sure. Perhaps it was only his imagination that had red-lined and then entered into overdrive. For several days now, they had been sailing up the west coast of Scotland. The engines were performing as they should be, surprisingly, even the diesel monkeys have not issued any imminent warnings about any of the important equipment being on its last legs, about ready to break down.

Cinds, armed with tea along with the obligatory nutritious delights, had just entered the bridge. Gareth asked if that was the double cheese with Azari red onions and the quadrupled filtered latte with the Himalayan Mountain goat's milk. Cinds' informed him that he can have what everybody else is eating, unless he can perform a vault through time. She dumps his food on the desk, adding, "If you can, could you get me a few portions of French fries and four double cheeseburgers. Alwyn is driving me nuts about this and all of the other food that he badly misses."

Gareth promised her that he would find out where the special suit is stored. That would enable him to travel back to when things were normal, and she would be the first to know. He did not look at what culinary delights were on offer, and it was lamb, the same as it was yesterday, no doubt it would be more than likely the same tomorrow. Gareth asked if his adopted grandsons, Bob and Ed, had managed to say any words yet.

Cinds' shook her head as he knew dam well fine that they were still way too young to even attempt to speak. She asked him if he had visited his grandsons recently, and could he tell the difference between the pair of them. Gareth answered a definite no to both of the questions, confessing that he was really only enquiring about their general health and well-being.

Cinds' took the helm and allowed Gareth to eat while the food was reasonably warmish. She updated the info as he stuffed his face. Both mothers had just about fully recovered and were up on their feet. "Do you remember their names?" Gareth, now with a mouth full of food, shook his head and indicated that his reply was, as per normal, a most definite no. Cinds' was going to ask him if he knew her name, but decided against it.

She changed the subject and asked Gareth if he had a chart available to give a rough indication of where they were. Cinds' pointed to the shore, "It was either a huge inlet, or we had reached the top of Scotland. I would suggest that we find someone who can read a chart or start asking the passengers how many had booked for an all-around exclusive trip to Iceland." Gareth had a look at the landfall and, on seeing the lighthouse on the very edge of the finger of land, and agreed that they should had someone come and advise. As much as he did not want to disturb Leena, Gareth felt that he should seek her expert advice. "Okay, Cinds, I guess that I would have to go and inform the captain," Cinds told him not to bother and stood at attention as Leena entered the bridge. Leena asked Cinds if Gareth had put her up to this. Cinds' still standing at attention, replied, "No, Captain sir, it was all my own idea."

Leena dismissed her and informed Cinds that she was so full of shit that you could easily smell it a hundred miles away. Gareth still had his eyes glued onto the binoculars, looking for any tell-tale clues on the landfall to indicate where exactly they were. Leena asked if it would be okay if she could be allowed a view of the headland. Gareth handed over the vison-aid and stood at ease. Leena asked him to give her some space, indicating that he should stand over beside the other trainee sea cadet. She looked at Gareth almost issuing him with a dare to salute. He moved away without any of the formality and smirked, and he stood at ease with Cinds'. As she scanned the horizon, she informed them that the pair of them were most definitely not funny, but she would forgive them if a hot brew arrived in five minutes.

Captain Leena informed Gareth that they had completed the easy part of the voyage. As they had passed all of the island's west coast, they were now at the top of Scotland, and if all went well, they would had fair weather to pass through the Pentland firth. Gareth asked her how dangerous it could be. Leena, not taking her eyes from the weather, told him that on a scale of one to ten this stretch of water can easily be a fifteen. Captain Leena continued, "One minute, it could be fine and then, without any warning, it can turn instantly into a nightmare. Gareth, please go down to the dungeon dwellers and ask them to give us every ounce of power available. It was better that we go through this at full steam ahead. The quicker we pass through, the quicker we get it out of the way." Gareth saluted as he passed Cinds' on the way to the engine room. Cinds' now on the bridge, asked Leena why Gareth was so happy all of a sudden. "Oh, nothing really, but perhaps it was because we were now at the top of Scotland, and one way or another, we would all be going onshore pretty soon."

The women talked about how they still had no real idea where they were going or if they would actually find any of the groups that Gareth had hoped to join up with. Leena confessed to Cinds' "Even if we find a group; there was no guarantee that they would welcome us in and permit us to join their community. It was not as if we had been in contact with them, and they had issued an open invitation to come and join them. At this moment we do not know if they even actually exist, and if they do, nor do they know of our existence." Cinds assured Leena that all would turn out well, "Gareth took control of the group we were with when no one wanted the job. He had looked after and protected us all during the bad times. He saved many lives and built up our community out of nothing. Seriously, Leena, if there were people there, Gareth would be able to talk to them. If there was no community there to join up with, Gareth would come up with another plan, and with this, he would make sure that we all had a fair chance at surviving whatever was in front of us."

Leena added, "Well if that was the case and we really don't know what was actually there, the quicker we arrive, the sooner we would find out. Cinds' another brew and some scran would be wonderful, and Cinds' please, no more saluting or standing at ease waiting for the admiral to issue instructions to load the eighteen pounders and get ready for boarding." Cinds agreed to her wishes, then left to go and fetch the grub. Leena felt the change in vibration and indicated that Gareth had delivered the message for the diesel monkeys to turn up the volume to eleven.

Captain Leena studied the charts in front of her, then made a slight course change. She hoped that they would manage to complete the dangerous crossing before nightfall. Every sailor who has crossed this stretch of water thought that it was cursed, with the strong currents and the violent storms that can appear out of nowhere. These waters had claimed many lives and many ships over centuries, and Leena had no intention of this ship, along with all the crew, being added to the lost at sea statistics. Gareth had arrived back on the bridge; he handed over a hot brew. "Thought you might need this." Leena asked, "No salute this time?" Gareth explained that Cinds had made him do it and added that she would get stroppy if he did not play along.

Leena explained where they were she showed him the plotted course on the charts. "Gareth, this was us now at the top of Scotland; sooner or later, we would be heading inland." Gareth knew that there was more to come and waited for Leena to continue. "We had no idea if there would be any group here or if they were even willing to let us stay. Please tell me that if none of this works out, that you had an alternative plan." Gareth told her straight up that he did not know if there was a group up here. If there was a group, there were no guarantees that they would speak to us, never mind let us join them. But even if there was no one there, even if there was, they decided not to listen or take us on. Then, at the very least, we had tried to join up and take on the invaders. If all failed, there would not be enough of us to take the invaders on. I guess that would mean that we would have to set sail for some foreign land. Even at that, there would be no guarantee that things would be any different there." He took her hand, "Leena, I know there will be people there; once they listen to what I tell them, they would let us in. All we have to do is find them, and the rest will be easy."

The captain took him at his word but informed him that they would not be able to search forever, and at some point, if nothing was found, they would have to make a decision. "Gareth, between us, we were responsible for lots of people; we had to give them hope, and we had to take care of them. Just remember that, before you make any decisions that we may all live to regret." He promised her that everything would work out fine and assured her that if he had any doubts, he would let her know as soon as possible. They sailed on for the full day and steamed as fast as possible through the firth. At the end of the day, Leena calculated that they were now about at the top of the northeast coast. She intended that they stop for the night, then ordered a full stop on all engines and dropped the anchor. Leena and Gareth were fast asleep in their cabin when just after dawn. One of the crew knocked on the door and informed them that they had just spotted a fishing vessel that was heading towards land, possibly it was returning towards the homeport.

Chapter 16

Uno, accompanied by his two unexpected passengers, had made great time travelling up north. As the vehicle ate up the miles, he had seen no one following them, nor had they come across any hostile natives. His passengers had not really said much in the way of conversation. When truth came to shove the old man had uttered the odd grunt here and there. This usually occurred when a toilet stop or a stretch-the-legs stop was required. The little girl did not speak to Uno at all; anything that she said was passed on via the old man in their private whisper mode. From the very start of their journey, this was the way that their conversations had progressed. Uno had tried very hard to get some rapport going, but it was a fruitless exercise. He had asked the old man his name, who had replied, "Macdhiarmada, do you want me to fucking spell it out for you?" Uno had initially wanted to stop the vehicle, with the intention of asking the pair of them to get the fuck out. Uno had changed his mind and asked the old man if he had a nickname. Macdhiarmada had amazed him with his reply, "You could call me Bryan if you really have to." Uno instantly surrendered, giving up any further attempt to try an establish a conversation. If he had a sound machine onboard, it would now be blasting out at full volume.

At several points during the journey where there was a choice of direction, the little girl had, through grumpy chops, advised which way to travel. Uno never asked why or how; she just seemed to know the way. If the truth be known both of them freaked him out some, it was not the fact that they were odd. This alone was saying something, as the swamp people had some weird and wonderful ways. Not to mention the varied assortment of weird and wonderful people. These two, residing in the back of the vehicle, would have without even a mere morsal of doubt freaked out the whole of the now-dead-and-gone community.

Most of the time, they were asleep or as Uno suspected, they were pretending to be sleeping. He thought it was strange that they always appeared to wake up every time they arrived at a road junction. Then proceeded to inform him in that matter-of-fact way, in which direction to continue. The one time that stood out as a complete freak out in his memory was when he was advised to turn off at the next left. It was no more than an overgrown country track; he had asked them if they were sure that this was the road to take. Uno was astonished when Bryan Mac, whatever the fuck his name was, coldly informed him that there was a storm coming and as the wipers did not work. They would all be safer to rest for a couple of days. Uno, not having any of it, pulled the lever and much to his surprise the windscreen wipers never even moved. He accepted the result, never even attempting to fathom out how they knew about the mechanical malfunction.

Eventually, the vehicle had pushed its way through the nearly impassable undergrowth and arrived at a little dilapidated shack. Bryan informed Uno that they had arrived and then requested that he stop the vehicle. The old man and the little girl just sat in the back, looking at Uno. He eventually caught on that he had to go out and check that the shack was safe to enter. This, he thought was odd? they had told him about the storm, then about the wipers, but strangely enough, he had to go and check that the house was safe. Uno took the safety off the weapon, then cautiously walked towards the dwelling. He checked around the house and, upon seeing no signs of recent habitation, entered the abode. The interior was devoid of any former dead occupants, a little on the dusty side but fit enough for a temporary stopover. Uno opened the front door, giving them the signal that all was good and it was safe to enter.

The old man, accompanied by his equally strange companion, exited the vehicle, making their way into the house. Uno melted into one of the big comfy chairs, rescued the makings from his pocket and rattled together a homemade cigarette. He was just about to spark it up when Bryan informed him that he should not get too settled as they needed firewood. Uno looked at him, just about to deliver the slave for today's speech. When Macdhiarmada confided in him that if he could kindly gather the material for the fire, he would go out and arrange something for dinner. Uno, not wishing to pursue any additional conversation, nor having the energy to argue over the finer points and without offering any form of resistance, agreed and then went outside.

He had been gathering the sticks and then piled them at the door for quite a while. Uno thought that he had supplied enough to keep the fire going for some time and sat and lit up his homemade cigarette. He had only taken the first draw when Macdhiarmada returned from his excursion. Uno thought that Bryan had no weapons and had perhaps conjured the rabbits into jumping into his arms. Macdhiarmada looked at the pile of wood and shook his head. "Did you forget that there was a storm coming? It would be easier if you were to collect more wood while it was still dry." Uno had listened to what old misery guts had told him. Several times, he looked up at the sky. It was a bright blue sky with not a cloud in sight.

If it was not for the fact that he was starving, Uno would have jumped back in the car, leaving them there and then. Now more than a little miffed at his mysterious passengers' behaviour, he collected more wood until he was informed that dinner was ready. Macdhiarmada had somehow managed to cook the animals over the open fire. Uno did not complain; it was not the best meal that he had ever tasted, but it was more than sufficient to fill his empty belly. Macdhiarmada supplied Uno with a bottle of beer that had an unreadable label to wash the meal down.

The storm suddenly appeared right out of nowhere. Uno, in the big, comfy chair, struggled to keep his eyes open and fell fast asleep as the rain battered unrelentingly against the windows and the corrugated tin roof. When he woke up, Uno was as stiff as five-week-old socks. The old bastard that he was an unpaid acting chauffeur to, informed Uno that he snored like a pig and smelled like a well-seasoned community cesspit. He thought that perhaps during his period of absence, the ancient one had formed a committee to rigorously uphold the expected standards of suitable attire and personal grooming techniques.

Uno was going to inform the newly self-elected cleanliness invigilator that his people had been eliminated, and during the rush to escape he had been rather inconsiderate in forgetting to pack a change of clothes along with his bag of assorted boutique grooming accessories. Now extremely pissed off at the ungrateful old fuckers' attitude. Uno stripped off, emptied his pockets, and marched outside into the rain. He deliberately stood in full view and washed himself and all of his clothes in the torrential rain. Although he knew that it was childish, Uno made a point of attempting to squeeze all the water out of his clothes before putting them back on. Now fully dressed and ready for inspection, he stormed back into the house.

Macdhiarmada and the little girl just looked at the nutjob in front of them. Uno informed them that he hoped that he had passed the inspection. Macdhiarmada's face showed nothing, "Your clothes would dry quicker if you had placed them in front of the fire." Uno stared at the cantankerous old bastard, "They would dry quicker if I keep them on." He rattled a number together, then stood facing the fire and remembered to rotate himself approximately every fifteen minutes.

In the morning, he found himself all on his own. His rather difficult to get on with passengers were absent. Uno spotted the food and drink that had, and he assumed, been left out for him. He was still fucked off at both of them, especially at the old fuckers' attitude. Uno put his pride away and devoured the gift from his missing passengers. He would like to ask them how much longer the journey was going to last, and on the other hand he would just like to get in the vehicle then drive away. Uno just couldn't figure out what to do. His previous leader, Tally, would have just run them over at the initial meeting. Although it would have been tempting, he knew that it would had just not been the right thing to do under any circumstances. He settled on the idea that he would take them up north, and after that, they could do their own thing. Uno had to deliver a message to the woman who ran naked through the forest. He did not know, nor did he care, why they wished to travel in the same general direction.

Noticing that the weather had changed and it was no longer pissing it down from the heavens. He sat outside smoking, wondering if and when his non-talkative passengers were going to show up. Uno was now thinking, even if it was fundamentally not correct if they did not show by the time he finished smoking, he was going continue the journey without them. The squeaking noise of the window being rolled down in the back of his vehicle gave the game away. Macdhiarmada, full of his charismatic morning charm, shouted, "Whenever you 're ready, we could continue our journey sometime today." Uno, not in the mood to listen to any more shit from the old reprobate stared straight at him. He lit up another homemade cigarette from the end of the one he had just finished and then proceeded to crack open the emergency tin of fizzy juice.

For the final act of defiance, Uno covered both of his eyes with his hands and then covered both ears and then delivered stereo middle fingers. "When I finish my juice and my smoke, I would top up the tank, and then we would be ready to go," Macdhiarmada informed him that the tank had been already topped up. Uno shrugged his shoulders, "We will leave when I am ready. If you are not happy with that, I can hand over the keys, and you can go without me. Either way, I am not moving until I finish." Macdhiarmada muttered something that Uno couldn't quite make out, something along the lines of twisted, stubborn mother fucker. Uno smiled as he heard the window being rolled back up and was pleased with the fact that at least he would get to finish his breakfast in relative peace and quiet.

Uno was now happy that, if anything, at the end of today, he would be one day closer to his final destination. If this was the passenger's termination point, then that was fine, and if it was not, well, that was just tough shit and no longer his problem. The vehicle took a little persuading before it started, but Uno spoke nice to the machine. He saw

Macdhiarmada and glared at him in the mirror before the war of words erupted, and the vehicle finally coughed into life. The old bastard promptly pretended to fall back asleep as Uno manoeuvred the near scrapyard-grade vehicle backwards and forwards to get into the exit position. He drove carefully through the overgrown bushes that had attempted over years of neglect to reclaim the road. The vehicle stopped before venturing onto the main road. Macdhiarmada asked why they had come to a halt. Uno curtly informed his passengers, "As I am not the fucking resident clairvoyant, I thought that at the very least you could inform me whether to take a right or to take a left."

Macdhiarmada spurted out, "Take a fucking right." Uno replied, "Thanks, very fucking much," then accelerated as soon as the wheels touched the tarred surface. He thought about asking them to play "eye-spy," but a grumpy old bastard who pretended to be asleep all of the time would take way too long to supply his guesses. Uno got settled in for the long day ahead, and he hoped Rubthadug was doing well and that, after all this time, he would remember him from the old days. Rubthadug had left the settlement to go up north after they had rid the land of the evil people. Uno now had the task of informing Rubthadug, along with the group that he now stayed with, that there was an army coming to get them.

He hoped deep down that the people had left the area, even perhaps that they had left the country. In the event that he did find them, he must tell them that it would be better to die in battle than to be captured.

The woman who ran through the forest naked would listen to him. She would understand. Rubthadug would listen, but Uno was not too sure if he would understand the risks involved. Sure, Rubthadug had been in lots of battles with tribes similar to the swamp people, but never against a fully equipped army. The worst possible thing that could happen would be that he would arrive there too late to warn them. Uno squeezed a little more power out of the vehicle. If the passengers noticed they never let on. The roads were empty. Either they had all been cleared, or no one had used them. Occasionally, he slowed down to pass by an old wreck or squeeze between a couple of abandoned vehicles. Misery-guts in the back, had just spoken to inform him to take a left at the next junction. Uno intentionally pissed him off by switching on the indicator early, then switching it off late.

As far as Uno was concerned, little pleasures don't come very often in this world. He thought that he was fully entitled to piss off the old fucker in the back of the vehicle as often as he could. Uno sneezed and was unable to get his hand to cover his mouth in time, and the snot decorated the inside of the windscreen. It was totally unintentional; Uno was mortified, and just as he was about to apologise when Macdhiarmada, the moaner, started to complain. "You really are a piece of shit, anyone else would have put their hand over to curtail the spread of the germs. Going by your appearance and your extremely lackadaisical approach to life, fuck knows what fucking germicides you had exposed us to with spreading your ultra-infested snot in this confined space."

Uno switched on the hazard warning lights, pressed the brake pedal and pulled over to a stop. He turned around in his seat, taking great pleasure in wiping his snot-covered face with the sleeve of his jacket. "Ahh, I needed that. Now you listen, and you listen well. The sneeze came out of nowhere, and I guess it was a summer cold. If not, we would all be dying already. This was your last chance; I am sick of your fucking attitude. Where you treat me as your unpaid fucking tour guide whose sole purpose in life was to drive you from A to B without any of the normal day-to-day niceties that you seem to had fucking forgotten all about. If you were unhappy with the service provided, you can get out now and fucking walk. From now on, I would appreciate a left, please, a right, please or even a 'Could you please pull over.' That was all I request, nothing more, nothing less."

Macdhiarmada stared at him, and he was about to say something when the little girl crept in close to him and then whispered something. "Could you please continue to drive straight ahead? Thank you." Uno muttered something about him being a self-centred, ungrateful mother fucker, flipped on the indicator and continued to drive. They made good time for several miles then the number of abandoned dead vehicles gradually started to fill up the road and reduced their speed to almost a crawl. Uno constantly weaved in and out of the static traffic, forever searching for a suitable space to squeeze past. After a considerable time, he announced to no one in particular that this was a futile exercise. "Sooner or later, we were going to had to abandon the vehicle and start walking." The vehicle was soon after stuck, merged into a mess that looked as if it continued forever.

Uno switched off the engine. As he rolled a cigarette, the other two didn't say a word and just sat there in silence. When he finished the job in his hand, Uno stretched down and pulled the lever to open the bonnet and the boot. There was no point in discussing what needed to be done. Uno lights up and then searched in the boot for the tools to disconnect the battery. After what seemed like forever, he had stowed the power source and the other bits and pieces that were needed into the rucksack. Not wanting the old man and the little girl to think that he was a complete arsehole, he handed them two bottles of water. Uno was going to inform the couple that it had been an absolute pleasure travelling with them. Not really wanting to lie to them, nor wanting to spoil the day, he waved them bye-bye and walked away.

Where they would go or how they would get there, he did not care. Uno had had enough of them, and if he was going to be really honest about it, they were about the strangest people he had ever met. The swamp people had, over the years, attracted its fair share of nutters, undesirables and eccentrics. The two specimens that he had just left behind fell into their own unique category. Uno did not hear them getting out of the car, and maybe they were under the impression that he was going to return and get them. That was a big mistake on their behalf; he was off and had no intentions whatsoever of even looking back, nevermind going back to get them. With every step a step farther away from them he marched forward.

Then he heard the little girl screaming, without hesitation he dropped off his backpack and then retrieved his weapon. Uno took the safety off and cursed as he walked back towards them. He really thought that this was going to be a pleasant day, with no one criticizing his every move and questioning every syllable that he uttered. Uno checked that the weapon had one in the pipe ready to go, then walked a wee bit quicker back towards where he had last seen his favourite couple. He fished out and fitted the suppressor before he got too close. It was one thing to shoot someone, then again, another thing entirely different to announce to everyone and their dog in the vicinity you had just shot someone. One could not be too careful these days, as just like the old days someone always wanted something for nothing.

There were three of them. Two were harassing the old man, and the bravest one was questioning the little girl. They noticed him approach, and the little girl was dragged over and deposited with the pair that were holding the old man. The leader looked as if he should be flying out to a country in the Mediterranean to get a completely new set of gnashers. Uno had spotted an orphan off-white one in amongst the multi coloured assortment currently inhabiting his gob. Uno stood still with his hands behind his back as the leader approached. "The old days were gone, and in these new days, one had to do what one had to do to survive. I would suggest that you fuck off, turn back around and mind your own business." Uno just ignored him and took another few steps forward. Now that he was closer, he thought that the leader could forget about a new set of enamels and just opt for a new head. He was covered in open sores, and his skin was a funny colour, and the smell was almost overpowering.

Uno took a step back, and the leader thought that he was in charge and delivered another statement. "That right, you just keep walking and get to fuck away from me. This is our turf, and now you just fuck off back to whatever hole in the ground that you crawled out off. Now go on, scaddle out of here before I have to show you who was the boss around here." By this time, he had stepped forward, puffing out his chest out and pointing as he spoke. Uno calmly brings the gun out front and puts one in the leader's head. The two holding his ex-passengers didn't know what to do. While they were running through the various options, Uno walked forward and delivered a single shot in each of their brains. He looked at the slightly ruffled couple, "I am going now. I don't possess enough bullets to continue coming back to rescue you, so I would suggest that if you were coming, you should get a move on." Uno turned around and then started to walk back away to pick up his backpack and restart his journey.

He knew that he was stuck with them now. He just wishes that they would perhaps talk to him like he was a normal human being. Out of all the things that had disappeared when the world changed, he missed the art of conversation. Uno remembered living on the web, talking to people all over the planet. Now, here he was, stuck with an old man and a young girl who hardly said a single word. Now that he had saved them from the bad guys, perhaps they would open up and then maybe say a few words every once in a while. Uno charged on and hoped that the sea of dead and redundant traffic would finally ease off, giving him the opportunity to acquire a new carriage.

He walked on, and this time, for some strange reason, he looked behind him every once in a while, just to check that the couple was actually following him. Uno weaved in and out of the already rusting beyond recognition collection of abandoned cars that stretched for as far as he could see. The light was starting to fade and as he did not want his passengers roaming about in the dark, Uno now started to find them somewhere suitable to safely bunk up for the night. As there were no buildings of any sort within the vicinity, Uno was thinking that they would have to sleep in a vehicle. All he had to do was find a reasonably clean one, and perhaps a mini-bus or some sort of van would do. He had already started rummaging in a few vehicles and gathered up some food and liquid. These he had chucked into his getting heavier-by-the-minute rucksack.

By the time they had caught up with him, he had the accommodation all sorted and ready. It was not as per say a luxurious five-star, with all of the trimmings overnight stay, but for now, it would do. The van had been abandoned in a reasonably clean state. All he had to do was remove the long-dead occupants from the front seats and supply a few travel rugs. These, he thought, would keep the couple warm. If not, they could always go and search for additional coverings that would be readily available in the abundant dormant vehicles. Uno welcomed them to their temporary abode, pointing to the selection of tins he asked them to take their pick. As none of them had any translatable labels, they could contain anything. Uno thought that at least some of them should contain human delicacies, and if they were really unlucky, they could be hiding premium cat or bargain basement dog food.

He had checked the cans and then discarded the ones that were rusty and the ones that were severely bashed. The sell-by dates were no longer applicable and thus were no longer part of the equation. As he was resolutely sure that the manufacturers blasted them with radiation prior to releasing them to be consumed by the general public. A few weeks, a few months, or a few years won't really matter; as long as the contents were not black and smelly, they would be edible. Uno looked at them and wondered why they had not selected dinner; the old man informed Uno that he needed a tin opener.

Uno thought that he was going to have to apologise for the a-la-carte selection not being available this evening. Ignoring his previous thought, he produced had wonder tool. Then proceeded to show thcm how to open the tin with a spoon. Uno was delighted with himself, and if he had to display any more of these ad-hoc demonstrations, he could perhaps be a master-class chef. The old man and the young girl looked at him as they surveyed the newly revealed contents of the tin. By the looks and the smell of it, the displayed semi-solid pinkish flesh could be cat food or some type of fish. Uno, not being too fussy, assumed ownership of the uncertain foodstuff and scooped it out of the tin into his mouth. "I think it was fish, not too sure what type, but it was definitely not cat food."

The odd couple just continued to stare at him and the remaining selection of tins. Uno informed them that just to help themselves, as he had been reliably informed that he snored like a pig, he would source out alternative accommodation. Uno assured them that they would be safe and not to worry as he would be nearby should they require his assistance. As usual, they had said just about nothing.

Uno wondered why he had bothered to save them. He grabbed his rucksack, bid them a good night, then walked away.

Initially he had intended to keep on walking, but the better half of his soul got a grip on him, warning his conscience that if he had done this, he would only regret his action forever. A hundred yards up the road, he started checking for a suitable vehicle. The first one he found was fine; the bones wrapped up in clothes were ejected. Uno treated himself to a handmade cigarette, adjusted the seat into relaxation mode and puffed away. He wondered what delights they would face tomorrow. Hopefully, the new vehicle was not that far away, as he was getting tired of lugging the heavy rucksack every step of the way.

He must had fallen asleep pretty easily as he, emerging from the Christmas dream from a gentle tap on the windscreen. As he slowly opened his eyes, Uno moved the weapon to line up with his vision and looked out the window. The old man and the little girl were standing there, and much to his surprise they were bearing gifts. Uno opened the door, and at first, he was a trifle disappointed that they were not bearing gifts of Frankincense, myrrh and gold. On accepting the alternative presents, the odd couple informed him that they were going to keep on walking. He watched them walk away, and if he was indeed a dog, he would now be licking his lips, wagging his tail in anticipation of the savoury delights stored in the can. The tin of foodstuff was launched over his shoulder into the back of the vehicle. The once tin of red-coloured fizzy juice was examined. The corrosion on the base was quite extensive. As he did not have the constitution of a shark's stomach, the tin of fizzy was unceremoniously sent to join the dog food. Uno removed a bottle of water from the backpack, sparked up a smoke and then set off to overtake them and take pole position. It was very nice of them supplying breakfast but if he had consumed the offerings, Uno was sure that food poisoning would have been the least of his worries. He would lie through his teeth when he caught up with them and declared that the breakfast was wonderful. Maybe the next time, Uno would just tell them that he had already eaten. He easily reached them, and already there was good news, Uno spotted a clearing in the distance. He roughly calculated that by around lunchtime; they could be the proud owners of a newish vehicle.

Macdhiarmada had also spotted the break in the traffic. He pointed and informed Uno that the little one had told him that they were nearly there. "She also told me that the people you seek would be pleased to see you, but you had to be careful as you approach their territory. Lots of things had changed since you last saw them, and they, like everyone else in this cursed life, had to take precautions." Uno wondered how Macdhiarmada could say this and look totally convinced. Uno had said very little about who he was going to try and find. The more he thought about he had said almost nothing about his friends and he did not know where they were located. Now, all of a sudden, they knew where they were going and also knew who he was going to meet. Perhaps they had consumed some contaminated food, and their dreams were in hyper-mode, hallucinating the answers prior to being asked the questions.

Uno couldn't wait to get in the next vehicle and couldn't wait till he dropped them off. As of yet the couple had given him no indication, no clues of their final destination. Wherever it was, he hoped it was near, and more than that, he wished that it was soon. Uno marched ahead with the mindset of driving as far as possible for the rest of the day. The one thing he was not looking forward to was the syphoning of the foul liquid. He had always been hopeless at this task. Every time that Uno had attempted it in the past, he had always ended up swallowing the fuel. He must remember to remove the hose from his mouth before the gas flows through the tube. Otherwise, he would be vomiting for hours on end. Uno did not think the old man or the young girl would be any better at performing this task, so he would just have to take his time and be careful not to swallow the once premium-grade octane-loaded fuel.

At the other end of the country, five hundred miles away, it was all business. After she had forwarded the two-letter, two-number encrypted message the Baroness had set about having the debris cleared from the runway. The main terminal at the capital's airport was beyond a doubt unrecoverable, damaged way beyond repair. Where the aeroplanes had once all neatly lined up, ready to take on passengers and cargo, was now in complete disarray. Several aircraft were now embedded into the structure of the terminal; a result of the would-be pilots not quite having mastered the finer art of getting off the ground.

The departure gates were equally messed up, with hundreds of dead passengers. Some with their tickets firmly grasped in their now skeletal fingers were still patiently waiting to breathe a sigh of relief at the announcement to commence boarding. Lesqueth wondered how long they had waited, hoping that they would be safe once they had fastened the seat belts and the plane was taxing to the runway. She thought that was a genetic trait of these primitive bipeds, to still be full of eternal optimism even when everything was dead and dying all around you.

The Baroness of Kindeace-Shire had gathered up every available body to sweep clean the runway. Once they got to the end, they would be forced to start all over again. They would all do this exercise right up until the last possible minute, and she was taking no chances. All it would take was one discarded nut or bolt, and then disaster would be upon them. Everything that she had worked for, everything that her family had fought for would be gone. Tesporo, the current, still living keeper of the records, had been warned that he, along with his braindead followers, would be held accountable for any mishaps. Lesqueth watched as the white-upon-white walked behind the droves of sweepers and rechecked every millimetre of the runway.

With Miasnikov away on a mission to finally erase the remaining fragments of the Hidden and with the unexpected demise of John Josiah Atkin. Lesqueth had revised the game plan, changing all the previous arrangements and the envisaged time scale. She very much doubted that Vladimir Miasnikov would arrive back in time for the departure. The future of their species came first. Everything else, including family, friends, lovers and entrusted commanders, did not even come a close second. Lesqueth doubted that Miasnikov would survive his latest mission, and even if he did manage to make it back, there would be nothing remaining here for him. All that would await his arrival would be chaos and a decaying regime. If the planned restructuring of the country had been accomplished, then things would have been different. She could have followed the original criteria that had been meticulously detailed and had taken years to formulate. Unfortunately, it was one mishap after another and in the end, Lesqueth had no choice but to cut her losses. She was not running away, merely relocating her base of operations ahead of plan.

The American contingent up until now, had been dealt a relatively free hand in achieving all of the perceived objectives. Any arising setbacks had been delt with accordingly, quickly dismissed the risks by eliminating the issues prior to them and developed further into becoming a major problem. The Abe Hubstien situation involving the Kunupenny clan had inadvertently almost resolved itself. With one almost eliminating the other, all the American contingent required to do now was to sweep up the waifs and strays. Lesqueth had no intention of brokering a deal for peaceful coexistence with any other factions or people groups. The survivors would all be part of her envisaged future, and the ones that were not privy to inclusion would be hunted to the point of extinction.

Once Lesqueth had initiated the grand plan, her armies would sweep every habitable region of this planet and then eradicate any would-be opposition. The Baroness envisaged that by this time, there would be no requirement nor any reasoning for the original inhabitants to be permitted to roam freely on the surface. The ones that were allocated a breathing permit would only be used for the services that required expendable resources. The Baroness had issued the revised instructions to the technicians overseeing the twelve hundred infants. She liked the fact that she did not have to issue any kind of details, no amazon forest worth of health and safety protocols. In the old days, Lesqueth would have had a full department working for months on all of the now null and void paperwork. The Baroness would almost have been umbilically connected to her smartphone, ensuring that every T was crossed and every I was dotted.

If it was possible, she would have much preferred to undertake the journey onboard the Magno-L. Even though the family's wealth was unimaginable, it was not possible to extend the electro-rail line across the Atlantic due to the available technology. In the future years, perhaps once the whole of the planet had been completely colonised with her species, then, and only then, would she interconnect every continent. Her father, along with her ancestral lineage, had planned so, so much for the future. Now it was down to her and her alone to bring all their ideas to fruition, transport them all out from the sketches then transform them all into the real world. The Baroness was acutely aware that it would be impossible to make everything that was envisaged in the far distant past happen overnight, but she was going to give it her best shot. As her father had told her often, sometimes you had to sacrifice a few pieces to ensure the true path of the queen.

The colonies stationed in Merica would find out soon enough what it was like to serve under her rule. No doubt, some of them would perish in the line of duty, while others would rise above the trial by fire and join her in ushering in the new age on this planet. The runway, for sure, was spotlessly clean, and perhaps she could torture Tesporo and his self-mutilated followers to recheck while wearing a clean set of sterile, clean white gloves. Lesqueth had not got long left to wait before the arrival of the transport. In the remaining hours, she intended to perform a spot check and visit every part of the planned operation to ensure that this stage would be a resounding success. The medical technicians in charge of the future twelve hundred troopers had been summoned to present their reports. The Baroness was not interested in their family names nor in their former family's precious pedigree. All she wanted to know was that they were all fit and that they were all healthy.

Their brains had been continuously bombarded with facts, figures and what was expected of them since they had opened their eyes. All of their paternal leanings would hopefully have been eradicated from their minds, and the only family loyalty they would show would be to their new family and their species. Even if her son, Marshall was to display any hint of weakness. Any inclination of anxiety associated with the absence of maternal bonds; she would have him exterminated without any hesitation. All of the children were being indoctrinated into becoming rank and file members of her future army and were subjected to the same rules. Marshall would have had to realise that being the only son of the Baroness carried no dispensations, nor awarded him any special treatment. Lesqueth had quietly pulled the instructors aside, warning them that her son had to be pushed to the very limits of his endurance. Lesqueth now walked with the instructors and reviewed the training schedule.

As they walked through the galley, she noticed a few additional empty spaces that contained no child. All that was there was an empty chair, facing an upturned plate and cup blatantly advertising that failure carried its very own special reward. After finishing viewing the stats with the accompanying graphs, Lesqueth nodded giving the seal of approval to the instructors' efforts. They collectively breathe a sigh of relief at passing her strict inspection. They silently nodded to each other and acknowledged the fact that they were going to live another day as she marched off with her security team.

Next on her list was the medical team, the Baroness had warned them in advance of the required changes. The chief medical technician stood before her; the task she had been presented with was in her opinion a rather tall order. In this day and age where supplies were fairly limited, she had to beg, borrow and steal all of the items needed to accommodate the latest demand from the Baroness of Kindeace-Shire. The chief medical technician had inherited the position after her superior had mysteriously launched himself through a window on the upper floor. The official line was that even though he had bound hands and feet. The subject in question had somehow still managed to run across the room and throw himself through the reinforced glass.

As she was not permitted to use her real name, Med. Tech. 141 stood waiting for the questions that would follow once the great leader had finished reading the presentation. Lesqueth, who had not even acknowledged her presence, and issued the odd grunt and sighed as she scanned quickly through the information. "So, tell me, how did you test the serum?" Med. tech. 141 did not dare look at the Baroness, "I tested the various solutions on the available prisoners, then once we found a suitable application. We then diluted the solution as per the weight, height and age of the infants." Lesqueth said nothing and stared at her and wanted more facts. "The children that were earmarked as failures were tested with the solution, and all of the procedures were a resounding success." Lesqueth now demanded to see where the serum was kept and a demonstration of how it was administered.

Med. Tech. 141 led the way to the storage room on the upper floor, where all the concoctions were stored. She pointed to the door, "We keep them all in there to ensure that they were kept in a temperature-controlled environment and safe to use on the day. That way, we can assure you that they would all perform exactly the same way when they were used." Lesqueth curtly reminded the technician that the door had to be opened and that she wanted a demonstration of how the potion was delivered.

Med. Tech. 141 was slightly hesitant to perform the first part of the request. Lesqueth suspected that she had something to hide but, for the moment, let it go. The room was entered, and the Baroness was shown the refrigerated unit where all the requested medication was stored. Med. Tech. 141 pointed at all the items stored on the lower shelves, "These were all the ones that you wanted to inspect. The device for administering the dose to the patients was next door. If you would care to follow me, I would show you how they function." Lesqueth noticed that the technician wanted out of the room as soon as possible and knew without any doubt that 141 was hiding something. The medical technician proudly demonstrated how the device worked, "It was self-venting, did not draw blood, nor create bruising and as far as we were aware, it was relatively painless. Each unit can administer doses to fifteen children." The Baroness stared at her, 141 and felt that she had said used the incorrect terminology, corrected the word children and changed it to trooper. Lesqueth handled the device and then passed it over to one of her guards to play with.

Chapter 17

'So, tell me, Med. Tech. 141 When you tested the substandard troopers, how did you dispose of them when the serum was signed, sealed and delivered? 141 hesitates, then mutters incoherently that the inadequate troopers were disposed of immediately once the testing was verified. Lesqueth sighed, "Did you witness their final moments?" 141 replied that she had just summoned the guards for that task. Lesqueth shakes her head and as she walked towards 141, she looked her straight in the eye. "Why Chicken, you have motherhood written all over you. I don't think that you disposed of the unwanted troopers. How about we call all of your staff into this room, then ask some questions. Do you think they would testify, confirming the exact same sequence of events of your version?"

Lesqueth ordered her guards to round up all of the staff in the medical facility. Now, with only the two of them there, the Baroness ignored her as they waited for the others to arrive. Lesqueth wondered why the room contained several patients hooked up to drips and monitors that irritated her as they constantly bleeped away. The guards marched in 141's co-workers and then had them stand in a line. Lesqueth repeated word-for-word the medical technician's version of the events. Then issued instructions for them to go and stand alongside 141 if they agreed that this was the truth, the whole truth and nothing but the truth. First there was one, then another followed and eventually they had all hobbled over to stand with their leader. Lesqueth announced that she loved the idea of loyalty no matter what, as all the medical staff absorbed what had just been said. The Baroness clapped her hands to attract their undivided attention, "Just to inform you all, now that you have made your choice, there would be no chance to change your minds."

She ordered the guards to start searching the building, beginning with the room where the serum was stored. Lesqueth watched the worried expressions appear on their faces. It always amused her that this species, even in the face of impending doom, always reverted to a murmured prayer in the hope of divine intervention. One of the guards approached and informed her that they had found evidence to support the fact that 141, along with her co-worker's version of the truth, was colourful and somewhat magical.

The Baroness ordered the guards to retrieve and then display the evidence for everyone to see. Six rejected troopers who had been allocated for testing, then allegedly eliminated were presented to the company. Lesqueth looked at them, then at the medical facility staff. "It looks as if you all had been busy, and you must have had lots of spare time to dress them all up in non-regulated attire. I am by no means an expert in boutique clothing, but I would hazard a guess in stating that some of these clothes look handmade." Lesqueth now stared at the rejected troopers and informed them to go and stand by their adopted parent, the one who took care of them. At first the children were reluctant to look her in the eyes and hesitant to do as they were told.

The Baroness, now getting angry shouted out her instruction to be obeyed. The children did not move, and some of them started sobbing, Ellen Corrigan, AKA Med. Tech. 141 stepped forward and ushered all the infants to gather in beside her. Lesqueth was shocked that the rejected troopers unashamedly, without any hesitation, took part in a maternal group cuddle.

Ellen looked directly at the Baroness, "You seem bitterly disappointed at the emotion on display. Anyone else in this day and age would view this as quite something, considering all that had been lost and all that was left behind. What difference could this possibly make to your plans, your envisaged version of the future. What a place that would be with emotionally cold children and sterilised parents devoid of all parental feelings. We would almost be like unfeeling electrobio mannequin, following an unforgiving set of rules, where all choice and rational thinking were not permitted. Is this really the only hope that you had for future generations. You could turn a blind eye and allow these children to go, allow them to venture out into the outside world, what possible harm could they do to you or your regime? For once you could just show some compassion, some feeling towards your subjects."

Lesqueth held up her hand requesting silence, as she walked towards the seemingly bedridden patients. "This country was doomed to fail; everything was wrong, and nothing was ever going to change that certainty. More than anything, the bleeding-hearted liberals broke this country. Minor problems that should have been quashed and then removed from the public eye were heralded towards the front-page news." The Baroness crushed the breathing tube of the first patient, and the monitor issued all sorts of warnings until she disconnected the power. "The unemployed, the ones who did not want to work, the ones who refused to work had all between them squeezed every penny they could by abusing the welfare system. They were allowed to breed without any form of statutory control, subsequently adding to the already overloaded system."

"This country took in every waif and stray that were expelled from their mother country because they had been deemed a menace to society. Yet the faint-hearted do-gooders proclaimed that it was inhumane to leave a person stateless and without some form of safety net. The first thing that they did was to bring over their entire family network and then proceed to milk the system for all that it was worth. Word got out, come to the UK, plead persecution on political grounds, religious grounds, anything as long as you got adopted by a prominent bleeding-hearted liberal, all would be okay." Lesqueth viewed the next patient, and this one had an assortment of tubes inserted into the arm and body. She produced her flame initiator and gently heated the plastic tubing until it collapsed on itself, creating a permanent blockage.

Now, at the next patient, the Baroness placed her hand over their nose and mouth. She continued speaking to her captive audience. "Every system had limits, and I am not reactivating the National Health Service. Therefore, if the body was not fit for purpose, then it had no place in the system." She showed no emotion nor any sign of interest as the patient started to get cold and turn blue. "We cannot save everyone; the way that I see it was quite simple: you work until you have been deemed unsuitable for employment."

Lesqueth ordered her troopers to open one of the double windows, then to throw the last bedridden patient and his bed out of the window. The Baroness waved them goodbye as they sailed through the opening.

"Medical technician 141, I suppose you think that I am cruel, brutal and emotionless. Perhaps I am truly guilty of all of these qualities. We had to forge a new world out of these ashes and start afresh. In my world we would be a species, with no imperfections and within that realm we would have no room for stragglers." Lesqueth withdrew her sidearm and started shooting the medical fraternity along with the failed troopers. She reloaded her weapon and walked towards them, and added a round in each of their heads to ensure that they were all dead. Lesqueth then issued orders for the serum to be transported to the airport and made ready. The Baroness felt no remorse nor had any misgivings in regards to her actions, she was here to lead her species into their undeniable future and that perfection was required no matter what the cost.

At the other end of the country, Murray had been roped into Okolo's plan to check all the houses, shops and buildings in the area for all the items that would be needed by future generations. He had no problem going into the shops and rummaging about, digging out the useful items. Murray loaded up the trolley with the sewing kits and the medical supplies, along with the other things that would be of use to someone in their community. He tried going into one of the houses but found the whole process heartbreaking, almost as if he was peering into the former owners' souls. The faded photographs displayed the occupants' favourite memories that haunted him and overcame him with emotion. Murray had tears running down his face as he looked at the family pictures, displaying happier times.

The mother and daughter, the family events, Christmas and holiday snaps all displaying happier times were really wrenching his heart and soul. As he entered the room full of children's toys, it just rips a huge hole inside him. Murray closed the door and then walked straight out of the house. He couldn't help it, as the tears flowed down his face, he was in bits and was crying uncontrollably. Murray couldn't do this, the loss in this house alone was so overpowering it had hammered home the fact that one day, all that would remain of him would be a faded memory displaying happier times.

He was determined to leave his children many happy memories, all full of laughter and joy about the times when they had done this along with all of the times that they had done that. Murray thought if they could get hold of a camera, then possibly he could gather memories for everyone. They were all entitled to a picture or two of their relations, their friends and even their dogs. At the thought of the dogs, Murray broke down again, imagining what life would be like without Charlie and Romulus. Even worse than that, he thought he would be utterly inconsolable without a picture of his beloved pets. Murray did not know how he was going to do it exactly, but hc intended to set something up for everyone to have a keepsake of happier times. As he wiped his eyes and face, he smiled and thought that when Rebecca make-up counter face heard about it, she would be at the front of the queue every day. Murray thought that either Mark or Alicia would be able to clue him up about what equipment was required. He did not know if it would be possible but even if his idea failed and he fell flat on his face then at least he had tried.

Murray informed the rest of the crew that he had got to go, jumped into his loaded vehicle then drove home. The house was quiet for a change, and as soon as he entered, Cha knew that there was something wrong with him. She looked at him and knew that he had been crying his eyes out. Cha asked him if he had some bad new, over a cuppa and a smoke, Murray opened his heart and emptied all the emotional upheaval that he experienced during the search for the house. He ran the idea of taking pictures for everyone.

Cha put her arms around him and informed Murray that he was just a big softie and that was why she loved him so much. She had listened to his plan; Cha would run it past Alicia when she returned. Cha looked at him, feeling his distress, "You have the time to run through to Marks, he had everything and if he had not got the equipment you need, he would be able to point you in the right direction, but before you go, just one thing." Murray knew what she was going to say and promised not to mention a word of his idea to Rebecca make-up face. They laughed at this and all of her previous performances. He promised to be home before it got dark and, put his arms around her and told her that he loved her more every day. Cha told him to stop it or she would cry, then kissed him again before he left.

Down the road, south of there Uno had at last found a suitable vehicle for them to continue the journey. Macdhiarmada sat with the little girl, and they talk away to themselves as Uno did all of the necessary tasks in order for the vehicle to move. It bothered Uno that the old bastard had never once offered to help, but as they had told him that they were nearly there, he held his tongue. It would have been the easiest thing in the world to lash out and give the pair of them some as far as he was concerned a more than well-deserved verbal lashing. Uno now thought, what was the point? Soon, they would be nothing but a distant memory. He brightened up at the fact that he would hopefully and with a fair deal of luck be reunited with Rhubradug. It had been a really long time since he had seen him. Uno hoped that his old friend was happy, healthy and living a good life far removed from the abject squaller of their previous existence.

As soon as he had completed the work, He was tempted to shout out, "Okay fuckface, yeah, you with the hard-to-pronounce name and your strange companion, it is time to go." Uno's better side took control and opened the vehicle's door, then started up the engine. It was a surprise when the beast started the first time. Uno took this as a sign that it was going to be a good day. He did not expect the almost non-existent conversation to change into a free-flowing, matter-of-fact chit-chat with many jokes and amusing anecdotes. At last, maybe even later on today, his passengers would depart for adventures unknown and that would be the best present ever. The odd couple took their time in getting their shit together and then entered the vehicle. All this was done in complete silence, and not once did they even mutter anything about thanks for doing all the work to enable them to continue the journey.

Uno would not class himself as a mechanic, but today, they had been lucky. He had on many previous occasions wrestled with various uncooperative monsters, even trying to bribe them to persuade them to come back to life. As they approached the first junction, Uno very nearly stalled the vehicle as the old fart announced, "Please, take a left." He performed the instruction without comment, fully aware that the old bastard had reverted back to pretending to be dead or sleeping.

He thought that either version was acceptable as both of them do not require any conversation. The journey had not been unpleasant, but it had been well and truly awkward. If he was being really honest, he would have had more conversation if he was travelling on his lonesome. On a positive note, the dynamic duo had not supplied him with any food residing within a rusty, bashed tin today. The roads were almost clear and enabled them to eat up the miles with relative ease, and all was going well. Uno intended to pull over in an hour or so for a much-needed piss and smoke break. If his passengers wished to get out the vehicle that was fine and if they wished to stay in the vehicle that was fine also. Uno if he was on his own would be singing and dancing to entertain himself. As the old codger in the back seat would only complain, Uno danced a little to the imaginary songs playing out in his head.

He slowed down to navigate through the abandoned vehicles, and as he did so, he immediately noticed a change in the car. Uno knew that they had acquired a puncture. It was no big deal, as he made sure that there was a spare prior to setting off. He pulled in once they were clear of the debris, making sure that he annoyed the old fucker in the back by indicating well before he drew to a halt. As expected, he received no offer of help. Uno sparked up as he gathered up the kit, then set about changing the tyre. Once he had completed the changeover, he checked the other wheels fully aware that if they had another problem, they were fucked, and if that was the case, then they would need another vehicle.

Uno offered a silent prayer to the God of motor vehicles and wished for a continued, unhindered journey. He did not know if there was a God for unwanted passengers, but just in case, Uno also offered them a prayer and hoped that his guests departed like real soon. He took the last drag from his homemade cigarette and flicked the roach away, exhaled and got back into the driver's seat. The pair in the back had not moved a muscle, and perhaps they were unaware that the vehicle had actually come to a stop or they were more likely just plain mother fucking rude.

He restarted the vehicle and couldn't help smiling as he heard a sigh of complaint as he indicated to move off. The road ahead was still pretty clear, and taking full advantage, Uno put the foot down. Any time that had been lost was made up. The miles zoomed past rapidly, and before they knew it was time to stop for a break, Uno, being stiff and uncomfortable, wished to stretch his legs. The youngest passenger whispered in Macdhiarmada, Bryan, or whatever the fuck he was called ear, "I don't know why you were stopping; we were nearly there!" Uno put all of his manners firmly back in the box. "I need to piss, stretch my legs and a couple of other things. If you were unhappy at that, you can do one and fuck right off." Uno slammed the door as he exited the vehicle; one minute, they were almost hibernating, and then the next minute, they were Bonafide tour guides with a rigidly tight time schedule to be followed to by the letter.

He totally ignored them and set about doing his business; his pee almost lasted forever as he washed the tyre with his spent liquid after wiping his hands on his jacket. Uno delved into his bag for some juice, and all of a sudden, he was very thirsty. As luck would have it, he was in possession of a solitary can of fizzy juice. He muttered to himself, "Just what the doctor ordered." He cracked it open and took a huge swallow. Uno rattled one up and finished the fizzy, then stretched his legs by walking about taking in the view of the countryside. He had always been a high-rise dweller and never fully understanding the attraction of miles of uninterrupted open space without a single twenty-four-seven take away shop within walking distance.

Uno was unaware if his unofficial tour guides had taken the opportunity to get out and stretch their legs or they were still being huffy and sitting in the same place. Either way he could not care less. He fished inside his bag and was pretty disappointed that his tin selection had been depleted. Uno preferred to cut out his tongue, rather than lower himself to ask his non communitive companions if they had any spare nosh. He treated himself to another homemade smoke and, this time, sat down and tried to take in the scenery. Uno being a city dweller in his previous life, tried very hard to appreciate what was all around him but was still unable to grasp the beautiful panoramic setting. Uno needed to pee again and just unzipped and let if fly where he stood. He had been doing this more frequently and was now starting to think that perhaps he had some sort of infection. Uno opened his memory banks and the alarm went off at the fairly recent drunken encounter with Buggy Annie. He was now one hundred percent positive that she had given him a gift that would require a course of fairly strong antibiotics.

The passengers had not moved during his unauthorised absence, and Uno ignored the about fucking time comment issued from the old bastard in the back seat. He switched on the engine followed by indicator; this Uno was left on for ages just to infuriate the frequent complainant in the back. Uno wondered if Rhubradugs' new digs would have a doctor hopefully, they would not give him an examination. If he was unfortunate enough to have to submit himself for one, he would have just to declare his predicament. They drove on an easy road accompanied with a perfectly clear blue sky; all that was needed were some sounds and it would be nearly perfect. A voice piped up from the backseat, "Take the next right." Uno looked for the next turning, checking for a tarmacked exit. Not seeing one, he continued on.

The voice in the back asked him to stop and reverse back to the exit. "You missed the turn-off point," Uno replied that he had never seen the road nor the sign. "It was an unsigned country track." Uno reversed back until he found what they were looking for, "Will this one be okay, or would you like me to keep travelling backwards." The old bastard snarled, "Just turn onto the fucking track, would you, and follow the instructions without comment." Uno did not bite back at his ungrateful passenger and drove onto the track. He travelled at a speed that he knew would deliver a rather uncomfortable journey, which would make them all bounce about. The old bastard informed Uno that if he did not slow down, he was going to puke. Uno gave in, decreasing the speed, and to avoid any additional complaints, he switched off the indicators.

He was tempted to ask what the fuck his name was. If he was now content and, when he filled out the travel companies' happy sheet, would he give him a glow-in-the-fucking-dark, five-star report? Uno did not get the chance as he was kindly requested to take the left and the third right. "If you drive slow, I would tell you when to turn, and that would avoid any drastic manoeuvres." Uno blanked him and offered no form of reply. Eventually, after the unexpected safari, they re-joined the main road. The voice in the back informed him to take a right and to drive really slowly. Uno did not understand why, as the road ahead was clear as far as they could see. He was just about to ask a question when a vehicle suddenly slid across the road in front of them. Uno was about to slam the vehicle into reverse and hightail it out of there when he was informed that he would only be wasting his time. He wondered what the fuck was going on when another vehicle appeared behind them, blocking them in completely. Macdhiarmada informed Uno that he would get brownie points if he switched off the engine and dropped his weapon out of the window.

They sat in silence; Uno, for one, would like to know what was fucking happening and to calm his nerves, he made a smoke. The way he saw it, if he had cut off the motor and dropped his weapon, then surely, they would not be upset if he had a smoke while they decided what they were going to do with them. Whoever they were, they had done nothing yet, Uno thought that if it was a hold-up, they were going to be terribly disappointed. Uno rolled down the window and then opened the door from the outside. He kept his hands in view as he gently pushed the door out with his feet. When he had made enough space, he squeezed himself out. Uno slowly stood upright and then lifted his hands and displayed the homemade cigarette and the lighter. He sparked up thinking that if they were going to shoot him, he would refuse the blindfold. A voice came out of nowhere, "Raise your hands and walk away from the vehicle," if you make any sudden movements, you will be shot. Uno followed the instructions, puffing away with the homemade cigarette clenched in his lips.

He had only cleared his vehicle when someone put a gun to the back of his head, and several masked figures appeared in front of him pointing weapons. One of them stepped forward and searched him, then cuffed him. A hood was roughly placed over his head, and then he was dragged away and chucked into the back of a truck. Uno had heard some of them climbing in with him. None of them said a single word as the vehicle accelerated away. The journey only lasted about ten minutes; it was mostly uphill, and he bounced about a fair bit in the back of the truck. The vehicle came to a sudden stop, and then he was unceremoniously dragged out. Uno fell and was pulled upright and frogmarched into a room.

He was still wearing the hood as they forced him onto a chair. The cuffs were removed, and the shirt was ripped from his back. Uno told them clearly that he had no tattoos on his back and was most definitely not one of them. He was asked what he knew about the group of people with the insignia tattooed on their backs. Uno replied that they had attacked his people, and as far as he was aware, he was the only member of his tribe who was still breathing. He added that he could breathe a lot easier as they took the fucking hood off. There was no answer given. His interrogators had left the room and left him to sweat it out in silence. The people who were questioning him had taken the interrogation as far as they could. Their training had revolved mainly around checking the prisoners back to ascertain that they did not belong to the group that was carving up the country. They had sent word down to the grown-ups that they needed some help and guidance with the captive. On reaching Murray's house, they told them about the recently captured prisoner; as Mr Black was unavailable, Cha asked the twins to watch the children. On the way over to where the captive was being held. She had spotted Robbo, and Cha roped him in to come along and then assisted in the interrogation. Robbo was hesitant at first, but Cha delivering her version of the famous Black stare insisted that his help was required and he was coming with her.

Uno started to think that if they left him unattended for much longer, he was going to apply for lonely money. Just at the door opened, Uno recognised the voice of Rhubradug immediately and asked him if he could kindly remove the hood from his head, it would be greatly fucking appreciated. Cha vaguely remembered Uno from the castle adventure but never the less agreed with Robbo to untie him. Uno looks at Rhubradug, "You look healthy; your hair was different, but there was no way that anyone could impersonate that voice. I could murder some liquid refreshments, and a smoke would be nice." Robbo popped outside for a moment and asked nicely if they could bring in some tea, juice or water. Robbo came back into the room, introduced Cha and also informed Uno that they called him Robbo now, "It's a long story, so don't ask." Uno nodded and held his hand out for some smoke.

Robbo obliged with a ready-made. Uno sparked up, confessing that he was really pleased to see him. "I was worried that I would be too late to pass on the news, and you would either be dead or long gone away from here." Robbo was perplexed at his statement and asked him if he could explain why he thought that he could be dead or gone. The knock on the door interrupted the conversation. They waited until the juice was placed on the table and the delivery person left before recommencing the chat.

Robbo told Uno to help himself. Uno replied that he was doing nothing until he received a cuddle from his long-lost brother. Both of them stood up, performed a bear hug and spoke in what Cha assumed was the standard swamp people greeting. Now satisfied, Uno cracked open one of the tins, gulped down almost the entire contents and, relighted his joint and started to deliver the bad news.

"I am the last remaining member of the swamp people; every one that you knew was dead. The liberation army, or whatever the fuck they call themselves, arrived and attacked at dawn. Those who were not killed during the battle were rounded up and systematically killed. These people were truly evil; they took great pleasure in slowly eliminating every member of the swamp people. The lunatic in charge told everyone that it was just a reward for murdering his sister. He tied them all up and then had them force-fed with poisoned food. None of them had a chance, and he put a bucket over their heads, then had it beaten like a drum to drive them insane. Just as the poison was taking its effect, he had nails driven into them to slowly finish them off. No one escaped; no one survived." Uno helped himself to another tin of juice and bums another smoke.

"I was taken prisoner, then they made me watch everything. Their leader pulled me aside, informing me to tell you that he was coming to annihilate all of you, and he was going to kill Okolo last. I dumped the vehicle that they gave me and used one of the swamp people's escape cars. I also checked that I was not being followed, but I am so happy I got here in time to warn you. Rhub, sorry Robbo, they were hundreds of them, they had tanks and all sorts of military shit, they were a fucking army of them, and you were not going to beat them. They had uniforms, do all that saluting shit, they were completely ruthless and would show you and yours no compassion nor any kind of mercy." Cha asked him about the old man and the young girl that he travelled with.

Uno explained that he had almost run them down, and then the next minute, they were in the vehicle and gave him directions on how to get here. "They just knew where you were, they were kind of strange, nothing at all like me."

Chapter 18

Robbo vouched for Uno's character and declared that he was no threat to their community as he took him up to the medical facility for an examination. Robbo updated Uno on how his life had changed for the better. Uno was over the moon at the fact that his old friend had found happiness and that he was living in a healthy environment. Light years away from the former community that only clawed out an existence on a continual day-to-day basis. Uno talked non-stop informing Robbo that they had built a shrine to the woman who ran naked through the forest. "I think that Tally was really quite jealous of the number of people in her fan club. They never stopped talking about her, and the stories about her exploits grew arms and legs." Robbo looked at him and wondered if Uno had anything to do with the extended versions of her daring adventures in the never-ending fight against injustice and tyrannical regimes.

They had at last reached Cora's domain; Robbo told Uno to just be himself and, for once, try and exhibit no outrageous behaviour. One of the doctors' staff opens the door, and they walk through and enter Cora's office. Robbo introduced them, then informed the doctor that Uno was here for a medical. Robbo explained that everyone in the community gets one, and he should just answer all the questions as honestly as possible. Uno had gone quiet, which Robbo thought was not like him at all. He just stood there saying nothing as Robbo explained that he was going to get him some fresh clothes, then arrange for somewhere for him to stay. Robbo asked Uno what was bothering him and said he should relax, clear the air then just get whatever it was that was bothering him off his chest.

Uno took a deep breath and confessed to all present that he was suffering from Buggy Annie Syndrome and was pissing razor blades. As Cora had not come across this topic in any of her medical reference books, she looked dumbfounded, requiring an explanation. Robbo stepped up to the plate and explained that Mr Uno had contracted a venereal disease. Cora asked if, by chance, they knew which one. Robbo replied that going by Buggy Annie's reputation and standing within the swamp people community, it was probably multiple infections covering several known variants of the sexually transmittable diseases. "I was thinking that you could just give him some of the super-duper antibiotics that kill everything. Don't worry, Uno; Cora can provide a cure; you will be right as rain before you know it. In the meantime, you need some new clothes, somewhere to stay. I would leave you here, then come back and get you when I had it all sorted." Cora informed Uno that he would need to shower prior to the examination taking place. Uno asked her if it was a proper shower with hot water, soap and shampoo. Cora nodded her head, adding that there would also be a nail brush, a toothbrush and toothpaste. Uno remarked that he had not had this luxury for quite some time.

Robbo walked back towards the house; the old battered crow perched above gave him a greeting. Robbo informed his old friend that it would not be long. Cha had just sent Alicia up to interview Uno's passengers, and she must inform every one of the approaching imminent danger. She has sent out orders for the patrols to be doubled on all fronts and spoking to herself, and she wished that Murray would be home soon.

Murray had travelled to the farmhouse community. Now that they were in possession of the high-powered binoculars, the checkpoints waved him through quickly. He was delighted at not having to go through the various identification checks and confirmations. Mark, on hearing of his friend's arrival had insisted that Murray joined him for lunch. "Well, bud, you were looking well." Murray thanked Mark for the compliment and remarked that he imagined that it would be a different picture if you had a look at him from the inside. He came clean for the reason for his visit. Mark listened and thought that it was a great idea, he promised to get someone on it. "I don't know if we would be able to source the items locally but I promise I would try." A shiver ran down his spine just imagining how brutal and unforgiving life would be outside of their fairly stable community. Murray somehow knew what he was thinking and confirmed that he would much prefer not to have to travel over the bridge to acquire the items.

Ellie came over and joined them at the table, and she was disappointed that Cha had not accompanied him. Murray promised Ellie that he would pass on her regards. "Maybe one day, when the children were older, cured of the travel sickness, we could bring the whole tribe over for a little break," Mark informed his friend that he could come over anytime; no invitations were required. Mark updated Ellie on the idea that Murray was currently working on, and she listened and then blurted out where they may find the items required. Murray told her that he always knew that she was the brains in the family. Ellie also added that she thought that it was a great idea, "I would try and get you some of the items before the end of the day; some of our people had talked about this a while back. We may not be able to get you every piece of equipment that was required, but we should be able to get you enough kit to get started."

Mark looked serious and asked Murray if Rebecca's makeup face knew about it. "You know that as soon as she gets wind of this, she would be wanting a full portfolio." They all chuckled at this and remembered the rumour that she got up at dawn to apply the multiple-layered array of cosmetics before she even opened her eyes. With the lunch now over, Mark asked Murray if he had time to go and visit the mechanics. "Murray, if they find out that you were here and did not visit them, you know I would get non-stop earache, so please just go and see them." Murray agreed to the request and then set off to entertain his one-time students. He entered the workshop; all was good, and it was functioning as it should be. One of the new trainees passed and informed him that if he was looking for a job, then he would need to fill in an application form.

Murray ignored him and walked around the shop and said hello to all the familiar faces, shooting the shit where and when required. Mark hurriedly entered the workshop, and, catching Murray's attention, he waved him over. They go outside, away from all the prying eyes and ultrasensitive ears. Mark looked worried, "The fishing crew had just returned. They had just informed me that a large boat was spotted at anchor a day away from here. I don't know what this means, but a little voice inside my head was telling me that I should tell you this immediately." Murray replied that it could be nothing, but all the same, he would have to go and inform his people just in case. "You never know what kind of people they would be and what gifts they had to offer. It could be people who were lost, people who were trading, we won't know until we see them. Mark, they might never land anywhere near here, but as soon as I receive any news, I will pass it on straight away." Murray gave his friend a bear hug and added that he would see him soon.

All the way home, he thought that as soon as Okolo found out, she would remember the words of the old woman with the hooded cloak and would be already loading her guns. He really hoped that it all turned out to be nothing, but even if it turned to shit, he was duty-bound to give her the news. Murray was at the home checkpoint before he knew it. The journey had passed quickly with his head full of the pending woe if the old woman's prediction turned out to be true. Okolo was one of his closest friends, he really hopes and prays that it remains that way. Cha rushes to him as soon as he opens the door, "Thank goodness that you are home; we had some bad news." Murray told her he knew about the ship that had been spotted offshore, and he did not know if it was good news or bad news. Cha shook her head, "No, we had some visitors, and they had told us that there was an army heading our way. By all accounts, they were coming to destroy us, to wipe us from the face of the earth."

Cha continues, "Uno, you may remember him from the castle that we visited a while back. He was up at Cora's just now. I had asked Robbo to bring him down here once he had been given the all-clear." Murray asked if the rest of the team knew, and she replied that as soon as he got here, they would call a meeting so that they could all hear what he had to say. Murray told her about the ship, Cha thought about the forewarning from the old woman and knew instantly that he was worried about Okolo's reaction to the news. Murray just gave her it straight: it could be nothing, but you never know who was on the ship, and you never know what they want. "I will speak to Okolo about it as soon as time permits, better to get these things out the way as soon as possible." Cha updates him, "Alicia was up interviewing the old man and the young girl that had travelled with Uno. Okolo would be with the children. "Maybe you should go and give her the news just now," Murray asked her to make some nice tea and he would go and get her.

Okolo could tell by the look on his face that she knew something was bugging him. Murray persuaded her to bring the children to his house so that they could talk and smoke at the same time. Okolo wanted to know if it was good news or bad news. Murray told her the truth and admitted that right now, he did not know, but either way they would have to talk about it. Okolo had deposited the children with the favourite, number one auntie as Cha entertained them and then placed them with the others. Okolo was now outside with Murray, and he gave her a peace offering in the form of a ready rolled. Then, before he uttered a single word, she asked him just to spit it out. Murray knew that she could read him like a book, and she noticed immediately that he still had something worrisome on his mind. Murray initiated the flame device, and then after they sparked up, he just let it flow. "You will, no doubt remember the old woman with the hooded cloak warning about the arrival of a ship?" Okolo nodded and was vividly aware of every word that was said. "Well, the fishing boat just arrived back at port, and they reported seeing a ship at anchor a day away. As of yet, we don't know anything about who they are, what they want and for all we know, it could just sail straight past." Okolo exhaled and asked him what happened next.

Murray replied that she was one of his closest friends, and no matter what happened, he hoped that it remained that way forever. Murray continued, "I had always trusted you, but taking into consideration the words in the dream, we have to be careful." Okolo nodded, "Until the ship arrives, there was no point worrying about it. We should have had a patrol monitoring the coast, and then, should the vessel arrive, we should be there for them coming ashore. We were assuming that they would be friendly, what if they were actually part of the group that Uno had warned us about." Murray agreed, and he thanked her for listening to his worries. Okolo stubbed out her smoke and then informed him that he is still a wanker. Inside the house, the children were all grouped together, watching everything around them. Charlie, along with Romulus, was lying among them and acted as their personal guard dogs, ready to instantly protect them against anything. Okolo looked at all of the little bundles of joy and remarked to Murray, "Don't you wish it could just be like this forever." Murray agreed but inwardly worried about what the future held for all of them.

The deep thoughts were interrupted by the arrival of Robbo accompanied by his long-lost soul mate. Uno almost fell to his knees at seeing Okolo. "It has been so long; the swamp people never forgot about you," Okolo told him that he could relax, he was among friends now. "We were waiting for the others to arrive, "grab a cuppa, then when everyone gets here, you could tell all of them all of what you had seen and witnessed." Uno did as he was told, and before he asked, Robbo helped himself, then passed him over one of Murrays' ready rolled.

Uno made to spark up there and then only to be informed that he had to take it outside. Okolo accompanied him. Uno was almost shaking with excitement at being reunited with his heroine. Uno talked non-stop and revealed all of the details about the shrine that was dedicated to her memory. "Tally was really not happy with your popularity. He wanted the shrine moved away as far as possible, but the people refused, then threatened to leave." Okolo thanked him for everything, then told him that here she was just a normal person with two children to take care of. Uno offered her a belated congratulations and added that she would be a great mother. Okolo held up the flame initiator, and Uno calmed down enough to relight his homemade cigarette. Robbo came out to join them, and he asked Okolo to give him the news. "Uno until we find you somewhere to stay, you would be staying with us for a while. The children would probably try and bite you but don't worry about it. Once they get to know you, you would like them. We also have a sound system, and I hope you were not a purveyor of the same shit that Robbo listens to."

Uno laughed and confessed that he used to listen to classical music, "Even my parents thought I was a snob." Okolo informed Uno that if he wanted to listen to classical music, then that would be okay. "If Robbo even attempts to complain, just tell him the management informed you that it was cool," Robbo confessed that Okolo and Alicia had ganged up on him since day one, and he really was a housebound domestic slave, perpetually assigned cleaning duties on a twenty-four-seven basis. Okolo informed Uno that Robbo was a complete wanker and that he should not believe a single word that spewed from his lips as it was all lies.

At the other end of the country, the aeroplanes had started to arrive. Lesqueth had never bothered to inform the keeper of the records. The crew that was employed to clean the runway ran to escape being obliterated by the huge wheeled monsters coming into land. Tesporo had lost a few of his brethren who had unfortunately not been quite agile enough and had gone down, subsequently being squashed beneath the gigantic smoking black tyres. He would be extremely foolish if he were even to admit to thinking that the Baroness should have informed him prior to the transatlantic arrivals. One by one, the airliners came to a stop; immediately, Lesqueth's troopers appeared and persuaded all the unessential personnel to vacate the airport. The Baroness did not care where they went, just so long as they left the immediate area. At the gates, the loading bridges were out of operation due to the piles of dead bodies and the damage that had taken place during the ensuing chaos during the last few hours of the airport's operation.

To resolve this problem, Lesqueth had the appropriate number of mobile passenger steps on standby, ready to be wheeled into place as soon as the main doors opened. Commander Bryan was the first of the transatlantic cousins to set foot on the tarmac. She was more than aware of the expected quick turnaround and went from plane to plane and ensured that the refuelling was underway. The huge bladders full of jet fuel were all hooked up, ready to refill the almost empty tanks. All she needed was the pumps, which, by her reckoned, should have been in place as soon as they arrived. Commander Bryan looked around her and eventually saw the machines slowly making the journey toward the waiting aeroplanes. Her mechanics immediately connected all the hoses as soon as the vehicles were in position. Commander Bryan ordered the overly curious ragtag ground personnel to stand back and warned them not to interfere with the refuelling operation. The crew onboard the aircraft constantly monitored all the ongoing activities, anxiously scanning all the dials and gauges and ensured that a smooth transition was underway. As the contents of a bladder were depleted, the empty receptacle was unloaded from the aircraft. The calculated weight for the flight was almost at its maximum, and any excess had to be removed prior to commencing the return journey.

Through the high-powered vision aid, Lesqueth watched the work in progress. At last, the doors opened and the mobile personnel steps were wheeled towards the planes. This was part of the laid-out security protocol, where she was checking out that the cousins were loyal and totally trustworthy. None of her essential people would be allowed to board until the craft was checked and then secured. Although the Americans were allegedly loyal to the core, as one had not seen them for a considerable time. One had to be careful, just in the off chance that they had another idea about who was actually in charge. The Baroness's security gave the all-clear signal, and the twelve hundred members of her future army were marched out to the waiting transport. All of the trainee soldiers had been allocated a ticket that displayed the assigned aircraft, seat number and order of embarkation. The little troopers displayed no excited chit-chat associated with their age group as they lined up to board by the numbers. They file onto the aircraft, the extended lines of two by two like giant snakes slowly making their way up the stairway and board the aircraft. As soon as the members of Lesqueth's future fighting force took the first step onto the craft, they immediately received the specially prepared serum, which was injected into their necks. The fully indoctrinated children then followed the directions to their allocated seating arrangements.

As per their issued orders, one by one, they almost automatically fastened the seat belts and attached the headsets, then closed their eyes. The vehicles containing the sealed boxes from Lesqueths home, medical equipment, emergency supplies and treasured artifacts, stood by and awaited permission to proceed to the aircraft. Tesporo had painstakingly packed all of the records that go all the way back for untold generations and depicted all of the associated families' daring deeds, skulduggery and treachery. He watched as he stood with all of the brethren and noted that he had not received any boarding information. Tesporo hoped that in the future, the keeper of the records and all of their followers would once again hold some esteemed positions and, with that, the recognition that he firmly believed they truly deserved. In days of old, they were consulted and guided the family heads in times of change; now, they were merely book keepers and funeral arrangers.

Tesporo intended to change this and once again retain its measure of importance in the fabled corridors of power.

At the other end of the country, Leena had got everybody moving. They hauled up the anchor and then set off in pursuit of the fishing vessel. Gareth was of the opinion that if they did not lead them to a like-minded community, then perhaps they could point his crew in the right direction. Both of them were aware that they were taking a big chance. As there was no guarantee that the settlements that they came across would not attack them, never mind actually converse with them. Gareth had explained to Leena and the crew that if they had remained in their previous lands, they would all be dead or slaves. The ship now up to nearly full power, followed the alleged route of the fishing vessel. The crew posted on the prow of the vessel scanned the horizon for any signs of life. Even travelling at maximum knots, there was no way that the smaller craft would have been able to outrun them. Leena passed the message that if they did not spot them within the remaining daylight, then their quarry had already docked, and they would have to double back and then send search parties ashore. A few hours later, one of the crew announced that the fishing vessel had just been spotted heading inland. Their ship now ploughed through the swell and followed the course of the smaller craft.

Gareth, along with the rest of the crew, had scanned every inch of the shore and reported that they had spotted no one watching them, no signs of life. He nevertheless hoped and prayed that the group that they found would at least listen to what they had to say. If they do not, he would have to come up with an alternative plan very quickly. Leena followed the course and now entered the inlet where the fishing vessel had taken. She continued forward keeping to the middle of the channel. Now, at the end of the main inlet, they had the choice of turning to port or turning to starboard. Leena turned to the right. She passed out the order for all the crew on duty to keep watching the shoreline for any unwelcome activities. Leena thought that they should have spotted the fishing vessel by now, and perhaps it had indeed turned to the port. As they were in uncharted waters, she had no choice but to continue forward just in case the vessel had docked further up the coast.

At the watermill Murray had gathered all the gang together to inform them of the bad news. They were all sitting at the table, waiting for Robbo and his long-lost cousin to make an appearance. They all listened as Alicia informed them about the strange old man, along with the equally strange little girl who, for some reason, made the hair on the back of her neck stand up. Alicia took it a step further and informed all that there was something not quite right with the girl. "It was not what she says, nor the way that she says it. I think there was something that she is not telling us. Some dark secret that she was very reluctant to part with. It was not as if we could torture her to find out the truth. So, I would suggest that, for the time being, we keep them segregated until we find out more. I, for one, don't want her mixing with the other children."

There was a knock on the door, and Robbo, with Uno in tow, entered the house. Uno looked totally unrecognisable, almost as if he had fallen into an industrial washing machine. Even Robbo had to admit that he would most likely have walked past him if he had seen him in the street. Uno reacquainted himself with everyone, almost giving the impression that he wished to throw himself to the ground in front of Okolo. She took in her stride, "It was great to see you again, Uno. Going by the faces, my children made when I present them food, I don't think they would agree to sending me any fan mail." Uno nodded, understanding that the old days had sadly gone. He refused the offer of food and explained that his system was readjusting to digesting real food after all the years of processed junk. Uno gladly accepted the cold of fizzy juice and the smoke.

He tried to keep the story true, not adding in anything or missing any of the details. Uno told all of the assembled about the demise of the swamp people. "They killed everyone, no one was spared, I am the last. Their leader pulled me aside; he told me to inform you that he was coming to kill you all. For you, Okolo, he delivered a special message, and he intends to save you till the very last. Once you have witnessed the demise of all of your people, he promised to torture you in ways that you could not possibly imagine." Uno told them all about the size of the advancing army, about all of the tanks and all the weaponry. "These people were not some disgruntled tribesmen; they were real soldiers with all the training, the uniforms, the saluting and the chain of command."

"I don't think you will be able to defeat them. If it was up to me to make the decision; I would be voting to run away. I don't think that the type of cruelty that they displayed was a new tactic; I think that is just the way that they are." Cha thanked Uno for telling them and added that he was welcome to stay here for as long as he wanted. Okolo informed the group that the patrols had been extended and that there had been nothing reported indicating the invading army's advancement in this region. Cha was worried about the tanks. A previous attack had been a couple of old tanks operated by ex-taxi drivers. A whole regiment of modern tanks, manned by well-trained and rehearsed crews, was altogether a far different scenario. Murray came clean and confessed that he did not want to run away, nor did he know how to take on a fully trained mechanised army.

Beth and her other half threw their thoughts into the ring. Uno, unaccustomed to the way they spoke, moved his head from one to the other every time they spoke. "We could blow the bridge over at the animal kingdom, then blow the bridge closer to home. But what if they don't come that way? It would just be a waste of explosives. Then, if they come from the other direction, we would just be erasing our escape route." Cat, who had listened to everything that had been said and informed them all that until they knew which direction the army was coming from, they would only be guessing. "We don't have any multiple options in any action we decide to take. Whatever we decide to do, we would only get one chance and one chance only. I suggest that we think about this very carefully, adding in a contingency to escape if it does not go according to plan."

Murray asked Alicia to draw up plans for extending the patrols and placing them further afield. "This, at least, would give us some form of early warning. In the meantime, we could look at what we would need to destroy the bridge. As

I am sure that, you geniuses would be able to make something that would be suitable out of all that stored weaponry." Murray was about to continue when there was a knock at the door. One of the patrols was delivering a report that a fairly large ship had just been spotted travelling up the fourth heading in their direction. Murray and Okolo looked at each other, thinking of the old woman's words and their recent conversation. Cha knew where this might lead to and told everyone that it could be nothing. Okolo nodded and agreed with what she had said but was going to get her weapons just in case.

The twins were, much to their annoyance, left in charge of the infants. The others jumped into the vehicles and then drove down to the shore. Cha watched the vessel through the magnified vision aid and informed them all that the people on the ship were not wearing uniforms. "They are not displaying any weapons, nor did they look as if they were lost. I get the feeling that they are looking for us." Murray was astonished when Cha broke cover and walked forward, then waved in the direction of the ship.

She turned around and informed Murray that there was no point in worrying about the unknown, "Better to get these things out into the open." Murray did not know what to say. None of them knew what to say. The love of his life has just exposed herself to possible danger. As he could not face one single day without her, he walked over to where she was standing and took her hand. Okolo, having no intention of missing out on any of the fun, walks over towards them. She did not wave nor hide her weapons. Onboard the ship, they had seen the woman waving. Leena changed her heading and then reduced speed and steered towards them. The ship came to a halt a couple of hundred meters from the shore. Not knowing the depth, it was better to be safe than sorry. Gareth volunteered himself, Alwyn and Cinds for the advanced shore patrol. He looked at Leena, "If all of this goes tits up, crank up the engines and get out of here as quick as possible. I am hoping that these are the good guys. I am hoping that they want to listen. Keep the engines running. If anything happens, promise me that you will go immediately and not look back."

Gareth puts his arms around her, "Maybe the next time we are on a boat, we will be heading towards a sun-drenched island." Leena hid a tear as he exited the bridge and headed towards the inflatable that had just been lowered over the side. Gareth climbed down the rope ladder and joined his two companions. As soon as he was seated, Cinds' opened up the throttle and then headed towards their date with fate. Gareth told them that he would do all the talking all they had to do was watch. Alwyn joked that the group on the beach would be nothing like King David as they had no numbers or initials stencilled on their clothing. Cinds and Gareth just looked at him and wondered where the fuck that statement had come from.

Chapter 19

Across the pond on the other side of the Atlantic Ocean, Blink, along with her crew, had finally finished all of the island hopping and, at last, reached the fabled shores of the USA. Their motor launched slowly and glided up the coastline, and with the sudden halt of human interference, super colonies of birds had reappeared. The huge sways of pink and yellow birds almost ignored the boats as they sailed gently past. The Everglades still looked somewhat uninviting and most likely full of dangerous animals. All the former settlements that they had passed by recently had been destroyed, leaving only burnt-out hulks that were once fine homes. As for signs of life, not one living soul had been spotted. Blink had still not received any signs from the old woman, and it was only her gut instinct that had made her travel this route. The Gulf of Mexico, for her, seemed a realistic choice as opposed to venturing northwards into the Atlantic Ocean. Sekoyaz and the rest of the crew had not complained and never asked any awkward questions that she did not know the answers to.

Blink wished that she could have presented them with the outline plan detailing what was ahead of them. As she did not know it was impossible, all Blink really could be one hundred percent sure of was that this was what she had been training her whole life for. All she could do for now was to travel onwards, looking for signs of Enunsha's whereabouts. The woman that she had only briefly met in her dreams could be located anywhere in this vast landscape. As the day would be drawing to a close soon, she informed the crew to keep an eye out for somewhere safe to rest for the night. Blink had, along with her crew, noticed all the signs of desolation. All of the people of this region were long gone. She thought if there were any bad guys residing here, they would have seen them, or they would have indicated their presence by now.

Sekoyaz indicated a suitable place up ahead. Blink nodded her approval, and the group moved inshore to the safe haven. The pier has not been used for quite a long time; the arrows embedded in various locations indicated that the last human activity was far from friendly. Sekoyaz was detailed to organise several scouting parties to ensure that this area was indeed safe and secure enough to settle down for the night. The sight of the arrowheads had worried Blink and gave her thoughts that there had been a purge carried out in this place. As of yet, there have been no dead or living humans spotted in the area. Sekoyaz returned a while later and informed Blink that they were the only people who were there. All of the locals must have left a very long time ago.

This region was notorious for snakes that would attempt to eat anything. The once-household pets that had outgrown their glass cases than had been unceremoniously dumped in the Everglades. Here, they had met up with other similarly disposed members of their species. The abundant food supply had enabled their kind to multiply into becoming the apex predator in the region. It was not until the missing person list had steadily increased that the authorities had finally realised that they had a highly aggressive, invasive species that thrived in the Everglades. Blink gathered her team together, "Okay, people, no wandering off on your own. Many people had vanished in this area. The animals that hunt here make no noise and would snuff you out in minutes. Also, don't even think about going for a quick dip. The waters around here were far from safe. The animals that reside there would quite happily wait for hours for some poor soul to venture too close to the water's edge. Get some rest, as we will be moving at first light."

Several hundred miles away, Jackson, assisted by Perry, had gone through the plan for about the fiftieth time. Jackson had thought that they were taking too big of a chance, with way too many unknown possibilities. Perry had enlisted the help of Abe to persuade him to help convince Jackson that the time to fight back was here. Perry gave Jackson his now standard speech, "We could sit and wait, then before we know it, the bad guys would be on top of us rounding up the ones that were still alive. I hate to think what would happen to the people that were captured. They don't seem the forgiving kind who would welcome us into their world with open arms." Jackson had heard enough, "Looks like I am outvoted on this one, but at least check the area again before you deploy our forces."

Perry replied that the area was undergoing a final check as they speak. Abe, still not happy at being denied involvement in the action, stood looking at the huge map on the wall. Once all of this nonsense has been taken care of, he would really like to venture out into this vast country. Abe thought that Enunsha could have a word or two with her father and persuaded him to permit his people to settle in a region where they could start afresh. As far as he was concerned, his people couldn't possibly survive in this desert region. They needed green fields, forests and flowing rivers. Perry's troops carefully scanned the area and looked for signs of anything out of the ordinary. They were aware that the group who had scuppered their hydro station build to produce ample amounts of green electricity had access to hi-tech devices that could instantly thwart and eliminate any threat. Every patch of ground, every bush and every tree had been meticulously examined to ensure that they contained no hidden devices. They followed Perry's instructions to the letter then, when all the preliminary work was complete, they settled into their concealed position.

Commander Green had approached G-Flem and highlighted the facts in the recent report that Abe, along with his traitors, were planning to attack. G-Flem had listened to the details. At first, she had fobbed him off. "As you were aware, our great leader would be arriving on these shores. The last thing that we need, the last thing that I need, was for her ladyship to get irritated with some disturbing news about Abe Hubstien and his band of renegades causing chaos." Commander Jack Green cautiously reminded her that she had promoted him because his predecessor was weak and indecisive. Green continued, "I am not asking for extra troopers. My units were more than capable of taking care of the riff-raff."

"Just think of the compliments that our great leader would bestow on you if the first thing that she sees when entering the great hall was Abe, along with all of his compatriots held fast in chains." G-Flem thought about what he had said, "What do you want, Commander Green, and more to the point, what do you get out of this." Jack assured his leader that all he wanted was some specialist equipment and for their species to be finally rid of the indigenous bipeds once and for all. G-Flem asked him if he had a list of what was required, and Jack handed her over the previously prepared details.

She informed him that his requirements constitute quite an extensive list. Commander Green agreed but highlighted the fact that this equipment would enable him to capture all of the rebels in one single swoop. "Just think, no more manpower being wasted in fruitless patrols, no troopers, no machines allocated to the wasteland. Once this little problem was cleared up, all of our resources could be put to work on our great leaders' projects." G-Flem gave in and informed Green that he could have the toys, but he should take into consideration that if his plan failed, she would personally cut him up and then feed him piece by piece to the hungry regimental pets in the canal. Commander Green assured her that his operation would be, without any doubt, a resounding success, guaranteeing a positive result. G-Flem replied that she would hold him to that, "Good news, I could deliver to the Baroness. Any bad news, I would have to sort out prior to her arrival."

Commander Green was dismissed, G-Flem thought that he was a cocky fucker. She would have to keep an eye on him, and in her world, cockiness, along with its overconfident cousin, delusions of grandeur go together hand in hand. Flemings would have to dispose of him before he gets confident enough to attempt to remove her from power. It was a pity, really, as he was so full of promise compared to the washout that held the position before him. She removed all thoughts of Green from her head and then returned to review the preparations for the arrival of the Baroness and her extensive entourage. If she failed to have everything ready, G-Flem expected that she would be dismissed immediately. The Baroness was not noted for tolerating failure. She was noted for brutally dismissing failure with the gun or swift flash of the blade. Flemings was confident that all that was required would be ready and available for her arrival. Her technicians had been put through that many dress rehearsals, and she thought that they could carry out all that was required of them in their sleep. G-Flem was taking no chances and would continue to make all of the allocated personnel go through every single step of the process until the very last moment when the Baroness arrived.

In Scotland, Miasnikov's vast convoy was making steady progress traveling northwards. His forward patrols had frequently returned with prisoners. Vladimir had taken an active part in all of the interrogations; he was bitterly disappointed in the lack of information that had been disclosed. Miasnikov had to admit that some of the stories had amused him as the people under torture had sworn on all things holy that the people up north ate children and kept dragons as pets. Some of the condemned had even claimed that the northerners were ten feet tall and performed black magic rituals to conjure up the devil. The most revealing fact that he had managed to extract was that the people he was searching for resided somewhere on the other side of the ugly bridge. Miasnikov had tried getting the condemned to pinpoint this location on the maps, only to be disappointed in the fact that they could not read due to poor vision induced by overindulging in various experimental concoctions derived from wood alcohol.

Now totally exasperated by the whole process of attempting to extract some useful information from the repugnant biped. Miasnikov ordered Essmie to remove the aroma and then dispose of him somewhere far enough away to ensure that the smell did not come back to haunt them. Subcommander Essmie returned a while later to enquire if

Vladimir had any additional orders. Miasnikov was tempted to request some decent food, some decent alcohol, and a prisoner that could speak in truths, not another one reciting fucking drunken campfire stories. He told her just to keep him up to date, "If anything changes and we happen to find someone who was not into fairy tales, please let me know. If any of the captured locals were related to the last prisoner, just dispose of them there and then. Essmie, I need an update for Lesqueth. Use your imagination and add in some of the very big-sounding words that she thrives on. Leave it out for me to sign, preferably before you send it." Essmie felt an explosive Miasnikov moment approaching and saluted, then quickly disappeared out of sight.

She thought that her boss was not coping well with being out in the field for this extended tour. He was, in her opinion, far more comfortable sitting in his office directing the operations. Their great leader expected results, and all they had done up till now was obliterate a couple of tribes who made the mistake of being located. The tanks had surrounded one of the settlements, there was no communication exchanged. Miasnikov just sat eating his breakfast while the well-trained crews started bombarding the buildings. He would be expecting this to be reworked into the report, citing valour along with the heroic deeds of his troopers as they held back wave after wave of determined, well-armed hostiles. The truth would be somewhat different; any survivors to emerge from the salvo had run out waving once white pieces of cloth. It did not matter that they were all unarmed, men, women and children, as they were all mercilessly gunned down. Miasnikov had shown no interest whatsoever in the massacre, and the only comment was that, for a change, his breakfast was nearly edible.

At the airport, Tesporo watched as the queues of Lesqueths' future killing machines got smaller and smaller as they disappeared into body the aircraft. The last youngsters went on board, and then immediately, all the doors were closed. Tesporo, now fully aware that the Baroness had no intentions of including him nor any of the brethren on the journey across the ocean, walks away from the runway. One of his disciples caught up with him, very perplexed as to why they were not going to be boarding the aircraft. The keeper of the records informed his followers that the Baroness no longer had any requirement for their services. The disciple looked as Tesporo pointed to where they were loading the cargo and included all the records that their order had meticulously updated for centuries. Several of the keeper of the records followers had gone onboard the aircraft, in view of adequately securing their archived material. They were immediately beaten up and then unceremoniously dumped on the runway.

As the engines all fire up, Lesqueth waved bye-bye to Tesporo. His followers, who had been ejected from the hold, scramble to escape out of the way of the aircraft as the engines increase speed and taxi up the runway. One by one, they accelerated until they reached take-off speed then all of them, in a perfectly choreographed movement, gracefully climbed up into the heavens. Tesporo was, of course, disappointed at not being included in her perceived future of their species. The keeper of the records gathers his flock together, issuing instructions that would guarantee their place in the future.

Lesqueth unbuckled her seatbelt. For the next ten hours, she was going to be onboard this craft. The crew manning the galley approached and then stood at attention before her. Lesqueth requested a bottle of the finest champagne and some privacy. It was going to be a long haul across the ocean; she had much to think about, and the last thing she needed right now was to be constantly interrupted by a flight crew who had been instructed to cater to her every need. The Baroness asked for the one in charge and informed them that if she required anything, she would press the service button.

Until then, she wished to be left alone and completely undisturbed.

In sunny Scotland, Gareth, accompanied by Cinds and Alwyn, approached the shore. He had told them that he would do the talking, but still not knowing what to expect, he told them, "All fingers and toes crossed on this one." As he was the first to leave the craft and set foot on the land. Cha, Murray and Okolo watched as the trio from the ship hauled their craft onto the shore and then walked towards them. Okolo to make sure that there were no misunderstandings, blatantly inserted a fresh magazine into her weapon, then flicked the switch setting on to fully automatic. Cha and Murray looked at Okolo, knew that if the approaching people appeared to be anything but true and honest, she would gun them all down in an instant.

Gareth knew that every word he said, along with every facial gesture, was going to be scrutinized and that the person holding the gun could very well be their judge, jury and executioner. Gareth held up his hands, then lifted up his jacket to reveal that he was not armed. Okolo, with her finger ready to pull the trigger, watched every single move. Gareth asked if they could step closer as he did not want to shout and would rather speak face to face. Okolo nodded, granting permission for them all to walk forward. Once the shouting distance was null and void, the woman with the gun spoke, "Okay, that's far enough, I suggest you start talking and avoid any sudden movements." Gareth introduced himself and his companions; Cinds' said hello, and Alwyn seemed frozen in time and just stared at the woman pointing the gun at them.

Gareth spoke, "Our country was invaded, and our community was destroyed. We fought back, killing many of the invaders, but they sent reinforcements and hunted us down like animals. Many of our people were killed, and all that remains of our group was aboard that ship. We were seeking shelter, but we also wanted to fight back against the invaders. We knew that they had been working their way up the country. The people that they did not kill were taken away and never returned. It was only a matter of time before they would arrive here and forcibly, without any compassion, introduce your community to their harsh regime. We seek a community that would let us rejoin the fight, and together, we might be able to defeat the invaders. We have weapons, we have supplies, and we have the experience of fighting the forces who wanted to crush the people of this country. If you are not the group that we seek to join, then perhaps you could point us in the direction where we could meet up with a like-minded group." Gareth supplied the listeners with some details on what he and his people had witnessed.

Okolo had listened to every single word, but she still had to be sure that the newcomers were who they said they were. "We have also experienced what these invaders were capable of. Just to make certain that you and yours were not imposters, I need all of you to remove your shirts." Alwyn had snapped out of his state of deep freeze and muttered something to Gareth and Cinds'.

Gareth curtly told Alwyn he should keep quiet and let the grow-ups speak. Alwyn did not pay heed to what his boss was saying and made a further attempt at speaking. Murray, who had stayed silent until now, informed Alwyn to remove his shirt or Okolo was going to kill him. "Right now, we need to know if you were one of them, so get undressed and let's see your back." Alwyn removed his clothes, and then, along with Gareth and Cinds' they displayed their nontattooed backs to the inquisitors. Okolo, now satisfied that they were not the bad guys, asked Alwyn what was so important that he had risked the prospect of being shot. He looked at Gareth, who just told him to get it over with and say what he had got to say.

Alwyn looked at Okolo, "I have met you before."

Okolo shook her head and then replied that if she had met him, she would have remembered. Alwyn shook his head, "I saw you that day you shot the woman that you had the car accident with. You shot her in the head, then just started walking away, even before she hit the ground." Okolo looked at him again, "There was no one there that day, only me and the woman." Alwyn shook his head, "I was hiding over in amongst the abandoned cars. I was there, and I know what I saw." Murray, along with Cha were now standing beside Okolo and ready to support her instantly should the need arise.

Okolo addressed the younger of the two men, "What you thought you witnessed and what you actually witnessed were two entirely different things altogether. You thought that I killed the woman because of a traffic accident. What if the woman I killed was actively involved in the manufacture of the virus that killed most of the population? She was one of them, one of the groups who were slowly eliminating or enslaving any survivors that they had come across. If I had to relive that day again, I would have no hesitation whatsoever in shooting her again. She was bad to the core of her being, and I had to end her, there and then." Alwyn held his hands up, "I was only telling what I had witnessed. How was I meant to know that she was one of them? I was only trying to tell my people that I had seen you before." Okolo asked Alwyn if he had killed any of the invaders, "Well, kiddo, a minute ago, you stood there, right in front of me, judging me for my alleged crimes. So, what about your crimes?" Gareth spoke on his behalf, "My group, the people I fought with, killed hundreds of the invaders, and if it was not for Alwyn's help, we would not have been so successful. He had paid his dues in full, and you could take it from me that he is up for the fight."

Okolo looked at the youngster, "What, you had a magic wand, cast a spell and made all the bad people disappear?" Gareth bluntly answered her, "Alwyn designed all of the explosives that blew up their vehicles and destroyed the dam, which drowned many of the attacking forces, enabling my people to escape. So why don't you cut him some slack and save your anger for the ones who truly deserve it? Are we going to talk like this for days before you and yours decide to inform us if we have found the right group? We want to fight. If the group we were seeking was located elsewhere, point us in the right direction, and we will be on our way. I have several hundred people on that ship who have travelled for days to reach here. Make up your mind. Either you want our help, or you don't want our help." Cha took over and spoke directly to Gareth, "We would like to find out more of what you know. Send a message to your ship that we were going to continue to talk. As a measure of good faith, as a measure of trust, two of my people would go onboard your ship until the talking was finalised."

Murray knew without being told that Alicia and himself would be nominated to take part in the exchange. He nodded to Alicia, "I hope that they have some seasickness tablets." Alicia told him not to worry as the ship was stationary and the movement would be minimal. Cha told them that she would see them in the morning and gave Murray a quick cuddle before he departed with Cinds' who had been nominated to take them to the ship. Okolo relaxed a little and put the weapon on safe mode as they headed back home towards the watermill. Gareth asked Cha if they were going to be kept in a cell. Cha replied that she was thinking about dinner, "That's unless you think we should just inundate your brain with lots of questions. I thought that we all could have a civilised conversation without the need for implementing her group's advanced torture and interrogation techniques." Alwyn piped up that he was starving. Gareth informed everyone that he thought Alwyn had an infestation of worms as he was always hungry.

Gareth and Alwyn were escorted up towards the medical facility. None of the locals gave them a second glance as they continued with their tasks. Cha, along with Okolo, received many smiles and warm greetings on the walk up to Cora's. Gareth got the strong impression that this was a happy community with no patrols of armed guards ready to beat up the inhabitants at a moment's notice. Okolo had somehow reached inside his brain and informed him that they did not need armed guards as everyone here was free and they were not forced to do anything. One of Cora's staff, the alleged ex-member of the secret police, opened the door and then escorted them to the doctor.

Cora thanked the head nurse and Okolo informed her that the two new chaps were here for a quick medical. As Gareth underwent the inspection, Okolo sat and watched the procedure. Cora performed her tests understanding that there was a stranger in front of her, and Okolo was just ensuring that no matter what transpired, she had Cora's and the community's best interests covered. Alwyn sat in the waiting room, chatting away almost non-stop to Cha. He explained at length that when he had joined Gareth's community, Scruffy had a very much different approach in confirming that he was not a disguised member of the invading armed forces attempting to infiltrate their group. Cha listened as Alwyn informed her that Gareth had already disposed of several less-than-honest people who had tried to surreptitiously work their way into their group.

Cha began to think that Alwyn could breathe through his ears as he talked incessantly about all of his adventures when he joined up with Gareth. Alwyn relayed the tale about King David and his misaligned quest for amassing as much gold and precious stones as possible. Cha asked him if she and all of her friends should adopt stencilling identification symbols. Alwyn replied that he did not think that was a good idea, "Why change things when all of the people I have seen here seem to be happy? More importantly, they appear to be content and relaxed. To have achieved this, I think that you must be one of the good guys. Otherwise, your people would be miserable and in chains." Cha very nearly got up and cheered as Cora announced that Gareth's check-up was complete and he could swap places with Alwyn.

Cha informed Gareth that his companion spoke very highly of him but couldn't help but to ask if he could breathe through his ears. Gareth admitted that Alwyn could talk the hind legs off a donkey. She asked him how the procedure went, and Gareth coldly replied that if the doctor had found even a trace of a family tattoo, her friend, the assassin in waiting, would have already killed him. Cha smiled, "Okolo was very protective, partly due to all that she had seen what these people could do. If it was of any consolation, everyone who arrives here is given a medical. We have to be one hundred percent sure that everyone is who they say they are. It would only take one of the bad guys to infiltrate our group to unleash all sorts of terror."

At that, Alwyn appeared and was accompanied by his bodyguard, Okolo. Cha addressed the pair of newcomers, "It looks as if we will be having dinner. After all, the twins are be the cooks tonight. Think yourselves lucky if my other half was doing the cooking, and you would confess all your sins immediately." Gareth asked if his cooking was really that bad, Okolo replied that his culinary skills were way much worse than that.

Murray felt like he had been awarded the short straw. No sooner than he had climbed aboard the boat, Murray felt his stomach issuing the red alert. Cinds started the outboard, and Murray instantly puked over the side. Cinds' looked at Alicia, "Oh, don't worry about me. Murray just does not like water. Rumour has it that he was even sick when he took a bath." Cinds' ignored her comments, and opened the throttle up and then travelled as quickly as possible across the relatively calm water. In the short time it took to reach the ship Murray's face was displaying a vibrant shade of sea-green.

Leena had watched the scene unfolding on the beach through the vision aids. On seeing the man puking she had asked one of the crew to go and locate a bucket. Cinds' climbed onboard and then waited for the couple to catch up with her. Alicia helped steady Murray as he slowly pulled himself together; they were taken to the bridge where Leena was waiting to meet them. There was no lengthy introduction, and there was no introduction at all. Murray was presented with a mug of overloaded sweet tea and a bucket. Leena almost scolded him, "Better to get the liquid down as quick as possible. The quicker it goes down the quicker we will find out if it was going to come straight back out." In a normal situation, Murray would have thanked her for her underlying compassion and understanding, but on this occasion, he reached for the bucket and ejected the foul liquid. Cinds' left the bridge and then returned a short while later. She handed Murray the sea sickness tablets, "They were well past their sell-by date, but they seemed to work on all of the other landlubbers." Murray dry swallowed a bundle of them down and mentioned that a cuppa without one grain of sugar would be gratefully appreciated. Leena ordered one of the crew to accommodate their guest's request.

Murray sparked up and asked the captain if she would like him to remove his clothes now or if it would be okay if he drank his tea first. Leena got straight to the point, "I think you were one cheeky bastard. You kidnap my friends, puke your way onto my ship, smoke without asking, then offer to remove your clothes, but only once you have finished your smoke and tea." Leena asked Okolo if he was always this polite and charming. Alicia laughed and then confirmed that her companion was probably the most honest straight forward individual she has ever met, and if everyone was like him the world would surely be a far better place.

Chapter 20

At the other end of the UK, Tesporo had taken a while to assemble all of the paperwork required. Now accompanied by the entire brood of his brethren, they had arrived unannounced at Buckingham Palace. The guards that were on duty, curtly informed Tesporo that as he was not on the official register, they were unable to grant him and his entourage permission to enter the grounds. Tesporo hissed a reply stating that the Baroness had tasked the brotherhood to maintain law and order in her absence. "Of course, you could refuse to allow us entry, but take into consideration that I have sealed orders addressed for the immediate attention of your commander from the Baroness. Just imagine what would happen, when our great leader returned and her orders had been ignored. Perhaps this was the moment that you summoned your superior, informing him that their presence was urgently required."

The trooper in charge of the gate, dispatched one of his subordinates to go and inform the commander of the situation. Tesporo, accompanied by his nest of vipers, stood in place, and none of them said a word and just stared at the guard detail. The troopers tried to ignore them, quietly hoping that the commander would issue orders to dispose of the keeper of the records along with all of his sycophantic followers. As soon as the commander appeared, Tesporo nodded to one of his acolytes to walk forward and hand over the sealed orders. The keeper of the records did not even wait until the commander had finished reading and asked him if he would like to see the precise orders that had been personally issued to him by their great leader.

The commander had, as expected, ignored him, but nevertheless, Tesoro's faked document was thrust towards him. Once he had finished reading the signed and sealed letter, he gave the order for the brotherhood to be permitted entry into the palace. The commander stood to attention and saluted, "The instructions from our great leader would be obeyed without question." He then ordered the troopers to assist and the keeper of the records in performing the duties that had been deemed to be of great importance by the Baroness. The rank and file of Tesoro's followers march into the building as if they were born there immediately set up shop in the great banqueting hall.

Once they had unpacked all of their equipment, Tesporo ordered the troopers to go and gather up all of the staff. All of the cleaners and gardeners, along with all the other forms of human dross were persuaded at gunpoint to assemble in the adjacent room. One by one, they were dragged into the great hall. Each of them was then branded, named and numbered. Tesporo's lackeys had rearranged all of the furniture so that when the domestic staff entered the room, they were presented by the sight of the supreme justice accompanied by his deputies sitting at the high table. The commander of the palace guard detail had been persuaded that Lesqueth would look favourably upon his presence at the judging table and perhaps even promote him for taking an active part in the proceedings.

The first prisoner was dragged in and then forced to kneel before the tribunal. The troopers not on duty accompanied by the keeper of the records' brethren have taken up all of the seating in the gallery. They hissed and then jeered, calling for severe punishments to be dealt out for even the most trivial of charges. The cleaner who was being charged for squandering much of her working schedule on idle gossiping does not truly understand any of the proceedings. She was foreign and had not quite mastered the new language. This, of course, made no difference to her alleged misdemeanours or her punishment. Tesporo, on hearing all the evidence, "In view of our laws and customs, I hereby order your tongue and ears to be removed. Perhaps this would act as a deterrent, and the absence of the said body parts would serve as a constant reminder. In years to come of your failure to perform the duties that were unfortunately neglected in your preferred choice of participating in endless gossip."

She was led away in shackles, blissfully unaware of what had been said and what was about to happen to her. As the next prisoner was led in to stand before the court. Tesporo had to postpone the proceedings for several minutes until the screaming subsided from the adjacent room. Tesporo covered his mouth and hid his lips from the condemned, on his knees before him. He whispered to one of his aids, "Cut the tongue out first the next time. Otherwise, I will end up with a severe headache before this day is through." The aide bowed and promised to deliver a much-improved service to the next participant. The prisoner now before him was accused of being a spy whose sole aim was to dismantle the fair and just governance that the Baronesses had set up to ensure, above all else, equality for all.

The crowd in the gallery issued calls for the death penalty, and Tesporo held his hands up to restore order in the court. "I sentence you to death. First, you would be chained up, and from here in, you would witness every punishment issued by these proceedings. This would be the last thing you see. As once all the crimes have been justly rewarded, your eyes would be removed, and then you would be executed. The manner of in which you would meet your last breath, I would leave to the judgement of your executioners." The prisoner screamed and complained about the unfairness of his trial and the barbarity of the court. Tesporo ignored the unfounded outburst and then called for the next prisoner.

At the end of the day, every single surviving member of the human baggage that was employed at the place was now without a tongue. Tesporo was of the opinion that, without question, justice had to be duly served upon the ungrateful. He had no choice; the humans truly deserved all of the punishments. As per the evidence laid out before the court, they were all guilty. The prisoner, who had been forced to watch all of the punishments being issued, was hauled back into the court. Tesporo was now in receipt of the proposed method of death, which had been decided by the executioners. He passes the paper among the panel of judges, who all added their signatures and approval without any hesitation.

Tesporo approached the prisoner; the pen that he had used to note all of the crimes and sentences was plunged into the prisoner's eyes. As he lay there clutching his now defunct viewing organs, Tesporo raised his hands and announced for justice to be carried out. The prisoner was now surrounded by the troopers and keeper of the records brethren, who now take it in turns of kicking and stomping the prisoner. The blind groundkeeper, come alleged spy, was beaten unmercifully by the mob. His broken and misshapen corpse was put on display and served as a constant reminder to the primitive bipeds that all crimes against the state were justly rewarded.

As he felt that Lesqueth had abandoned him and, with Miasnikov somewhere up the north of the country, crushing the rebels. Tesporo has taken the opportunity to increase his brethren's status within the remnants of the Baronesses forces. In the foreseeable future, he intended to inspect the remaining biped population that was currently employed in the various state-sponsored industries. Tesporo was of a mind that routine on the spot inspections, checking for subversive activities, would root out all of the conspirators. The troopers that were involved in these manoeuvres would be generously rewarded. Tesporo would grant them certain privileges that were deemed unacceptable and punishable under Lesqueths rules. He, as acting leader in her absence, would bend the rules, ensuring that the troopers would become supporters and loyal subjects of the brotherhood. In the last few days, several of the local commanders who were opposed to his new plans had unexpectedly perished or have been found guilty of serious crimes against the state. These commanders were immediately replaced by one of the many troopers that had been swayed, bribed and coerced to swear loyalty to the keeper of the records.

At the watermill, the two refugees were treated to a sumptuous meal. Beth, along with Debs, had gone to town in the kitchen and prepared a rather fancy meal. They had been annoyed that they had not been included in the welcoming committee, and rather than let the anger fester, they had channelled the negative energy into producing a meal of five-star quality. On entering the house, Gareth could not help noticing the spread on the table and asked if they always ate like this. Okolo could not help herself, "We always lure waifs and strays into a false sense of security before we torture them." Alwyn was reassured by Cha that her friend was only joking.

Cat sat at the table, saying very little as she observed the newcomers. Gareth and Alwyn were introduced to everyone. Okolo asked Alwyn if he had met any of them in his travels. He smiled and then replied that up till now, she was the only one that he had crossed paths with in the previous life. Cha thanked the twins for the meal and then informed everyone to dig in. Gareth did not know where to start. Alwyn had no issues helping himself to a portion of every dish on the table.

The twins have calmed down some and graciously accept all of the compliments for their culinary expertise. Uno was still having issues with digesting real food that was not fermented in an enclosed environment and ate very little. He went for the liquid option, filled up a teapot, then went outside to sit and smoke. He thought that the newcomers along with his hosts would have lots to discuss. Uno thought that this was a private matter and that he should have no input into the discussion.

Cat had noticed that as soon as her daughter entered the house and then joined the rest of the infants the humming had started again. This time it only lasted for a brief period, as now Sammarra and the rest of the children were almost looking in the direction where the old man and the young girl were being held. She thought that this was just a figment of her imagination. If she were to mention it to Cha or any of the others, they would no doubt inform her that she was being silly. Cat had caught a glimpse of Okolo and had thought for an instant that she was almost thinking exactly the same. The conversation at the table evolved around the two newcomers, and they talked freely about their experiences with the invaders. Cha had listened to Alwyn's methodology relating to the explosive mixtures that had been used in the field with devastating effect. She had even complimented his choice of ingredients, where the options were indeed very limited.

Okolo found the stories about King David's empire amusing and laughed at the stencilling of his initials along with the identification numbering on all the things that he seemed to think belonged to him. She thought that he must have been fairly stupid to think that everything was going to return back to normal and even stupid to think that he was going to be in a position of wealth. She also thought that he had surrounded himself with weak people who would be so gullible into listening to King David's waffle in the first place. If she had the unfortunate experience of being in his company, Okolo thought that she would have shot him within the first ten seconds of his spiel.

As the exchange of ideas and what they could do together to defend themselves against the enemy passed around the table. Cha thought that these people could help them and join them in the fight. She would have to run it past the others, but as Okolo had not shot them, she thought that there was a fair chance that her group would accept their help if they came to an agreement that was beneficial to both parties and the newcomers would all have to receive a medical check.

Even though Gareth had informed her that all of his people had been checked, she would insist that this procedure had to be carried out. If, for some reason, Gareth and his entourage refused, then there would be no deal, and they would have to leave. Cha took the bold step and offered Gareth a provisional agreement. Okolo gave her the briefest of nods and indicated that for the moment, and, she approved as the others got into the nitty gritty about what the two groups could do to take on the invaders. She had noticed that Uno had been missing for a while. Okolo slipped away from the table. Uno had just poured the last of the tea, and he was just about to savour the brew when Okolo appeared beside him. Uno handed her a ready rolled and noticing the handiwork, Okolo commented that either Robbo had been practicing or that the homemade cigarette was his own work. Uno pleaded guilty and confirmed that he also thought that Robbo's joints frequently resembled a burst couch.

She laughed at his observation, and then, as she sparked up, Okolo informed him that he should come and join them. Uno confided in her that he thought the conversation was privy to them as they stayed here and he was only a visitor. Okolo replied that he was the last of the swamp people and would always be an honoured guest. "Uno, you need to come in and tell the newbies what happened to your people. It was your place to tell them that we have all lost something. You have lost more than others. So, once we finish these smokes, you could come in and join us and tell them what happened. I will make you a fresh brew, and hey, just be you and tell them what you have seen." Uno thanked Okolo for the kind words and agreed to join all of them at the table. They finish up, enter the house then join the others at the table. Okolo introduced Uno to the newcomers, as he was being a little reticent to speak. She gave him a kick under the table and gently persuaded him to tell them what had happened to his people and how the invaders had relished every moment of killing all of his kin.

Robbo had spent his time interviewing the old man and the young girl who had made the journey with his old friend. Macdhiarmada was reluctant and far from cooperative in answering any of Robbo's questions. At one point, Macdhiarmada had asked if this was an interview for an emergency social security payment and if Robbo wanted his national insurance number, but he was unable to help him as he could not remember it. Robbo asked Macdhiarmada, Bryan or whatever the fuck he wanted to be informed as to what he had done in the old world.

The old man calmly replied that he had opted out of the system a long, long time ago. "I had seen the corruption that was blighting society many years ago and walked away from it all. I never registered as unemployed never gave any of the governmental agencies the pleasure of my time, nor my existence. I travelled the land conversing with fellow thinkers, free and unattached to all of the poison that had contaminated the rest of the blind and deaf population." The young girl, who had said absolutely nothing since Robbo had entered the room and, tugged at the old man's sleeve. Macdhiarmada leaned down closer to hear what she was whispering in his ear.

"My companion thinks that you would have very much enjoyed this lifestyle. Rather than having spent your woeful existence being chained to the chair in the bank, persuading people to take out loans that you knew they would default on." Robbo was taken aback; he had never mentioned his previous life in the old world. Macdhiarmada continued, "You have former office dweller stamped all over you. You may have yearned for freedom, but you never acquired the balls to go and look for it." Macdhiarmada just sat and stared at Robbo. He could have told him that he was just stating the obvious and he did not wish to partake in any confrontation, but on reflection, he also thought that he was almost a prisoner here and why the fuck he should be helpful. The old fucker continued to annoy Robbo and stated for the record that he and his companion had done nothing wrong, and even though they were no threat to his community, they were still confined to this room. Robbo replied that as he was reluctant to tell them anything that would influence the group's decision to release him, then like it or lump it, he stayed here.

Plus, the given fact that his companion only whispered and had never actually talked with anyone since they had arrived. Macdhiarmada asked Robbo if he and his compatriots thought that the little girl was a danger to his community, and if that was the case, why couldn't they just let them go? Macdhiarmada, now on a roll, continued, "Just let us go, let us go to freely wander this land. What would be the harm in that." Robbo replied that it was dangerous out there and added that if anything was to happen to them, he, along with his friends would carry the guilt for evermore. "I can't change anything. If you don't tell me anything, how could I be sure that you were who you say you are?"

The young girl started to speak. The words were way above her age and went straight into his soul. "You sit there armed with your misguided perception in judging us for being something other than what we are. I wonder if you had ever been this inquisitive when you were dolling out the many mortgage applications that the recipients would willingly sink every penny they had into. In you knowing full well that with their current financial situation, there would be an almost definite one hundred percent chance of failure."

"We were in possession of no skillsets that could anyway connect to a perceived threat to you or yours. As Macdhiarmada has already informed you, we are innocent travellers just looking for a place to rest and possibly settle. You could come and question us every single day for all of eternity, and the replies to your questions would always be the same. As my friend has stated, if you want us to stay, let us out of this cell. If you don't want us to stay, then let us go."

"Think deeply about what possible threat an old man and a young girl could possibly present that would put your community in danger. You should go now and meet the new people who have arrived." At that, the young girl cuddled snugly into Macdhiarmada, and they both nodded off and indicated that the questioning for today was well and truly over.

Robbo was shocked. The young girl who had never even revealed her name has almost reached into his soul. To reveal his dark secret that he was bitterly ashamed of his past life, so much so that in his dreams, he still saw the desperate young couples' dreams fall apart when unemployment and then divorce came knocking along with the red warning letters that slowly destroyed their world. He made his way back to the house. Okolo noticed the look on his face immediately and knew that something was wrong. Robbo was introduced to Gareth and Alwyn, joining in with the conversation but secretly waiting patiently for this first opportunity to inform Okolo of what had transpired.

Uno was still going through the story depicting the demise of the swamp people. Robbo sneaked out for a much-needed smoke. Okolo joined him moments later and informed him that he looked like shit. Robbo disclosed what had been discussed while he was interviewing the odd couple. Okolo agreed with him and also thought that there was something that was not quite right about them. "We would run it past the others when the new people leave," Robbo asked if the newbies were suitable and trustworthy.

Okolo replied that she would not know until she had seen all of them. "We don't have room for them here, but Mark could possibly let them stay at the farmhouse. I guess that Murray would have to go and ask him if he has room for some lodgers. We have been talking for most of the day, and they have agreed that they would undergo a medical. Do you think you could persuade Cora to go onboard their ship to perform these procedures? That way, if there were any problems, we could deal with them on the ship."

Robbo remembered the old woman in the hooded cloak's words of warning, knowing full well that Okolo remembered them also. He asked her if she was going to accompany Cora on her expedition, and coldly, Okolo replied that she would not miss it for the world. "I am thinking that I would ask Cat to join us." Robbo agreed, even though she had not actually asked him. As the meal and the talks were over, Cha informed the visitors that they could stay the night. Robbo, at Okolo's prompting, has volunteered to show them where they would be bedding down for the night. Cha told Gareth that tomorrow, Cora and their doctor would come aboard the ship and test everyone. Once that was done, we would sort out some accommodation for all of your people and then make plans to defend our communities. Gareth and Alwyn thanked everyone for listening to their plea, not forgetting to compliment the twins on the best meal they had had in like forever and some. Robbo took them over to where Cat and Frank used to reside. "It was nothing special, but it was clean. The door would not be locked, and you are free to wander about. The galley was next door. Frank puts on a fairly decent spread, but please don't mention the twins cooking." Robbo bids them farewell and leaves them to it.

When he returned to the house, Uno had retired for the evening, leaving them to discuss today's events. Okolo had just finished informing the group of the strange experience that had happened to Robbo when he was interviewing the odd couple. All of them agreed that there was more to their story, especially the young girl who was reticent even to disclose her name. Cat told them that when the children were awake, she had the feeling that they were looking towards where the odd couple were stationed.

"I know that you would all think that I am being silly to mention this, but the hairs were standing on the back of my neck. I would not go as far as to state that Sam was communicating with the girl, but I am sure that they were aware of each other's existence. There was no proof that this was nothing more than my imagination but there was definitely something happening between them. It also may just be a mother's instinct, but it was almost as if the girl was saying, I know something that you don't know."

Okolo agreed that she, too, had felt that something had transpired when the humming was going down but couldn't quite put her finger on it. Cha informed everyone that the humming was only noticeable when all of the children were together. Cat piped up that they all knew the humming intensified when Sammarra was in the room. "I am not saying that she seems to be the leader. Perhaps she was just the catalyst that brings them all together." The twins had not yet added their input, so Okolo asked them straight out what they thought.

Beth and Debs spoke in their accustomed manner, where one started the sentence and the other one finished. "Sometimes, especially since Uno's passengers have been here, we have been dreaming about the people who used to be in charge of the castle. None of Uno's people were in the dream, only the rulers who regularly hunted down and then tortured the locals who had survived. We don't know if this was related or not, but several times, we woke up in the middle of the night. Much to our surprise, both Terina and Lyla had been sitting staring wide-eyed at us. Almost as if they were waiting for us to tell them the story about the castle and its people. I know, we know that it all sounds terribly farfetched and almost strange, but that was what we have been experiencing." Beth and Debs asked the others if they had any similar dreams. All of them confessed to having nothing similar. Cha admitted that sometimes she woke up sweating in the middle of the night, having just dreamt that Murray had opened up a restaurant chain.

Okolo looked at the clock, and it was still stuck on the same numbers as it was when Murray and Cha had first moved into this house. She informed Robbo that they would need to take their little dumplings next door and bed them down. Okolo gave Cat a huge cuddle and reassured her that she would not let anything happen to the children. Cha asked the twins what they really remembered about the dream, "Are there any parts that were repeated, or were that just the same people you see in the same places." Beth and Debs replied that they had just seen the man, his artwork and the crazy woman. "There was no dialog, no sound, only the same pictures. The man stands with his hands on his hips, almost waiting to be drawn into the horrendous artwork displayed on the walls. The crazy woman, who should have been locked in a secure ward, runs about the castle grounds, hunting the locals. She does not say anything. She just searches the area like a wild animal, almost sniffing the ground, hoping to pick up a fresh scent of the quarry. That's all we know. That was all we see. Cha, we really need to ask you something." Cha told them to go ahead and ask. "If Murray opens up an eatery, do we really have to dine there?" Cha smiled and then replied that in the world where Murray comes from, takeaways were the norm. "So don't worry, you could always order a takeaway then discretely place them in the incinerator when he was not looking."

Cha invited Cat to stay the night, "Sammarra was out for the count, as always, cuddled in between Mark and Alfie and surrounded by the dogs. Why disturb them?" Cat accepted her offer and thanked her for listening to her worries. Cha replied that her worries were her worries, "If you ever have any doubts about anything, you could come to me any time of day or night. We will always be here for you no matter what happens." The woman mucked in and tidied up. Murray's ears must have been burning bright as they all joked about his alleged restaurant and all the court appearances defending the charges of malicious food poisoning.

Onboard the ship, Murray was sent to the sick bay; even though the ship was stationary in the water, he was still suffering from motion sickness. Leena asked Alicia if he was like this when he took a bath. Alicia replied that Murray had only to look at the tub, and he turned instantly green. Leena saw no point in hanging about the sickbay and took Alicia on a guided tour. Most of the people on the ship said hello, and the smartasses among them stood and saluted. Scruffy was the main offender. He has taken it a step further and marches towards her and addresses Leena as captain. Leena asked him straight up if Gareth had anything to do with this. She told him to fuck right off when he stood to attention again, then replied no, mam. Leena ordered Scruffy to go and get some weights and then to see how long he could hold his breath underwater. She spotted Cinds' and motioned for her to come over and join them. Leena, although they had already met, introduced them. This was Cinds' she was Alwyn's other half. "They pretend that there was nothing going on, but for fucks sake, we were on a ship." Cinds' pleaded guilty to all charges and informed them that the galley was open. The eatery was packed, and the hubbub of the conversations going on was all about going onshore and walking on land. Alicia asked if they were not all sailors, and Leena shook her head. "One or two of them were fishermen at one point, and the rest were just waifs and strays. As we stayed on the coast, my crowd had no option but to learn. Gareth's team, not one of them apart from Cinds', had been on anything larger than the paddle boat at the local pond. The only one who had ongoing issues with seasickness was Gareth. He should get on well with your guy in sickbay."

Alicia replied that Murray was not her guy and added that he was much too posh for her tastes. Leena thought that this was a good answer and thought that she would get on with the one with piercing green eyes and wild red hair. Alicia confessed that she thought that Murray must be feeling terrible as this was the longest time that she had ever seen him without smoke in his hand. Leena replied that some people were just not meant to go to sea, and her friend should avoid going on a boat forever. "I guess that Gareth must be doing okay, and all is going well, and your friend should be returning to dry land tomorrow." Alicia agreed and thought that if it had not turned out well, Cat would have been already on board, accompanied by her best friends killing her people.

Chapter 21

Blink was not sure where she was; the ground around her was enveloped in a swirling mist that gathered around her feet all the way up to the lower half of her legs. The people were oblivious to her presence as she moved around and in amongst them. The old woman in the hooded cloak beckoned her to come closer. She pointed at all of the people marching about in uniforms and waited for their great leader to arrive. This, she informed Blink, would be a time of great danger not just for her but for everyone on the planet. The old woman in the hooded cloak encouraged Blink to pay close attention to all of the activities taking place. Blink was drawn from location to location as they witnessed all of the strange devices, along with all the accompanying strange machinery, being carefully lifted into place and then meticulously connected together.

Men and women dressed in spotlessly clean overalls were directed by people in uniforms to perform the allocated tasks. They were all like robots as they jumped to it, working with the various tools required to complete the task at hand. The people did not look unhappy; they all looked more like they were all part of the regime that was putting the finishing touches to a plan that had been in place for a long, long time. As she watched all the synchronised movements, the old woman in the hooded cloak informed her that it was now impossible to halt this process. 'What would come after this would be unbelievable; it would disrupt the future.' 'Your friends across on the other side of the ocean would also be affected by this event.' They had moved to another location; the old woman warned her that Enunsha was now in great danger if you moved quickly, you may be able to save her. You would not be able to save everyone; saving Enunsha was important for the future of you and yours. Blink had no idea where Enunsha was to be found and looked at the old woman in the hooded cloak almost pleading to her for some form of directions. This time, they had moved to a huge room where the maps covered all the walls. Commanders ordered troopers who moved various markers on the board. A huge clock on the wall, with increments marked out in bold red and yellow, almost glared at her. Blink was instructed to look at the map where the markers were placed out in the shape of a circle.

Now awake, Blink checked her feet, already knowing that even though she had slept with her boots on, they would be ingrained with dirt. She washed away the dirt and then made plans for the next part of the journey. The name of the place where they were going still eluded her, but at least she knew what direction to travel. Sekoyaz reported in, and at least this time, Blink would be able to provide some information on where they were going. She drew a rough map in the sand, pointing at where they were presently situated and then indicating to where they were going. Sekoyaz knew without being told that all of their people would not survive this journey. She listened to everything that Blink could tell her, and then, having absorbed all of the information, she went and welcomed all of the sleeping members of the crew to a brand-new day.

Commander Green had been busy, having obtained all of the items on his wish list. He had set about, painstakingly putting all of the pieces into place. This was not an easy task as some of the equipment was ultra-sensitive and had never been used by his troopers. To speed up the process some, Jack had even joined the techs who were translating the operation manuals into trooper speak. Commander Green made them all go through the whole process of how to connect the items, where to place them, how they worked and the possible inhibiting factors that could cause a malfunction or a false positive.

If he had not required every single trooper on this mission, Jack reckoned that he would have disposed of at least thirty percent of them by now. He fully appreciated that none of them had ever used this kit before. Everyone was expected to learn, and everyone was expected to learn quickly. He thought that some of his team would have difficulty ascertaining which was their left hand and which was their right hand. Jack thought that if this was the best people they had to offer, then in the future, the company would have to supply them with slip-on boots labelled with a large L and a large R.

Commander Green had persuaded some of the excess workforce into joining his regiment. G-Flem was not informed of this action, which was strictly forbidden and deemed a category double A offence. As in all of his surreptitious activities, Jack had no intention of leaving any proof which could be traced back to reveal his involvement. As far as he was concerned, who would actually care enough to notice that fifty of the primitive bipeds had disappeared from the work detail. Even if someone were to question this discrepancy, the numbers could be easily attributed to the frequent industrial accidents or the summary executions for insubordination. Jack had at one time been fond of using the phrase, outgrown their useful lifespan. The commander had used it many times in the past but even he thought that he would be pushing it if he used the same excuse for the disposal of fifty of the smelly, bothersome bipeds.

Prior to the great change, Jack had suffered the misfortune of having to immerse himself in the multi-cultural, multi-faceted sphere of the biped's existence. They had elevated themselves into being something that they had no right to be. They incessantly complained about anything and everything. This firm that he had been placed in proclaimed to be at the forefront of human expansion. They bent over backward to accommodate all of the new fads and trends, proclaiming that this was a new golden age. At this point, the bipeds were issuing proclamations to anyone who listened that they were able to recategorize their identity. It amused Jack to no end that one of the employees had voiced their opinion that they wished to be identified as a box.

The company, in view of all the social media platforms, even though they were mostly artificial, pulled out all of the stops to accommodate the new identity of the worker. They changed everything to suit; the clock card was changed to the box, and the bank details were changed to the box. Green was laughing now that the box even had the audacity to declare that they were now allergic to plastic, and the company spent untold sums of money in the hope of appeasing the employee and finding a suitable alternative.

The box played the game to the full, on social media and now claimed that the company's delay in finding a solution had accelerated his allergies to the point where he was now in the process of being allergic to all oil-based products. At his desk in the HR department, Green had been allocated to the unenviable position as the first point of contact for the box. Jack had constantly reassured the box that the company was doing everything possible and that they were in consultation with experts all over the world to find an acceptable solution. The box was having none of it and ridiculed the company at every opportunity, even proclaiming that Jack Green was, without any reasonable doubt, solely responsible for all of his ills.

The social media platforms were updated regularly and depicted the alleged atrocities that Jack had committed on behalf of the company. The bleeding-hearted liberals were anything but shy when they righteously jumped on the bandwagon. They supported the claims that the box was being ridiculed, persecuted then punished for expressing his God-given right to be recognised and fully accepted without prejudice in his chosen identity classification.

As his media exposure expanded, the box was invited to various talk shows where he put on the performance of a lifetime. In listing all of the companies' failures encapsulated in his custom-built allergy free habitat. He put on a rather convincing tear-jerking routine, vilifying the HR's conduct, especially the Greens' extreme right-wing fascist attitude that he felt had put him over the edge. The box now claimed to have almost lost the will to live and to address his suicidal tendencies, attended a shrink on a daily basis.

Jack could do nothing about it; his bosses called him in regularly to deal with issues arising from the media circus following the box had acquired. Who were in the process of attempting to obtaining an interview with the company prior to releasing the damming statements. They told him that the company had every faith in him and this nightmare would eventually all blow over. Mr Green persevered with his posting in the real world, and then, out of the blue, he received the encrypted communication that informed him to tidy his affairs and then report for duty. He informed the head of the HR department that he had to take some emergency leave for a family problem. Green had no family as such, nor had any problems that he was aware of.

Now that he had received the heads-up, the score had to be settled. Jack, with the resources available to him, had kept a careful eye on the box. Fully aware of his home address, his social circle and his habits. Jack packed a few of the essentials required and then headed across town. Green put his locksmith skills to good use, then, with the expertise of a seasoned burglar, opened the door to the box's residence. The apartment was occupied by Box, his partner and another couple, and Jack did not feel the need to introduce himself as he incapacitated all of them with the stun gun.

He was a little perplexed and unable to figure out why all of the company present were dressed in swimming costumes along with Stetsons and cowboy boots. Even more perplexing was the fact that none of them were adorned in cardboard. Green quickly secured them with cable ties, then changed the channel on the wall-to-wall state-of-the-art media screen. He helped himself to the extensive, well-stocked drinks cabinet and then smoked while waiting patiently for his audience to re-enter the real world. Jack had to admit that it was one hell of an apartment that the box stayed in; you name it, they had it, and more than that, they had the best version available. One by one, the occupants came around; understandably, the box was a little upset, and through the inaudible muffled sounds, Jack could have sworn he had heard his name being issued, connected in some undistinguishable sounds associated with the word bastard.

Now that they were all awake, Jack informed them of the rules appertaining to this evening's planned entertainment package. The first item on the agenda was all of their social media passwords, along with all their user names. One of the guests, Green, never asked what their name was, who they were, nor who they stole from to maintain this opulent standard of living had strongly objected to disclosing any of the requested information. Jack complimented them on their defiant stance of non-cooperation, "Toes or fingers, you can choose what you were prepared to lose." He never waited for a reply; he calmly removed the hammer and the rather fine carpenter chisels from his holdall. To lure them all into a false sense of security. Jack had then lied through his teeth and informed them that he was only joking and that the items he had put on the table were just props.

Five minutes later, he informed them that he had changed his mind. Everyone present was one at a time, roughly manhandled into position, and Green then proceeded to remove all of their little fingers. As they all shook with fear, Jack placed the fingers on the table. "Do I need to resume removing more of your body parts, or were you going to grant me free unrestricted access to your social media catalogue." Through the muffled group response and the red lined rapid head movements. Jack was pleased to announce that from now on, he would only hack their media profiles and not their bodies. One by one, he ungagged them and then extracted all of the details that were required to open up their preferred web pages and the accompanying platforms. Jack streamed the data onto the large screen. The box was the first to open a new post, which was linked to all of the popular mind-numbing media presentations.

'My dear friends, I would like to thank all of you for supporting my quest for change. As you can appreciate this has been rather a difficult time for myself and my closest friends. Without all of your help and encouragement, I would not have been able to survive the cruel treatment that I had received from my employers. We were in the process of winning this war on the established mega companies entrenched in modern society who steadfastly refuse to address nor encourage change. As you can all imagine, this has depleted lots of my energy, and to enable me to fight in this epic battle, I had come to the conclusion that to continue in the righteous cause, I would need to recharge my batteries. My tribe and I were going to go into a self-imposed state of hibernation. Sadly, this would equate to my regular posts on the media being absent for a short period of time. If you fully support our quest for justice, please feel free to join our righteous cause. Our affiliated sponsors will be streaming very soon all the details that would enable you to build your very own hibernation box. I hope you all fully understand, and again, thank you all for the more than generous support.'

Green asked his captives what they thought about the latest post; unable to make out what they were saying, he ignored whatever point of view they were put across. He continued with the additional posts. The other three people in the apartment immediately released updates on their respective web pages and declared their undying support for the box. Jack chuckled as he got right into it and added that in full support and their heartfelt belief that Box was a true martyr of this modern age, they were also going into a self-imposed state of hibernation. They encouraged all the other supporters of the box to join them in their quest for recognition of the new species.

Jack watched and was almost mesmerised as the like numbers slowly increased along with the pitiful messages of encouragement, hope and lots of brightly coloured cardboard boxes. He commented that the box should be paying him for all the hits that were now inundating his web page. Green apologised for being a bad host and hinted that he should have offered them some adequate nutrition. The holdall was placed on the table, 'I had some of your old favourites here, and I really hope that you all enjoy this as much as I will.

'Here were the rules: you eat, I watch, and if you don't eat, you will be punished.' The box watched as Jack ripped the cardboard into strips and then placed them in a bowl. He untied all of their hands and wished them all bon appetite.

Green displayed the hammer and chisel, asking them if perhaps they required an incentive. Slowly the guests started to chew on the tasty treats. Jack continued to shred more of the corrugated paper, 'Just pretend this was the second course.' None of the guests said anything in return. He thought that they should be relishing the delights that were on offer, 'Look, people, I had spent a very long time sweating over a hot stove to make you this sumptuous meal.' 'If you don't consume more, I will be more than seriously offended.'

One of the guests, the woman with the face reminiscent of a bulldog chewing a wasp, muttered that they were full and could not possibly eat any more. Jack sighed and then stuck the chisel into the side of her throat, and as she bled out, he stuck a bundle of the already shredded cardboard into her mouth. The remaining guests consume more of the meal. Jack encouraged them to clear the entire plate, only to be disappointed as he constantly replaced the dwindling contents. The box issued a comment that the food was very dry and was guessing that they would require a drink to wash it all down would be very much appreciated.

Green profusely apologised, explaining that he had not expected so many thirsty guests and had only brought enough drinks for one. He then proceeded to kill the extra two guests with repeated hammer blows to the head. Jack looked at the box, 'You wanted a drink and a drink you shall have.' The box was dragged over to the table; Jack opened the bottle and forced the engine oil down his throat. The box tried to resist; the more he resisted, the more Jack forced the contents down his throat. Two bottles of 10WX or-something oil, immediately followed up by two bottles of high-octane petrol and the box had ceased breathing. These were the good old days and boy, he surely missed them.

Commander Green now finished reminiscing, thankfully did not have to score points on any of the now-defunct social media platforms. He only has to keep his current boss happy, and more importantly, he had to keep her well out of the way. He received word that all of the key players were in position and now requested the green light. Jack transmitted the good-to-go code.

Lesqueth had calculated that the journey across the ocean must nearly be over; she freshened up and pressed the service button. The head of the flight crew appeared immediately. The Baroness requested a small breakfast accompanied by a pot of English breakfast tea. The lead steward called on one of his assistants and instructed them to gather up all of the debris. Lesqueth does not have to wait for long before being presented with the morning meal. As she played with the food, Lesqueth couldn't help but think how healthy the mass of water below looked, what a difference the removal of millions of bipeds had made. In a relatively short space of time the ecological systems had rebounded and then replenished all of the marine life. That had been slowly suffocating under all of the man-made pollution.

The Baroness, now having lost all interest in her food, pressed the buzzer and informed the person in charge to take it away. The teapot was refreshed; Lesqueth smoked and contemplated the day ahead; who would have thought that she would actually be going to be the leader of this world? Her ancestors had built the idea of a new regime for their species, but it was her determination that steered the plan to fruition. She had no regrets about disposing of all the non-essential elements, whether it be humans or even members of her own species. It did not matter; they all had to be permanently removed.

Some of the American families were guilty of being less than honest about their true intentions and blatantly lied to attempt to disguise their true aspirations. These people had been sealed up in their allegedly secure underground kingdoms and witnessed their family's demise as they succumbed to the disease. Lesqueths thoughts were interrupted as she was informed that they should be landing in thirty minutes. The Baroness was ready for whatever her trans-continental cousins threw at her. She suspected that they would, for all intent and purpose, appear to be nothing but true and loyal.

One way or another, they would all be brought into line, she would govern and advance their species without any interference nor dissenters to her unquestionable, absolute rule. The view of the landscape below changed as the aircraft made a gentle turn and slowly started to descend. Lesqueth lit up another smoke, and she had thought that she would have felt like one of the early explorers seeing the great continent for the first time. Unfortunately, this did not happen. Lesqueth just saw this as one of the necessary journeys that would have to be undertaken to ensure that all of her destiny had all the required sequence of events in place at the correct time.

There was no marching band nor a ticker-tape parade awaiting her arrival. General Flemings was waiting at the bottom of the steps to welcome the supreme leader. She stood to attention as Lesqueth escaped confined of the aircraft and then bounded down the walkway to reach firm ground. The Baroness informed the general that would be enough saluting for the day, adding that she expected everything to go as planned. G-Flem confirmed that all of the arrangements were in place. As the general was speaking, the transportation started to arrive, and several vehicles broke off from the main convoy. The armoured personnel carrier, along with a couple of heavy-duty trucks, drew to a halt beside Lesqueths aircraft.

The Baronesses private guard detail and replaced the drivers, then moved towards the now lowered cargo bay door. As the precious cargo was being loaded onto the waiting transport, the children belonging to Lesqueths future army started to disembark simultaneously from all of the aircrafts. Prior to landing, the guards had administered the wake-up injection that curtailed any effects of jetlag and sparked some life into the little cherubs. They all now marched towards their allocated transport as per the details on their issued landing cards.

G-Flem, who had no motherly inclinations whatsoever, thought that what she witnessed was a truly exceptional stroke of genius. She believed that every one of their species had a part to play in their collective future, and to be allocated to one's particular part at this early age was nothing short of inspirational. The Baroness had noticed the generals' reaction of awe and wonder. Thought that at least this one would not be expressing any concerns over depriving the troopers of the allegedly important childhood development years.

The Baroness, in previous years, had travelled to many countries and met countless diplomatic delegations and their transparent associates. She was fully aware that this was all part of the game, to persuade them to give her family's company sole extraction rights on their country's precious minerals. The one thing that she absolutely abhorred was the endless lines of knuckle crushing, where she was viewed to be strong, weak or acceptable as a leader, solely on the type and strength of her handshake.

G-Flem opened the door to one of the many identical all-terrain vehicles. The Baroness informed her that as she would be travelling in the same vehicle. She assumed that the general had opened the door for herself. The Baroness got in the vehicle and joined her in the back seat. G-Flem got down to business and updated the great leader on all of the current activities being carried out by the various groups. "Commander Green was at present out in the field, hopefully he would be apprehending Abe Hubstien and his renegades within the next twenty-four hours. It had taken longer than expected to track them down, and with this group's activities coming to an abrupt end. We can say for sure that all of the bipeds who managed to survive the great sickness had all been eliminated." Lesqueth was handed the report detailing the recent demise of the great Indian nation. As she perused the document G-Flem received a message over his comms. "It appears that an unlisted piece of cargo has been located inside the landing gear on one of the planes," Lesqueth asked for some details and then was informed that the culprit was clothed in once white-on-white robes.

She denoted that he was one of Tesporos brain-dead brethren. The Baroness asked G-Flem what was the current method of disposing of unwanted bags of flesh and bone. The general replied that the popular trend at present was feeding them to the regimental pets that inhabited the canal. Lesqueth nodded her approval and added that she would like to witness the proceedings. G-Flem issued the change of orders over her comms device. The Baroness noted that the request was instantly obeyed without any returning stupid questions arising and G-Flem must be running a well-trained crew, who do what was required when they were ordered to. Lesqueth thought this one may perhaps be the one she should have had running her forces in the UK. JJ had shown lots of promise and had the correct breeding, the correct education, and training, only to be stopped in his tracks by ex-miners and sheep shaggers. Miasnikov, unfortunately, had a limited skillset and, hopefully, a limited lifespan.

The motorcade grinded to a halt at the canal. The white-robed figure had already been delivered to the location. He looked a little worse for wear and tear as he had suffered broken legs when he was drawn into the aircraft's landing mechanism. Lesqueth looked at him without feeling any sympathy for his predicament. G-Flem asked her leader as she wished to have the unregistered cargo questioned. The Baroness stepped forward and then asked the broken figure of a man if he happened to have a name. He almost hissed that his name was Extorpz; he had thought about disclosing that he had been inadvertently drawn into the landing gear while trying to escape being crushed. Extorpz had overheard the troopers jokingly pointing at him and then shouting at the water creatures informing them that the take away had arrived. He thought that there was no point in saying anything further, then pushed himself off his seat and rolled into the water. Lesqueth was very impressed and awarded the late Extorpz ten out of ten for his presentation and entertainment for not succumbing to fear, thus saving her ears and her time.

The motorcade continued on its journey towards station A. In the slight detour, the transport carrying the future army had already arrived and was now boarding the train in an orderly fashion. The Baroness commented on the alleged efficiency of the Magno-L. G-Flem politely informed the great leader that the journey from station A to the CCP was around one thousand miles, and it would take just less than an hour to reach their destination. G-Flem added, "You would not notice any of the momentum as the system was rail-less, frictionless and one hundred percent motionless. The only thing you might notice was the hum of the magnetic particles energising and then de-energising. It was a really pleasurable, quick and efficient way to travel. I only wished that we had seen the foresight and had the necessary funding to extend the system worldwide. I appreciate that the world was different then, but perhaps in the future, every destination on this planet would only be a few hours away."

The Baroness replied that the future held many possible advancements for their species. Without any political restraints or the many intolerable human ethical considerations holding them back, they can now do anything, absolutely anything at all. "It was no longer a matter of time but now more of a matter of when and how."

G-Flem talked non-stop about all the possible innovations that the techs had been working on and praised the Baroness for her foresight into the possible use of this new technology. All of which would have seemed far-fetched and pure science fiction only several years ago. The general apologised for giving the Baroness earache and then announced that the journey was nearly over. Lesqueth, if she listened very carefully, she could almost hear the hum of the demagnification process. Arriving at the CCP as expected, all of the preparations had been made. The young troopers marched off the Magno-L as they diligently followed their instructions to the required assembly points. There, they would be met by the section head, who would escort them to the barracks. G-Flem thought that it was amazing that none of the children uttered the horrible noises associated with their various age groups.

Lesqueth was taken on a tour of the Central Command Post, G-Flem showed her great leader where all of the various departments were situated and introduced her to the person who was nominated as first point of contact. As Lesqueth absorbed all the relevant information, the people who were involved in all of the processes to enable this complex to function went about their normal tasks. Not once has Lesqueth caught any of the worker ants staring at her;

again, she was more than impressed with the general's firmly held grasp on discipline.

The biggest shock was that she had not seen one group of workers engaged in idle chit-chat. Everything she had witnessed up till now all seemed to be serious work-orientated discussions, no laughing, no raised voices and most of all, no lazy workers sauntering about almost as if they were providing a great service for just turning up. The Baroness issued G-Flem with praise and complimented her on running a tight ship. The general gracefully accepted the praise but admitted that it was the dedicated teamwork that made them a cohesive force.

The next section that they entered was the control centre; Lesqueth saw the large clock on the wall with the bold red and yellow increments. In the very near future, she would be in this very room, orchestrating the most advanced technological breakthrough that this planet has ever witnessed. If the theoretical physics worked and, it would propel her and her species into the future, the beginning of a new era and making them completely invincible.

Chapter 22

Gareth, along with his second, had survived the night, and no one bothered them as they walked around the community. Like everyone else who had newly arrived at the watermill, they had ended up in the Orangery. Cat had just happened to bump into them when she was out with Remus. Gareth was not what you called an animal lover, but it had been noted by anyone who mattered that Alwyn had more than a soft spot for animals, especially dogs. Remus almost ignored Gareth and treated Alwyn like a long-lost friend and dropped the once-yellow ball as an invitation to play. Cat informed Alwyn that he must be okay as this was quite an honour. He lay on the ground with Remus and delivered a much-appreciated belly rub and commented that dogs had always sort of adopted him. Gareth joined in the conversation and added that it was just confirmation to the latest to fact that it was not a rumour and Alwyn did truly stink. The man, along with his new best friend continued to bond and ignored the cruel remarks. Cat reminded them that they were more than welcome to have breakfast in the galley, and if they went now, then it was possible that they would avoid the rush hour. They took her up on the advice. On entering the galley,

Frank greeted them like he had known them forever. Alwyn, as expected had some of everything that was on offer. Gareth, as always, thought that his companion had hollow legs that stored all the food he consumed; anyone else would have easily weighed twenty-one and a bit stone. Okolo entered the galley and grabbed a cup of something hot. She wished them a good morning and informed them that when they were ready, she would accompany them down to the shore.

Murray was now awake and was slightly confused as he looked around him not quite sure of his surroundings. Now, remembering that he was on the ship and then recognised the bucket that the pirate queen had almost awarded him with as a star prize. Alicia sat across from him and offered congratulations for sleeping the whole time that they were on the ship. Murray asked if he had really slept all the way through. Alicia confessed that was almost true, except for the puking, frequently cursing Neptune, and snoring like the dead. Murray informed her that he should have told her that he hated the water.

"I don't mind getting washed, but as far as the sea goes, count me out. Water, fish and boats just don't appeal to me." Alicia smiled, and Murray asked her what was with the smile, "Oh, nothing really, but Cha told me a long time ago that you wanted to be buried at sea."

He replied that Cha must have been angry with him that day, and he would have come back and haunted them if they had deposited him into the murky depths to spend all of eternity with the slimy creatures who lived down there.

The pirate queen had arrived, and she looked at him and remarked that he looked sort of different when his skin was not green. "Anyway, good news, Gareth and Alwyn were on the shore. Cinds' was on the boat, ready to take you both home." Alicia thanked Leena for everything; Murray just ignored her as he could not wait to get back to dry land. He kept his eyes closed and just pretended that he was somewhere else, anywhere else but here, as the small craft bobbed up and down on the water heading towards the shore. The gang was there to meet them; Cha looked at Murray, who was still in the process of concentrating very hard and did not quite notice that the boat had come to a halt and was actually back on dry land.

Cha touched him on the shoulder, "Murray, you are now on dry land; if you don't open your eyes, I will ask Okolo to shoot you." Murray, not quite believing her, opened his eyes one at a time just to confirm the truth. He said hi to everyone, "I was really enjoying that journey; there was just something so relaxing about being on the water." Everyone looked at him, amazed at his sheer bravado, now accompanied by the projectile vomiting as he took his first steps onshore. Gareth, along with Alwyn, helped Cinds' put the craft back into the water and then headed back towards the ship.

Okolo informed Murray that sometimes he was so full of shit, but most of the time, he was okay as she helped him up onto his feet. She handed him a lit number, he inhaled some of the smoke and then announced to anyone who was interested, "That feels better." Cha filled Murray in on all that he had missed. Okolo asked him if he had noticed anyone who was pretending to be someone that they were not supposed to be. Alicia announced that as he never left the confines of the cabin, and that there was really not that much to observe in the bottom of the bucket. She also thought that it was highly unlikely that Murray had even noticed his shadow. She then added that all of the people that she had come across seemed friendly enough.

Cha gave Murray the good news that while the people on the ship were being examined, he had been tasked with going through to the farmhouse to ask Mark if he could accommodate the waifs and strays. Murray nodded and accepted the challenge but wanted to freshen up some. He instantly regretted his words as the gang all had a hand over their faces and pretended that he was that smelly. Okolo, along with Cha and Alicia, then pretended that the stench was bad and that they were dying. Murray held his hands in the air and, surrendered and agreed to go and shower immediately. They gave him a round of applause as he set out on the walk of shame. The rest of the gang sat and waited for an answer. Gareth and Alwyn had provisionally accepted the terms but had to run the conditions through Leena and the rest of the people onboard. If they all agreed, Cora would carry out the examinations prior to letting them join their communities.

Murray had just opened the door and received a warm welcome from his closest friends. While he was getting licked to death by Charlie and Romulus, Robbo appeared. 'I was just dropping off my charges with the twins.' Murray nodded, then asked him if he was getting the old man and the young girl to say anything meaningful. Robbo just confirmed that Macdhiarmada was awkward and was still trying to infuriate him at every opportunity. "The little girl, now she was something else, and I could swear that she was trying to get into my head," Robbo added that once things were settled with all the newcomers, maybe he would like to come and talk to Uno's travelling companions. Murray agreed that once he had some spare time, he would help him out. Robbo headed off and left Murray to it; the children were all excited to see him and bitterly disappointed that he did not have any time to perform any of his now-famous animal impersonations. Beth, along with Debs, spoke to him in their accustomed way and informed him that all of the children were fine. "Well, that was apart from the humming; we think that it seems to be growing stronger." Murray could hear it but did not notice any change, and he asked them to mention it to Cha and the gang when they returned. A quick run about the shower and an even quicker change of threads, then Murray was going to make his way over to Marks. He was not quite sure as to how he was going to ask this favour; somehow, Murray would just have to slowly bring it up into the conversation without blurting it straight out.

Gareth, now having arrived back on the ship, presented the terms and conditions for joining up with the group onshore. Leena thought that it was a bit on the strange side that the new group wanted to examine all of their people, given the fact that they had all been checked out previously. She had asked Gareth if he thought that they should join them. He admitted that given the fact that they really don't have much in the way of other options, he thought that they didn't have any other choice but to agree to the tests. "If we don't agree, we will have to leave, leaving us with the question of where do we go from here. I think we should take them up on their offer; we stay and fight. Once it was all over, we could always move away from here."

Leena told him not to even mention the sun-drenched island, which at this present time could as well be a million miles from here in not-so-sunny Scotland. Gareth suggested that they gather their people together and then asked them what they would like to do. "We can give them the options that we presently had available, the good, the bad along with the uncertain future with each and every option." Leena gathered everyone in the galley and then started to deliver the news. "The leaders of this new community had offered to let us stay and join the fight. First, we all had to undergo a medical for them to check that there were no infiltrators hiding among our group. Just so that you all know, Gareth and Alwyn have already been checked; if you have any questions about the tests then go ahead and ask them. If the vote goes against staying, then we would be back to square one. I, for one, would be voting to stay. Please have a think about it, while we organise the voting process."

Murray had just cleared all of the checkpoints and arrived at the farmhouse. Mark greeted him with, "Just the chap I was wanting to see. The last time you were here, you asked about the process of taking pictures. Well, we had good news, and I can get the bits and pieces put in your vehicle while we have some tea." Murray asked if the equipment came with the very easy-to-operate instruction booklet designed specifically for luddites like him. Mark laughed telling him just to give the paperwork to Alicia. They drank tea and smoked, then Murray just got to the point and asked Mark if he had room for some waifs and strays. Marks gave him some numbers; he could accommodate some of them, but unfortunately, not all of them. "As these buildings had not been occupied for quite some time, they all need some form of repair work carried out. I would get my people to start to prepare the habitable ones, ready to take in the new people. If the numbers change, I will let you know immediately." Mark saw Murray back to his vehicle, winding him up on the new bio-med scanners that they intend to install at the checkpoints. Murray gave his friend a bear hug and thanked him for everything, and as he got in his vehicle to depart, he told Mark that he knew what he could do with the new scanners.

Miasnikov's convoyed had progressed further northwards, and he was disappointed that the resistance from the inhabitants they had encountered had been weak. Vladimir had expected an army or even a reasonably well-equipped militia to be waiting, ready to attack. A few modified pickup trucks had been blown to smithereens as they approached the convoy, and then the various groups of armed peasants who made the mistake of crossing their path had been eliminated without hesitation. If this was all that the locals had to offer then he would be back at Blackpool sooner than expected. He summoned Essmie and informed her that they required some prisoners to be shipped back to his headquarters for interrogation. Miasnikov looked forward to inviting Lesqueth to view the newly designed and installed entertainment package. Vladimir summoned his scribe to update the Baroness on the recent events and instructed them to put their vivid imagination into gear to make the report sound really interesting and full of the rather long, unpronounceable words that she liked to torment him with.

His thoughts were interrupted by one of the other commanders informing him that they had received a note from a group of the local partisans. Miasnikov initially thought that he would just shoot them and then have a nice, quiet, undisturbed lunch. He changed his mind and held his hand out for the note. The barely legible scrawl informed him that one of the local groups wanted to join his forces. They professed to know the area well and were seeking to be part of the winning team. Miasnikov sets out to make arrangements to have a pow-wow with their leader. He shouted out for Commander Essmie. She had been ordered to go and locate the chap who wished to sign up and join his illustrious forces. "Make sure you extract all the useful information; if it was just waffle and campfire stories, send him along with his commandos to the entertainment facility in Blackpool." Essmie did as she was told and half expected to be called back immediately with a change of orders.

As per her instructions, Essmie arrived alone where the subject was last spotted; she left out a message and gave him guaranteed safe passage to attend a face-to-face meeting. Essmie retreated to the secure location and waited patiently for the mystery guest to show up; she had snipers positioned covering every approach to eliminate any unexpected surprises. A sole representative of the group who wanted to join up appeared on the outskirts of the tree line and moved cautiously towards her. Essmie spotted the lone figure approaching and then waved to confirm that she was alone and that it was safe for them to continue. As the distance between them closed, Essmie prepared her stall to welcome the stranger that would hopefully get them to relax enough to talk away like they were reunited, long lost friends. The stranger had arrived, and Essmie offered the woman some tea along with some of the food. To alleviate any suspicions,

Essmie tasted the food from each plate and drank some of the liquid from each cup. The woman's appearance was rough, and the scars on her face were a mix of old and new ones. Lorrie noticed Essmie looking, "Some guys just don't accept no for an answer." The commander nodded, appreciating that the old courtship rules were no longer applicable.

The women talked away, and Essmie lied through her teeth and stated that she was part of a group that wanted to bring back law and order. Lorri admitted that she was tired of foraging and all the other problems that were inherited from scraping by on a day-to-day existence. Essmie poured more tea and then produced the map. Lorrie pointed out the location of the ugly bridge. She was just getting to pointing out areas where she thought other groups were located when her head exploded. Essmie immediately dived for cover and thought that there was another sniper in the area. The sound of the oncoming vehicle abruptly returned her to reality. Miasnikov rolled down the window and beamed. He informed her that the interviews were over for the foreseeable future. The advance patrols had located the group that he wished to destroy. Vladimir looked at the now-dead Lorrie, "That was a good shot, even if I had to say so myself. Pack up all your stuff; we start the advance now, so chop-chop or, as the locals used to say, Tally-Ho."

Murray had returned from the farmhouse; he had then gently persuaded the twins to set up all the equipment for taking the pictures. Murray had asked more than a few questions. The twins were gobsmacked at his complete lack of knowledge in view of how the digital world actually worked. Murray was perplexed, "No fix, no tub of water and no developer?" Beth and Debs wondered if he had actually stayed in a box for years that had somehow denied access to basic technological advancements. As part of the deal, he had agreed that they, along with their children, should get their family portraits done first.

Once the twins were satisfied that Murray understood what buttons to press and, more importantly, the buttons he had not to press, they proceeded with the family pictures. Murray halted the shoot for a second, opened the door, and had a quick look. He informed them that he was just checking that Rebecca's make-up face was not waiting outside. Armed with trunks full of clothes that would enable her to dress for the occasion in every imaginable scenario for her artistic modelling portfolio. Murray returned back to his appointed task and took his new role as the portrait impresario seriously. He repositioned the group, "A little closer, Debs darling be a good girl, show your teeth, do not snarl like an animal, put on a smile to light up the heavens." Beth asked him if he had taken any pictures yet. Murray replied that he had taken many and now wanted to know how many empty slots were remaining on the imaginary roll of film.

Beth, along with Debs, asked him nicely to move away from the equipment, and they would take over the technical part. Murray was transfixed as they brought up the pictures on the computer. He had, in fact, taken almost a hundred pictures, albeit some were of the walls, the ceiling, some were of the furniture and several which, upon closer inspection, could be a close-up of one of his fingers, but he had actually taken several good shots of the twins and their bundles. Murray complimented himself on the great pictures and blatantly ignored the vague assortment of the ones that had gone skewwhiff. The twins selected the ones that they required, printed them off then placed them in the machine that covered them in the plastic material that would enable them to keep the cherished pictures forever and ever. Murray behaved like a pedantic five-year-old who wanted a picture of him and the dogs but insisted on being suitably attired for what he has named the authentic shoot.

The twins were mystified as to why Murray had darted up the stairs. He returned with the sheepskin rug that he swiped from the bedroom floor. Murray asked the portrait photographers of the year to be patient as he draped himself with the animal skin, then pulled in Charlie and Romulus for the snap. He spoke to his best friends like they understood every word and informed them that they had to look a little on the serious side. Debs had just pressed the button when the rest of the gang arrived, they had got tired of waiting for the boat people to announce their decision and had decided to come and wait in the house. Murray asked them all to wait for their turn, and amazing asked Cha to go and beg, borrow or steal another animal's skin so that she could join the family photograph.

Cha thought that it was perhaps time to take Murray to the doctor, but Okolo saved the day and any awkward conversations by borrowing a rug from next door. Murray asked them all to keep quiet and not to interrupt, as he would like the perfect family photograph to be captured. Debs gave them the thumbs up and informed the participants that the image had been captured for posterity. Murray now over the moon, picked up young Mark along with Alfie to join in with the posing. The remaining children had even stopped humming and were just as mystified as the adults in the room and almost wondered what was actually happening.

Murray held aloft the now plasticized pictures like he was holding the double prize-winning international lottery tickets for all to see. Alicia and Okolo, along with their brooding infants, were the next family to undergo the family photograph. Okolo hated getting her mug shot taken and had difficulty in obtaining the correct pose. Debs had tried all the proverbial portrait pleads and said cheese, only got a reply of I don't like the fucking stuff from Okolo. Murray witnessed the developing situation and shouted out loud and clear that he would make dinner. The look on Okolo's face was priceless and enabled Debs to capture the perfect snap. Alicia gave him the nod of approval but had to ask him that when he was in his old job, did he have to resort to entertaining the workers.

Murray smiled, "you had no idea the number of jokes and tricks that I had to perform to get the guys on the shop floor to work. To cheer them up one time, I told them that I was dying. They were all over the moon, and production increased exponentially that month. I was only playing the sympathy card, unfortunately I had to lie and inform them that the doctor had read the wrong report. They just hated me even more for that, which I thought was great. They can hate me, but as long as they all worked, I never had a problem with that." Okolo could not help herself, "Was your name Murray the bastard then?" Murray shook his head, "They actually named me Murray the smart bastard, which, as you can imagine, I took to be a term of endearment."

Okolo asked if he would go and swap out with Robbo while he took part in the portraits. Murray agreed to do the necessary, and as he went to the door. Okolo called him just to inform him that he was still a wanker. Murray faced her and then delivered a flamboyant bow and an equally flamboyant hand gesture of one finger. Alicia informed all the children to ignore Murray's hand gestures, "If he does that again, he will have to reside in the naughty corner for the foreseeable future." The children and the dogs just look at her, wondering what planet she is actually from.

Murray's happiness was shattered when he heard the sound of the first shell exploding. He immediately about turns and runs back to the house, barged in and interrupted the ongoing hilarity. "We were under attack; get the people evacuated to the shelter. Then get all the ones that had been trained to gather at the assembly points." Cha informed him that Cat was still down at the shore, awaiting the arrival of the boat people. Murray asked her to help with the evacuation and informed her that he would go and get Cat.

Karen has also heard the explosion, and straight away, she informed her workers to abandon the task at hand and go to their muster stations. She then took several crews up to Coras to help pack then transport the emergency medical supplies required. The people in the community all ran to take cover, the start of a queue had started to form at the stairs. Alicia was already there and informed the crowd to remain calm and refrain from panicking and shoving their way forward. "There was plenty of room for everyone, the shelling was not here; please take your time and gently make your way forward."

Murray arrived just in time to witness the next shell arriving. The first target looked to be the ship, with the next incoming shells getting closer to the vessel. Murray checked that Cat was safe and unharmed and then signalled the ship to come towards the shore. He did not know how close they could reach, but he hoped that they would stand a better chance of disembarking all of the passengers and crew before they suffered a direct hit. Murray scans the hillside opposite and can see no signs of any of the guns; Cat informs him that they could be miles away. She elaborated, "All they need was a group of spotters to direct the coordinates." Murray thought about crossing the bridge to locate them when the next volley of shells started exploding near the centre of the crossing. Eventually, the directions improved and one-by-one the shells got a direct hit on the bridge, and then, slowly, with each shell, started to demolish the structure. In no time at all; all that remained of the crossing was now several uneven stumps that protruded above the waterline.

The ship had started to move slowly at first, and then, with the engines at full blast, it headed at full steam to reach the shore. The explosions followed the ship as she steered towards the land. Leena had instructed her crew that the women with children get off first, and if they had to shoot anyone who argued with that, then just shoot them. Gareth asked her what he could do to help, "Get everyone to put off a life vest, tell them to hold on to something and brace for impact." Leena had no sooner finished issuing the instructions when the ship contacted with the rocks beneath the water and then came to an abrupt halt. The pirate queen abandoned her post on the bridge and then went to help her people. There was chaos all around her, and people were pushing each other out of the way to get on the available small boats. Leena fired a round in the air, "Women with children in the boats. If anyone disagrees with this, please let yourself be known. Anyone who can swim, jump overboard now and make your way to the shore." The shells had been getting closer, and one had just hit the stern of the ship. The explosion rocks the vessel; the metal groans in protest and then separates, sending shrapnel in all directions.

Her crew was busy pushing swimmers and non-swimmers over the side; Leena heard one woman protesting that she couldn't swim. She curly informed her that the crew member would teach her, then pushed the two of them overboard. Leena frantically did what she could to save as many of the people as possible. She spotted Gareth ushering up the last people out and up onto the deck; they only made eye contact when the next volley achieved a perfect score, with every shell making a direct hit. The ship was now just a smoking, misshapen hulk of distorted metal.

Murray, now with help from his people, dragged the sailors ashore and, pulled them out and away from the water's edge then pointed them in the direction of shelter. There was not much he could do for the seriously wounded, as there were too many people struggling in the water. More of his people arrived, and he saw Cha, Okolo, Robbo, and Alicia chest-deep in the water, pulling the survivors ashore. He grabbed Gareth and stopped him from going under again; all Gareth could do was mouth some words. Murray was helped by Cinds' who joined in and pulled him ashore. She went closer and made out the words, "Go and find Leena, and something about an exotic island in the sun." She closed her eyes and then immediately returned to the water to pull in any remaining survivors.

There had been a momentary lull in the shelling, and the people were frantically directed away from the shore. Those who couldn't walk were helped up the stairs where the transport that had been organised by the twins awaited them. The ones that needed urgent medical treatment were gathered up and then delivered to Cora's makeshift facility. The others who could walk unaided were directed up toward the underground shelter. Murray, who had done all that he could on the shore, shouted above the racket and told everyone that as soon as he found out what was happening, he would let them know. "Until then, you all know as much as I know. Remain calm, and we will get back to you as soon as possible." Cora had put out the word that anyone with any medical training was required to help out with the causalities. Several hands went up, and Murray's people took them in hand and ushered them towards the medical facility.

Cinds' and Alwyn were among the volunteers; they admit that they do not know much, but if they could help in any way, they would be happy to stay. One of Cora's nurses instructed them to follow her as they went to gather up more furniture to rearrange into makeshift beds. Cinds' spotted

Leena lying still on the ground, and she took a moment to tell her that Gareth loved her and would meet her on the exotic island. Cinds closed Leena's eyes and then got back to helping, lugging about the desks, wardrobes and anything else that could be utilised for the ongoing emergency.

The shelling continued, bombarded the shoreline and ignored the now defunct vessel and now concentrating on the land. The explosions indiscriminately pepper the hill overlooking the water. All that remained of the lookout post was an indescribable mess of cement and bent and broken reinforcement steel wire. Murray couldn't figure out why the shells were not being directed over the brow of the incline. Cha informed him that whoever was in charge was just letting them know that there was no way out in that direction, and they were holding them in place. Murray clicked on it straight away and noted that the attack would come from the other direction. He wondered why they had not received any news from the advance patrols. Cha informed him that they are not due back until tomorrow, "We should send someone out to find out what was happening."

Murray agreed and walked away, and Cha asked him if he thought that he had do everything on his own. He replied that there was no way that he would allow her to come. Okolo stepped forward, "Looks like it was you and me then."

Murray gave in and knew fully well that Okolo would not be swayed, persuaded or coerced into staying. He asked if he was still a wanker, and she replied, "Oh, that's for sure, one hundred percent accurate, but at least you are a wanker; that is on my side." They grab the first available form of transport and then move towards the area where they thought that the patrols should be operating in. Okolo gave him directions to avoid the numerous landmines that had been sporadically placed to deter and slow down the invading forces.

Okolo asked Murray to stop, "I think it would be better if I drive; I would hate for you to get your right mixed up with your left." Murray wanted to say something, Okolo told him that she knew that she was also a wanker. She laughed. "But at least this wanker knows where the landmines were located." Quite chuffed at the cutting remark, she pressed the gas pedal, and now happy that Murray was not going to get them blown up, they went off in search of the patrols.

Chapter 23

On the other side of the world, Blink, along with her crew, had travelled all day and all of night to reach this nameless god forgotten place. The engine power on their crafts had been maxed out as they crossed the Gulf of Mexico. As she had calculated that it was impossible to cover this vast distance in one go, Blink had roughly triangulated the huge expanse of water into a manageable journey comprising of two legs. The first stop had been fairly uneventful, where most of the brief time ashore was spent locating and then bunkering the fuel. She knew that the crew were tired, almost at the outermost limits of their endurance, but she had to press them on. "A day late and they would be too late." This she had kept telling them, hitting home the sad but true fact that there was a great danger out there. One that would alter the lives of everyone on the planet, and they were the only ones who could made a difference. Blink spurs them on, informing them that once back on the water, they could take shifts on who stays awake, then who gets to sleep. "This was the last leg of our long journey. After this, I hope we could all take it easy for a while."

Sekoyaz like the rest of the crew was functioning on vapour. A sleep, a meal, and a wash would be greatly appreciated by all, especially her, but for now, she had to step up to the plate and join in with Blink to push everyone forward. She joined in pulling the containers onboard to refuel their crafts, but at least this was the last leg. As for a rest at the end, she, like the others, would just have to wait it out and see what happened. She did not think that Blink knew exactly what would happen when they arrived at the final destination; the only thing that Sekoyaz could guarantee was that she would stand side by side with Blink no matter what challenges they faced. Blink waited for the signal to confirm that all the crafts were ready to move. With everyone accounted for, she gave the order to move on out. The crafts edged out into the expanse of water and gradually increased speed, now all at full throttle, they headed towards where Blink had told them that they would be desperately needed to combat against the great evil that intended to engulf the whole of the planet. Blink had prayed to the old woman in the hooded cloak that she would help and guide them to ensure that they arrived in time.

Perry had arrived at the forward position where his best troopers had been waiting for days to lay on a surprise attack on the invaders. The guys were very frustrated that they had seen no action; they had trained non-stop for this for weeks on end. The heat, the flies were annoying, and the snakes, along with all of the other horrid little insects that could inflict serious damage, were pretty scary. Up till now, they had all been lucky, a couple of close calls with the venomous reptiles that had to be quietly removed. It was the silence that bothered Perry up until now; the bad guys had followed a strictly adhered to pattern. So many days on station where they searched, followed by so many days of inactivity and then a constantly repeated process. The only problem was that the repeated process had not been followed; for several days now, his troopers had not even seen a suspect plume of dust in the vicinity. According to the plan, they should have arrived here days ago. Perry was about to call them all in and return to base when a tell-tale plume of dust was spotted in the distance.

At first, it was just an indistinguishable speck of disturbed sand and dirt moving across the semi-barren landscape, but through the magnification of the high-powered vision aids, Perry was able to view the oncoming convoy. He was taken aback that the enemy had chosen this form of advancement; their previous movements had all been surreptitiously carried out in the dead hours. They had moved metre by metre and left almost no obvious signs of their recent infiltration into a new area. These guys were perhaps overly confident that they were invincible. They just appeared to have thrown caution to the wind, then were now almost announcing their imminent arrival to one and all. Perry, much to his consternation, thought that there was something not quite right about the way the bad guys approached. If he ordered his troopers to withdraw, with the lack of available cover, they would be exposed to enemy fire and easily mown down. Perry readied his weapon, and as per their training, his troopers, without hesitation, followed suit. The faint, almost inaudible mechanical noises of the weapons selection switch being moved out of the safe position blended into the ambient background noise. The only sound that was now present and rang out in everyone's ears was the noise of the approaching vehicles. Perry waited until the last possible moment before he gave the appropriate hand signal to detonate the concealed shaped charges.

The two vehicles at the front of the convoy were exposed to the full blast of the plastic explosives. They somersaulted through the air, then the severely distorted personnel carriers rolled over a few times before coming to a sudden halt. The vehicles that were travelling way too close behind them tried desperate manoeuvres to avoid a collision with the now dead and defunct transport. They swerved this way and then tried to move in the other direction, only to be caught in the crossfire that Perry's troopers were unrelentingly laying down on upon them. The ambush was almost a perfect textbook example of how a well-planned covert operation should be performed.

Perry thought that the whole performance was just way too perfect, given the fact that the victims of the onslaught had not even fired a single shot in return. Adding to this, the fact that the enemy convoy had failed to observe even the basic formation rules when travelling at high speed.

This was a fatal mistake as it removed any possibility of countering even a minor assault or sudden interaction by insurgents. He ordered his guys to check in amongst the now bullet-ridden misshapen hulks for information and any survivors of the attack. One of his guys approached, "You were not going to like this." The trooper handed his leader a fully loaded magazine, all of the rounds were blanks. Perry thought that someone had just pissed down his leg and they were now trying to convince him that it was raining cats & dogs. He rounded up his troopers, "Saddle up guys, we need to quick time it back to base, I think that we had just been well and truly fucked over. Forget all about the laid-out procedures for travelling, pump that gas pedal straight to the floor and don't even think about sparing the horses. Let's go, guys, move it on out, we are going to be needed at the base. I hope we get there in time."

Lesqueth had settled in for what now is home within the vast complex of the CCP. She had been constantly checking for flaws in their operus morandi, running tests and random inspections. As far as she could see and in view of all that she had witnessed, it was a flawless setup. G-Flem should have been taken to the side and perhaps even congratulated in public for running a very tight ship. Lesqueth really hated performing to the masses; she had no problems performing an odd execution or two. It was the addressing of the crowds that she despised. Knowing fully well that a fair percentage of the people attended would at that precise moment would be wishing or praying very hard that they were in an entirely different location. Lesqueth could not really blame them for that, as they were all guilty of doing this in one form or another. The Baroness issued a quiet sigh, and all this would change soon, no hesitations, no debilitating thoughts where the perpetrators would have any seeds of doubt, colliding with conscious and unconscious thoughts floating about unregulated in their grey matter.

It has taken a fair amount of time, lots of planning and required the implementation of shedloads of new technological advances to be brought forward and utilised not quite in the way their inventors had envisaged. As her father used to quote and quote often, 'Who the fuck were they, to tell us how a new tool should be used, they only invented it. We paid for all of the research, we paid for all of the equipment, we got you out of the swamps, we will decide the optimal usage of this invention.'

Lesqueth's father was truly inspirational and set the example for how things should be done. 'For everything we do, there was a reason; this reason may not be perceived by others as rational or even logical, but that did not matter now, and it would not matter in the future. Nothing mattered, just as long as we win.' The Baroness inwardly thanked her father for the words of wisdom and then turned to take the corridor that would lead her to the so-called research and development section of the vast underground complex. The squadron of guards, on seeing her approaching, immediately stood to attention and performed the salute of fingers set at double vee, placed across their hearts. Lesqueth was not remotely impressed by the said performance; she was, in fact, very annoyed that she had not been stopped for an identification check.

The Baroness walked down the line and, on reaching the very last sentinel, she asked why she was not challenged. Trooper Tierney replied that they had been informed of her arrival. Lesqueth, still not impressed, informed Tierney that she could have very well been an impostor. Someone who had sought out to damage the state-of-the-art equipment behind these very closed doors. "Ma'am, with all due respect, the cameras record everyone, and our comms receive up-to-date information. We were given a heads-up about your movements only minutes ago. If you were an impostor, the security systems that are all over this complex would have picked you up, then highlighted you as an intruder, and you would have been restrained, then eliminated well before you reached this part of the facility."

Lesqueth thought that his answer was the correct one, one that he along with the rest of the hive had been rehearsing for hours on end to get perfect. She moved closer to Tierney and headbutted him, as his body reacted to the surprise assault, Lesqueth delivered a swift kick to his private parts, then kicked his legs out from under him. "I don't care if you had been informed over your headset that god almighty and all his little angels were coming down this corridor to deliver in person everlasting redemption certificates to all that were present. From this moment on, you would ask for and check everyone's identification; there will be no exemptions. Even if it was the ghost of your mother and spectres representing your aborted embryos, you would question them. Trooper Tierney, was that clear?" The trooper who had just managed to pull himself back upright utters a resounding "Yes, ma'am, I understand." The Baroness informed him to go and tidy himself up, and the next time he appeared to look shabby, she would have him arrested on the spot.

Lesqueth entered the room, reminiscent of a gunfighter walking into the roughest saloon in town. A sole figure wearing an ill-fitting white lab coat cautiously approached. By the look on his face, she was unsure as to whether he wished to vomit or shit himself on the spot. Professor Vassorob started to deliver the welcoming speech, he only reached, "It was a great honour" when she told him to shut the fuck up and show her what she was here for. Vassorob, without showing any giveaway facial gestures, regurgitates his spent breakfast as he unquestionably obeys the request. He pointed to all the mini reactors that the teams of technicians were fussing over. The Baroness looked at them, then redirected her stare towards him, and asked a few questions.

Vassorob replied that the muon thorium-saturated fuel cells had been tested and that all of the results were very favourable. "The final analysis vastly exceeded the projected theoretical yield. Way, way beyond the expected numerical values, so much so that the team had to recalculate the whole process." Vassorob signalled for one of the other white suited mutants to come over. He instructed them to acquire the summary information for GRE-1 all the way through to GRE-14. While they waited for the data sheets to arrive, on the display. Vassorob now with a visible shake, pointed to all the functioning desk jockeys and painstakingly explained their primary and secondary functions in the proposed great leap forward. As he rattled off all of the information, Lesqueth remembered who he actually was. The esteemed Professor Vassorob had more degrees and letters after his name than anyone else living or dead. A child prodigy who had gained the unheard-of admission into one of the top universities in America at the tender age of twelve based solely on his adept knowledge of theoretical atomic structure.

Once he had started collecting the various degrees, he had declined all of her company's approaches to come and work in the private sector. His rebuttal came in the form that he had way too many important lectures to present, along with the vast numbers of students who required his steerage throughout the complexity of their chosen somewhat difficult field of advanced scientific theorems. The vast sums of dollars being offered for him to jump ship did not appeal to him one little bit.

It was only when he returned home one night to be greeted by Lesqueth in his apartment that he had fully realised what was actually on offer. The work that her company proposed to carry out was, at that time, only a theorised conception that only existed on paper and had still to be proven. They had talked well into the night, with Lesqueth sweetening the deal with the limitless offer of all sorts of equipment that could be manufactured on request. The laboratories that he would be in sole charge of would attract the finest brains available to assist him on his quest. Lesqueth had told him that the splitting of the atom would in the future be viewed as mere child's play compared to the complex equations still to be discovered, equations that he would unravel. This had soothed his unquenchable ego as well as the offer of governing the Hawaiian island chain once all of his work was complete.

To finalise the deal, Lesqueth placed her phone on the table. The sound could have been better, but even so, it clearly recorded the unequivocal moans of mutual satisfaction. The streamed images were of great quality showing the man, who was strapped to a table wearing nothing but a pair of high heels, enjoying unprotected anal sex with a donkey. The Baroness assured him that if he were to reconsider the more than generous offer to come and work for the company, the movie and the donkey could miraculously vanish overnight. Professor Vassorob immediately handed in his notice to his employers and now completely hidden from the prying eyes of the various governmental agencies to whom the learned professor, for all intents and purposes, had unexplainably vanished from the face of this earth.

The requested paperwork arrived, and as he attempted to hand it over to Lesqueth, she asked him if she really needed to read it. "If you tell me it would work, then why could I possibly doubt you. Just think, Erno, you could very soon be relaxing at your chosen destination very soon." Professor Vassorob was acutely embarrassed; none of the people who worked here knew his first name, and although he hated to admit it, the way the Baroness had formed her lips when she pronounced it had given him a huge erection.

Lesqueth ignored the sheaths of highlighted numbers, statistical frequency graphs and digital version of same information being triumphantly heralded on the big screen. She informed him that now she would like to view the bio-cryogenic chambers. The professor nodded and almost wetting himself, sort of squeaked confirming in a roundabout way that they would need to suit up. Vassorob silently praised the Gods for the provision of separate changing rooms; otherwise, he would have been unable to hide his still engorged member. He led the way and pointed to the control room. The professor informed the Baroness that everything that was required had already been laid out for her, and all she had to do was follow the instructions as per the stipulations on entering the cryo-suite. Vassorob was now delighted to be well away from her and relished the comforting cold shower that would normalise his acute embarrassment.

The pair of them were now suited up like deep space explorers about to venture onto an unexplored planet. As they exited the decom rooms, Vassorob guided Lesqueth over to view row upon row of the bio-cryogenic chambers. Twelve hundred completely identical cylindrical liked coffins lay out in regimental fashion, and stretched as far as their eyes could see. The various tubes that supplied the power, nutrients, water, enhanced amino acids and protein multipliers hang from the mezzanine like dormant tentacles waiting for their unsuspecting prey to alert their heat sensors. Vassorob pointed to the sheets of tubes, "These were all self-venting and specifically designed to freely compensate for each and every individual participant's needs. In every change that each child went through, their intake was adjusted to suit the uniformity of the group, to guarantee that the end results would produce a concise and accurate end product that would all have more than comparable characteristics."

The Baroness had previously read the ins and outs of the pioneering growth enhancement process, she rather bluntly informed the professor that she fully understood how it all worked, and he should proceed with the walkthrough. Vassorob guided Lesqueth over to a separate unit in the building. He pressed the red button, which exposed an encrypted control panel. "The occupants in here were the gutter snipes that were collected from various slums across the world. They had been processed and thoroughly indoctrinated." Vassorob asked the Baroness if she would like to question them, see them perform or view the edited highlights. Lesqueth asked if the process actually worked on the uncultivated street urchins. Vassorob curtly responds, "They were all speaking the same language, possessed all of the required aggressive responses, and also the unquestionable loyalty. All this information has been recorded and was stored in the archives."

The Baroness nodded and understood all that had been said and pointed at the panel. She asked, "What was the difference between the buttons with marked X1 and X2?" The professor calmly informed her that X1 would release them from the enclosed building and X2 would release them from ever having to breathe again. Lesqueth instructed Vassorob that he should press X2 as the experiment was over; without blinking an eyelid, he obeyed her command. She continued her questioning, "If the exercise to prove that the theory works had used twelve subjects, then I am presuming that all the resources required had been multiplied to accommodate the next intake." The professor confirmed that the calculations had been checked. All of the stages had been run through the quadruple quantum liquefied bio-computer, which controlled the process from start to finish, and subsequently, all of the imputed numerical values had been approved. The Baroness of Kindeace-Shire, now satisfied that the professor had done all that he had been asked to do, ordered him to proceed to the final stage immediately.

Professor Erno Vassorob escorted Lesqueth back towards the decom rooms. He informed her that the process would be initiated from within the main control room. The professor was waiting for the Baroness as she exited the decom process. "I, along with everyone who has been involved in this project since day one, would consider it a great honour if you were to turn on the machines to start this great leap forward into the future. Lesqueth thanks him for the offer but informs him that, as he had done all the hard work transforming this project from the scribbles on a notepad, then to turn it into a fully functional project." Professor, the honour of switching on the machines was yours and yours alone."

The Baroness excused herself to remedy a noticeable error. She approached trooper Tierney, who had just recently returned to duty after a brief visit to the medical facility to have his broken nose manipulated. Lesqueth stood face to face with a trooper who had a fairly large plaster covering his repaired breathing tubes. "Did we not have a discussion recently, deliberating about the necessity for conducting identification, as well as verification checks on all personnel traversing this corridor?" Tierney confirmed the validity of the statement. Lesqueth matter-of-factly pointed out that traffic flowed in, and unfortunately for him, traffic flowed out. The Baroness shouted that this equated to validating the entering and the exiting. Lesqueth suddenly turns about and delivers an expertly performed spinning hook kick. Tierney's body impersonated a disregarded sack of unwanted potatoes, issuing a dull thud as it connected with the floor. The Baroness informed the still-standing troopers that there would be no more warnings issued, nor any further infringements of security protocol would not be tolerated.

She calmly walked away, totally unperturbed at the pool of blood emanating from Tierney's irreparably damaged head that was now inhabiting an increasing surface area as it expanded slowly in several directions over the highly polished floor. Professor Erno Vassorob had remained motionless on the spot where she had left him, akin to an electro-mechanical mannequin that had been placed in safe mode. Lesqueth, now almost displaying an overload of electrical energisation, walked straight past the still figure. Vassorob sprang into action and reacquired the position of senior tour guide as he increased his pace and led the way towards the main control section. The word must have spread rapidly as the troopers impeded the odd couple's entry into the underground facility's nerve centre, asking them to produce valid identification.

The Baroness, as a rule, carried no documentation, but submitted to an undertaking of a retinal-bio-scan. The handheld device beeped for a few microseconds before displaying the green indication. The troopers saluted her, and then the stern-looking female behind the reinforced plexiglass enclosure selected and depressed the appropriate touch screen authentication confirmation that opened the doors into the control hub. A huge clock on the wall, with increments marked out in bold red and yellow, almost glared at her, subconsciously daring her to reach out and grasp the future for her species. General Flemings issued the command to stand to. By the numbers, the uniformed officers, along with the white coated technicians, instantly ceased their collective activities and stood to attention.

Lesqueth leaned closer and then whispered in the professor's ear that there was a drove of Jacks and Jennets braying incessantly, awaiting patiently for his return to Hawaii. "The sooner you initiate the process, the sooner you will be able to reunite with your loved ones." Vassorob stepped forward to the main control array, louder than necessary, and announced, "Activate the clock." The gathered resume work at their stations and double checked all the displayed data that inextricably interconnects, challenging the laws of physics, reconfiguring the phased developments of biological growth and inherent genetic traits.

The main screens now displayed the twelve hundred infants that had been ordered to form up into their required groupings. They all marched on the spot, as one section moved forward towards the exit. The next section was hot on their tail, blatantly advertising forced, choreographed, and regimented movements. They marched in perfect formation towards the exit. As the line increased, the doors opened and allowed the children to enter the corridor, which would enable them to rapidly transcend Lesqueth's armed forces of the future. The squadron of seasoned troopers stood at attention and saluted the children as they marched down the length of the vaulted corridor. A single drumbeat was pounded out, and the reverberated sound broke the silence as its ethereal tone encapsulated the mind and soul of all present. Tierney's blood spillage had been sprinkled with an absorbent medium to curtail the spread. Inadvertently, the youngerlings step on his now defunct carcass, which would act as a last-minute reminder that failure was not a viable option.

As they reached the yellow stop line, following the memorised instruction, children at the front came to a halt and stood to attention. The drum beat increased in tempo, indicating that the children had to make a left turn into the preparation area. A pair of infants stepped up to the first post, where they underwent a biometric scan. As they moved to the second post, the next pair had already taken up their position at the first post. The first pair of children, on reaching the second post, were instructed to remove their uniforms and place the discarded clothing in the reclamation receptacle.

The third post was where the future armed forces received a series of injections that nullified and then voided their senses. After the minimum permissible time, they were moved forward to the last post, where they were fitted with a temporary breather that would allow them to safely enter into the inert atmosphere contained within the transformation hall. Every post had a pair of attending infants, and the repetitive procedure was performed in perfectly synchronised movements as the first pair proceeded towards their allocated bio-cryogenic chambers. A pair of suited-up technicians removed their temporary breather and then assisted and guided them up the steps that allow easy access into the bio-cryogenic chamber.

The first technician hooked up the hoses inside the chamber as per the sequential order and locked them up to the pre-surgically emplaced connectors that protrude from various parts of the infant's body. The second technician adhered to the stringent sequential order and connected the self-venting tubes that hang from the mezzanine. As soon as the specially formulated breathing mix tube was interconnected, the technician in the nerve centre was notified automatically. She watched as all the other indicators switched from inactive to active, and the green lights appeared on her viewing screen. As all of the tubes distributing the enhanced amino acids, protein multipliers, and nutritional supplements were registered on her display. The last connection that took place was the power supply, which transferred all the incoming data onto the large screen. The swarm of suited-up technicians steadily moved from one bio-cryogenic chamber to the next, gradually interconnecting every individual's life and soul into the enhancement project.

Vassorob moved swiftly from work-station to work-station inside the nerve centre, noting and checking that every change from every data port was activated on the large screen. On reaching the unit that controlled the compact reactors, he informed the operator to activate the insertion of the saturated fuel source. The small units, which each emulated the intense power of the sun, had all started to energise, and the status of each calibrated module was verified and then confirmed through the emergency control panel.

Professor Vassorob was completely satisfied that all was going to plan and now ordered that all of the compact reactors be brought up to the five percent capacity hold point. The Baroness issued a prayer to the fallen, the vanquished and the forgotten as Professor Erno Vassorob ordered the excited muons to be with bombarded with the additional thorium-saturated ions. Which would start, then suspend the expanding motion of the substructure decay, thus producing a steady stream of intensified nuons. These would then be transformed into a controlled oscillation, which would kick-start and bring the enhancement project from an obscure theoretical exercise into an all-encompassing force. That would challenge the fundamental laws of physics.

Chapter 24

Several thousand miles away in not-so-sunny Scotland, Miasnikov had quickly brought Commander Essmie up to speed. "We had good news, my dear, what one of the patrols had thought was just a pile of smelly, weather-beaten rags. Actually, turned out to be a lost, bewildered soul who had wandered extensively throughout the whole area. Much to our surprise, he could talk in an understandable dialect. After some jolts of electricity, he was gently coaxed into looking at the maps. Al's mind would wander from time to time, but after removing some of his fingers and then threatening to feed his testicles to the dog, he eventually revealed the elusive prizes that we had been searching for. As Al was suspected of being a mental defective, he was persuaded to go on a little jaunt. He pinpointed where the people we were after reside, along with the exact coordinates of another group who allegedly helps and supports them."

"Obviously, Al had used up all of his credits and now was nothing but a heap of rags at the side of the road." Their vehicle draws to a halt. "Listen, my dear, what you could hear were our shells; we had cut off their escape route by destroying the bridge." Miasnikov quickly ran her through the plan, detailing the structure and the part she would take. "Essmie, after we crush the Hidden, on my recommendation, our great leader would most likely promote you to the rank of general." Commander Essmie thanked Vladimir for the possible promotion exited the vehicle, striding away to take charge of her troopers by leading the assault.

Murray sat in the passenger seat, anxiously watching for any sudden movements. The patrols that were sent out to search the area for the invaders had still not been located. Both of them know that this could very well be more than a problem; it could be catastrophic and consequently lead to their community's sudden demise. One of their people broke cover and directed them to pull over. She informed them that they had just detected a large group forming up, relatively close by, and they would need urgent reinforcements. Murray asked Okolo to return back to the watermill to inform Cha, then possibly muster up some support. She quickly turned the vehicle around, then sped off at full tilt.

At the watermill, Cha had quickly put the emergency plan into operation. The people who had been trained to fight were supplied with arms and ammunition were all now waiting at their assembly points. The ones who were not trained to fight, the old along with the young, were ushered into the relative safety of the underground shelter. Okolo had just arrived back; she was just delivering the news that the invaders were forming up, ready to attack, when a messenger from the farmhouse approached them. He informed them that their community was under attack from all directions, and it did not look good. Cha was about to send the messenger to Cora when the chap dropped dead at her feet.

Cat had been delegated to go and assess the survivors from the ship that had been attacked before all of the passengers had made it safely on land. She had to shout to attain their full attention. "I know that you are all shocked, but we need anyone who was capable of fighting to volunteer and take up arms." Alwyn and Cinds' had stepped forward. Cat curtly shot them down in flames by informing them that she had no time for niceties and only required people who were capable of taking up arms. Alwyn curtly informed her that he knew the ones who could fight, and all she had to do was point them in the direction of where the weapons were stored. Cinds' quickly helped sort out their people, the ones who couldn't fight who were either being sent to assist Frank in the galley to prepare and deliver food, or to the underground shelter.

The fighters from the ship were being issued with weapons, then assembled, ready to be allocated into one of the fighting groups. Anna, along with Olga and their children, were in the midst of having a shouting match with Alwyn and Cinds'. All Cat caught was, "We could fight, but we need someone to look after our children." Cat approached, and on reaching the two women, the hairs on the back of her neck stood up. She asked what was going on, and in between the harsh words of the ensuing conversation between Cinds' and the women.

Cat detected that the women were not exactly who they were portraying themselves to be. She delivered a question in a language and dialect that she strongly suspected one of them would understand. In the guttural tones associated with the regional dialect used south west of Azerbaijan, Cat told them straight that they were not as innocent as they were pretending to be. Cinds' made an executive decision, walked away, and left them to it. Olga replied in the same tongue and informed Cat that the pair of them would fight for this community, but the safety of their children had to be settled before they did anything. She added, "Regardless of our dubious backgrounds, you know that we have attributes and skills that could be put to good use." Cat was acutely aware that they would need every capable fighter, informs them to follow her and not to forget their children.

Alicia was ripping Robbo to bits for bringing the little girl who had accompanied Uno on his journey up to where the rest of the children were gathered. "What on earth possessed you to bring her up here of all places? Sometimes I think that you are so selfish, incapable of taking the feelings and perceptions of others into consideration." Alicia had halted the verbal onslaught, along with the twins and Robbo, and they watched as all the children settled in with the little girl. Much to the twins' surprise, Terina and Lyla had been allocated pole position and looked almost adoringly at the newcomer amidst in their group. Robbo was just about to admit that he had somehow thought it was one of his better ideas, possibly subconsciously aided and abetted by the strange little girl.

He was stopped prior to issuing the first syllable when Cat entered the house unannounced with two of the boat people, accompanied by their precious little bundles. Alicia caught on straight away. Cat, fully aware of what she was about to say, informed her that she would take care of any issues presented by Okolo. The children were placed beside the others. All of them noticed that the hum had abruptly stopped, then restarted without any noticeable changes in the frequency. Cat asked the women from the boat if they were satisfied with the childcare arrangements. Tears ran down the women's faces as they gave their children a final hug, then, with heads bowed, they followed Cat out the door.

Robbo asked Alicia whether she was going to bring this up with Okolo, and she hissed that she won't have to, as he would no doubt inform her at the first available opportunity. Robbo did not address the aggressive statement but muttered something about going to go and recruit Macdhiarmada and Uno into the fight with the invaders. Alicia ignored him as he nearly ripped the door off its hinges as he stormed out. The twins were tasked to look after all of the children as she set out to pack up a few of the essentials that would be required if they had to leave in a hurry.

Cha, with Okolo at her side, directed the armed members of their community to move out to take on either the forces attacking from the farmhouse or to go and reinforce Murray's position. They came across Cat with the two women who had survived the shelling directed at the ship. Cat pre-empting Okolo's attack, "Whatever you had in mind to do could wait until we return, right now we have more important matters to take care of." Okolo, having placed himself ready to draw a weapon, calmly informed Cat that Murray was not here to protect her. Cha knew fully well that if she did not intervene, Okolo would be easily disposed of, somethings in life were not meant to be messed with, Cat and her best friends were at the very top of that list.

Cat informed Cha, along with her friend, that unless they had any objections, someone would have to go across the water and eliminate the spotters. Cat told Olga and Anna to pick out whatever weapons they needed. Okolo just stared at the pair of them, wishing that she could just finish them right now. Cat asked the woman if they had gathered everything that was required. The women replied that all they needed now was a boat to get across the water. Cat thought that she knew where they could borrow one from. As she looked directly at Okolo, Cat informed her that she would see her later, with the look that made it crystal clear that it would not matter if Murray was present or not.

Cha and Okolo watched them leave. There were about a million things that Cha could say, and equally, there were about a million things that she should not say. The group led by Gareth and Cinds' moved off to stand against the invaders who would be attacking from the farmhouse direction. Then the group led by Robbo moved out to reinforce Murray, Cha, along with Okolo, rushed about the watermill and checked that the remaining fighters were manning the defensive positions. They see Karen in the distance directing the people who had been seconded to ferry the emergency supplies to the escape vehicles. They had rehearsed over the years for this scenario and streamlined the process into a perfect operation. Not once during this time had any of them ever thought that they would have to put it into practice. Karen had seen Cha along with Okolo making sure that the defensive posts were all crewed up and equipped, she just gave them a nod as none of them had any spare time to exchange words.

Cat, along with the two women that Okolo wished to remove from the planet, cautiously made their way towards the waterfront. The occasional shell exploded almost as if the attackers were just letting them know that they were still there, and they were watching, just waiting for them to made any foolhardy moves. They moved from shell hole to shell hole in the hope of locating a suitable form of transport that would enable them to get across the stretch of water. The trio had spotted the boats that Gareth's people had intended to use to ferry their people back and forth. These were now nothing but distorted shapes and shredded pieces of fabric that lay across the front. Some dangled in the remaining trees along with the other parts of the crafts that move backwards and forward, half floating in amongst the bloated, misshapen bodies in the water.

Anna, not quite as gentle as it should be, prods Olga in the ribs. She handed over the vision aid and pointed in the direction of the demolished stone pillars that had supported the bridge until very recently. The fast-moving craft was spotted moving across the water heading towards their side of the now defunct bridge. Cat signalled the women to advance towards the point where the invaders would be landing. They ran, ducked and dived for cover as the incoming shells landed about them, on reaching the location where the craft had already beached. One of the invading troopers guards the craft, and the others were nowhere to be seen. Cat did not need to issue orders as they set about to try to locate the invaders before they started to redirect the shell fire. In hushed tones, she told them that they would deal with the sentry last. The three of them search for the likely whereabouts of the spotters, who, if not apprehended, would start to redirect the bombardment upon the dwellings at the watermill complex. Olga had managed to sneak up on one of them, and Cat along with Anna, appeared at her side. Olga informed the other enemy combatant that she would cut his companion's throat unless they dropped their weapon. The trooper who was more terrified of his commander, told them to go and fuck themselves then puts his weapon to his head and blew his brains out. Olga saw no point in pursuing a meaningful conversation and slit the throat of the trooper she was holding. They quickly moved down towards the sentry, who was left to guard the small craft. As they closed in on their position, Cat made a decision, they could slowly move towards them, taking a considerable amount of time to cover the relatively short distance, or they could just shoot them. As it was highly unlikely that the sentry would give them any information, Cat calmly broke cover, dropping the sentry with a single shot to the heart.

They climbed into the small watercraft and travelled on the opposite sides of the stubs that once supported the bridge. The spotters had given them no information, but Olga pointed out that as they had used the opposite side to get there. Then it could be possible that the unit they intended to signal to was positioned on the side of the hill overlooking that vantage point, on reaching the opposite side of the stretch of water. Cat told her companions to spread out when they broke cover and take a run across the stretch of shingle. They broke left, right, and Cat moved straight ahead and dove behind the huge pile of rocks that had been put in place to stop the incoming tides reclaiming the land. She moved steadily forward, stopped, and then rapidly climbed over the abutment, then ran to take cover in a natural depression on the other side of the road.

Down by the border, Commander Jack Green had waited for what seemed like a lifetime. As the technicians transferred then correlated the data that had been downloaded from the nano-insectoids. These were the items that he had to sign over his soul to get G-Flem to agree to having them released. The items were let loose miles away from the suspected location of the camp that Abe Hubstien and his happy band of rebels now occupied. The first batch of nano-insectoids scanned the area grid by grid, gradually eliminating areas that held no significant points of interest. On reaching their limits of operation, the self-programmed units joined together in the specified configurations to form a hub that enabled all transmissible data to be streamed back to base.

When this part of the process was complete and all the good-to-proceed lights flicked up on the panel, the next batch was released. Jack was getting frustrated and wished to release the complete hive. He was addressed like an impetuous school boy when the lead technician informed him that it did not work that way, and General Flemings would be none too happy to find out that the whole hive had been lost. Jack bit his tongue, outwardly displaying the patience of a saint. While inwardly fantasising about disembowelling the lead technician right now, where he sat.

As time relentlessly marched on, the incoming data started to accumulate, gradually building up a complete picture of Hubstien and company. This depicted not only the temporary location of Abe's camp but also all of the activities of the people who lived and worked there. This provided Jack with all of the information that he required and enabled him to plan the attack by the numbers. He now had a fairly accurate list of all the people who resided there, a detailed account of all of their day-to-day activities and more importantly, a comprehensive schedule of the manned patrols sanctioned by the Perry chap. Commander Green was impressed by the quantity of information the nano-insectoids were able to extract from the maps on the wall and all of the notebooks that had been casually left open on the desks.

Jack thought that for sure, the one named Abe was a certifiable halfwit, taking all of his orders and instructions from Jackson and the Enunsha woman. He also thought that Abe was so gullible that he would accept commands from the dog if it could speak. If it were up to him, he would happily cut Abe up, then place him on a leaking boat to gradually sink in the canal that was inhabited by the regimental pets. Commander Green's orders had stipulated, making it clear in no uncertain terms that the great leader had ordained that the one called Abe was to be captured alive. Jack knew that failure to do so would most likely nominate himself for free entry into the involuntary swimming competition with ravenous water creatures. The Jackson fellow, he hoped, would accidentally on purpose be mislaid and take up residence in one of his secretive places that specialise in medieval information extraction techniques.

The Perry chap had been drawn into the trap, as suspected, Jack had clearly thought out his next moves, patiently waiting for Perry to swallow them hook, line and sinker. Green actually applauded the movements of Perry's troopers as they eliminated the donkeys that he had hoodwinked into thinking that it would be a great idea to put on a uniform. The lead technician stepped forward, congratulating Commander Green on a well-planned operation. Jack, in view of all the other staff, accepted his slimy handshake, while inwardly resolutely declaring that the public display of grovelling would not save him.

The people in the mobile control watch the screens, and Green provided the commentary as Perry encountered one setback after another. Jack wished that he could communicate with the leader of the patrol. To issue torrents of vile abuse to Perry as he came across all of the dead patrol units that had been placed in the reserve positions. Commander Green issued an insult at the screen, "So much for all your planning, all your training, just wait till you receive your next surprise."

Perry had ordered his crew to double time it back to the drop-off point, where they would pick up the transport, then return to the camp. As his group made their way back, they discovered that all of the patrols and observation posts had all been eliminated. Every single member that they came across was all lined up, grouped together for a macabre photo shoot. All of them had been shot, then placed in the sitting position holding their now decapitated heads. Perry shouted at his group and informed them that there was no time for grief, and they had to keep moving.

At the farmhouse, Miasnikov's troopers had staged a double-pronged attack. The mechanised units had arrived facing the front of the enclosure. On the brow of the hill, the tanks then proceeded to direct several salvos of concentrated fire, which obliterated the gates, the walls, as well as anyone who was hopelessly trying to defend them. At the same time, Commander Essmie followed Miasnikov's plan to the letter and led an attack against the back entrance of the farmhouse community. The gates maintained little or no resistance as the armoured vehicle charged straight through them. On seeing the movements of Essmie's units charging inside the community and creating chaos, the barrage ceased, and the troopers positioned there now advanced forward to join the battle. What had once been a self-efficient hub of humanity surviving against all odds was now a smoking ruin. Miasnikov's troopers had been unleashed and were now in the process of killing anything that breathed. Men, women, children and even all the domestic animals were slaughtered at will. The orders stipulated that everything living had to perish, with no permissible exceptions.

Alwyn and Cinds' group had arrived too late and witnessed the carnage now underway from a safe distance. Cinds' asked Alwyn they should retreat, returning to the watermill. Alwyn replied that they should attack, as once the animals had finished here, they would be heading towards the people who had kindly agreed to let them stay. Cinds' gave the order, and the group advanced on Miasnikov's troops, who were so engrossed in the ongoing slaughter that none of them noticed their approach.

The first group to receive their attention was the rear guard that had been posted to protect the mechanised unit. The animals were now subjecting the remainder of Mark's sentries to all sorts of barbarity. Cinds' crew descended upon them and despatched them to join their ancestors in hell. Alwyn tasked his crew with checking all of the stationary vehicles for enemy combatants. When he found the machines unattended, he ordered them to be manned by their own group. The new crew quickly familiarised themselves with the controls as Cinds', along with Alwyn, led the search and rescue party headlong into the fight.

At first, Miasnikov's troopers did not notice the arriving forces; they were too busy enjoying themselves slaughtering the innocents. Essmie spotted a few of her troopers being gunned down and issued the alert. It was too little and too late. Cinds had identified her as the leader, then directed the trooper with the rocket launcher to blow her to hell. Essmie had only just issued the command and was now in the process of mustering her troopers as the high explosive projectile detonated, splattering the nearby walls with her remains.

As the combined forces of Alwyn and Cinds' people rallied, then advanced throughout the farmhouse. Several of the armoured vehicles belonging to Commander Essmie attempted to made a break for freedom. They only made it halfway up the hill before the tanks that had been repossessed by the Alwyn crew opened fire and destroyed them. Cinds' group worked their way throughout the buildings, now at the repair facility, they had encountered a group of unarmed mechanics being tortured. Miasnikov's troopers had hung several of the workers from the overhead crane and were now in the process of placing bets on which one would issue the final kick. Cinds' troopers mercilessly mowed down the attackers, allocating a some of the first aiders of her crew to lower the hoisting mechanism in the hope of saving some of the mechanics.

Alwyn was on the other side of the complex, frantically searching the offices for survivors and eliminating any of the invaders who were still resisting capture. He entered one office, the man with cropped blonde hair has been subjected to a severe beating was in the process of being gang raped. The naked woman that Alwyn assumed to be his partner lay naked with her throat cut, unmoving, on the floor in front of him. Alwyn, without any hesitation, gunned down all of the assailants. As he helped the man with the cropped blonde hair to his feet, he sobbed as he told Alwyn that without Ellie, he was nothing, absolutely nothing at all. Alwyn was helpless as he picked up one of the discarded weapons, pointed it at his heart, then smiled and pulled the trigger.

Cinds' had only managed to save one of the hanging men; all of the others were dead before they were lowered to the ground. She told the survivor to hold on and that they would send someone to help him, then ordered her troopers to search every nook and cranny. "Any of the invading forces that you find, there was no need to ask them any questions, just kill them." In the background, she heard only sporadic issues of gunfire, indicating that the battle was almost over.

Alwyn spotted her and then headed over to meet her. "Most of the people who stayed here were all dead; we had only found a couple of survivors." Cinds' informed Alwyn that her group, up till now, had only found one of the locals still alive.

Alwyn looked at her, "What were we going to do with all of the prisoners?" Cinds' did not reply to his question and inserted a fresh magazine into her weapon. Alwyn copied her action and added that he had hoped that this would be her reaction. Together they walked towards the tied, bound and defeated remnants of Miasnikov's forces. Cinds' issued orders for all of the prisoners to be stripped of all of their clothing. Once they were all naked, she nodded towards Alwyn, fingers on the trigger they made their move on the prisoners and gunned them all down without or any remorse or compassion.

Cinds' took the lead in ordering one of the drivers to return to the watermill to inform them that the mechanised unit that would be arriving shortly was no longer part of the invading forces. She asked Alwyn if he would take control of the tanks and lead them to defend their new home. Alwyn told her that he was on it, then departed with the remainder of his squad to take up his new position. Cinds' requested that her people carry out a full sweep of the farmhouse complex to double-check for any survivors.

Cat, along with the two women from the ship, had moved out from the natural depression and were now moving towards where they thought the spotters were located. It was slow going as they crawled from their concealed position to the next place that would offer them a piece of relatively safe cover. They had been progressing slowly, but had now halted as they had overheard some voices nearby. The sound of the resuming conversation was located on the other side of a small clump of bushes up ahead of them. Cat delivered her guests the appropriate hand signals and depicted that they fan out, covering both of the approaches. Anna and Olga gave her the thumbs-up sign, then crawled forward to attempt to take up position on the spotters without revealing themselves. Cat moved in the opposite direction and hoped that she did not make any unnecessary noise that would give away her presence. Olga, accompanied by Anna, had already eliminated the spotters and were now searching through their things as Cat approached. Olga tossed her the map, clearly showing the planned attack. She looked at it, Olga rotated the folded paper up the other way, pointing as she spoke, "Both of the communities on the map were going to be attacked, the guns or tanks that were positioned near here were only waiting on coordinates before they unleashed hell. It would be a good idea if we were to eliminate them, completely removing them from the equation." Olga had been promoted to the position of pathfinder, and together they moved forward to where the heavy guns were located on the map.

Cat and Anna take up the flank positions as they move forward, aware that there could be several additional checkpoints whose coordinates had not been noted on the map. A short while later into their journey, Anna spotted the first barely concealed position. One of the troopers has decided to go and relieve himself. As he breathed a sigh of relief, Anna shouted out in the accepted dialect used by Miasnikov's forces. "I could have shot you, but if you give me some of your spare cigarettes and vodka, I would not report you. The trooper replied, "Hey bitch, go and ask your mama who was now on all fours entertaining the troopers if she has earned enough to share." Anna replied that her mother was never sober enough to go on all fours, then placed her silenced pistol in his mouth. She forced him backwards into the dilapidated shelter, where she promptly executed him and his companions. As she exited, she informed Cat and Olga that the occupants would no longer be a problem.

The trio continued their journey to locate the heavy weaponry. As they reached the top of the next incline, they carefully peered over the edge. There, below them, were all of the tanks, mobile rocket launchers, and artillery pieces. All lined up on the road, their elevated barrels pointed towards the watermill. Cat asked Olga if it was possible to destroy them all. In her natural language, she replied that anything was possible; they would just have to be very careful and get it right the first time, as it was highly unlikely that they would live long enough to get a second chance. Olga pulled a pen out of her pocket, then started to mark up the map.

Chapter 25

Murray heard them starting to approach, ordering his nervous troops to hold their fire until he gave them the order. Macdhiarmada complained again, this time blatantly reassuring Murray that in the days of old, he would have easily found employment press-ganging defenceless people into a life on the ocean waves. Murray without even looking at the issuer of the complaint, asked Uno why he did not just shoot him or dump him in some feral inner-city ghetto. Macdhiarmada now lets the pair of them know that they were nothing but a pair of bastards, devoid of any emotion or compassion. On cue, and in matching stereo they both delivered the message and told the old bastard to shut the fuck up. Their scolding of Macdhiarmada, Bryan or whatever the fuck they were meant to address him as was halted when the armoured personnel carriers started to break out through the tree line. As he had not been informed of their presence, Murray thought that they must have been parked up there, for God knows how long, just waiting for the order to attack. The tracked vehicles, for some strange reason, do not start to open fire immediately. They collectively create an atmosphere of abject terror as the attached twin barrels on each carrier menacingly traverse left, then right.

Some of the defenders, who were scared shitless made a break for it. Murray shouted for everyone to hold their ground, but the sound of the fifty-cal machine guns decimating those who had abandoned their positions drowned out his voice. An eerie silence developed, but not for long, as the tanks moved forward from their concealed positions, passing through the gaps in the line of the armoured personnel carriers.

These machines did not hesitate; they opened fire, purposely aiming for the trees, attempting to create as much damage and fear as possible. The displaced tree trunks suddenly crushed the defenders along with the lethal, life-destroying splinters that indiscriminately rained down upon them. Murray passed out the word that those armed with the handheld rocket launchers were to take aim at the tanks. The order was obeyed immediately, as streams of munitions streak through the air from both sides in an attempt to kill off and destroy as many of each other as possible. Murray was dismayed as he witnessed several of the projectiles that had been launched from his side hit their targets, then almost bounce off. These direct hits had totally unaffected the ability of the killing machines to rain hell down upon his motley crew. Uno ignored the issued order and pointed his weapon at one of the personnel carriers, pulled the double fire release mechanism, and then whooped in delight as he scored a direct hit. On receiving reports that they had now depleted their heavy weapons, Murray ordered a retreat back towards the secondary line of defence.

Just like the rest of his troopers, he ran at full pelt; the explosions were deafening, several of them knocked him off his feet, but none of them were close enough to inflict any damage. The tracer rounds penetrate through the dust and smoke, and the following hail of bullets cuts to ribbons any unfortunate souls who were caught in the deadly crossfire. Murray thought that it was highly unlikely that there would be any wounded survivors as distorted body parts fell all around him and the fleeing combatants. Several troopers who were next to him were picked off as they made their way up the steep incline to the second and final defence line. Murray looked around him, knowing that without even getting the remnants of his crew to call out the numbers, they had lost at least fifty per cent of the fighting force. He summons Uno, "Go back to the watermill and tell Cha that it was not looking good and they should start the evacuation." Uno wanted to stay and pretend that all of a sudden, he had gone deaf. With hand gestures, he strenuously indicated that with all the shelling, he thought that he had burst eardrums. Murray shouted out, asking if Robbo was still with them in the land of the living. Robbo, on hearing the summons, replied to all that he was one of the swamp people, and as he well knows, they cannot be gotten rid of that easily.

Murray had to give it to him; here they were being obliterated by a superior force, and Robbo had delivered an inspirational speech to rally to almost worn-out defenders. Murray asked him if he had finished speaking to the masses, and if he was not too busy, could he make his way towards him. Robbo squeezed up the line; sometimes he pretended he was the visiting five-star general here to egg on the troops. He addressed a group of troopers, "Where were you guys from?" They mentioned the placenames from where they and their families had originated from, 'Yoker, Budapest, Govan and Shettleston were the replies. Robbo shook his head, then retorted back that he had never heard of any of these places. He saluted, then told them to keep up the good work. Murray had heard the guffaws of laughter as he had approached.

Robbo was now beside him; he could have said something about his antics in the face of adversity, but withheld any comments as he thought that Robbo would only deliver another smartass comment. "I need you to return to the watermill, tell Cha the truth that we are not doing too well and that she should start the evacuation." Robbo accepted the order without hesitation. Uno, now knowing that it was non-negotiable, got up and moved to join Robbo. Bryan, Macdhiarmada or whatever the fuck he was called caught Murray's eye. He informed the two remaining members of the swamp people tribe that they might as well take this chap along with them. Uno looked at Murray as if he had been handed the poisoned chalice. "He was not too good at fighting, but he may be able to entertain and calm the children with stories of old in the dark nights to come." Murray watched them go, wondering if this was the last time that he would set eyes upon them.

The remaining force of tanks and armoured personnel carriers was unable to drive up the steep incline. Murray watched as the mechanised units about turned then headed in the direction of the main roads. Hopefully, the landmines and the ad hoc explosive devices would render some of them inoperable. Miasnikov's troopers were now fanning out and making their way towards the final defence line. Murray ordered his remaining troopers to launch the Molotov cocktails: "Don't light the fuses, just throw them unlit." The crashing sound of the glass impacting solidly amongst the rocks and trees was unheard above the sound of the resounding gunfire. A few rifles equipped with telescopic scopes had now been distributed to the best shooters. Murray heard them popping away at the incoming targets, the odd 'Got-yee-ya fucker' was occasionally overheard above the diminished breaks in the ensuing firefight. A huge explosion reverberates from the direction of the road, followed by a large plume of smoke.

Murray's troopers gave a cheer and hoped that the occupants of the chosen vehicle were trapped and were now being burned alive. Murray was also aware that no matter how efficient Karen and Okolo were at planting explosive devices, they just never had enough to combat the vastly superior forces that were now relentlessly driving towards them. Mr Black had a quick swatch at the oncoming forces, which were now spread over the incline in small groups. He fished in his pocket for the flame initiator, and the first thing he located was a long-lost, long-ago forgotten homemade cigarette. Thought that it must be fate indeed, he continued fishing until he found the lighter. Murray sparked up the joint, took a long drag, then lit the fuse on the petrol bomb. Murray launched the hot bottle, as Mr Black was exhaling the plume of smoke, he heard the sound of the impacting glass upon the rock below, then the whoosh of the petrol ignited, followed by the screams of the now burning invaders. Murray ordered his forces not to shoot the frantically dancing men and women, "Let them burn merrily in front of their all their comrades."

Once the troopers completed the unchoreographed routine, along with their pitiful screams for help and salvation. The whole area slowly developed an uneasy silence. Murray told his forces that the bad guys had not given up this easily; therefore, as they were no doubt up to something, they must keep focused. Murray watched intently and looked for any slight movements that would give the game away and reveal what they were about to try next. The explosions start to rain down upon them, the only reason that the invaders had ceased moving forward was for to allow the mortars to be moved into position before they recommenced the attack. Murray was just about to issue the order to retreat when a salvo started to rain down upon their position and the surrounding woodland.

Across the Atlantic Ocean at the CCP, overflowing with pride at the onset of a successful operation, the Baroness intently watched as Professor Vassorob moved the sliders. He looked almost biometrically attached to the control panel as the power increased to the twenty-five percent mark. Vassorob had a quick look at the huge clock with the increments marked in bold yellow and red and ensured that the changes were all following the scheduled synchronisation. The mini-reactors all vibrated and then emitted a slight humming noise as the muon thorium-saturated fuel cells were gently coerced into releasing the required increased output. An almost ethereal hue enveloped the whole of the control room; no static electric barrier was visible, but to those who could see it, the faint glow was most definitely present.

Lesqueth drew the professor's attention away from the panel with a single finger and indicated that she had a question. Vassorob immediately withdrew from the required surveillance. As he approached her, the professor deferred to her esteemed position, bowed his head and with all due diligence, respectfully asked how he could be of assistance. Lesqueth pointed out the faint blueish hue that populated the atmosphere around them. He nodded immediately, understanding her question, "That was what was described in the old world as Tesla's blue. I could assure you that it was nothing to be alarmed at. The faint distortion that was slightly visible was nothing more than the absorption of the miniscule Penta emissions released from the compact reactors."

He complimented the great leader, "Not everyone can see it, only those gifted with more than perfect eyesight could detect it's presence." Lesqueth thanked him for the explanation. Vassorob asked if there were no other questions, may he return to his work. Lesqueth barely moved her head and dismissed him like an errant school boy, seeking permission to attend the toilet outside of the permitted break times. The professor diligently moved between the various stations that monitor and cross-reference all of the activities displayed on the motherboard. Vassorob checked the incoming data related to the increase in power levels. He almost released an enthusiastic air punch as the growth levels increased evenly within the bio-cryogenic chambers. All the indicators register an overall evenly placed spread, consistent with the theorised projected numbers.

This confirmed that the brains, bones, flesh and skeletal structured of the enclosed infants were advancing in the precise increments required. Vassorob was fully aware that if the bio-cryogenic chambers were opened and an enormous head attached to a small body was revealed, then the thought of no more donkeys would be the least of his worries. The professor requested that the stations involved in the biometrical analysis of the chemically induced enhanced growth solutions run a full inspection on a random sample. The technicians interfered with the required buttons to initiate the processing of the relevant information flow. Lesqueth summoned General Flemings and asked the officer to accompany her outside of the control hub.

Lesqueth then ordered Flemings to lead the way to the nearest vacant office. G-Flem marched forward, not knowing what the great leader had in mind, but nevertheless with an air of confidence, strides forward resolutely self-assured that she had committed no punishable offence. General Flemings, without knocking, entered the first available office and then ordered the occupants to leave. Lesqueth followed her inside, she reached inside her pocket and produced a packet of her small cigars and then delved in another pocket to rescue the small hip flask. G-Flem is not waiting to be asked, raked about the drawers in the desk for some vessels to hold the fluid. She found a suitable container. Lesqueth informed the general that they would require two containers.

"I thought it was about time we raised a toast to your success and the initiation of the enhancement project." Lesqueth poured two large measures into the grubby plastic cups. She raised her container to the general, "Here's to you and your success, and from now on, you will retain the rank of Field Marshall in charge of all the armed forces in the realm." Flemings thanked Lesqueth for the promotion. Excused herself for one minute, Flemings stood on the desk, then hastily decommissioned the smoke detector attached to the ceiling. On descending back to ground level, she produced a flame machine, and together they lit up the small cigars. As they smoked, FM-Flem knew without asking that it would be disrespectful, possibly developing into a near-death situation if she were to ask about the future plans once the enhancement project had come to fruition.

She deferred to the great leader, letting her take the lead in the subjects of the ensuing conversation, blissfully aware that this, like everything else, was just part of the constant, never-ending testing that the Baroness employs to maintain all of her subjects' unquestionable loyalty. Lesqueth, in between puffs of the cigar, informed G-Flem that she had all the add-ons for her newly assigned rank and had asked the uniform tailor to report to her at the soonest. "I suppose that with your promotion, you would be expecting double time on a Sunday?" FM-Flem, fully au fait with the workings of post-industrial terms and conditions practised in the former United Kingdom, laughed, adding that it would be greatly appreciated if she also received time and a half, then the additional double time after twelve o'clock on a Saturday.

Lesqueth pretended to agree, but wanting the last word on the subject, she warned her that if she formed a trade union, she would feed her and all her Bolshevik membership to the regimental pets. They raised their cups in a toast to the statement, then drained the last of the brandy.

As they returned to the control hub, Professor Vassorob was glued to the clock and watched for the dial to move from one of the bold yellow and red increments onto the other. The indicators, along with the dial, moved simultaneously, declaring to all that the fifty per cent stage of the process has now been reached. Vassorob listened carefully as the increased volume of saturated fuel was injected into the compact reactors. The hum emitted from the machines was hardly discernible; only Vassorob noticed the slight variation displayed by his children. On noticing the Baroness, he asked her if she wished to see the details of the growth that was increasing exponentially within the bio-cryogenic chambers. Not wanting to disappoint him, Lesqueth, along with FM-Flem in tow, accompanied the professor to the work station involved in monitoring the progress. Vassorob pointed to all of the indicators, selecting various sections to be highlighted, then painstakingly explaining this particular part of the process.

"This one here indicates the data that was being subconsciously fed into the developing brain calls. Every individual hub was closely monitored, the technicians checking that all the collective growth was equal and constant." He then pointed to a fluctuating numerical display, "These were the resulting changes required to maintain equilibrium." The Baroness asked what age had the inhabitants of the bio-cryogenic chambers had reached. Professor Vassorob pressed a few buttons that equated to the growth per age, "They were all at approximately thirteen years of age, and if I may be as bold as to add, not one of them has inherited the attributes of a surly, rebellious teenager." The Baroness pretended to be amused at his absurd form of a joke; her lips moved the required amount necessary to simulate a smile, but her eyes had retained the appearance of belonging to the dead, devoid of any expression, staring straight through him.

Thousands of miles to the east, across the stretch of water near the watermill. Olga went through the plan, as Cat did not know how to operate a tank, she had been elected to deal with the ammunition dump. Once the trio was all satisfied with the proposed incursion into the heart of the invader's territory, Cat took the lead and moved them into position. She may not be able to operate any of the mechanised weaponry, but she was more than certain that with the assistance of her best friends, she was more than capable of removing any sentries attempting to curtail their intentions. Cat alerted the former boat people to stop in their tracks. She hunkered down, then disappeared completely from sight, fully utilising the natural geographical highs and lows of their present location. Anna and Olga wait patiently for her return. Cat appeared a while later and caught them off guard as she approached them from a different direction. Cat stood before them, covered in blood that both Anna and Olga knew without asking that it did not belong to her. "Sorry, I kept you waiting. There were a few more in the way than I had thought, but we could go now." Anna nor Olga asked Cat how many she had eliminated; they followed behind as Cat led the way forward.

The heavy weapons were all set up on the road; what had once been the major north and south expressway was now like a military outpost. Artillery pieces, mobile rocket launchers and tanks lined a fairly large section of the road. Cat had travelled along this route, which now seemed so long ago that it could have very well belonged to a previous life. The invading forces had set up a rudimentary camp, which through the vision aids looked like they had a couple of fairly large, roughly put together tent-like structures where they ate, slept, drank and most likely fight among themselves.

As they looked at what lay before them, dispensing with any uncertainty, Cat addressed her companions. "There was no point in talking about what we need to do, see you both at the muster point." Cat, now resplendent in the attire of one of the bad guys, gently pushed her best friends into place in the legs of the boots, then made her way to join Miasnikov's mechanised unit. Cat possessed this uncanny ability that enabled her to blend into any situation without drawing any unwanted attention. She attributed this skill to the years she had spent living day-to-day amongst the gutter snipes. Who scraped an almost meagre existence begging and stealing in some of the major cities in western Europe. On entering the enclave, Cat claimed ownership of a wheelbarrow half loaded with several boxed items, along with a clipboard detailing the contents and the alleged recipients. She calmly wheels the contraption throughout the unsuspecting inhabitants of the makeshift camp, never once drawing a suspicious look or being questioned about her activity.

Cat reached the location of her first stop, and Olga, aided by Anna, had spent a considerable amount of time explaining what the place would look like and, more importantly, what was required once she entered. Cat pushed the wheelbarrow inside. The officer in charge, who was presently being serviced by an underling, uttered some harsh words. The semi-naked couple looked in disbelief as Cat walked towards them with the clipboard. "I need your signature for the items." More harsh words were issued by the woman bent over the desk. Cat ignored her, removing her best friend. She killed both of them quickly, then dragged their bodies out of sight where they would be hidden from view.

Olga had described in great detail the stored ammunition that, if dismantled correctly, would provide her with the necessary components to destroy all of the munitions. Cat searched the boxes looking for the stored tube-like objects, most of the labels looked like joined-up matchsticks. Even if they were labelled displaying normal lettering, it still would not have made any sense to her. Cat searched for the tube-like items, which, according to her advisor, should be packed individually in long, slender packing crates. She was disturbed that someone had entered the storage area; they informed her that they were looking for the officer in charge. Cat raised her eyes then shrugged her shoulders and in a guttural tone informed them that she had fucked off for a quick shag with her current sex slave. The man laughed, then left. Whatever he wanted was not important enough to disturb the officer participating in her favourite pastime. Cat returned the dagger with the yellow semi-precious stone in the pommel back home into her boot, then continued on with her search. After what seemed like hours upon hours, she had finally found the required items. Cat quickly prised open the lid of the packing crate, and she was bitterly disappointed as the tubes had been shipped without the propellant charges.

Olga had told her that this was a possibility and not to panic, as the launch boosters would be stored nearby. The words of advice played in her head, 'These people were lazy, and they would have stored all the components together.' Cat almost wanted to have a celebration when she located the boxes that contained the items that looked like solid-packed sand, emblazoned with the skull and crossbones warning.

After pulling out several of the packages, she stomped on them, reducing the solid structure of the propellant into a semi-powdered substance that would be easier to distribute in and about all of the other crates. Cat quickly spread out the contents and placed lumps of the solid white sand at points where she hoped it would create the most damage. All of the trails of highly inflammable breadcrumbs lead to a central point. Now searching in and around the desk, she grabbed the bottles of vodka and the reams of paperwork that had been casually dumped in the corner. Cat crunched up the paper into a pile in the centre of the storage area, and she sprinkled the vodka, which was so potent that it emitted fumes similar to rocket fuel over the mound of paper.

As she was making her way to the doorway, the trooper who had been previously looking for the officer in charge had returned. Cat rushed towards him and stabbed him several times before he uttered one word. She dumped his body in the corner, lit the paper trail soaked in the inflammable liquid. Then steered her contraption out of the storage area. Olga watched her for her progress through the vision aids, and, upon seeing Cat exit from where the ammunition was stored, she informed Anna that it was time to buckle up. They made their way to the tank that was situated at the southernmost point in the row of heavy weapons. The crew of the tank thought nothing of it as the two women approached; they were delighted in hopefully entertaining the seemingly slightly drunk troopers. Their dreamt of carnal pleasure sadly did not come to fruition as Anna, at the last possible moment, produced a silenced pistol and dispatched all of them with a well-aimed shot to the head.

Cat moved in on her secondary targets, the fuel dump and as expected, was guarded. She walked into their tent unannounced, dumped the two bottles of vodka on the table and with a sultry look on her face, started to unbutton her tunic. Now that she had their full undivided attention. Cat suggested that they could save a considerable amount of time if they were to start removing some of their clothes. As they scrambled about undressed, voiced opinions of who was going to do what and then argued amongst themselves about who was going to go first. Cat unleashed her best friends and ended them all in less than thirty seconds. She did not waste any time, disconnecting the hoses that were linked up to the storage containers containing the fuel. Cat made her way across, going from one vessel to the other, indiscriminately slashing at the hoses, then opening the valves a quarter turn. The various fuels gather on the uneven ground then streams of the foul-smelling liquid form into small puddles before they follow the contour of the terrain as they flow steadily down the hill. Cat buttoned up her tunic and then casually made her way to the previously agreed-upon muster point.

Olga, now in the driving seat, had already selected the preheat function to activate and now waited patiently to hit the ignition switch. Anna, sitting below her, had already run a quick check on the auto loader and ensured that the shells were all placed correctly. She exercised her hands, ready to activate the gunnery controls to life. A single explosion rocked the compound, and as the other stored munitions detonated, creating panic and chaos throughout the makeshift camp. Olga switched on the engine and as they belched out smoke, she increased the revs, then manoeuvred their borrowed vehicle into position. Anna had automatically moved the fire control system from standby to the active position. She hit the load button, then rotated and elevated the barrel for the first target. As the troopers ran about like headless chickens, the officers tried to return some sense of order while assessing the situation. Anna saw the officers attempting to restore order and activated the machine gun, which instantly cut down anyone in its path.

She depressed the fire button, and the vehicle shuddered slightly as the projectile exited from the smooth bore barrel, scoring a direct hit on the nearest tank. As the reload function took over, Olga moved forward to the next position. Anna fired at every available target that presented itself. The mobile rocket launchers were engulfed in flames as some fool had built a little shelter underneath it, and the liquid that Cat had let loose had accumulated in a quantity enough to produce a huge fireball when ignited. The ensuing flames spread easily from one closely parked vehicle to the next. They had been lucky that some of the munitions from the ammunition storage facility had obliterated some of the mechanised unit's equipment. They either had been parked way too close and had been engulfed by the resulting explosions, or they had received a direct hit from the hot rounds that were being ejected at force from the excessive heat that was spreading uncontrollably through the storage area.

Olga trundled over dead and wounded troopers as she continually repositioned her tank to enable Anna to line up another prospective target. Some rounds fired from hand-held weapons ping then ricochet from the turret until Anna located their position, then unleashed a hail of bullets. The ones that were ducking behind the barrier in between shots attracted her attention, and she shouted for Olga to turn slightly to the left and run over the top of them.

A rogue tank was in the process of manoeuvring into a suitable position to light them up. Olga spotted it just in time and stomped her foot on the accelerator. Their vehicle lurched forward, the incoming round not having the correct angle of contact, and glanced off the heavily armoured sloped surface. Olga told Anna to take out the offenders before they get a chance to realign their sights. Anna fired before Olga had finished the sentence, the perfectly placed shot scored a direct hit, the round blowing the opposition's turret thirty feet into the air. They continued down the hill and dispatched men and machines without incurring any additional attempts by the former occupants of the camp returning fire.

A solitary tank was spotted moving down towards where the bridge used to be located. Anna adjusted the elevation, then fired. The round had misfired and detonated just after it had left the barrel. Olga was dazed but managed to pull herself together. Then, would all of her strength, she dragged and pushed the now unconscious Anna out of the vehicle prior to them receiving a hot round.

Chapter 26

Robbo, Uno, along with Macdhiarmada, had returned back to the watermill. Cha on noticing their arrival, asked Robbo why Murray was not with them. Robbo told her straight that he had been ordered to return here and informed her that their situation was not looking good, and that he was here to help with the evacuation as ordered. Alicia and Okolo had overheard the conversation, Alicia coughed then asked the three wisemen if they could stop standing there like they were waiting for the arrival of the number forty-eight bus, then they could help place the children in the waiting vehicles. Macdhiarmada muttered something under his breath. Alicia told him that if he did not have the balls to say it out loud, then he should not say anything at all. She shouted at them to get a move on. Once they entered the house, they found the children all dressed and ready to leave.

The twins had them all organised and passed them over one at a time to their sponsors. Cha grabbed a quick cuddle with her children, informing them that she was just waiting for Daddy to return, and then she would join them. The vehicles, now loaded up with the precious cargo, departed. Robbo, who knew the route, took the lead, followed by Uno, then lastly by Macdhiarmada, who volunteered to drive. Uno had asked him why he never gave him a spell during the drive to reach here, Macdhiarmada curtly replied that he had never fucking asked him.

Cha stood with Okolo, "You should have left with the children; there was no need for you to stay here." Okolo looked at her, "Listen here, honey, you are one of my best friends, if you stay, I will stay. We shall wait for Murray together, and once you finish scolding him for causing all of the unnecessary strain and worry, I will have a turn." Cha thanked her for the kind words as they moved forward and took up position within their community's defences.

They hear Miasnikov's forces before they see him, the tank's tracks squeak and issue metallic groans as they churn up the road surface. They drove up past the houses and laid waste to the woodland as the heavy mechanised vehicles crashed through the trees. The buildings that had sheltered and kept all of their people safe were systematically blown apart. Miasnikov, now satisfied with the planned introduction, ordered his tank to crash into and drive over the buildings.

Robbo, Uno, the twins, and Alicia had returned to help with the last-ditch effort of defending their homes. Okolo had seen him return. Cha smiled as he heard her say, "Just you wait till this was all over." Several of the members of the community had stayed back to aid their family and friends who had volunteered to be part of the defence force. These people were now attacking the tanks. They had very little in the way of heavy weapons and actually achieved modest gains with their assortment of homemade explosives. Much to Miasnikov's annoyance, several of his vehicles were now without tracks. Vladimir issued orders for the barrage to begin. The first place to receive his attention was the medical facility. Cora's pride and joy was blasted at near point-blank range, and the remaining tanks opened up on all of the houses and buildings.

Cha waited until the last possible moment before she fired the last portable rocket launcher. It was a direct hit, but only put a small dent in Miasnikov's tank. He ordered the bombardment to cease, then, on his mark, the machine guns opened up and unleashed their firepower in every conceivable direction. Cha and Okolo were joined by the last of the survivors and took refuge in one of the last standing buildings. Cha looked around her. This house has brought so much happiness into her life. She looked at the clock, and surprisingly, it was still set at three o'clock. The exit behind them was inaccessible as the falling debris had completely blocked it off. Miasnikov sensed that the Hiddens' demise was almost at hand and switched on the sound system to torture the remaining survivors with military marching music. General Vladimir Miasnikov opened the top hatch and proudly laid his eyes on all that he had laid to waste. He ordered his remaining forces to advance forward.

On the other side of the Atlantic Ocean, Perry had at last reached the vehicles, desperate to return to the camp, he abandoned any and all safety protocol as he and his remaining troopers load into the transport. Commander Green was again complimented by the sycophantic technicians; Jack ignored them completely as he watched the live feed displayed on the screen. As Perry's convoy ate up the miles on the dust track, Jack could be heard saying, "Come on, just a little closer." Commander Green waited until the transport was within half a mile of the camp. When he started to detonate the explosive charges that had been planted in the vehicles. As the transport behind him started, one by one, to erupt into fireballs, Perry ordered his men to jump.

Jack Green pressed the big red button and ordered his main force to commence the attack. The camp was caught completely off-guard as his troopers rushed in from the front, the rear and the additional entry points that had been simultaneously created to allow an all-points-of-entry break.

Jackson was alerted by the sounds issued by the sporadic gunfire, knowing somehow that their defences had been overwhelmed. He ordered Abe and Enunsha to get the hell out of here before it's too late. Jackson grabbed a weapon and stepped out, hoping that at least he would give them enough time to escape. He did not even have time to remove the safety from his weapon as someone whacked him on the back of the head. Jackson was subjected to a severe beating, then dragged to join the rest of the prisoners, and woke up just in time to see Enunsha and Abe frog marched at gunpoint to come and join them before he slumped back into unconsciousness.

Blink and her crew had pushed their motor launches to the very limit to reach the location that the old woman in the hooded cloak had shown her in the dream. They had arrived early in the morning; Blink had steadfastly reassured her crew that this was the place. "All we had to do was find them." Sekoyaz, along with all of the other members of her crew, thought that it was great to be back on dry land, but like the others, she found it equally hard going. Blink pushed them on relentlessly, never slowed down and never stopped for a rest long enough to fully recover. It was not till late in the afternoon that they arrived at the camp.

Sekoyaz had thought that if it weren't for the stray dog that had befriended Blink, they would not have found the place. Blink had watched, unable to do anything, as the vastly superior forces stormed virtuously unopposed into the camp. After a brief firefight, all the prisoners were cuffed and assembled in the main courtyard as their leader strutted about like a prize peacock and delivered a speech about what it truly means to conquer an adversary, and alas, what it truly means to be one of the conquered. Blink watched them being loaded into trucks, noting which one Enunsha was placed in. She delivered the latest plan to her crew, then pushed, for what she hoped was the final time, egging them on to hopefully get them into position.

At the CCP Lesqueth watched as the single arm on the big clock with the bold yellow and red increments approached the last remaining section. Professor Vassorob anxiously scratched his face and looked perplexed as he studied the incoming numbers. The indexed data should line up perfectly with the collective stream of information, automatically updating the given and selected parameters many thousands of times per second. The compact reactors had been set to the higher limit to induce more of the saturated fuel source. Vassorob checked the growth indicators associated with each individual bio-cryogenic chamber. All of the infants were at the same stage, and not even a miniscule difference had been detected.

This in itself was quite an achievement as the modular programme was capable of calculating down to point zero, zero something of a percent. Lesqueth had been viewing his movements and knew by his uncharacteristic mannerisms that something was bothering him. She worked her way towards him, constantly changing her intercept course as he moved from work station to work station. As she finally caught up with him, she caught Professor Vassorob off guard as she asked him if there was anything at all to be concerned about. Vassorob took a deep breath and announced that all the growth was beyond expectations. All of the children enclosed within the bio-cryogenic chambers would share identical levels of intelligence, aptitude. They would be a major part of the future that she has envisioned.

Lesqueth took his complimentary remark with a pinch of salt, "So what was bothering you? I had seen you move frantically between the work stations, punching in numbers and standing there expecting something to change. May I take this opportunity to remind you that as soon as you complete the work here. The transport, which was now placed on standby, would fly you immediately to your chosen destination. Vassorob, Hawaii patiently awaited your return, so start talking and tell me right now what seems to be the problem." The professor explained that by now, the infants should have reached the maximum permissible growth, and all of the machinery controlling the enhancement project should have automatically registered this and subsequently shut down. The Baroness informed him that he could tweak the compact reactors to produce an increase in power.

She coldly informed him that, like all things that were made in the UK, these were designed to work at one and a half times the guaranteed limitations. She grew impatient with his inability to make a decision; he stood still, frozen on the spot. Lesqueth stepped towards the power control, then informed the technicians to shout out the numbers as she advanced the sliders, pushing the power over the one hundred percent mark. The technician beside her shouted out the increasing percentage. Lesqueth informed him that he did not need to shout these out quite so loud, as she was standing right next to him. As the power output reached one hundred and fifty percent, another technician shouted out that the growth rate had started to move towards the expected limit.

Vassorob has decided to join in, and as he moved from work station to work station, he shouted out that the enhancement project was back on schedule. Professor Vassorob then proceeded to announce the decreasing percentage required to reach completion. Lesqueth would have shot him, but she did not want to risk inflicting damage on the sensitive equipment that lined the room. As every notable stage of all the various governing factors associated with the enhancement project reaches ninety-seven percent, Tesla's Blue magnified exponentially. The now highly visible bright blue rays were rapidly emitted in a continuous flow out of every compact reactor and cover a full spectrum of three hundred and sixty degrees.

Alwyn, along with Cinds', had just arrived at the watermill with their recently confiscated mechanised unit. They would have arrived sooner, but several groups of Miasnikov's troopers who were denying defeat had to be dealt with along the way. One of Miasnikov's commanders had attempted to surrender. She stood in front of the approaching tank, frantically waving a white piece of cloth. Cinds' suspected that this action was nothing but a not-so-subtle ruse to draw them into a trap, increased acceleration to the maximum and crushed the one in the wrong uniform beneath the tracks of her vehicle. Alwyn had insisted that they change into the uniforms and, addressing what remained of his crew, he told them that he did not know what to expect when they arrived at the watermill.

As they drove in formation into the once-happy settlement, they witnessed firsthand the devastation that had taken place. The place that was going to be their new forever home was now nothing more than a burned-out village, dead bodies littered the street, most of the semi-demolished houses smouldered away, and several distorted vehicles, including a few decapacitated tanks, lay abandoned in the main street. Miasnikov had activated the PA system and now gloats at his army's success. "*You there in the house, there was no possible means of escape. The tanks that had just arrived had destroyed the nearby community. All your friends were now dead or dying, and there will be no rescue, no one is coming to help you. If you surrender now, I will spare all of your children.*"

Miasnikov had now arrived at the part in the speech where he praised his illustrious leader, who would conquer and rule this world. He did not get any further as Alwyn was assisted by Cinds' opened fire at close range and decimated his remaining tanks. Vladimir Miasnikov was furious, having come all this way, then had victory snatched out of his hands at the very last moment. He launched a one-man attack on the last remaining house.

Lesqueth was transfixed as the data displayed on the huge screen indicated by the flashing indications that the enhancement project was now one hundred percent complete. The growth assessments confirmed that each of the bio-cryogenic chambers contained a healthy and fully developed twenty-five-year-old. Vassorob approached the Baroness, and he kneeled before her. "The world now lies at your feet for the taking, may you have a long and illustrious reign." As the rest of the occupants in the control hub joined Vassorob in acknowledging the supreme leader. The blue light suddenly increased in height as it almost reached the high ceiling, and the compact reactors developed a high-pitched hum. As the hum settled into a stabilised frequency, the extended blue light rapidly expanded outwards. From every part of the outside surface of the compact reactors, the light was projected all around the world in a microsecond. As each beam of light encircled the globe and returned to the compact reactors, the reactors shut down one by one. All that could be heard in the control room was the repeating thud of the mechanism withdrawing the fuel cell and then the clicked of the machine's automatic programmed response coming into play, activating the off switch.

Every person in the world has been temporarily incapacitated; well, that was everyone with the exception of

Blink. She was twenty-five years old, and the light that had appeared then disappeared in less than a second did not affect her at all. Blink looked at all of her crew; they were all sleeping and looked several years younger. She did not forget why she was here and set off to rescue Enunsha. The vehicle that she had been roughly placed in had not travelled far before it came to a sudden stop.

The dog was at her side, happily wagging its tail, almost perceiving the fact that together they were going to rescue its best friend. Blink, accompanied by the dog, races to find the vehicle with the corresponding number. She forced open the door and located Enunsha, and then gently carried her out. Blink manhandled her over her shoulder and took her away to a place of relative safety until she recuperated and was able to move under her own steam. The dog sat and stared at her, the big eyes peering into her very soul, expecting Blink to know what they wanted. The dog, not receiving the required reaction, moved towards her and darted away. Blink talked to the dog as if it understood every word: "Okay, dog, show me what you want." Spotty led the way back to where there was another stationary vehicle full of prisoners. The dog sat by the door, this time staring at the handle. "Oh, so you want me to rescue another body?" Spotty moved his head slightly to the side and scraped the door with his paw, letting her know that she had to hurry. Blink did as she was instructed, no sooner than she had prised open the door, Spotty darted inside. Blink followed the dog in and found the canine sitting beside a man who looked like more than a little worse for wear and tear.

Spotty gently hits her leg several times in quick succession, "Okay, I will get this one out." The dog waited for her outside and attempted to help her save him by grabbing his trouser leg, then pulling in the same direction where they had placed Enunsha. Blink struggled for a while but eventually managed to place him in a fireman's lift. She had just reached Enunsha when everyone started to wake up.

At the watermill, Alicia was the first to stir back to life, and the first thing that caught her attention was Robbo. He looked so much younger, his eyes almost as radiant as the blue light that had momentarily passed through all of them. The twins look about the same. Okolo and Cha had shed some years and look even more beautiful. She smiled as she cast her eyes upon Uno and the Macdhiarmada chap, it did not matter if these two had lost a few years. They still retained that look of down-and-outs, that would not be out of place begging outside an off-sales, harassing passers-by for any spare change for the elusive bus fare home. Her inner thoughts were instantly invaded by many voices that belonged to people she did not know. The voices were questioning many things, not in an overtly aggressive manner, not in an overly friendly manner, but very demanding and very inquisitive.

Miasnikov's voice distracted her and rudely dragged her back to reality. "There was an old saying. Do not celebrate winning until you have passed the finish line." He pulled the pins out of a pair of hand grenades and then lobbed them through one of the missing panes of glass in the window. Almost frozen in time, Alicia watched as they slowly arced through the air, bounced, and then rolled across the floor. Robbo gave her a cheeky wink and roused Uno with the swamp people's battle cry. Even though Uno had just opened his eyes a second ago, he immediately latched on to Robbo's intentions. The pair of them, knowing what had to be done quickly collected the hand grenades, held them close then dived to the floor on the other side of the room. The muffled explosions sounded more like subdued thuds as the bodies of Uno and Robbo juddered as they absorbed the full impact of the detonations. Their unselfish action had, without a shadow of a doubt, saved them all.

Macdhiarmada, along with all the woman, looked in disbelief at what had just happened before their eyes. Alicia, full of rage with her flowing red hair almost electrified, now nearly standing on end, rushed forward and propelled herself through the damaged window frame. She caught Miasnikov by complete surprise, and before he had a chance to react, Alicia subjected him to the full spectrum of her mixed martial arts. The years of extensive training were put to their fullest use. In a flurry of moves, the majority of them being highly illegal, she, without respite, broke many of his bones and shattered various organs with the unleashing of precisely aimed kicks and punches. The last full force kick expertly landed in the underarm area and paralysed him.

Miasnikov, who had briefly returned to being a spritely twenty-five-year-old, now lay on the ground, barely able to move a muscle, and stole his last few breaths. Okolo had just witnessed Alicia unleash her wrath, and although Miasnikov was dying, she did not think that he had been subjected to enough pain and discomfort. Okolo lowered her trousers, positions herself perfectly, then defecated on his face. She sang away quite happily to herself as she used her fingers to force her excrement down his throat and up into his nostrils. Okolo removed the waste from her hands by wiping them on his face. Vladimir, being unable to close his eyes, looked at her through the brownish-tinted vision. She patted his head like a postman who was about to drown the unconscious family pet, that frequently used to bite his hands and snapped at his heels. "Where I come from, we had a special gift for special people like you." As Miasnikov struggled with his final breath, she asked if he was savouring every single bite of the West African version of Pirozhki for one.

About the Author

This is book number 6 in the series, and if you send a nice, pleasant email, you will get a nice, pleasant email in return. croftengrebe@gmail.com.